Praise for *New York Tim*
Tess Gerritsen

"Tess Gerritsen...throws one twist after another until the excitement is almost unbearable."

—*San Jose Mercury News*

"Ms. Gerritsen is a master!"

—*RT Book Reviews*

"Riveting... Gerritsen knows how to fashion credible, dimensional characters."

—*Los Angeles Times*

"Gerritsen is tops in her genre."

—*USA TODAY*

Praise for *USA TODAY* bestselling author Rita Herron

"Herron understands the bonds between mother and child and presents a touching and terrifying tale of evil and redemption."

—*RT Book Reviews* on *Unbreakable Bond*

"This story will totally captivate the reader. A tale packed solid with suspense and excitement with a new surprise at the turn of every page... An absolutely fascinating read that is definitely recommended. Rita Herron is an extremely gifted writer."

—*FreshFiction* on *Forbidden Passion*

IN THEIR FOOTSTEPS

NEW YORK TIMES BESTSELLING AUTHOR

TESS GERRITSEN

HARLEQUIN® SELECTS™

ISBN-13: 978-1-335-40654-5

This edition published by arrangement with Harlequin Books S.A.

For questions and comments about the quality of this book, please contact us at CustomerService@Harlequin.com.

Harlequin Enterprises ULC
22 Adelaide St. West, 41st Floor
Toronto, Ontario M5H 4E3, Canada
www.Harlequin.com

Printed in U.S.A.

CONTENTS

Internationally bestselling author **Tess Gerritsen** is a graduate of Stanford University and went on to medical school at the University of California, San Francisco, where she was awarded her MD. Since 1987, her books have been translated into thirty-seven languages, and more than twenty-five million copies have been sold around the world. She has received the Nero Award and the RITA® Award, and she was a finalist for the Edgar Award. Now retired from medicine, she writes full-time. She lives in Maine.

Books by Tess Gerritsen

Call After Midnight
Under the Knife
Never Say Die
Whistleblower
Presumed Guilty
In Their Footsteps
Thief of Hearts
Keeper of the Bride

Visit the Author Profile page at Harlequin.com for more titles.

IN THEIR FOOTSTEPS

Tess Gerritsen

Prologue

Paris, 1973

She was late. It was not like Madeline, not like her at all.

Bernard Tavistock ordered another café au lait and took his time sipping it, every so often glancing around the outdoor café for a glimpse of his wife. He saw only the usual Left Bank scene: tourists and Parisians, red-checked tablecloths, a riot of summertime colors. But no sign of his raven-haired wife. She was half an hour late now; this was more than a traffic delay. He found himself tapping his foot as the worries began to creep in. In all their years of marriage, Madeline had rarely been late for an appointment, and then only by a few minutes. Other men might moan and roll their eyes in masculine despair over their perennially tardy spouses, but Bernard had no such complaints—he'd been blessed with a punctual wife. A beautiful wife. A woman who, even after fifteen years of marriage, continued to surprise him, fascinate him, tempt him.

Now where the dickens *was* she?

He glanced up and down Boulevard Saint-Germain. His uneasiness grew from a vague toe-tapping anxiety to outright worry. Had there been a traffic accident? A last-minute alert from their French Intelligence contact, Claude Daumier? Events had been moving at a frantic pace these last two weeks. Those rumors of a NATO intelligence leak—of a mole in their midst—had them all glancing over their shoulders, wondering who among them could not be trusted. For days now, Madeline had been awaiting instructions from MI6 London. Perhaps, at the last minute, word had come through.

Still, she should have let him know.

He rose to his feet and was about to head for the telephone when he spotted his waiter, Mario, waving at him. The young man quickly wove his way past the crowded tables.

"Monsieur Tavistock, there is a telephone message for you. From *madame*."

Bernard gave a sigh of relief. "Where is she?"

"She says she cannot come for lunch. She wishes you to meet her."

"Where?"

"This address." The waiter handed him a scrap of paper, smudged with what looked like tomato soup. The address was scrawled in pencil: 66, Rue Myrha, #5.

Bernard frowned. "Isn't this in Pigalle? What on earth is she doing in that neighborhood?"

Mario shrugged, a peculiarly Gallic version with

tipped head, raised eyebrow. "I do not know. She tells me the address, I write it down."

"Well, thank you." Bernard reached for his wallet and handed the fellow enough francs to pay for his two café au laits, as well as a generous tip.

"Merci," said the waiter, beaming. "You will return for supper, Monsieur Tavistock?"

"If I can track down my wife," muttered Bernard, striding away to his Mercedes.

He drove to Place Pigalle, grumbling all the way. What on earth had possessed her to go there? It was not the safest part of Paris for a woman—or a man, either, for that matter. He took comfort in the knowledge that his beloved Madeline could take care of herself quite well, thank you very much. She was a far better marksman than he was, and that automatic she carried in her purse was always kept fully loaded—a precaution he insisted upon ever since that near-disaster in Berlin. Distressing how one couldn't trust one's own people these days. Incompetents everywhere, in MI6, in NATO, in French Intelligence. And there had been Madeline, trapped in that building with the East Germans, and no one to back her up. *If I hadn't arrived in time...*

No, he wouldn't relive that horror again.

She'd learned her lesson. And a loaded pistol was now a permanent accessory to her wardrobe.

He turned onto Rue de Chapelle and shook his head in disgust at the deteriorating street scene, the tawdry nightclubs, the scantily clad women poised on street corners. They saw his Mercedes and beckoned to him eagerly. Desperately. "Pig Alley" was what the Yanks used to call this neighborhood. The place one came to for quick delights, for guilty pleasures. *Madeline,* he thought, *have you gone completely mad? What could possibly have brought you here?*

He turned onto Boulevard Bayes, then Rue Myrha, and parked in front of number 66. In disbelief, he stared up at the building and saw three stories of chipped plaster and sagging balconies. Did she really expect him to meet her in this firetrap? He locked the Mercedes, thinking, *I'll be lucky if the car's still here when I return.* Reluctantly he entered the building.

Inside there were signs of habitation: children's toys in the stairwell, a radio playing in one of the flats. He climbed the stairs. The smell of frying onions and cigarette smoke seemed to hang permanently in the air. Numbers three and four were on the second floor; he kept climbing, up a narrow staircase to the top floor. Number five was the attic flat; its low door was tucked between the eaves.

He knocked. No answer.

"Madeline?" he called. "Really now, this isn't some sort of practical joke, is it?"

Still there was no answer.

He tried the door; it was unlocked. He pushed inside, into the garret flat. Venetian blinds hung over the windows, casting slats of shadow and light across the room. Against one wall was a large brass bed, its sheets still rumpled from some prior occupant. On a bedside table were two dirty glasses, an empty champagne bottle and various plastic items one might delicately refer to as "marital aids." The whole room smelled of liquor, of sweating passion and bodies in rut.

Bernard's puzzled gaze gradually shifted to the foot of the brass bed, to a woman's high-heeled shoe lying discarded on the floor. Frowning, he took a step toward it and saw that the shoe lay in a glistening puddle of crimson. As he rounded the foot of the bed, he froze in disbelief.

His wife lay on the floor, her ebony hair fanned out like a raven's wings. Her eyes were open. Three sunbursts of blood stained her white blouse.

He dropped to his knees beside her. "No," he said. *"No."* He touched her face, felt the warmth still lingering in her cheeks. He pressed his ear to her chest, her bloodied chest, and heard no heartbeat, no breath. A sob burst forth from his throat, a disbelieving cry of grief. *"Madeline!"*

As the echo of her name faded, there came another sound behind him—footsteps. Soft, approaching...

Bernard turned. In bewilderment, he stared at the pistol—Madeline's pistol—now pointed at him. He looked up at the face hovering above the barrel. It made no sense—no sense at all!

"Why?" asked Bernard.

The answer he heard was the dull thud of the silenced automatic. The bullet's impact sent him sprawling to the floor beside Madeline. For a few brief seconds, he was aware of her body close beside him, and of her hair, like silk against his fingers. He reached out and feebly cradled her head. *My love,* he thought. *My dearest love.*

And then his hand fell still.

Chapter 1

Buckinghamshire, England
Twenty years later

Jordan Tavistock lounged in Uncle Hugh's easy chair and amusedly regarded, as he had a thousand times before, the portrait of his long-dead ancestor, the hapless Earl of Lovat. Ah, the delicious irony of it all, he thought, that Lord Lovat should stare down from that place of honor above the mantelpiece. It was testimony to the Tavistock family's sense of whimsy that they'd chosen to so publicly display their one relative who'd, literally, lost his head on Tower Hill—the last man to be officially decapitated in England—unofficial decapitations did not count. Jordan raised his glass in a toast to the unfortunate earl and tossed back a gulp of sherry. He was tempted to pour a second glass, but it was already five-thirty, and the guests would soon be arriving for the Bastille Day reception. *I should keep at least a few gray cells in working order,* he thought. *I might need them to hold up my end of the chitchat.* Chitchat being one of Jordan's least favorite activities.

For the most part, he avoided these caviar and black-tie bashes his uncle Hugh seemed so addicted to throwing. But tonight's event—in honor of their house guests, Sir Reggie and Lady Helena Vane—might prove more interesting than the usual gathering of the horsey set. This was the first big affair since Uncle Hugh's retirement from British Intelligence, and a number of Hugh's former colleagues from MI6 would make an appearance. Throw into the brew a few old chums from Paris—all of them in London for the recent economic summit—and it could prove to be a most intriguing night. Anytime one threw a group of ex-spies and diplomats together in a room, all sorts of surprising secrets tended to surface.

Jordan looked up as his uncle came grumbling into the study. Already dressed in his tuxedo, Hugh was trying, without success, to fix his bow tie; he'd managed, instead, to tie a stubborn square knot.

"Jordan, help me with this blasted thing, will you?" said Hugh.

Jordan rose from the easy chair and loosened the knot. "Where's Davis? He's much better at this sort of thing."

"I sent him to fetch that sister of yours."

"Beryl's gone out again?"

"Naturally. Mention the words 'cocktail party,' and she's flying out the door."

Jordan began to loop his uncle's tie into a bow. "Beryl's never been fond of parties. And just between you and me, I think she's had just a bit too much of the Vanes."

"Hmm? But they've been lovely guests. Fit right in—"

"It's the nasty little barbs flying between them."

"Oh, *that.* They've always been that way. I scarcely notice it anymore."

"And have you seen the way Reggie follows Beryl about, like a puppy dog?"

Hugh laughed. "Around a pretty woman, Reggie *is* a puppy dog."

"Well, it's no wonder Helena's always sniping at him." Jordan stepped back and regarded his uncle's bow tie with a frown.

"How's it look?"

"It'll have to do."

Hugh glanced at the clock. "Better check on the kitchen. See that things are in order. And why aren't the Vanes down yet?"

As if on cue, they heard the sound of querulous voices on the stairway. Lady Helena, as always, was scolding her husband. "*Someone* has to point these things out to you," she said.

"Yes, and it's always you, isn't it?"

Sir Reggie fled into the study, pursued by his wife. It never failed to puzzle Jordan, the obvious mismatch of the pair. Sir Reggie, handsome and silver haired, towered over his drab little mouse of a wife. Perhaps Helena's substantial inheritance explained the pairing; money, after all, was the great equalizer.

As the hour edged toward six o'clock, Hugh poured out glasses of sherry and handed them around to the foursome. “Before the hordes arrive,” he said, “a toast, to your safe return to Paris.” They sipped. It was a solemn ceremony, this last evening together with old friends.

Now Reggie raised his glass. “And here’s to English hospitality. Ever appreciated!”

From the front driveway came the sound of car tires on gravel. They all glanced out the window to see the first limousine roll into view. The chauffeur opened the door and out stepped a fiftyish woman, every ripe curve defined by a green gown ablaze with bugle beads. Then a young man in a shirt of purple silk emerged from the car and took the woman’s arm.

“Good heavens, it’s Nina Sutherland and her brat,” Helena muttered. “What broom did *she* fly in on?”

Outside, the woman in the green gown suddenly spotted them standing in the window. “Hello, Reggie! Helena!” she called in a voice like a bassoon.

Hugh set down his sherry glass. “Time to greet the barbarians,” he said, sighing. He and the Vanes headed out the front door to welcome the first arrivals.

Jordan paused a moment to finish his drink, giving himself time to paste on a smile and get the old handshake ready. Bastille Day—what an excuse for a party! He tugged at the coattails of his tuxedo, gave his ruffled shirt one last pat, and resignedly headed out to the front steps. Let the dog and pony show begin.

Now where in blazes was his sister?

At that moment, the subject of Jordan Tavistock’s speculation was riding hell-bent for leather across a grassy field. Poor old Froggie needs the workout, thought Beryl. And so do I. She bent forward into the wind, felt the lash of Froggie's mane against her face, and inhaled that wonderful scent of horseflesh, sweet clover and warm July earth. Froggie was enjoying the sprint just as much as she was, if not more. Beryl could feel those powerful muscles straining for ever more speed. She's a demon, like me, thought Beryl, suddenly laughing aloud—the same wild laugh that always made poor Uncle Hughie cringe. But out here, in the open fields, she could laugh like a wanton woman and no one would hear. If only she could keep on riding, forever and ever! But fences and walls seemed to be everywhere in her life. Fences of the mind, of the heart. She urged her mount still faster, as though through speed she could outrun all the devils pursuing her.

Bastille Day. What a desperate excuse for a party.

Uncle Hugh loved a good bash, and the Vanes *were* old family friends; they deserved a decent send-off. But she'd seen the guest list, and it was the same tiresome lot. Shouldn't ex-spies and diplomats lead more interesting lives? She couldn't imagine James Bond, retired, pottering about in his garden.

Yet that's what Uncle Hugh seemed to do all day. The highlight of *his* week had been harvesting the season's first hybrid Nepal tomato—his earliest tomato ever! And as for her uncle's friends, well, she couldn't imagine *them* ever sneaking around the back alleys of Paris or Berlin. Philippe St. Pierre, perhaps—yes, she could picture *him* in his younger days; at sixty-two, he was still charming, a Gallic lady-killer. And Reggie Vane might have cut a dashing figure years ago. But most of Uncle Hugh's old colleagues seemed so, well…used up.

Not me. Never me.

She galloped harder, letting Froggie have free rein.

They raced across the last stretch of field and through a copse of trees. Froggie, winded now, slowed to a trot, then a walk. Beryl pulled her to a halt by the church's stone wall. There she dismounted and let Froggie wander about untethered. The churchyard was deserted and the gravestones cast lengthening shadows across the lawn. Beryl clambered over the low wall and walked among the plots until she came to the spot she'd visited so many times before. A handsome obelisk towered over two graves, resting side by side. There were no curlicues, no fancy angels carved into that marble face. Only words.

Bernard Tavistock, 1930-1973
Madeline Tavistock, 1934-1973
On earth, as it is in heaven,
we are together.

Beryl knelt on the grass and gazed for a long time at the resting place of her mother and father. *Twenty years ago tomorrow,* she thought. *How I wish I could remember you more clearly! Your faces, your smiles.* What she did remember were odd things, unimportant things. The smell of leather luggage, of Mum's perfume and Dad's pipe. The crackle of paper as she and Jordan would unwrap the gifts Mum and Dad brought home to them. Dolls from France. Music boxes from Italy. And there was laughter. Always lots of laughter…

Beryl sat with her eyes closed and heard that happy sound through the passage of twenty years. Through the evening buzz of insects, the clink of Froggie's bit and bridle, she heard the sounds of her childhood.

The church bell tolled—six chimes.

At once Beryl sat up straight. Oh, no, was it already that late? She glanced around and saw that the shadows had grown, that Froggie was standing by the wall regarding her with frank expectation. *Oh Lord,* she thought, *Uncle Hugh will be royally cross with me.*

She dashed out of the churchyard and climbed onto Froggie's back. At once they were flying across the field, horse and rider blended into a single sleek organism. *Time for the shortcut,* thought Beryl, guiding Froggie toward the trees. It meant a leap over the stone wall, and then a clip along the road, but it would cut a mile off their route. Froggie seemed to understand that time was of the essence. She picked up speed and approached the stone wall with all the eagerness of a seasoned steeplechaser. She took the jump cleanly, with inches to spare. Beryl felt the wind rush past, felt her mount soar, then touch down on the far side of the wall. The biggest hurdle was behind them. Now, just beyond that bend in the road—

She saw a flash of red, heard the squeal of tires across pavement. Froggie swerved sideways and reared up. The sudden lurch caught Beryl by surprise. She tumbled out of the saddle and landed with a stunning thud on the ground.

Her first reaction, after her head had stopped spinning, was astonishment that she had fallen at all—and for such a stupid reason.

Her next reaction was fear that Froggie might be injured.

Beryl scrambled to her feet and ran to snatch the reins. Froggie was still spooked, nervously trip-trapping about on the pavement. The sound of a car door slamming shut, of someone running toward them, only made the horse edgier.

"Don't come any closer!" hissed Beryl over her shoulder.

"Are you all right?" came the anxious inquiry. It was a man's voice, pleasantly baritone. American?

"I'm fine," snapped Beryl.

"What about your horse?"

Murmuring softly to Froggie, Beryl knelt down and ran her hands along Froggie's foreleg. The delicate bones all seemed to be intact.

"Is he all right?" said the man.

"It's a she," answered Beryl. "And yes, she seems to be just fine."

"I really *can* tell the difference," came the dry response. "When I have a view of the essential parts."

Suppressing a smile, Beryl straightened and turned to look at the man. Dark hair, dark eyes, she noted. And the definite glint of humor—nothing stiff-upper-lip about this one. Forty plus years of laughter had left attractive creases about his eyes. He was dressed in formal black tie, and his broad shoulders filled out the tuxedo jacket quite impressively.

"I'm sorry about the spill," he said. "I guess it *was* my fault."

"This is a country road, you know. Not exactly the place to be speeding. You never can tell what lies around the bend."

"So I've discovered."

Froggie gave her an impatient nudge. Beryl stroked the horse's neck, all the time intensely aware of the man's gaze.

"I do have something of an excuse," he said. "I got

turned around in the village back there, and I'm running late. I'm trying to find some place called Chetwynd. Do you know it?"

She cocked her head in surprise. "You're going to Chetwynd? Then you're on the wrong road."

"Am I?"

"You turned off a half mile too soon. Head back to the main road and keep going. You can't miss the turn. It's a private drive, flanked by elms—quite tall ones."

"I'll watch for the elms, then."

She remounted Froggie and gazed down at the man. Even viewed from the saddle, he cut an impressive figure, lean and elegant in his tuxedo. And strikingly confident, not a man to be intimidated by anyone—even a woman sitting astride nine hundred muscular pounds of horseflesh.

"Are you sure you're not hurt?" he asked. "It looked like a pretty bad fall to me."

"Oh, I've fallen before." She smiled. "I have quite a hard head."

The man smiled, too, his teeth straight and white in the twilight. "Then I shouldn't worry about you slipping into a stupor tonight?"

"*You're* the one who'll be slipping into a stupor tonight."

He frowned. "Excuse me?"

"A stupor brought on by dry and endless palaver. It's a distinct possibility, considering where you're headed." Laughing, she turned the horse around. "Good evening," she called. Then, with a farewell wave, she urged Froggie into a trot through the woods.

As she left the road behind, it occurred to her that she would get to Chetwynd before he did. That made her laugh again. Perhaps Bastille Day would turn out more interesting than she'd expected. She gave the horse a nudge of her boot. At once Froggie broke into a gallop.

Richard Wolf stood beside his rented MG and watched the woman ride away, her black hair tumbling like a horse's mane about her shoulders. In seconds she was gone, vanished from sight into the woods. He never even caught her name, he thought. He'd have to ask Lord Lovat about her. Tell me, Hugh. Are you acquainted with a black-haired witch tearing about your neighborhood? She was dressed like one of the village girls, in a frayed shirt and grass-stained jodhpurs, but her accent bespoke the finest of schools. A charming contradiction.

He climbed back into the car. It was almost six-thirty now; that drive from London had taken longer than he'd expected. Blast these backcountry lanes! He turned the car around and headed for the main road, taking care this time to slow down for curves. No telling what might be lurking around the bend. A cow or a goat.

Or another witch on horseback.

I have quite a hard head. He smiled. A hard head, indeed. She slips off the saddle—bump—and she's right back on her feet. And cheeky to boot. As if I couldn't tell a mare from a stallion. All I needed was the right view.

Which he certainly had had of her. There was no doubt whatsoever that it was the female of the species he'd been looking at. All that raven hair, those laughing green eyes. *She almost reminds me of...*

He suppressed the thought, shoved it into the quicksand of bad memories. Nightmares, really. Those terrible echoes of his first assignment, his first failure. It had colored his career, had kept him from ever again taking anything for granted. That was the way one *should* operate in this business. Check the facts, never trust your sources, and always, always watch your back.

It was starting to wear him down. *Maybe I should kick back and retire early. Live the quiet country life like Hugh Tavistock.* Of course Tavistock had a title and estate to keep him in comfort, though Richard had to laugh when he thought of the rotund and balding Hugh Tavistock as earl of anything. *Yeah, I should just settle down on those ten acres in Connecticut. Declare myself Earl of Whatever and grow cucumbers.*

But he'd miss the work. Those delicious whiffs of danger, the international chess game of wits. The world was changing so fast, and you didn't know from day to day who your enemies were…

He spotted, at last, the turnoff to Chetwynd. Flanked by majestic elms, it was as the black-haired woman had described it. That impressive driveway was more than matched by the manor house standing at the end of the road. This was no mere country cottage; this was a castle, complete with turrets and ivy-covered stone walls. Formal gardens stretched out for acres, and a brick path led to what looked like a medieval maze. So this was where old Hugh Tavistock had repaired to after those forty years of service to queen and country. Earldom must have its benefits—one certainly didn't acquire this much wealth in government service. And Hugh had struck him as such a down-to-earth fellow! Not at all the country nobleman type. He had no airs, no pretensions; he was more like some absentminded civil servant who'd wandered, quite by accident, into MI6's inner sanctum.

Amused by the grandeur of it all, Richard went up the steps, breezed through the security gauntlet, and walked into the ballroom.

Here he saw a number of familiar faces among the dozens of guests who'd already arrived. The London economic summit had drawn in diplomats and financiers from across the continent. He spotted at once the American ambassador, swaggering and schmoozing like the political appointee he was. Across the room he saw a trio of old acquaintances from Paris. There was Philippe St. Pierre, the French finance minister, deep in conversation with Reggie Vane, head of the Paris Division, Bank of London. Off to the side stood Reggie's wife, Helena, looking ignored and crabby as usual. Had Richard *ever* seen that woman look happy?

A woman's loud and brassy laugh drew Richard's attention to another familiar figure from his Paris days—Nina Sutherland, the ambassador's widow, shimmering from throat to ankle in green silk and bugle beads. Though her husband was long dead, the old gal was still working the crowd like a seasoned diplomat's wife. Beside her was her twenty-year-old son, Anthony, rumored to be an artist. In his purple shirt, he cut just as flashy a figure as his mother did. What a resplendent pair they were, like a couple of peacocks! Young Anthony had obviously inherited his ex-actress mother's gene for flamboyance.

Judiciously avoiding the Sutherland pair, Richard headed to the buffet table, which was graced with an elaborate ice sculpture of the Eiffel Tower. This Bastille Day theme had been carried to ridiculous extremes. *Ev-*

erything was French tonight: the music, the champagne, the tricolors hanging from the ceiling.

"Rather makes one want to burst out singing the 'Marseillaise,' doesn't it?" said a voice.

Richard turned and saw a tall blond man standing beside him. Slenderly built, with the stamp of aristocracy on his face, he seemed elegantly at ease in his starched shirt and tuxedo. Smiling, he handed a glass of champagne to Richard. The chandelier light glittered in the pale bubbles. "You're Richard Wolf," the man said.

Richard nodded, accepting the glass. "And you are…?"

"Jordan Tavistock. Uncle Hugh pointed you out as you walked into the room. Thought I'd come by and introduce myself."

The two men shook hands. Jordan's grip was solid and connected, not what Richard expected from such smoothly aristocratic hands.

"So tell me," said Jordan, casually picking up a second glass of champagne for himself, "which category do you fit into? Spy, diplomat or financier?"

Richard laughed. "I'm expected to answer that question?"

"No. But I thought I'd ask, anyway. It gets things off to a flying start." He took a sip and smiled. "It's a mental exercise of mine. Keeps these parties interesting. I try to pick up on the cues, deduce which ones are with Intelligence. And half of these people are. Or were." Jordan gazed around the room. "Think of all the secrets contained in all these heads—all those little synapses snapping with classified data."

"You seem to have more than a passing acquaintance with the business."

"When one grows up in this household, one lives and breathes the game." Jordan regarded Richard for a moment. "Let's see. You're American..."

"Correct."

"And whereas the corporate executives arrived in groups by stretch limousine, you came on your own."

"Right so far."

"And you refer to intelligence work as *the business*."

"You noticed."

"So my guess is... CIA?"

Richard shook his head and smiled. "I'm just a private security consultant. Sakaroff and Wolf, Inc."

Jordan smiled back. "Clever cover."

"It's not a cover. I'm the real thing. All these corporate executives you see here want a safe summit. An IRA bomb could ruin their whole day."

"So they hire you to keep the nasties away," finished Jordan.

"Exactly," said Richard. And he thought, *Yes, this is Madeline and Bernard's son, all right. He resembles Bernard, has got the same sharply observant brown eyes, the same finely wrought features. And he's quick. He notices things—an indispensable talent.*

At that moment, Jordan's attention suddenly shifted to a new arrival. Richard turned to see who had just entered the ballroom. At his first glimpse of the woman, he stiffened in surprise.

It was that black-haired witch, dressed not in old jodhpurs and boots this time, but in a long gown of midnight blue silk. Her hair had been swept up into an elegant mass of waves. Even from this distance, he could feel the magical spell of her attraction—as did every other man in the room.

"It's her," murmured Richard.

"You mean you two have met?" asked Jordan.

"Quite by accident. I spooked her horse on the road. She was none too pleased about the fall."

"You actually unhorsed her?" said Jordan in amazement. "I didn't think it was possible."

The woman glided into the room and swept up a glass of champagne from a tray, her progress cutting a noticeable swath through the crowd.

"She certainly knows how to fill a dress," Richard said under his breath, marveling.

"I'll tell her you said so," Jordan said dryly.

"You wouldn't."

Laughing, Jordan set down his glass. "Come on, Wolf. Let me properly introduce you."

As they approached her, the woman flashed Jordan a smile of greeting. Then her gaze shifted to Richard, and instantly her expression went from easy familiarity to a look of cautious speculation. *Not good,* thought Richard. *She's remembering how I knocked her off that horse. How I almost got her killed.*

"So," she said, civilly enough, "we meet again."

"I hope you've forgiven me."

"Never." Then she smiled. What a smile!

Jordan said, "Darling, this is Richard Wolf."

The woman held out her hand. Richard took it and was surprised by the firm, no-nonsense handshake she returned. As he looked into her eyes, a shock of recognition went through him. *Of course. I should have seen it the very first time we met. That black hair. Those green eyes. She has to be Madeline's daughter.*

"May I introduce Beryl Tavistock," said Jordan. "My sister."

* * *

“So how do you happen to know my uncle Hugh?” Beryl asked as she and Richard strolled down the garden path. Dusk had fallen, that soft, late dusk of summer, and the flowers had faded into shadow. Their fragrance hung in the air, the scent of sage and roses, lavender and thyme. He moves like a cat in the darkness, Beryl thought. So quiet, so unfathomable.

“We met years ago in Paris,” he said. “We lost touch for a long time. And then, a few years ago, when I set up my consulting firm, your uncle was kind enough to advise me.”

“Jordan tells me your company’s Sakaroff and Wolf.”

“Yes. We’re security consultants.”

“And is that your real job?”

“Meaning what?”

“Have you a, shall we say, *unofficial* job?”

He threw back his head and laughed. “You and your brother have a knack for cutting straight to the chase.”

“We’ve learned to be direct. It cuts down on the small talk.”

“Small talk is society’s lubricant.”

“No, small talk is how society avoids telling the truth.”

“And you want to hear the truth,” he said.

“Don’t we all?” She looked up at him, trying to see his eyes in the darkness, but they were only shadows in the silhouette of his face.

“The truth,” he said, “is that I really am a security consultant. I run the firm with my partner, Niki Sakaroff—”

“Niki? That wouldn’t be Nikolai Sakaroff?”

"You've heard the name?" he asked, in a tone that was just a trifle too innocent.

"Former KGB?"

There was a pause. "Yes, at one time," he said evenly. "Niki may have had connections."

"Connections? If I recall correctly, Nikolai Sakaroff was a full colonel. And now he's your business partner?" She laughed. "Capitalism does indeed make strange bedfellows."

They walked a few moments in silence. She asked quietly, "Do you still do business for the CIA?"

"Did I say I did?"

"It's not a difficult conclusion to come to. I'm very discreet, by the way. The truth is safe with me."

"Nevertheless I refuse to be interrogated."

She looked up at him with a smile. "Even under torture, I assume?"

Through the darkness she could see his teeth gleaming in a grin. "That depends on the type of torture. If a beautiful woman nibbles on my ear, well, I might admit to anything."

The brick path ended at the maze. For a while, they stood contemplating that leafy wall of shadow.

"Come on, let's go in," she said.

"Do you know the way out?"

"We'll see."

She led him through the opening and they were quickly swallowed up by hedge walls. In truth, she knew every turn, every blind end, and she moved through the maze with confidence. "I could do this blindfolded," she said.

"Did you grow up at Chetwynd?"

"In between boarding schools. I came to live with

Uncle Hugh when I was eight. After Mum and Dad died."

They rustled through the last slot in the hedge and emerged into the center. In a small clearing there was a stone bench and enough moonlight to faintly see each other's face.

"They were in the business, too," she said, circling the grassy clearing slowly. "Or did you already know that?"

"Yes, I've…heard of your parents."

At once she sensed an undertone of caution in his voice and wondered why he'd gone evasive on her. She saw that he was standing by the stone bench, his hands in his pockets. *All these family secrets. I'm sick of it. Why can't anyone ever tell the truth in this house?*

"What have you heard about them?" she asked.

"I know they died in Paris."

"In the line of duty. Uncle Hugh says it was a classified mission and refuses to talk about it, so we never do." She stopped circling and turned to face him. "I seem to be thinking about it a lot these days."

"Why?"

"Because it happened on the fifteenth of July. Twenty years ago tomorrow."

He moved toward her, his face still hidden in shadow. "Who reared you, then? Your uncle?"

She smiled. "'Reared' is a bit of an exaggeration. Uncle Hugh gave us a home, and then he pretty much turned us loose to grow up as we pleased. Jordan's done quite well for himself, I think. Gone to university and all. But then, Jordie's the smart one in the family."

Richard moved closer—so close she thought she

could see his eyes glittering above her in the darkness. "And which one are you?"

"I suppose… I suppose I'm the wild one."

"The wild one," he murmured. "Yes, I think I can tell…"

He touched her face. With that one brief contact, he left her skin tingling. She was suddenly aware of her pounding heart, her quickening breath. *Why am I letting this happen?* she wondered. *I thought I'd sworn off romance. But now this man I scarcely know is dragging me back into the game—a game at which I've proved myself a miserable failure. It's stupid, it's impulsive. It's insanity itself.*

And it's leaving me quite hungry for more...

His lips grazed hers; it was the lightest of kisses, but it was heady with the taste of champagne. At once she craved another kiss, a longer kiss. For a moment, they stared at each other, both hovering on the edge of temptation.

Beryl surrendered first. She swayed toward him, against him. His arms went around her, trapping her in their embrace. Eagerly she met his lips, met his kiss with one just as fierce.

"The wild one," he whispered. "Yes, definitely the wild one."

"Demanding, too…"

"I don't doubt it."

"…and *very* difficult."

"I hadn't noticed…"

They kissed again, and by the ragged sound of his breathing, she knew that he, too, was a helpless victim of desire. Suddenly a devilish impulse seized her.

She pulled away. Coyly she asked, "Now will you tell me?"

"Tell you what?" he asked, plainly confused.

"Whom you really work for?"

He paused. "Sakaroff and Wolf, Inc.," he said. "Security consultants."

"Wrong answer," she said. Then, laughing wickedly, she turned and scampered out of the maze.

Paris

At 8:45, as was her habit, Marie St. Pierre patted on her bee pollen face cream, ran a brush through her stiff gray hair, and then slipped under the covers of her bed. She flicked on the TV remote control and awaited her favorite program of the week—"Dynasty." Though the voices were obviously dubbed and the settings garishly American, the stories were close to her heart. Love and power. Pain and retribution. Yes, Marie knew all about love and pain. It was the retribution part she hadn't quite mastered. Every time the anger bubbled up inside her and those old fantasies of revenge began to play out in her mind, she had only to consider the consequences of such action, and all thoughts of vengeance died. No, she loved Philippe too much. And they had come so far together! From finance minister to prime minister would be such a short, short climb…

She suddenly focused on the TV as a brief news item flashed on the screen—the London economic summit. Would Philippe's face appear? No, just a pan of the conference table, a five-second view of two dozen men in suits and ties. No Philippe. She sat back in disappointment and wondered, for the hundredth time, if she should have accompanied her husband to London. She hated to fly, and he'd warned her the trip would be tiresome. Better to stay home, he'd told her; she would hate London.

Still, it might have been nice to go away with him for a few days. Just the two of them in a hotel room. A change of scenery, a new bed. It might have been the spark their marriage so terribly needed—

A thought suddenly crossed her mind. A thought so painful that it twisted her heart in knots. *Here I am. And there is Philippe, alone in London...*

Or was he alone?

She sat trembling for a moment, considering the possibilities. The images. At last she could resist the impulse no longer. She reached for the telephone and dialed Nina Sutherland's Paris apartment.

The phone rang and rang. She hung up and dialed again. Still it rang unanswered. She stared at the receiver. So Nina has gone to London, too, she thought. And there they would be together, in his hotel room. *While I wait at home in Paris.*

She rose from the bed. "Dynasty" had just come on the TV; she ignored it. Instead she got dressed. *Perhaps I am jumping to conclusions,* she thought. *Perhaps Nina is really home and refuses to answer her telephone.*

She would drive past Nina's apartment in Neuilly. Check the windows to see if her lights were on inside.

And if they were not?

No, she wouldn't think about that, not yet.

Fully dressed now, she hurried downstairs, picked up her purse and keys in the darkened living room, and opened the front door. Just as she felt the night air against her face, her ears were blasted by a deafening roar.

The explosion threw her off her feet, flinging her forward down the front steps. Only her outstretched arms beneath her prevented her head from slamming against the concrete. She was vaguely aware of glass raining down around her and then of the soft crackle of flames. Slowly she managed to roll over onto her back. There she lay, staring upward at the fingers of fire shooting through her bedroom window.

It was meant for her, she thought. The bomb was meant for her.

As fire sirens wailed closer, she lay on her back in the broken glass and thought, *Is this what it's come to, my love?*

And she watched her bedroom burn above her.

Chapter 2

Buckinghamshire, England

The Eiffel Tower was melting. Jordan stood beside the buffet table and watched the water drip, drip from the ice sculpture into the silver platter of oysters below it. So much for Bastille Day, he thought wearily. Another night, another party. And this one's about run its course.

"You have had more than enough oysters for one night, Reggie," said a peevish voice. "Or have you forgotten your gout?"

"Haven't had an attack in months."

"Only because *I've* been watching your diet," said Helena.

"Then tonight, dear," said Reggie, plucking up another oyster, "would you mind looking the other way?" He lifted the shell to his mouth and tipped the oyster.

Nirvana was written on his face as the slippery glob slid into his throat.

Helena shuddered. "It's disgusting, eating a live animal." She glanced at Jordan, noting his quietly bemused look. "Don't you agree?"

Jordan gave a diplomatic shrug. "A matter of upbringing, I suppose. In some cultures, they eat termites. Or quivering fish. I've even heard of monkeys, their heads shaved, immobilized—"

"Oh, please," groaned Helena.

Jordan quickly escaped before the marital spat could escalate. It was not a healthy place to be, caught between a feuding husband and wife. Lady Helena, he suspected, normally held the upper hand; money usually did.

He wandered over to join Finance Minister Philippe St. Pierre and found himself trapped in a lecture on world economics. The summit was a failure, Philippe declared. The Americans want trade concessions but refuse to learn fiscal responsibility. And on and on and on. It was almost a relief when bugle-beaded Nina Sutherland swept into the conversation, trailing her peacock son, Anthony.

"It's not as if Americans are the only ones who have to clean up their act," snorted Nina. "We're none of us doing very well these days, even the French. Or don't you agree, Philippe?"

Philippe flushed under her direct gaze. "We are all of us having difficulties, Nina—"

"Some of us more than others."

"It is a worldwide recession. One must be patient."

Nina's jaw shot up. "And what if one cannot afford

to wait?" She drained her glass and set it down sharply. "What then, Philippe, darling?"

Conversation suddenly ceased. Jordan noticed that Helena was watching them amusedly, that Philippe was clutching his glass in a white-knuckled fist. What the blazes was going on here? he wondered. Some private feud? Bizarre tensions were weaving through the gathering tonight. Perhaps it's all that free-flowing champagne. Certainly Reggie had had too much. Their portly houseguest had wandered from the oyster tray to the champagne table. With an unsteady hand, he picked up yet another glass and raised it to his lips. No one was acting quite right tonight. Not even Beryl.

Certainly not Beryl.

He spied his sister as she reentered the ballroom. Her cheeks were flushed, her eyes glittering with some unearthly fire. Close on her heels was the American, looking just as flushed and more than a little bothered. Ah, thought Jordan with a smile. A bit of hanky-panky in the garden, was it? Well, good for her. Poor Beryl could use some fresh romance in her life, anything to make her forget that chronically unfaithful surgeon.

Beryl whisked up a glass of champagne from a passing servant and headed Jordan's way. "Having fun?" she asked him.

"Not as much as you, I suspect." He glanced across at Richard Wolf, who'd just been waylaid by some American businessman. "So," he whispered, "did you wring a confession out of him?"

"Not a thing." She smiled over her champagne glass. "Extremely tight-lipped."

"Really?"

"But I'll have another go at him later. After I let him cool his heels for a while."

Lord, how beautiful his baby sister could be when she was happy, thought Jordan. Which, it seemed, wasn't very often lately. Too much passion in that heart of hers; it made her far more vulnerable than she'd ever admit. For a year now she'd been lying doggo, had dropped out entirely from the old mating game. She'd even given up her charity work at St. Luke's—a job she'd dearly loved. It was too painful, always running into her ex-lover on the hospital grounds.

But tonight the old sparkle was back in her eyes and he was glad to see it. He noticed how it flared even more brightly as Richard Wolf glanced her way. All those flirtatious looks passing back and forth! He could almost feel the crackle of electricity flying between them.

"...a well-deserved honor, of course, but a bit late, don't you think, Jordan?"

Jordan glanced in puzzlement at Reggie Vane's flushed face. The man had been drinking entirely too much. "Excuse me," he said, "I'm afraid I wasn't following."

"The Queen's medal for Leo Sinclair. You remember Leo, don't you? Wonderful chap. Killed a year and a half ago. Or was it two years?" He gave his head a little shake, as though to clear it. "Anyway, they're just getting 'round to giving the widow his medal. I think that's inexcusable."

"Not everyone who was killed in the Gulf got a medal," Nina Sutherland cut in.

"But Leo was Intelligence," said Reggie. "He deserved some sort of honor, considering how he...died."

"Perhaps it was just an oversight," said Jordan. "Papers getting mislaid, that sort of thing. MI6 does try to honor its dead, and Leo sort of fell through the cracks."

"The way Mum and Dad did," said Beryl. "They died in the line of duty. And they never got a medal."

"Line of duty?" said Reggie. "Not exactly." He lifted the champagne glass unsteadily to his lips. Suddenly he paused, aware that the others were staring at him. The silence stretched on, broken only by the clatter of an oyster shell on someone's plate.

"What do you mean by 'not exactly'?" asked Beryl.

Reggie cleared his throat. "Surely… Hugh must have told you…" He looked around and his face blanched. "Oh, no," he murmured, "I've put my foot in it this time."

"Told us what, Reggie?" Jordan persisted.

"But it was public knowledge," said Reggie. "It was in all the Paris newspapers…"

"Reggie," Jordan said slowly. Deliberately. "Our understanding was that my mother and father were shot in Paris. That it was murder. Is that not true?"

"Well, of course there was a murder involved—"

"*A* murder?" Jordan cut in. "As in singular?"

Reggie glanced around, befuddled. "I'm not the only one here who knows about it. You were all in Paris when it happened!"

For a few heartbeats, no one said a thing. Then Helena added, quietly, "It was a very long time ago, Jordan. Twenty years. It hardly makes a difference now."

"It makes a difference to *us,*" Jordan insisted. "What happened in Paris?"

Helena sighed. "I told Hugh he should've been honest with you, instead of trying to bury it."

"Bury *what?*" asked Beryl.

Helena's mouth drew tight.

It was Nina who finally spoke the truth. Brazen Nina, who had never bothered with subtleties. She said flatly, "The police said it was a murder. Followed by a suicide."

Beryl stared at Nina. Saw the other woman's gaze meet hers without flinching. "No," she whispered.

Gently Helena touched her shoulder. "You were just a child, Beryl. Both of you were. And Hugh didn't think it was appropriate—"

Beryl said again, "No," and pulled away from Helena's outstretched hand. Suddenly she whirled and fled in a rustle of blue silk across the ballroom.

"Thank you. All of you," said Jordan coldly. "For your most refreshing candor." Then he, too, turned and headed across the room in pursuit of his sister.

He caught up with her on the staircase. "Beryl?"

"It's not true," she said. "I don't believe it!"

"Of course it's not true."

She halted on the stairs and looked down at him. "Then why are they all saying it?"

"Ugly rumors. What else can it be?"

"Where's Uncle Hugh?"

Jordan shook his head. "He's not in the ballroom."

Beryl looked up toward the second floor. "Come on, Jordie," she said, her voice tight with determination. "We're going to set this thing straight."

Together they climbed the stairs.

Uncle Hugh was in his study; through the closed door, they could hear him speaking in urgent tones. Without knocking, they pushed inside and confronted him.

"Uncle Hugh?" said Beryl.

Hugh cut her off with a sharp motion for silence.

He turned his back and said into the telephone, "It *is* definite, Claude? Not a gas leak or anything like that?"

"Uncle Hugh!"

Stubbornly he kept his back turned to her. "Yes, yes," he said into the phone, "I'll tell Philippe at once. God, this is horrid timing, but you're right, he has no choice. He'll have to fly back tonight." Looking stunned, Hugh hung up and stared at the telephone.

"Did you tell us the truth?" asked Beryl. "About Mum and Dad?"

Hugh turned and frowned at her in bewilderment. "What? What are you talking about?"

"You told us they were killed in the line of duty," said Beryl. "You never said anything about a suicide."

"Who told you that?" he snapped.

"Nina Sutherland. But Reggie and Helena knew about it, too. In fact, the whole world seems to know! Everyone except us."

"Blast that Sutherland woman!" roared Hugh. "She had no right."

Beryl and Jordan stared at him in shock. Softly Beryl said, "It *is* a lie. Isn't it?"

Abruptly Hugh started for the door. "We'll discuss it later," he said. "I have to take care of this business—"

"Uncle Hugh!" cried Beryl. "Is it a lie?"

Hugh stopped. Slowly he turned and looked at her. "I never believed it," he said. "Not for a second did I think Bernard would ever hurt her…"

"What are you saying?" asked Jordan. "That it was Dad who killed her?"

Their uncle's silence was the only answer they needed. For a moment, Hugh lingered in the doorway. Quietly he said, "Please, Jordan. We'll talk about it later.

After everyone leaves. Now I really must see to this phone call." He turned and left the room.

Beryl and Jordan looked at each other. They each saw, in the other's eyes, the same shock of comprehension.

"Dear God, Jordie," said Beryl. "It must be true."

From across the ballroom, Richard saw Beryl's hasty exit and then, seconds later, the equally rapid departure of a grim-faced Jordan. What the hell was going on? he wondered. He started to follow them out of the room, then spotted Helena, shaking her head as she moved toward him.

"It's a disaster," she muttered. "Too much bloody champagne flowing tonight."

"What happened?"

"They just heard the truth. About Bernard and Madeline."

"Who told them?"

"Nina. But it was Reggie's fault, really. He's so drunk he doesn't know what he's saying."

Richard looked at the doorway through which Jordan had just vanished. "I should talk to them, tell them the whole story."

"I think that's their uncle's responsibility. Don't you? He's the one who kept it from them all these years. Let him do the explaining."

After a pause, Richard nodded. "You're right. Of course you're right. Maybe I'll just go and strangle Nina Sutherland instead."

"Strangle my husband while you're at it. You have my permission."

Richard turned and spotted Hugh Tavistock reentering the ballroom. “Now what?” he muttered as the man hurried toward them.

“Where’s Philippe?” snapped Hugh.

“I believe he was headed out to the garden,” said Helena. “Is something wrong?”

“This whole evening’s turned into a disaster,” muttered Hugh. “I just got a call from Paris. A bomb’s gone off in Philippe’s flat.”

Richard and Helena stared at him in horror.

“Oh, my God,” whispered Helena. “Is Marie—”

“She’s all right. A few minor injuries, but nothing serious. She’s in hospital now.”

“Assassination attempt?” Richard queried.

Hugh nodded. “So it would seem.”

It was long past midnight when Jordan and Uncle Hugh finally found Beryl. She was in her mother’s old room, huddled beside Madeline’s steamer trunk. The lid had been thrown open, and Madeline’s belongings were spilled out across the bed and the floor: silky summer dresses, flowery hats, a beaded evening purse. And there were silly things, too: a branch of sea coral, a pebble, a china frog—items of significance known only to Madeline. Beryl had removed all of these things from the trunk, and now she sat surrounded by them, trying to absorb, through these inanimate objects, the warmth and spirit that had once been Madeline Tavistock.

Uncle Hugh came into the bedroom and sat down in a chair beside her. “Beryl,” he said gently, “it’s time… it’s time I told you the truth.”

“The time for the truth was years ago,” she said, staring down at the china frog in her hand.

“But you were both so very young. You were only

eight, and Jordan was ten. You wouldn't have understood—"

"We could've dealt with the facts! Instead you hid them from us!"

"The facts were painful. The French police concluded—"

"Dad would *never* have hurt her," said Beryl. She looked up at him with a ferocity that made Hugh draw back in surprise. "Don't you remember how they were together, Uncle Hugh? How much in love they were? *I* remember!"

"So do I," said Jordan.

Uncle Hugh took off his spectacles and wearily rubbed his eyes. "The truth," he said, "is even worse than that."

Beryl stared at him incredulously. "How could it be any worse than murder and suicide?"

"Perhaps...perhaps you should see the file." He rose to his feet. "It's upstairs. In my office."

They followed their uncle to the third floor, to a room they seldom visited, a room he always kept locked. He opened the cabinet and pulled a folder from the drawer. It was a classified MI6 file labeled Tavistock, Bernard and Madeline.

"I suppose I… I'd hoped to protect you from this," said Hugh. "The truth is, I myself don't believe it. Bernard didn't have a traitorous bone in his body. But the evidence was there. And I don't know any other way to explain it." He handed the file to Beryl.

In silence she opened the folder. Together she and Jordan paged through the contents. Inside were copies of the Paris police report, including witness statements and photographs of the murder scene. The conclusions were as Nina Sutherland had told them. Bernard had shot his wife three times at close range and had then put the gun to his own head and pulled the trigger. The crime photos were too horrible to dwell on; Beryl flipped quickly past those and found herself staring at another report, this one filed by French Intelligence. In disbelief, she read and reread the conclusions.

"This isn't possible," she said.

"It's what they found. A briefcase with classified NATO files. Allied weapons data. It was in the garret, where their bodies were discovered. Bernard had those files with him when he died—files that shouldn't have been out of the embassy building."

"How do you know *he* took them?"

"He had access, Beryl. He was our Intelligence liaison to NATO. For months, Allied documents were showing up in East German hands, delivered to them by someone they code-named Delphi. We knew we had a mole, but we couldn't identify him—until those papers were found with Bernard's body."

"And you think Dad was Delphi," said Jordan.

"No, that's what French Intelligence concluded. I couldn't believe it, but I also couldn't dispute the facts."

For a moment, Beryl and Jordan sat in silence, dismayed by the weight of the evidence.

"You don't really believe it, Uncle Hugh?" said Beryl softly. "That Dad was the one?"

"I couldn't argue with the findings. And it *would* explain their deaths. Perhaps they knew they were on the verge of being discovered. Disgraced. So Bernard took the gentleman's way out. He would, you know. Death before dishonor."

Uncle Hugh sank back in the chair and wearily ran

his fingers through his gray hair. "I tried to keep the report as quiet as possible," he said. "The search for Delphi was halted. I myself had a few sticky years in MI6. Brother of a traitor and all, can we trust him, that sort of thing. But then, it was forgotten. And I went on with my career. I think… I think it was because no one at MI6 could quite believe the report. That Bernard had gone to the other side."

"I don't believe it, either," said Beryl.

Uncle Hugh looked at her. "Nevertheless—"

"I *won't* believe it. It's a fabrication. Someone at MI6, covering up the truth—"

"Don't be ridiculous, Beryl."

"Mum and Dad can't defend themselves! Who else will speak up for them?"

"Your loyalty's commendable, darling, but—"

"And where's *your* loyalty?" she retorted. "He was your brother!"

"I didn't want to believe it."

"Then did you confirm that evidence? Did you discuss it with French Intelligence?"

"Yes, and I trusted Daumier's report. He's a thorough man."

"Daumier?" queried Jordan. "Claude Daumier? Isn't he chief of their Paris operations?"

"At the time, he was their liaison to MI6. I asked him to review the findings. He came to the same conclusions."

"Then this Daumier fellow is an idiot," said Beryl. She turned to the door. "And I'm going to tell him so myself."

"Where are you going?" asked Jordan.

"To pack my things," she said. "Are you coming, Jordan?"

"Pack?" said Hugh. "Where in blazes are you headed?"

Beryl threw a glance over her shoulder. "Where else," she answered, "but Paris?"

Richard Wolf got the call at six that morning. "They are booked on a noon flight to Paris," said Claude Daumier. "It seems, my friend, that someone has pried open a rather nasty can of worms."

Still groggy with sleep, Richard sat up in bed and gave his head a shake. "What are you talking about, Claude? Who's flying to Paris?"

"Beryl and Jordan Tavistock. Hugh has just called me. I think this is not a good development."

Richard collapsed back on his pillow. "They're adults, Claude," he said, yawning. "If they want to jet off to Paris—"

"They are coming to find out about Bernard and Madeline."

Richard closed his eyes and groaned. "Oh, wonderful, just what we need."

"My sentiments precisely."

"Can't Hugh talk them out of it?"

"He tried. But this niece of his…" Daumier sighed. "You have met her. So you would understand."

Yes, Richard knew exactly how stubborn Miss Beryl Tavistock could be. Like mother, like daughter. He remembered that Madeline had been just as unswerving, just as unstoppable.

Just as enchanting.

He shook off those haunting memories of a long-dead woman and said, “How much do they know?”

“They have seen my report. They know about Delphi.”

“So they’ll be digging in all the right places.”

“All the dangerous places,” amended Daumier.

Richard sat up on the side of the bed and clawed his fingers through his hair as he considered the possibilities. The perils.

“Hugh is concerned for their safety,” said Daumier. “So am I. If what we think is true—”

“Then they’re walking into quicksand.”

“And Paris is dangerous enough as it is,” added Daumier, “what with the latest bombing.”

“How is Marie St. Pierre, by the way?”

“A few scratches, bruises. She should be released from the hospital tomorrow.”

“Ordnance report back?”

“Semtex. The upper apartment was completely demolished. Luckily Marie was downstairs when the bomb went off.”

“Who’s claiming responsibility?”

“There was a telephone call shortly after the blast. It was a man, said he belonged to some group called Cosmic Solidarity. They claim responsibility.”

“Cosmic Solidarity? Never heard of that one.”

“Neither have we,” said Daumier. “But you know how it is these days.”

Yes, Richard knew only too well. Any wacko with the right connections could buy a few ounces of Semtex, build a bomb, and join the revolution—any revolution. No wonder his business was booming. In this brave new world, terrorism was a fact of life. And clients everywhere were willing to pay top dollar for security.

"So you see, my friend," said Daumier, "it is not a good time for Bernard's children to be in Paris. And with all the questions they will ask—"

"Can't you keep an eye on them?"

"Why should they trust me? It was *my* report in that file. No, they need another friend here, Richard. Someone with sharp eyes and unerring instincts."

"You have someone in mind?"

"I hear through the grapevine that you and Miss Tavistock shared a degree of…simpatico?"

"She's way too rich for my blood. And I'm too poor for hers."

"I do not usually ask for favors," said Daumier quietly. "Neither does Hugh."

And you're asking for one now, thought Richard. He sighed. "How can I refuse?"

After he'd hung up, he sat for a moment contemplating the task ahead. This was a baby-sitting job, really—the sort of assignment he despised. But the thought of seeing Beryl Tavistock again, and the memory of that kiss they'd shared in the garden, was enough to make him grin with anticipation. *Way too rich for my blood,* he thought. *But a man can dream, can't he? And I do owe it to Bernard and Madeline.*

Even after all these years, their deaths still haunted him. Perhaps the time had come to close the mystery, to answer all those questions he and Daumier had raised twenty years ago. The same questions MI6 and Central Intelligence had firmly suppressed.

Now Beryl Tavistock was poking her aristocratic nose into the mess. And a most attractive nose it was, he thought. He hoped it didn't get her killed.

He rose from the bed and headed for the shower. So

much to do, so many preparations to make before he headed to the airport.

Baby-sitting jobs—how he hated them.

But at least this one would be in Paris.

Anthony Sutherland stared out his airplane window and longed fervently for the flight to be over and done with. Of all the rotten luck to be booked on the same Air France flight as the Vanes! And then to be seated straight across the first-class aisle from them—well, this really was intolerable. He considered Reggie Vane a screaming bore, especially when intoxicated, which at the moment Reggie was well on the way to becoming. Two whiskey sours and the man was starting to babble about how much he missed jolly old England, where food was boiled as it should be, not sautéed in all that ghastly butter, where people lined up in proper queues, where crowds didn't reek of garlic and onions. He'd lived too many years in Paris now—surely it was time to retire from the bank and go home? He'd put in many years at the Bank of London's Paris branch. Now that there were so many clever young V.P.s ready to step into his place, why not let them?

Lady Helena, who appeared to be just as fed up with her husband as Anthony was, simply said, "Shut up, Reggie," and ordered him a third whiskey sour.

Anthony didn't much care for Helena, either. She reminded him of some sort of nasty rodent. Such a contrast to his mother! The two women sat across the aisle from each other, Helena drab and proper in her houndstooth skirt and jacket, Nina so striking in her whitest-white silk pantsuit. Only a woman with true confidence could wear white silk, and his mother was one who could. Even at fifty-three, Nina was stunning, her dark, upswept hair showing scarcely a trace of gray, her figure the envy of any twenty-year-old. *But of course,* thought Anthony, *she's my mother.*

And, as usual, she was getting in her digs at Helena.

"If you and Reggie hate it so much in Paris," sniffed Nina, "why do you stay? If you ask me, people who don't adore the city don't deserve to live there."

"Of course, you *would* love Paris," said Helena.

"It's all in the attitude. If you'd kept an open mind..."

"Oh, no, we're much too stuffy," muttered Helena.

"I didn't say that. But there is a certain British attitude. God is an Englishman, that sort of thing."

"You mean He isn't?" Reggie interjected.

Helena didn't laugh. "I just think," she said, "that a certain amount of order and discipline is needed for the world to function properly."

Nina glanced at Reggie, who was noisily slurping his whiskey. "Yes, I can see you both believe in discipline. No wonder the evening was such a disaster."

"We weren't the ones who blurted out the truth," snapped Helena.

"At least *I* was sober enough to know what I was saying!" Nina declared. "They would have found out in any event. After Reggie there let the cat out of the bag, I just decided it was time to be straight with them about Bernard and Madeline."

"And look at the result," moaned Helena. "Hugh says Beryl and Jordan are flying to Paris this afternoon. Now they'll be mucking around in things."

Nina shrugged. "Well, it was a long time ago."

"I don't see why you're so nonchalant. If anyone could be hurt, it's you," muttered Helena.

Nina frowned at her. "What do you mean by that?"

"Oh, nothing."

"No, really! What do you mean by that?"

"Nothing," Helena snapped.

Their conversation came to an abrupt halt. But Anthony could tell his mother was fuming. She sat with her hands balled up in her lap. She even ordered a second martini. When she rose from her seat and headed down the aisle for a bit of exercise, he followed her. They met at the rear of the plane.

"Are you all right, Mother?" he asked.

Nina glanced in agitation toward first class. "It's all Reggie's bloody fault," she whispered. "And Helena's right, you know. I *am* the one who could be hurt."

"After all these years?"

"They'll be asking questions again. Digging. Lord, what if those Tavistock brats find something?"

Anthony said quietly, "They won't."

Nina's gaze met his. In that one look they saw, in each other's eyes, the bond of twenty years. "You and me against the world," she used to sing to him. And that's how it had felt—just the two of them in their Paris flat. There'd been her lovers, of course, insignificant men, scarcely worth noting. But mother and son—what love could be stronger?

He said, "You've nothing to worry about, darling. Really."

"But the Tavistocks—"

"They're harmless." He took her hand and gave it a reassuring squeeze. "I guarantee it."

Chapter 3

From the window of her suite at the Paris Ritz, Beryl looked down at the opulence of Place Vendôme, with its Corinthian pilasters and stone arches, and saw the evening parade of well-heeled tourists. It had been eight years since she'd last visited Paris, and then it had been on a lark with her girlfriends—three wild chums from school, who'd preferred the Left Bank bistros and seedy nightlife of Montparnasse to this view of unrepentant luxury. They'd had a grand time of it, too, had drunk countless bottles of wine, danced in the streets, flirted with every Frenchman who'd glanced their way—and there'd been a lot of them.

It seemed a million years ago. A different life, a different age.

Now, standing at the hotel window, she mourned the loss of all those carefree days and knew they would never be back. *I've changed too much,* she thought. *It's more than just the revelations about Mum and Dad. It's me. I feel restless. I'm longing for... I don't know what. Purpose, perhaps? I've gone so long without purpose in my life...*

She heard the door open, and Jordan came in through the connecting door from his suite. "Claude Daumier finally returned my call," he said. "He's tied up with the bomb investigation, but he's agreed to meet us for an early supper."

"When?"

"Half an hour."

Beryl turned from the window and looked at her brother. They'd scarcely slept last night, and it showed in Jordan's face. Though freshly shaved and impeccably dressed, he had that ragged edge of fatigue, the lean and hungry look of a man operating on reserve strength. *Like me.*

"I'm ready to leave anytime," she said.

He frowned at her dress. "Isn't that... Mum's?"

"Yes. I packed a few of her things in my suitcase. I don't know why, really." She gazed down at the watered-silk skirt. "It's eerie, isn't it? How well it fits. As if it were made for me."

"Beryl, are you sure you're up to this?"

"Why do you ask?"

"It's just that—" Jordan shook his head "—you don't seem at all yourself."

"Neither of us is, Jordie. How could we be?" She looked out the window again, at the lengthening shadows in Place Vendôme. The same view her mother must have looked down upon on *her* visits to Paris. The same hotel, perhaps even the same suite. *I'm even wearing her dress.* "It's as if—as if we don't know who we are anymore," she said. "Where we spring from."

"Who you are, who I am, has never been in doubt, Beryl. Whatever we learn about them doesn't change us."

She looked at him. "So you think it might be true."

He paused. "I don't know," he said. "But I'm preparing myself for the worst. And so should you." He went to the closet and took out her wrap. "Come on. It's time to confront the facts, little sister. Whatever they may be."

At seven o'clock, they arrived at Le Petit Zinc, the café where Daumier had arranged to meet them. It was early for the usual Parisian supper hour, and except for a lone couple dining on soup and bread, the café was empty. They took a seat in a booth at the rear and ordered wine and bread and a *remoulade* of mustard and celeriac to stave off their hunger. The lone couple finished their meal and departed. The appointed time came and went. Had Daumier changed his mind about meeting them?

Then, at seven-twenty, the door opened and a trim little Frenchman in suit and tie walked into the dining room. With his graying temples and his briefcase, he could have passed for any distinguished banker or lawyer. But the instant his gaze locked on Beryl, she knew, by his nod of acknowledgment, that this must be Claude Daumier.

But he had not come alone. He glanced over his shoulder as the door opened again, and a second man entered the restaurant. Together they approached the booth where Beryl and Jordan were seated. Beryl stiffened as she found herself staring not at Daumier but at his companion.

"Hello, Richard," she said quietly. "I had no idea you were coming to Paris."

"Neither did I," he said. "Until this morning."

Introductions were made, hands shaken all around. Then the two men slid into the booth. Beryl faced Richard straight across the table. As his gaze met hers, she felt the earlier sparks kindle between them, the memory of their kiss flaring to mind. *Beryl, you idiot,* she thought in irritation, *you're letting him distract you. Confuse you. No man has a right to affect you this way—certainly not a man you've only kissed once in your life. Not to mention one you met only twenty-four hours ago.*

Still, she couldn't seem to shake the memory of those moments in the garden at Chetwynd. Nor could she forget the taste of his lips. She watched him pour himself a glass of wine, watched him raise the glass to sip. Again, their eyes met, this time over the gleam of ruby liquid. She licked her own lips and savored the aftertaste of Burgundy.

"So what brings you to Paris?" she asked, raising her glass.

"Claude, as a matter of fact." He tilted his head at Daumier.

At Beryl's questioning look, Daumier said, "When I heard my old friend Richard was in London, I thought why not consult him? Since he is an authority on the subject."

"The St. Pierre bombing," Richard explained. "Some group no one's ever heard of is claiming responsibility. Claude thought perhaps I'd be able to shed some light on their identity. For years I've been tracking every reported terrorist organization there is."

"And did you shed some light?" asked Jordan.

"Afraid not," he admitted. "Cosmic Solidarity doesn't show up on my computer." He took another sip of wine, and his gaze locked with hers. "But the trip isn't entirely wasted," he added, "since I discover you're in Paris, as well."

"Strictly business," said Beryl. "With no time for pleasure."

"None at all?"

"None," she said flatly. She pointedly turned her attention to Daumier. "My uncle did call you, didn't he? About why we're here?"

The Frenchman nodded. "I understand you have both read the file."

"Cover to cover," said Jordan.

"Then you know the evidence. I myself confirmed the witness statements, the coroner's findings—"

"The coroner could have misinterpreted the facts," Jordan asserted.

"I myself saw their bodies in the garret. It was not something I am likely to forget." Daumier paused as though shaken by the memory. "Your mother died of three bullet wounds to the chest. Lying beside her was Bernard, a single bullet in his head. The gun had his fingerprints. There were no witnesses, no other suspects." Daumier shook his head. "The evidence speaks for itself."

"But where's the motive?" said Beryl. "Why would he kill someone he loved?"

"Perhaps that is the motive," said Daumier. "Love. Or loss of love. She may have found someone else—"

"That's impossible," Beryl objected vehemently. "She loved him."

Daumier looked down at his wineglass. He said quietly, "You have not yet read the police interview with the landlord, M. Rideau?"

Beryl and Jordan looked at him in puzzlement. "Rideau? I don't recall seeing that interview in the file," said Jordan.

"Only because I chose to exclude it when I sent the file to Hugh. It was a…matter of discretion."

Discretion, thought Beryl. Meaning he was trying to hide some embarrassing fact.

"The attic flat where their bodies were found," said Daumier, "was rented out to a Mlle Scarlatti. According to the landlord, Rideau, this Scarlatti woman used the flat once or twice a week. And only for the purpose of…" He paused delicately.

"Meeting a lover?" Jordan said bluntly.

Daumier nodded. "After the shooting, the landlord was asked to identify the bodies. Rideau told the police that the woman he called Mlle Scarlatti was the same one found dead in the garret. Your mother."

Beryl stared at him in shock. "You're saying my mother met a *lover* there?"

"It was the landlord's testimony."

"Then we'll have to talk face-to-face with this landlord."

"Not possible," said Daumier. "The building has been sold several times over. M. Rideau has left the country. I do not know where he is."

Beryl and Jordan sat in stunned silence. So that was Daumier's theory, thought Beryl. That her mother had a lover. Once or twice a week she would meet him in that attic flat on Rue Myrha. And then her father found out. So he killed her. And then he killed himself.

She looked up at Richard and saw the flicker of sympathy in his eyes. He believes it, too, she thought. Suddenly she resented him simply for being here, for hearing the most shameful secret of her family.

They heard a soft beeping. Daumier reached under his jacket and frowned at his pocket pager. "I am afraid I will have to leave," he said.

"What about that classified file?" asked Jordan. "You haven't said anything about Delphi."

"We'll speak of it later. This bombing, you understand—it is a crisis situation." Daumier slid out of the booth and picked up his briefcase. "Perhaps tomorrow? In the meantime, try to enjoy your stay in Paris, all of you. Oh, and if you dine here, I would recommend the duckling. It is excellent." With a nod of farewell, he turned and swiftly walked out of the restaurant.

"We just got the royal runaround," muttered Jordan in frustration. "He drops a bomb in our laps, then he scurries for cover, never answering our questions."

"I think that was his plan from the start," said Beryl. "Tell us something so horrifying, we'll be afraid to pursue it. Then our questions will stop." She looked at Richard. "Am I right?"

He met her gaze without wavering. "Why are you asking me?"

"Because you two obviously know each other well. Is this the way Daumier usually operates?"

"Claude's not one to spill secrets. But he also believes in helping out old friends, and your uncle Hugh's a good friend of his. I'm sure Claude's keeping your best interests at heart."

Old friends, thought Beryl. Daumier and Uncle Hugh and Richard Wolf—all of them linked together by some shadowy past, a past they would not talk about. This was how it had been, growing up at Chetwynd. Mysterious men in limousines dropping in to visit Hugh. Sometimes Beryl would hear snatches of conversation, would pick up whispered names whose significance she could only guess at. Yurchenko. Andropov. Baghdad. Berlin. She had learned long ago not to ask questions, never to expect answers. "Not something to bother your pretty head about," Hugh would tell her.

This time, she wouldn't be put off. This time she demanded answers.

The waiter came to the table with the menus. Beryl shook her head. "We won't be staying," she said.

"You're not interested in supper?" asked Richard. "Claude says it's an excellent restaurant."

"Did Claude ask you to show up?" she demanded. "Keep us well fed and entertained so we won't trouble him?"

"I'm delighted to keep you well fed. And, if you're willing, entertained." He smiled at her then, a smile with just a spark of mischief. Looking into his eyes, she found herself wavering on the edge of temptation. *Have supper with me,* she read in his smile. *And afterward, who knows? Anything's possible.*

Slowly she sat back in the booth. "We'll have supper with you, on one condition."

"What's that?"

"You play it straight with us. No dodging, no games."

"I'll try."

"Why are you in Paris?"

"Claude asked me to consult. As a personal favor. The summit's over now, so my schedule's open. Plus, I was curious."

"About the bombing?"

He nodded. "Cosmic Solidarity is a new one for me. I try to keep up with new terrorist groups. It's my business." He held a menu out to her and smiled. "And that, Miss Tavistock, is the unadulterated truth."

She met his gaze and saw no flicker of avoidance in his eyes. Still, her instincts told her there was something more behind that smile, something yet unsaid.

"You don't believe me," he said.

"How did you guess?"

"Does this mean you're not having supper with me?"

Up until that moment, Jordan had sat watching them, his gaze playing Ping-Pong. Now he cut in impatiently. "We are definitely having supper. Because I'm hungry, Beryl, and I'm not moving from this booth until I've eaten."

With a sigh of resignation, Beryl took the menu. "I guess that answers that. Jordie's stomach has spoken."

Amiel Foch's telephone rang at precisely seven-fifteen.

"I have a new task for you," said the caller. "It's a matter of some urgency. Perhaps this time around, you'll prove successful."

The criticism stung, and Amiel Foch, with twenty-five years' experience in the business, barely managed to suppress a retort. The caller held the purse strings; he could afford to hurl insults. Foch had his retirement to consider. Requests for his services were few and far between these days. One's reflexes, after all, did not improve with age.

Foch said, with quiet control, "I planted the device as you instructed. It went off at the time specified."

"And all it did was make a lot of bloody noise. The target was scarcely hurt."

"She did the unexpected. One cannot control such things."

"Let's hope this time you keep things under better control."

"What is the name?"

"Two names. A brother and sister, Beryl and Jordan Tavistock. They're staying at the Ritz. I want to know where they go. Who they see."

"Nothing more?"

"For now, just surveillance. But things may change at any time, depending on what they learn. With any luck, they'll simply turn around and run home to England."

"If they do not?"

"Then we'll take further action."

"What about Mme St. Pierre? Do you wish me to try again?"

The caller paused. "No," he said at last, "she can wait. For now, the Tavistocks take priority."

Over a meal of poached salmon and duck with raspberry sauce, Beryl and Richard thrusted and parried questions and answers. Richard, an accomplished verbal duelist, revealed only the barest sketch of his personal life. He was born and reared in Connecticut. His father, a retired cop, was still living. After leaving Princeton University, Richard joined the U.S. State Department and served as political officer at embassies around the world. Then, five years ago, he left government service to start up business as a security consultant. Sakaroff and Wolf, based in Washington, D.C., was born.

"And that's what brought me to London last week,"

he said. "Several American firms wanted security for their executives during the summit. I was hired as consultant."

"And that's all you were doing in London?" she asked.

"That's all I was doing in London. Until I got Hugh's invitation to Chetwynd." His gaze met hers across the table.

His directness unsettled her. *Is he telling me the truth, fiction or something in between?* That matter-of-fact recitation of his career had struck her as rehearsed, but then, it would be. People in the intelligence business always had their life histories down pat, the details memorized, fact blending smoothly with fantasy. What did she really know about him? Only that he smiled easily, laughed easily. That his appetite was hearty and he drank his coffee black.

And that she was intensely, insanely, attracted to him.

After supper, he offered to drive them back to the Ritz. Jordan sat in the back seat, Beryl in the front—right next to Richard. She kept glancing sideways at him as they drove up Boulevard Saint-Germain toward the Seine. Even the traffic, outrageously rude and noisy, did not seem to ruffle him. At a stoplight, he turned and looked at her and that one glimpse of his face through the darkness of the car was enough to make her heart do a somersault.

Calmly he shifted his attention back to the road. "It's still early," he said. "Are you sure you want to go back to the hotel?"

"What's my choice?"

"A drive. A walk. Whatever you'd like. After all,

you're in Paris. Why not make the most of it?" He reached down to shift gears, and his hand brushed past her knee. A shiver ran through her—a warm, delicious sizzle of anticipation.

He's tempting me. Making me dizzy with all the possibilities. Or is it the wine? What harm can there be in a little stroll, a little fresh air?

She called over her shoulder, "How about it, Jordie? Do you feel like taking a walk?" She was answered by a loud snore.

Beryl turned and saw to her astonishment that her brother was sprawled across the back seat. A sleepless night and two glasses of wine at supper had left him dead to the world. "I guess that's a negative," she said with a laugh.

"What about just you and me?"

That invitation, voiced so softly, sent another shiver of temptation up her spine. After all, she thought, she was in Paris…

"A short walk," she agreed. "But first, let's put Jordan to bed."

"Valet service coming up," Richard said, laughing. "First stop, the Ritz."

Jordan snored all the way back to the hotel.

They walked in the Tuileries, a stroll that took them along a gravel path through formal gardens, past statues glowing a ghostly white under the street lamps.

"And here we are again," said Richard, "walking through another garden. Now if only we could find a maze with a nice little stone bench at the center."

"Why?" she asked with a smile. "Are you hoping for a repeat scenario?"

"With a slightly different ending. You know, after you left me in there, it took me a good five minutes to find my way out."

"I know." She laughed. "I was waiting at the door, counting the minutes. Five minutes wasn't bad, really. But other men have done better."

"So that's how you screen your men. You're the cheese in the maze—"

"And you were the rat."

They both laughed then, and the sound of their voices floated through the night air.

"And my performance was only…adequate?" he said.

"Average."

He moved toward her, his smile gleaming in the shadows. "Better than adquate?"

"For you, I'll make allowances. After all, it was dark…"

"Yes, it was." He moved closer, so close she had to tilt her head up to look at him. So close she could almost feel the heat radiating from his body. "Very dark," he whispered.

"And perhaps you were disoriented?"

"Extremely."

"And it *was* a nasty trick I played…"

"For which you should be soundly punished."

He reached over and took her face in his hands. The taste of his lips on hers sent a shudder of pleasure through her body. *If this is my punishment,* she thought, *oh, let me commit the crime again...* His fingers slid through her hair, tangling in the strands as his kiss pressed ever deeper. She felt her legs wobble and melt away, but she had no need of them; he was there to support them both. She heard his murmur of need and knew that these kisses were dangerous, that he, too, was fast slipping toward the same cliff's edge. She didn't care—she was ready to make the leap.

And then, without warning, he froze.

One moment he was kissing her, and an instant later his hands went rigid against her face. He didn't pull away. Even as she felt his whole body grow tense against her, he kept her firmly in his embrace. His lips glided to her ear.

"Start walking," he whispered. "Toward the Concorde."

"What?"

"Just move. Don't show any alarm. I'll hold your hand."

She focused on his face, and through the shadows she saw his look of feral alertness. Swallowing back the questions, she allowed him to take her hand. They turned and began to walk casually toward the Place de la Concorde. He gave her no explanation, but she knew just by the way he gripped her hand that something was wrong, that this was not a game. Like any other pair of lovers, they strolled through the garden, past flower beds deep in shadow, past statues lined up in ghostly formation. Gradually she became more and more aware of sounds: the distant roar of traffic, the wind in the trees, their shoes crunching across the gravel…

And the footsteps, following somewhere behind them.

Nervously she clutched his hand. His answering squeeze of reassurance was enough to dull the razor edge of fear. *I've known this man only a day,* she thought, *and already I feel that I can count on him.*

Richard picked up his pace—so gradually she almost didn't notice it. The footsteps still pursued them. They veered right and crossed the park toward Rue de Rivoli. The sounds of traffic grew louder, obscuring the footsteps of their pursuer. Now was the greatest danger—as they left the darkness behind them and their pursuer saw his last chance to make a move. Bright lights beckoned from the street ahead. *We can make it if we run,* she thought. *A dash through the trees and we'll be safe, surrounded by other people.* She prepared for the sprint, waiting for Richard's cue.

But he made no sudden moves. Neither did their pursuer. Hand in hand, she and Richard strolled nonchalantly into the naked glare of Rue de Rivoli.

Only as they joined the stream of evening pedestrians did Beryl's pulse begin to slow again. There was no danger here, she thought. Surely no one would dare attack them on a busy street.

Then she glanced at Richard's face and saw that the tension was still there.

They crossed the street and walked another block.

"Stop for a minute," he murmured. "Take a long look in that window."

They paused in front of a chocolate shop. Through the glass they saw a tempting display of confections: raspberry creams and velvety truffles and Turkish delight, all nestled in webs of spun sugar. In the shop, a young woman stood over a vat of melted chocolate, dipping fresh strawberries.

"What are we waiting for?" whispered Beryl.

"To see what happens."

She stared in the window and saw the reflections of people passing behind them. A couple holding hands.

A trio of students in backpacks. A family with four children.

"Let's start walking again," he said.

They headed west on Rue de Rivoli, their pace again leisurely, unhurried. She was caught by surprise when he suddenly pulled her to the right, onto an intersecting street.

"Move it!" he barked.

All at once they were sprinting. They made another sharp right onto Mont Thabor, and ducked under an arch. There, huddled in the shadow of a doorway, he pulled her against him so tightly that she felt his heart pounding against hers, his breath warming her brow. They waited.

Seconds later, running footsteps echoed along the street. The sound moved closer, slowed, stopped. Then there was no sound at all. Almost too terrified to look, Beryl slowly shifted in Richard's arms, just enough to see a shadow slide past their archway. The footsteps moved down the street and faded away.

Richard chanced a quick look up the street, then gave Beryl's hand a tug. "All clear," he whispered. "Let's get out of here."

They turned onto Castiglione Street and didn't stop running until they were back at the hotel. Only when they were safely in her suite and he'd bolted the door behind them, did she find her voice again.

"What happened out there?" she demanded.

He shook his head. "I'm not sure."

"Do you think he meant to rob us?" She moved to the phone. "I should call the police—"

"He wasn't after our money."

"What?" She turned and frowned at him.

"Think about it. Even on Rue de Rivoli, with all those witnesses, he didn't stop following us. Any other thief would've given up and gone back to the park. Found himself another victim. But he didn't. He stayed with us."

"I didn't even see him! How do you know there *was* any—"

"A middle-aged man. Short, stocky. The sort of face most people would forget."

She stared at him, her agitation mounting. "What are you saying, Richard? That he was following us in particular?"

"Yes."

"But why would anyone follow you?"

"I could ask the same question of you."

"I'm of no interest to anyone."

"Think about it. About why you came to Paris."

"It's just a family matter."

"Apparently not. Since you now seem to have strange men following you around town."

"How do I know he wasn't following you? You're the one who works for the CIA!"

"Correction. I work for myself."

"Oh, don't palm off that rubbish on me! I practically grew up in MI6! I can smell you people a mile away!"

"Can you?" His eyebrow shot up. "And the odor didn't scare you off?"

"Maybe it should have."

He was pacing the room now, moving about like a restless animal, locking windows, pulling curtains. "Since I can't seem to deceive your highly perceptive nose, I'll just confess it. My job description is a bit looser than I've admitted to."

"I'm astonished."

"But I'm still convinced the man was following *you.*"

"Why would anyone follow me?"

"Because you're digging in a mine field. You don't understand, Beryl. When your parents were killed, there was more involved than just another sex scandal."

"Wait a minute." She crossed toward him, her gaze hard on his face. "What do you know about it?"

"I knew you were coming to Paris."

"Who told you?"

"Claude Daumier. He called me in London. Said that Hugh was worried. That someone had to keep an eye on you and Jordan."

"So you're our nanny?"

He laughed. "In a manner of speaking."

"And how much do you know about my mother and father?"

She knew by his brief silence that he was debating his answer, weighing the consequences of his next words. She fully expected to hear a lie.

Instead he surprised her with the truth. "I knew them both," he said. "I was here in Paris when it happened."

The revelation left her stunned. She didn't doubt for an instant that it was the truth—why would he fabricate such a story?

"It was my very first posting," he said. "I thought it was incredible luck to draw Paris. Most first-timers get sent to some bug-infested jungle in the middle of nowhere. But I drew Paris. And that's where I met Madeline and Bernard." Wearily he sank into a chair. "It's amazing," he murmured, studying Beryl's face, "how very much you look like her. The same green eyes, the same black hair. She used to sweep hers back in this sort of loose chignon. But strands of it were always coming loose, falling about her neck…" He smiled fondly at the memory. "Bernard was crazy about her. So was every man who ever met her."

"Were you?"

"I was only twenty-two. She was the most enchanting woman I'd ever met." His gaze met hers. Softly he added, "But then, I hadn't met her daughter."

They stared at each other, and Beryl felt those silken threads of desire tugging her toward him. Toward a man whose kisses left her dizzy, whose touch could melt even stone. A man who had not been straight with her from the very start.

I'm so tired of secrets, so tired of trying to tease apart the truths from the half truths. And I'll never know which is which with this man.

Abruptly she went to the door. "If we can't be honest with each other," she said, "there's no point in being together at all. So why don't we say good-night. And goodbye."

"I don't think so."

She turned and frowned at him. "Excuse me?"

"I'm not ready to say goodbye. Not when I know you're being followed."

"You're concerned about my welfare, is that it?"

"Shouldn't I be?"

She shot him a breezy smile. "I'm very good at taking care of myself."

"You're in a foreign city. Things could happen—"

"I'm not exactly alone." She crossed the room to the connecting door leading to Jordan's suite. Yanking it open, she called, "Wake up, Jordie! I'm in need of some brotherly assistance."

There was no answer from the bed.

"Jordie?" she said.

"Your bodyguard stays right on his toes, doesn't he?" said Richard.

Annoyed, Beryl flicked on the wall switch. In the sudden flood of light, she found herself blinking in astonishment.

Jordan's bed was empty.

Chapter 4

That woman is staring at me again.

Jordan stirred a teaspoon of sugar into his cappuccino and casually glanced in the direction of the blonde sitting three tables away. At once she averted her gaze. She was attractive enough, he noted. Mid-twenties, with a lean, athletic build. Nothing overripe about that one. Her hair was cut like a boy's, with elfin wisps feathering her forehead. She wore a black sweater, black skirt, black stockings. Fashion or camouflage? He shifted his gaze ahead to the street and the evening parade of pedestrians. Out of the corner of his eye, he spied the woman again looking his way. Ordinarily it would have flattered him to know he was the object of such intense feminine scrutiny. But something about this particular woman made him uneasy. Couldn't a fellow wander the streets of Paris these days without being stalked by carnivorous females?

It had been such a pleasant outing up till now. Minutes after sending Beryl and Richard on their way, he'd slipped out of his hotel room in search of a decent watering hole. A stroll across Place Vendôme, a visit to the Olympia Music Hall, then a midnight snack at Café de la Paix—what better way to spend one's first evening in Paris?

But perhaps it was time to call it a night.

He finished his cappuccino, paid the tab, and began walking toward the Rue de la Paix. It took him only half a block to realize the woman in black was following him.

He had paused at a shop window and was gazing in at a display of men's suits when he spotted a fleeting glimpse of a blond head reflected in the glass. He turned and saw her standing across the street, intently staring into a window. A lingerie shop, he noted. Judging by the rest of her outfit, she'd no doubt choose her knickers in black, as well.

Jordan continued walking in the direction of Place Vendôme.

Across the street, the woman was paralleling his route.

This is getting tiresome, he thought. *If she wants to flirt, why doesn't she just come over and bat her eyelashes?* The direct approach, he could appreciate. It was honest and straightforward, and he liked honest women. But this stalking business unnerved him.

He walked another half block. So did she.

He stopped and pretended to study another shop window. She did likewise. *This is ridiculous,* he thought. *I am not going to put up with this nonsense.*

He crossed the street and walked straight up to her. *"Mademoiselle?"* he said.

She turned and regarded him with a startled look. Plainly she had not expected a face-to-face confrontation.

"Mademoiselle," he said, "may I ask why you're following me?"

She opened her mouth and shut it again, all the time staring at him with those big gray eyes. Rather pretty eyes, he observed.

"Perhaps you don't understand me? *Parlez-vous anglais?"*

"Yes," she murmured, "I speak English."

"Then perhaps you can explain why you're following me."

"But I am not following you."

"Yes, you are."

"No, I am not!" She glanced up and down the street. "I am taking a walk. As you are."

"You're dogging my every step. Stopping where I stop. Watching every move I make."

"That is preposterous." She pulled herself up, a spark of outrage lighting her eyes. Real or manufactured? He couldn't be sure. "I have no interest in you, *Monsieur!* You must be imagining things."

"Am I?"

In answer, she spun around and stalked away up the Rue de la Paix.

"I don't think I am imagining things!" he called after her.

"You English are all alike!" she flung over her shoulder.

Jordan watched her storm off and wondered if he had

jumped to conclusions. If so, what a fool he'd made of himself! The woman rounded a corner and vanished, and he felt a moment's regret. After all, she had been rather attractive. Lovely gray eyes, unbeatable legs.

Ah, well.

He turned and continued on his way toward the Place Vendôme and the hotel. Only as he reached the lobby doors of the Ritz did that sixth sense of his begin to tingle again. He paused and glanced back. In a distant archway, he spied a flicker of movement, a glimpse of a blond head just before it ducked into the shadows.

She was still following him.

Daumier answered the phone on the fifth ring. "Allô?"

"Claude, it's me," said Richard. "Are you having us tailed?"

There was a pause, then Daumier said, "A precaution, my friend. Nothing more."

"Protection? Or surveillance?"

"Protection, naturally! A favor to Hugh—"

"Well, it scared the living daylights out of us. The least you could've done was warn me." Richard glanced toward Beryl, who was anxiously pacing the hotel room. She hadn't admitted it, but he knew she was shaken, and that for all her bravado, all her attempts to throw him out of her suite, she was relieved he'd stayed. "Another thing," he said to Daumier, "we seem to have misplaced Jordan."

"Misplaced?"

"He's not in his suite. We left him here hours ago. He's since vanished."

There was a silence on the line. “This is worrisome,” said Daumier.

“Do your people have any idea where he is?”

“My agent has not yet reported in. I expect to hear from her in another—”

“Her?” Richard cut in.

“Not our most experienced operative, I admit. But quite capable.”

“It was a man following us tonight.”

Daumier laughed. “Richard, I am disappointed! I thought you, of all people, knew the difference.”

“I can bloody well tell the difference!”

“With Colette, there is no question. Twenty-six, rather pretty. Blond hair.”

“It was a man, Claude.”

“You saw the face?”

“Not clearly. But he was short, stocky—”

“Colette is five foot five, very slender.”

“It wasn’t her.”

Daumier said nothing for a moment. “This is disturbing,” he concluded. “If it was not one of our people—”

Richard suddenly pivoted toward the door. Someone was knocking. Beryl stood frozen, staring at him with a look of fear.

“I’ll call you back, Claude,” Richard whispered into the phone. Quietly he hung up.

There was another knock, louder this time.

“Go ahead,” he murmured, “ask who it is.”

Shakily she called out, “Who is it?”

“Are you decent?” came the reply. “Or should I try again in the morning?”

“Jordan!” cried a relieved Beryl. She ran to open the door. “Where have you been?”

Her brother sauntered in, his blond hair tousled from the night wind. He saw Richard and halted. "Sorry. If I've interrupted anything—"

"Not a thing," snapped Beryl. She locked the door and turned to face her brother. "We've been worried sick about you."

"I just went for a walk."

"You could have left me a note!"

"Why? I was right in the neighborhood." Jordan flopped lazily into a chair. "Having quite a nice evening, too, until some woman started following me around."

Richard's chin snapped up in surprise. "Woman?"

"Rather nice-looking. But not my type, really. A bit vampirish for my taste."

"Was she blond?" asked Richard. "About five foot five? Mid-twenties?"

Jordan shook his head in amazement. "Next you'll tell me her name."

"Colette."

"Is this a new parlor trick, Richard?" Jordan said with a laugh. "ESP?"

"She's an agent working for French Intelligence," said Richard. "Protective surveillance, that's all."

Beryl gave a sigh of relief. "So that's why we were followed. And you had me scared out of my wits."

"You *should* be scared," said Richard. "The man following us wasn't working for Daumier."

"You just said—"

"Daumier had only one agent assigned to surveillance tonight. That woman, Colette. Apparently she stayed with Jordan."

"Then who was following us?" demanded Beryl.

"I don't know."

There was a silence. Then Jordan asked peevishly, "Have I missed something? Why are we all being followed? And when did Richard join the fun?"

"Richard," said Beryl tightly, "hasn't been completely honest with us."

"About what?"

"He neglected to mention that he was here in Paris in 1973. He knew Mum and Dad."

Jordan's gaze at once shot to Richard's face. "Is that why you're here now?" he asked quietly. "To prevent us from learning the truth?"

"No," said Richard. "I'm here to see that the truth doesn't get you both killed."

"Could the truth really be that dangerous?"

"It's got someone worried enough to have you both followed."

"Then you don't believe it *was* a simple murder and suicide," said Jordan.

"If it was that simple—if it was just a case of Bernard shooting Madeline and then taking his own life—no one would care about it after all these years. But someone obviously does care. And he—or she—is keeping a close watch on your movements."

Beryl, strangely silent, sat down on the bed. Her hair, which she'd gathered back with pins, was starting to loosen, and silky tendrils had drifted down her neck. All at once Richard was struck by her uncanny resemblance to Madeline. It was the hairstyle and the watered-silk dress. He recognized that dress now—it was her mother's. He shook himself to dispel the notion that he was looking at a ghost.

He decided it was time to tell the truth, and nothing

but. "I never did believe it," he said. "Not for a second did I think Bernard pulled that trigger."

Slowly Beryl looked up at him. What he saw in her gaze—the wariness, the mistrust—made him want to reach out to her, to make her believe in him. But trust wasn't something she was about to give him, not now. Perhaps not ever.

"If he didn't pull the trigger," she asked, "then who did?"

Richard moved to the bed. Gently he touched her face. "I don't know," he said. "But I'm going to help you find out."

After Richard left, Beryl turned to her brother. "I don't trust him," she said. "He's told us too many lies."

"He didn't lie to us exactly," Jordan observed. "He just left out a few facts."

"Oh, right. He conveniently neglects to mention that he knew Mum and Dad. That he was here in Paris when they died. Jordie, for all we know, *he* could've pulled the trigger!"

"He seems quite chummy with Daumier."

"So?"

"Uncle Hugh trusts Daumier."

"Meaning we should trust Richard Wolf?" She shook her head and laughed. "Oh, Jordie, you must be more exhausted than you realize."

"And you must be more smitten than you realize," he said. Yawning, he crossed the floor toward his own suite.

"What's that supposed to mean?" she demanded.

"Only that your feelings for the man obviously run

hot and heavy. Because you're fighting them every inch of the way."

She pursued him to the connecting door. "Hot?" she said incredulously. "Heavy?"

"There, you see?" He breathed a few loud pants and grinned. "Sweet dreams, baby sister. I'm glad to see you're back in circulation."

Then he closed the door on her astonished face.

When Richard arrived at Daumier's flat, he found the Frenchman still awake but already dressed in his bathrobe and slippers. The latest reports on the bombing of the St. Pierre residence were laid out across his kitchen table, along with a plate of sausage and a glass of milk. Forty years with French Intelligence hadn't altered his preference for working in close proximity to a refrigerator.

Waving at the reports, Daumier said, "It is all a puzzle to me. A Semtex explosive planted under the bed. A timing mechanism set for 9:10—precisely when the St. Pierres would be watching Marie's favorite television program. It has all the signs of an inside operation, except for one glaring mistake—Philippe was in England." He looked at Richard. "Does it not strike you as an inconceivable blunder?"

"Terrorists are usually brighter than that," admitted Richard. "Maybe they intended it only as a warning. A statement of purpose. 'We can reach you if we want to,' that sort of thing."

"I still have no information on this Cosmic Solidarity League." Wearily Daumier ran his hands through his hair. "The investigation, it goes nowhere."

"Then maybe you can turn your attention for a moment to my little problem."

"Problem? Ah, yes. The Tavistocks." Daumier sat back and smiled at him. "Hugh's niece is more than you can handle, Richard?"

"Someone else was definitely tailing us tonight," said Richard. "Not just your agent, Colette. Can you find out who it was?"

"Give me something to work with," said Daumier. "A middle-aged man, short and stocky—that tells me nothing. He could have been hired by anyone."

"It was someone who knew they were coming to Paris."

"I know Hugh told the Vanes. They, in turn, could have mentioned it to others. Who else was at Chetwynd?"

Richard thought back to the night of the reception and the night of Reggie's indiscretion. Blast Reggie Vane and his weakness for booze. That was what had set this off. A few too many glasses of champagne, a wagging tongue. Still, he couldn't bring himself to dislike the man. Poor Reggie was a harmless soul; certainly he'd never meant to hurt Beryl. Rather, it was clear he adored her like a daughter.

Richard said, "There were numbers of people the Vanes might have spoken to. Philippe St. Pierre. Nina and Anthony. Perhaps others."

"So we are talking about any number of people," Daumier said, sighing.

"Not a very short list," Richard had to admit.

"Is this such a wise idea, Richard?" The question was posed quietly. "Once before, if you recall, we were prevented from learning the truth."

How could he not remember? He'd been stunned to read that directive from Washington: "Abort investigation." Claude had received similar orders from his superior at French Intelligence. And so the search for Delphi and the NATO security breach had come to an abrupt halt. There'd been no explanation, no reasons given, but Richard had formed his own suspicions. It was clear that Washington had been clued in to the truth and feared the repercussions of its airing.

A month later, when U.S. Ambassador Stephen Sutherland leaped off a Paris bridge, Richard thought his suspicions confirmed. Sutherland had been a political appointee; his unveiling as an enemy spy would have embarrassed the president himself.

The matter of the mole was never officially resolved.

Instead, Bernard Tavistock had been posthumously implicated as Delphi. Conveniently tried and found guilty, thought Richard. Why not pin the blame on Tavistock? A dead man can't deny the charges.

And now, twenty years later, the ghost of Delphi is back to haunt me.

With new determination, Richard rose from the chair. "This time, Claude," he said, "I'm tracking him down. And no order from Washington is going to stop me."

"Twenty years is a long time. Evidence has vanished. Politics have changed."

"One thing hasn't changed—the guilty party. What if we were wrong? What if Sutherland wasn't the mole? Then Delphi may still be alive. And operational."

To which Daumier added, "And very, very worried."

Beryl was awakened the next morning by Richard knocking on her door. She blinked in astonishment as he handed her a paper sack, fragrant with the aroma of freshly baked croissants.

"Breakfast," he announced. "You can eat it in the car. Jordan's already waiting for us downstairs."

"Waiting? For what?"

"For you to get dressed. You'd better hurry. Our appointment's for eight o'clock."

Bewildered, she shoved back a handful of tangled hair. "I don't recall making any appointments for this morning."

"I made it for us. We're lucky to get one, considering the man doesn't see many people these days. His wife won't allow it."

"Whose wife?" she said in exasperation.

"Chief Inspector Broussard. The detective in charge of your parents' murder investigation." Richard paused. "You do want to speak to him, don't you?"

He knows I do, she thought, clutching together the edges of her silk robe. *He's got me at a disadvantage. I'm scarcely awake and he's standing there like Mr. Sunshine himself.* And since when had Jordan turned into an early riser? Her brother almost never rolled out of bed before eight.

"You don't have to come," he said, turning to leave. "Jordan and I can—"

"Give me ten minutes!" she snapped and closed the door on him.

She made it downstairs in nine minutes flat.

Richard drove with the self-assurance of a man long familiar with the streets of Paris. They crossed the Seine and headed south along crowded boulevards. The traffic was as insane as London's, thought Beryl, gazing out at the crush of buses and taxis. *Thank heavens he's behind the wheel.*

She finished her croissant and brushed the crumbs off the file folder lying in her lap. Contained in that folder was the twenty-year-old police report, signed by Inspector Broussard. She wondered how much the man would remember about the case. After all this time, surely the details had blended together with all the other homicide investigations of his career. But there was always the chance that some small unreported detail had stayed with him.

"Have you met Broussard?" she asked Richard.

"We met during the course of the investigation. When I was interviewed by the police."

"They questioned you? Why?"

"He spoke to all your parents' acquaintances."

"I never saw your name in the police file."

"A number of names didn't make it to that file."

"Such as?"

"Philippe St. Pierre. Ambassador Sutherland."

"Nina's husband?"

Richard nodded. "Those were politically sensitive names. St. Pierre was in the Finance Ministry, and he was a close friend of the prime minister's. Sutherland was the American ambassador. Neither were suspects, so their names were kept out of the official report."

"Meaning the good inspector protected the high and mighty?"

"Meaning he was discreet."

"Why did your name escape the report?"

"I was just a bit player asked to comment on your parents' marriage. Whether they ever argued, seemed unhappy, that's all. I was only on the periphery."

She touched the file on her lap. "So tell me," she said, "why are you getting involved now?"

"Because you and Jordan are. Because Claude Daumier

asked me to look after you." He glanced at her and added quietly, "And because I owe it to your father. He was...a good man." She thought he would say more, but then he turned and gazed straight ahead at the road.

"Wolf," asked Jordan, who was sitting in the back seat, "are you aware that we're being followed?"

"What?" Beryl turned and scanned the traffic behind them. "Which car?"

"The blue Peugeot. Two cars back."

"I see it," said Richard. "It's been tailing us all the way from the hotel."

"You knew the car was there all the time?" said Beryl. "And you didn't think of mentioning it?"

"I expected it. Take a good look at the driver, Jordan. Blond hair, sunglasses. Definitely a woman."

Jordan laughed. "Why, it's my little vampiress in black. Colette."

Richard nodded. "One of the friendlies."

"How can you be sure?" asked Beryl.

"Because she's Daumier's agent. Which makes her protection, not a threat." Richard turned off Boulevard Raspail. A moment later, he spotted a parking space and pulled up at the curb. "In fact, she can keep an eye on the car while we're inside."

Beryl glanced at the large brick building across the street. Over the entrance archway were displayed the words *Maison de Convalescence.* "What is this place?"

"A nursing home."

"This is where Inspector Broussard lives?"

"He's been here for years," said Richard, as he gazed up at the building with a look of pity. "Ever since his stroke."

Judging by the photograph tacked to the wall of his room, ex-Chief Inspector Broussard had once been an impressive man. The picture showed a beefy Frenchman with a handlebar mustache and a lion's mane of hair, posing regally on the steps of a Paris police station.

It bore little resemblance to the shrunken creature now propped up, his body half-paralyzed, in bed.

Mme Broussard bustled about the room, all the time speaking with the precise grammar of a former teacher of English. She fluffed her husband's pillow, combed his hair, wiped the drool from his chin. "He remembers everything," she insisted. "Every case, every name. But he cannot speak, cannot hold a pen. And that is what frustrates him! It is why I do not let him have visitors. He wishes so much to talk, but he cannot form the words. Only a few, here and there. And how it upsets him! Sometimes, after a visit with friends, he will moan for days." She moved to the head of the bed and stood there like a guardian angel. "You ask him only a few questions, do you understand? And if he becomes upset, you must leave immediately."

"We understand," said Richard. He pulled up a chair next to the bedside. As Beryl and Jordan watched, he opened the police file and slowly laid the crime-scene photos on the coverlet for Broussard to see. "I know you can't speak," he said, "but I want you to look at these. Nod if you remember the case."

Mme Broussard translated for her husband. He stared down at the first photo—the gruesome death poses of Madeline and Bernard. They lay like lovers, entwined in a pool of blood. Clumsily Broussard touched the photo, his fingers lingering on Madeline's face. His lips formed a whispered word.

"What did he say?" asked Richard.

"*La belle.* Beautiful woman," said Mme Broussard. "You see? He does remember."

The old man was gazing at the other photos now, his left hand beginning to quiver in agitation. His lips moved helplessly; the effort to speak came out in grunts. Mme Broussard leaned forward, trying to make out what he was saying. She shook her head in bewilderment.

"We've read his report," said Beryl. "The one he filed twenty years ago. He concluded that it was a murder and suicide. Did he truly believe that?"

Again, Mme Broussard translated.

Broussard looked up at Beryl, his gaze focusing for the first time on her black hair. A look of wonder came over his face, almost a look of recognition.

His wife repeated the question. Did he believe it was a murder and suicide?

Slowly Broussard shook his head.

Jordan asked, "Does he understand the question?"

"Of course he does!" snapped Mme Broussard. "I told you, he understands everything."

The man was tapping at one of the photos now, as though trying to point something out. His wife asked a question in French. He only slapped harder at the photo.

"Is he trying to point at something?" asked Beryl.

"Just a corner of the picture," said Richard. "A view of empty floor."

Broussard's whole body seemed to be quivering with the effort to speak. His wife leaned forward again, straining to make out his words. She shook her head. "It makes no sense."

"What did he say?" asked Beryl.

"*Serviette.* It is a napkin or a towel. I do not understand." She snatched up a hand towel from the sink and held it up to her husband. *"Serviette de toilette?"*

He shook his head and angrily batted away the towel.

"I do not know what he means," Mme Broussard said with a sigh.

"Maybe I do," said Richard. He bent close to Broussard. *"Porte documents?"* he asked.

Broussard gave a sigh of relief and collapsed against his pillows. Wearily he nodded.

"That's what he was trying to say," said Richard. "*Serviette porte documents.* A briefcase."

"Briefcase?" echoed Beryl. "Do you think he means the one with the classified file?"

Richard frowned at Broussard. The man was exhausted, his face a sickly gray against the white linen.

Mme Broussard took one look at her husband and moved in to shield him from Richard. "No further questions, Mr. Wolf! Look at him! He is drained—he cannot tell you more. Please, you must leave."

She hurried them out of the room and into the hallway. A nun glided past, carrying a tray of medicines. At the end of the hall, a woman in a wheelchair was singing lullabies to herself in French.

"Mme Broussard," said Beryl, "we have more questions, but your husband can't answer them. There was another detective's name on that report—an Etienne Giguere. How can we get in touch with him?"

"Etienne?" Mme Broussard looked at her in surprise. "You mean you do not know?"

"Know what?"

"He was killed nineteen years ago. Hit by a car while crossing the street." Sadly she shook her head. "They did not find the driver."

Beryl caught Jordan's startled look; she saw in his eyes the same dismay she felt.

"One last question," said Jordan. "When did your husband have his stroke?"

"1974."

"Also nineteen years ago?"

Mme Broussard nodded. "Such a tragedy for the department! First, my husband's stroke. Then three months later, they lose Etienne." Sighing, she turned back to her husband's room. "But that is life, I suppose. And there is nothing we can do to change it…"

Back outside again, the three of them stood for a moment in the sunshine, trying to shake off the gloom of that depressing building.

"A hit and run?" said Jordan. "The driver never caught? I have a bad feeling about this."

Beryl glanced up at the archway. *"Maison de Convalescence,"* she murmured sarcastically. "Hardly a place to recover. More like a place to die." Shivering, she turned to the car. "Please, let's just get out of here."

They drove north, to the Seine. Once again, the blue Peugeot followed them, but none of them paid it much attention; the French agent had become a fact of life—almost a reassuring one.

Suddenly Jordan said, "Hold on, Wolf. Let me off on Boulevard Saint-Germain. In fact, right about here would be fine."

Richard pulled over to the curb. "Why here?"

"We just passed a café—"

"Oh, Jordan," groaned Beryl, "you're not hungry already, are you?"

"I'll meet you back at the hotel," said Jordan, climbing out of the car. "Unless you two care to join me?"

"So we can watch you eat? Thank you, but I'll pass."

Jordan gave his sister an affectionate squeeze of the shoulder and closed the car door. "I'll catch a taxi back. See you later." With a wave, he turned and strolled down the boulevard, his blond hair gleaming in the sunshine.

"Back to the hotel?" asked Richard softly.

She looked at him and thought, *It's always there shimmering between us—the attraction. The temptation. I look in his eyes, and suddenly I remember how safe it feels to be in his arms. How easy it would be to believe in him. And that's where the danger lies.*

"No," she said, looking straight ahead. "Not yet."

"Then where to?"

"Take me to Pigalle. Rue Myrha."

He paused. "Are you certain you want to go there?"

She nodded and stared down at the file in her lap. "I want to see the place where they died."

Café Hugo. Yes, this was the place, thought Jordan, gazing around at the crowded outdoor tables, the checkered tablecloths, the army of waiters ferrying espresso and cappuccino. Twenty years ago, Bernard had visited this very café. Had sat drinking coffee. And then he had paid the bill and left, to meet his death in a building in Pigalle. All this Jordan had learned from the police interview with the waiter. But it happened a long time ago, thought Jordan. The man had probably moved on to other jobs. Still, it was worth a shot.

To his surprise, he discovered that Mario Cassini was still employed as a waiter. Well into his forties now, his hair a salt-and-pepper gray, his face creased with the lines of twenty years of smiles, Mario nodded and said, "Yes, yes. Of course I remember. The police, they come to talk to me three, four times. And each time I tell them the same thing. M. Tavistock, he comes for café au lait, every morning. Sometimes, *madame* is with him. Ah, beautiful!"

"But she wasn't with him on that particular day?"

Mario shook his head. "He comes alone. Sits at that table there." He pointed to an empty table near the sidewalk, red-checked cloth fluttering in the breeze. "He waits a long time for *madame*."

"And she didn't come?"

"No. Then she calls. Tells him to meet her at another place. In Pigalle. I take the message and give it to M. Tavistock."

"She spoke to you? On the telephone?"

"*Oui.* I write down address, give to him."

"That would be the address in Pigalle?"

Mario nodded.

"My father—M. Tavistock—did he seem at all upset that day? Angry?"

"Not angry. He seems—how do you say?—worried. He does not understand why *madame* goes to Pigalle. He pays for his coffee, then he leaves. Later I read in the newspaper that he is dead. Ah, *horrible!* The police, they are asking for information. So I call, tell them what I know." Mario shook his head at the tragedy of it all. At the loss of such a lovely woman as Mme Tavistock and such a generous man as her husband.

No new information here, thought Jordan. He turned to leave, then stopped and turned back.

"Are you certain it was Mme Tavistock who called to leave the message?" he asked.

"She says it is her," said Mario.

"And you recognized her voice?"

Mario paused. It lasted just the blink of an eye, but it was enough to tell Jordan that the man was not absolutely certain. "Yes," said Mario. "Who else would it be?"

Deep in thought, Jordan left the café and walked a few paces along Boulevard Saint-Germain, intending to return on foot to the hotel. But half a block away, he spotted the blue Peugeot. His little blond vampiress, he thought, still following him about. They were headed in the same direction; why not ask her for a ride?

He went to the Peugeot and pulled open the passenger door. "Mind dropping me off at the Ritz?" he asked brightly.

An outraged Colette stared at him from the driver's seat. "What do you think you are doing?" she demanded. "Get out of my car!"

"Oh, come, now. No need for hysterics—"

"Go away!" she cried, loudly enough to make a passerby stop and stare.

Calmly Jordan slid into the front seat. He noted that she was dressed in black again. What was it with these secret agent types? "It's a long walk to the Ritz. Surely it's not *verboten,* is it? To give me a lift back to my hotel?"

"I do not even know who you are," she insisted.

"I know who *you* are. Your name's Colette, you work for Claude Daumier, and you're supposed to be keeping an eye on me." Jordan smiled at her, the sort of smile that usually got him exactly what he wanted. He said, quite reasonably, "Rather than sneaking around after me all the way up the boulevard, why not be sensible about it? Save us both the inconvenience of this silly cat-and-mouse game."

A spark of laughter flickered in her eyes. She gripped the steering wheel and stared straight ahead, but he could see the smile tugging at her lips. "Shut the door," she snapped. "And use the seat belt. It is regulation."

As they drove up Boulevard Saint-Germain, he kept glancing at her, wondering if she was really as fierce as she appeared. That black leather skirt and the scowl on her face couldn't disguise the fact she was actually quite pretty.

"How long have you worked for Daumier?" he asked.

"Three years."

"And is this your usual sort of assignment? Following strange men about town?"

"I follow instructions. Whatever they are."

"Ah. The obedient type." Jordan sat back, grinning. "What did Daumier tell you about this particular assignment?"

"I am to see you and your sister are not harmed. Since today she is with M. Wolf, I decide to follow you." She paused and added under her breath, "Not as simple as I thought."

"I'm not all that difficult."

"But you do the unexpected. You catch me by surprise." A car was honking at them. Annoyed, Colette glanced up at the rearview mirror. "This traffic, it gets worse every—"

At her sudden silence, Jordan glanced at her. "Is something wrong?"

"No," she said after a pause, "I am just imagining things."

Jordan turned and peered through the rear window. All he saw was a line of cars snaking down the boulevard. He looked back at Colette. "Tell me, what's a nice girl like you doing in French Intelligence?"

She smiled—the first real smile he'd seen. It was like watching the sun come out. "I am earning a living."

"Meeting interesting people?"

"Quite."

"Finding romance?"

"Regrettably, no."

"What a shame. Perhaps you should find a new line of work."

"Such as?"

"We could discuss it over supper."

She shook her head. "It is not allowed to fraternize with a subject."

"So that's all I am," he said with a sigh. "A subject."

She dropped him off on a side street, around the corner from the Ritz. He climbed out, then turned and said, "Why not come in for a drink?"

"I am on duty."

"It must get boring, sitting in that car all day. Waiting for me to make another unexpected move."

"Thank you, but no." She smiled—a charmingly impish grin. It carried just a hint of possibility.

Jordan left the car and walked into the hotel.

Upstairs, he paced for a while, pondering what he'd just learned at Café Hugo. That phone call from Madeline—it just didn't fit in. Why on earth would she arrange to meet Bernard in Pigalle? It clearly didn't go along with the theory of a murder-suicide. Could the waiter be lying? Or was he simply mistaken? With all the ambient noise of a busy café, how could he be certain it was really Madeline Tavistock making that phone call?

I have to go back to the café. Ask Mario, specifically, if the voice was an Englishwoman's.

Once again he left the hotel and stepped into the brightness of midday. A taxi sat idling near the front entrance, but the driver was nowhere to be seen. Perhaps Colette was still parked around the corner; he'd ask her to drive him back to Boulevard Saint-Germain. He turned up the side street and spotted the blue Peugeot still parked there. Colette was sitting inside; through the tinted windshield, he saw her silhouette behind the steering wheel.

He went to the car and tapped on the passenger window. "Colette?" he called. "Could you give me another lift?"

She didn't answer.

Jordan swung open the door and slid in beside her. "Colette?"

She sat perfectly still, her eyes staring rigidly ahead. For a moment, he didn't understand. Then he saw the bright trickle of blood that had traced its way down her hairline and vanished into the black fabric of her turtlenecked shirt. In panic, he reached out to her and gave her shoulder a shake. *"Colette?"*

She slid toward him and toppled into his lap.

He stared at her head, now resting in his arms. In her temple was a single, neat bullet hole.

He scarcely remembered scrambling out of the car. What he did remember were the screams of a woman passerby. Then, moments later, he focused on the shocked faces of people who'd been drawn onto this quiet side street by the screams. They were all pointing at the woman's arm hanging limply out of the car. And they were staring at him.

Numbly, Jordan looked down at his own hands.

They were smeared with blood.

Chapter 5

From the crowd of onlookers standing on the corner, Amiel Foch watched the police handcuff the Englishman and lead him away. An unintended development, he thought. Not at all what he'd expected to happen.

Then again, he hadn't expected to see Colette La-Farge ever again. Or, even worse, to be seen by her. They'd worked together only once, and that was three years ago in Cyprus. He'd hoped, when he walked past her car, with his head down and his shoulders hunched, that she would not notice him. But as he'd headed away, he'd heard her call out his name in astonishment.

He'd had no alternative, he thought as he watched the attendants load her body into the ambulance. French Intelligence thought he was dead. Colette could have told them otherwise.

It hadn't been an easy thing to do. But as he'd turned to face her, his decision was already made. He had walked slowly back to her car. Through the windshield, he'd seen her look of wonder at a dead colleague come back to life. She'd sat frozen, staring at the apparition. She had not moved as he approached the driver's side. Nor did she move as he thrust his silenced automatic into her car window and fired.

Such a waste of a pretty girl, he thought as the ambulance drove away. But she should have known better.

The crowd was dispersing. It was time to leave.

He edged toward the curb. Quietly he dropped his pistol in the gutter and kicked it down the storm drain. The weapon was stolen, untraceable; better to have it found near the scene of the crime. It would cement the case against Jordan Tavistock.

Several blocks away, he found a telephone. He dialed his client.

"Jordan Tavistock has been arrested for murder," said Foch.

"Whose murder?" came the sharp reply.

"One of Daumier's agents. A woman."

"Did Tavistock do it?"

"No. I did."

There was a sudden burst of laughter from his client. "This is priceless! Absolutely priceless! I ask you to follow Jordan, and you have him framed for murder. I can't wait to see what you do with his sister."

"What do you wish me to do?" asked Foch.

There was a pause. "I think it's time to resolve this mess," he said. "Finish it."

"The woman is no problem. But her brother will be difficult to reach, unless I can find a way into the prison."

"You could always get yourself arrested."

"And when they identify my fingerprints?" Foch shook his head. "I need someone else for that job."

"Then I'll find you someone," came the reply. "For now, let's work on one thing at a time. Beryl Tavistock."

A Turkish man now owned the building on Rue Myrha. He'd tried to improve it. He'd painted the exterior walls, shored up the crumbling balconies, replaced the missing roof slates, but the building, and the street on which it stood, seemed beyond rehabilitation. It was the fault of the tenants, explained Mr. Zamir, as he led them up two flights of stairs to the attic flat. What could one do with tenants who let their children run wild? By all appearances, Mr. Zamir was a successful businessman, a man whose tailored suit and excellent English bespoke prosperous roots. There were four families in the building, he said, all of them reliable enough with the rent. But no one lived in the attic flat—he'd always had difficulty renting that one out. People had come to inspect the place, of course, but when they heard of the murder, they quickly backed out. These silly superstitions! Oh, people claim they do not believe in ghosts, but when they visit a room where two people have died…

"How long has the flat been empty?" asked Beryl.

"A year now. Ever since I have owned the building. And before that—" he shrugged "—I do not know. It may have been empty for many years." He unlocked the door. "You may look around if you wish."

A puff of stale air greeted them as they pushed open the door—the smell of a room too long shut away from the world. It was not an unpleasant room. Sunshine washed in through a large, dirt-streaked window. The view looked down over Rue Myrha, and Beryl could see children kicking a soccer ball in the street. The flat was completely empty of furniture; there were only bare walls and floor. Through an open door, she glimpsed the bathroom with its chipped sink and tarnished fixtures.

In silence Beryl circled the flat, her gaze moving across the wood floor. Beside the window, she came to a halt. The stain was barely visible, just a faint brown blot in the oak planks. *Whose blood?* she wondered. *Mum's? Dad's? Or is it both of theirs, eternally mingled?*

"I have tried to sand the stain away," said Mr. Zamir. "But it goes very deep into the wood. Even when I think I have erased it, in a few weeks the stain seems to reappear." He sighed. "It frightens them away, you know. The tenants, they do not like to see such reminders on their floor."

Beryl swallowed hard and turned to look out the window. *Why on this street?* she wondered. *In this room? Of all the places in Paris, why did they die here?*

She asked quietly, "Who owned this building, Mr. Zamir? Before you did?"

"There were many owners. Before me, it was a M. Rosenthal. And before him, a M. Dudoit."

"At the time of the murder," said Richard, "the landlord was a man named Jacques Rideau. Did you know him?"

"I am sorry, I do not. That would have been many years ago."

"Twenty."

"Then I would not have met him." Mr. Zamir turned to the door. "I will leave you alone. If you have questions, I will be down in number three for a while."

Beryl heard the man's footsteps creak down the stairs. She looked at Richard and saw that he was standing off in a corner, frowning at the floor. "What are you thinking?" she asked.

"About Inspector Broussard. How he kept trying to point at that photo. The spot he was pointing to would be somewhere around here. Just to the left of the door."

"There's nothing to look at. And there was nothing in the photo, either."

"That's what bothers me. He seemed so troubled by it. And there was something about a briefcase..."

"The NATO file," she said softly.

He looked at her. "How much have you been told about Delphi?"

"I know it wasn't Mum or Dad. They would never have gone to the other side."

"People go over for different reasons."

"But not them. They certainly didn't need the money."

"Communist sympathies?"

"Not the Tavistocks!"

He moved toward her. With every step he took, her pulse seemed to leap faster. He came close enough to make her feel threatened. And tempted. Quietly he said, "There's always blackmail."

"Meaning they had secrets to hide?"

"Everyone does."

"Not everyone turns traitor."

"It depends on the secret, doesn't it? And how much one stands to lose because of it."

In silence they gazed at each other, and she found herself wondering how much he really did know about her parents. How much he wasn't admitting to. She sensed he knew a lot more than he was letting on, and that suspicion loomed like a barrier between them. Those secrets again. Those unspoken truths. She had grown up in a household where certain conversational doors were always kept locked. *I refuse to live my life that way. Ever again.*

She turned away. “They had no reason to be vulnerable to blackmail.”

“You were just a child, eight years old. Away at boarding school in England. What did you really know about them? About their marriage, their secrets? What if it was your mother who rented this flat? Met her lover here?”

“I don’t believe it. I won’t.”

“Is it so difficult to accept? That she was human, that she might have had a lover?” He took her by the shoulders, willing her to meet his gaze. “She was a beautiful woman, Beryl. If she’d wanted to, she could have had any number of lovers.”

“You’re making her out to be a tramp!”

“I’m considering all the possibilities.”

“That she sold out Queen and country? To keep some vile little secret from surfacing?” Angrily she wrenched away from him. “Sorry, Richard, but my faith runs a little deeper than that. And if you’d known them, really known them, you’d never consider such a thing.” She pivoted away and walked to the door.

“I did know them,” he said. “I knew them rather well.”

She stopped, turned to face him. “What do you mean by ‘rather well’?”

“We…moved in the same circles. Not the same team, exactly. But we worked at similar purposes.”

“You never told me.”

“I didn’t know how much I *should* tell you. How much you should know.” He began to slowly circle the room, carefully considering each word before he spoke. “It was my first assignment. I’d just completed my training at Langley—”

“CIA?”

He nodded. “I was recruited straight out of the university. Not exactly my first career choice. But somehow they'd gotten hold of my master's thesis, an analysis of Libyan arms capabilities. It turned out to be amazingly close to the mark. They knew I was fluent in a few languages. And that I had taken out quite a large sum in student loans. That was the carrot, you see—the loan payoff. The foreign travel. And, I have to admit, the idea intrigued me, the chance to work as an Intelligence analyst..."

"Is that how you met my parents?"

He nodded. "NATO knew it had a security leak, originating in Paris. Somehow weapons data were slipping through to the East Germans. I'd just arrived in Paris, so there was no question that I was clean. They assigned me to work with Claude Daumier at French Intelligence. I was asked to compose a dummy weapons report, something close to, but not quite, the truth. It was encoded and transmitted to a few select embassy officials in Paris. The idea was to pinpoint the possible source of the leak."

"How were my parents involved?"

"They were attached to the British embassy. Bernard in Communications, Madeline in Protocol. Both were really working for MI6. Bernard was one of a few who had access to classified files."

"So he was a suspect?"

Richard nodded. "Everyone was. British, American, French. Right up to ambassadorial level." Again he began to pace, carefully measuring his words. "So the dummy file went out to the embassies. And we waited to see if it would turn up, like the others, in East German hands. It didn't. It ended up here, in a briefcase. In this very room." He stopped and looked at her. "With your parents."

"And that closed the file on Delphi," she said. Bitterly she added, "How neat and easy. You had your culprit. Lucky for you he was dead and unable to defend himself."

"I didn't believe it."

"Yet you dropped the matter."

"We had no choice."

"You didn't care enough to learn the truth!"

"No, Beryl. We didn't have the choice. We were instructed to call off the investigation."

She stared at him in astonishment. "By whom?"

"My orders came straight from Washington. Claude's from the French prime minister. The matter was dropped."

"And my parents went on record as traitors," she said. "What a convenient way to close the file." In disgust she turned and left the room.

He followed her down the stairs. "Beryl! I never really believed Bernard was the one!"

"Yet you let him take the blame!"

"I told you, I was ordered to—"

"And of course you always follow orders."

"I was sent back to Washington soon afterward. I couldn't pursue it."

They walked out of the building into the bedlam of Rue Myrha. A soccer ball flew past, pursued by a gaggle of tattered-looking children. Beryl paused on the sidewalk, her eyes temporarily dazzled by the sunshine. The street sounds, the shouts of the children, were disorienting. She turned and looked up at the building, at the attic window. The view suddenly blurred through her tears.

"What a place to die," she whispered. "God, what a horrible place to die…"

She climbed into Richard's car and pulled the door closed. It was a blessed relief to shut out the noise and chaos of Rue Myrha.

Richard slid in behind the driver's seat. For a moment, they sat in silence, staring ahead at the ragamuffins playing street soccer.

"I'll take you back to the hotel," he said.

"I want to see Claude Daumier."

"Why?"

"I want to hear his version of what happened. I want to confirm that you're telling me the truth."

"I am, Beryl."

She turned to him. His gaze was steady, unflinching. *An honest look if ever I've seen one,* she thought. *Which only proves how gullible I am.* She wanted to believe him, and there was the danger. It was that blasted attraction between them—the feverish tug of hormones, the memory of his kisses—that clouded her judgment. *What is it about this man? I take one look at his face, inhale a whiff of his scent, and I'm aching to tear off his clothes. And mine, as well.*

She looked straight ahead, trying to ignore all those heated signals passing between them. "I want to talk to Daumier."

After a pause, he said, "All right. If that's what it'll take for you to believe me."

A phone call revealed that Daumier was not in his office; he'd just left to conduct another interview with Marie St. Pierre. So they drove to Cochin Hospital, where Marie was still a patient.

Even from the far end of the hospital corridor, they could tell which room was Marie's; half a dozen policemen were stationed outside her door. Daumier had not yet arrived. Madame St. Pierre, informed that Lord Lovat's niece had arrived, at once had Beryl and Richard escorted into her room.

They discovered they weren't the only visitors Marie

was entertaining that afternoon. Seated in chairs near the patient's bed were Nina Sutherland and Helena Vane. A little tea party was in progress, complete with trays of biscuits and finger sandwiches set on a rolling cart by the window. The patient, however, was not partaking of the refreshments; she sat propped up in bed, a sad and weary-looking French matron dressed in a gray robe to match her gray hair. Her only visible injuries appeared to be a bruised cheek and some scratches on her arms. It was clear from the woman's look of unhappiness that the bomb's most serious damage had been emotional. Any other patient would have been discharged by now; only her status as St. Pierre's wife allowed her such pampering.

Nina poured two cups of tea and handed them to Beryl and Richard. "When did you arrive in Paris?" she said.

"Jordan and I flew in yesterday," said Beryl. "And you?"

"We flew home with Helena and Reggie." Nina sat back down and crossed her silk-stockinged legs. "First thing this morning, I thought to myself, I really should drop in to see how Marie's doing. Poor thing, she does need cheering up."

Judging by the patient's glum face, Nina's visit had not yet achieved the desired result.

"What's the world coming to, I ask you?" said Nina, balancing her cup of tea. "Madness and anarchy! No one's immune, not even the upper class."

"Especially the upper class," said Helena.

"Has there been any progress on the case?" asked Beryl.

Marie St. Pierre sighed. "They insist it is a terrorist attack."

"Well, of course," said Nina. "Who else plants bombs in politicians' houses?"

Marie's gaze quickly dropped to her lap. She looked at her hands, the bony fingers woven together. "I have told Philippe we should leave Paris for a while. Tonight, perhaps, when I am released. We could visit Switzerland..."

"An excellent idea," murmured Helena gently. She reached out to squeeze Marie's hand. "You need to get away, just the two of you."

"But that's turning tail," said Nina. "Letting the criminals know they've won."

"Easy for you to say," muttered Helena. "It wasn't your house that was bombed."

"And if it was my house, I'd stay right in Paris," Nina retorted. "I wouldn't give an inch—"

"You've never had to."

"What?"

Helena looked away. "Nothing."

"What are you muttering about, Helena?"

"I only think," said Helena, "that Marie should do exactly what she wants. Leaving Paris for a while makes perfect sense. Any friend would back her up."

"I *am* her friend."

"Yes," murmured Helena, "of course you are."

"Are you saying I'm not?"

"I didn't say anything of the kind."

"You're muttering again, Helena. Really, it drives me up a wall. Is it so difficult to come right out and say things?"

"Oh, please," moaned Marie.

A knock on the door cut short the argument. Nina's

son, Anthony, entered, dressed with his usual offbeat flair in a shirt of electric blue, a leather jacket. "Ready to leave, Mum?" he asked Nina.

At once Nina rose huffily to her feet. "More than ready," she sniffed and followed him to the door. There she stopped and gave Marie one last glance. "I'm only speaking as a friend," she said. "And I, for one, think you should stay in Paris." She took Anthony's arm and walked out of the room.

"Good heavens, Marie," muttered Helena, after a pause. "Why do you put up with the woman?"

Marie, looking small as she huddled in her bed, gave a small shrug. *They are so very much alike,* thought Beryl, comparing Marie St. Pierre and Helena. Neither one blessed with beauty, both on the fading side of middle age, and trapped in marriages to men who no longer adored them.

"I've always thought you were a saint just to let that bitch in your door," said Helena. "If it were up to me..."

"One must keep the peace" was all Marie said.

They tried to carry on a conversation, the four of them, but so many silences intervened. And overshadowing their talk of bomb blasts and ruined furniture, of lost artwork and damaged heirlooms, was the sense that something was being left unsaid. That even beyond the horror of these losses was a deeper loss. One had only to look in Marie St. Pierre's eyes to know that she was reeling from the devastation of her life.

Even when her husband, Philippe, walked into the room, Marie did not perk up. If anything, she seemed to recoil from Philippe's kiss. She averted her face and looked instead at the door, which had just swung open again.

Claude Daumier entered, saw Beryl, and halted in surprise. "You are *here?*"

"We were waiting to see you," said Beryl.

Daumier glanced at Richard, then back at Beryl. "I have been trying to find you both."

"What's wrong?" asked Richard.

"The matter is…delicate." Daumier motioned for them to follow. "It would be best," he said, "to discuss this in private."

They followed him into the hallway, past the nurses' station. In a quiet corner, Daumier stopped and turned to Richard.

"I have just received a call from the police. Colette was found shot to death in her car. Near Place Vendôme."

"Colette?" said Beryl. "The agent who was watching Jordan?"

Grimly Daumier nodded.

"Oh, my God," murmured Beryl. "Jordie—"

"He is safe," Daumier said quickly. "I assure you, he's not in danger."

"But if they killed her, they could—"

"He has been placed under arrest," said Daumier. His gaze, quietly sympathetic, focused on Beryl's shocked face. "For murder."

Long after everyone else had left the hospital room, Helena remained by Marie's bedside. For a while they said very little; good friends, after all, are comfortable with silence. But then Helena could not hold it in any longer. "It's intolerable," she said. "You simply can't stand for this, Marie."

Marie sighed. "What else am I to do? She has so

many friends, so many people she could turn against me. Against Philippe…"

"But you must do something. Anything. For one, refuse to speak to her!"

"I have no proof. Never do I have proof."

"You don't need proof. Use your eyes! Look at the way they act together. The way she's always around him, smiling at him. He may have told you it was over, but you can see it isn't. And where is he, anyway? You're in the hospital and he scarcely visits you. When he does, it's just a peck on the cheek and he's off again."

"He is preoccupied. The economic summit—"

"Oh, yes," Helena snorted. "Men's business is always so bloody important!"

Marie started to cry, not sobs, but noiseless, pitiful tears. Suffering in silence—that was her way. Never a complaint or a protest, just a heart quietly breaking. *The pain we endure,* thought Helena bitterly, *all for the love of men.*

Marie said in a whisper, "It is even worse than you know."

"How can it possibly be any worse?"

Marie didn't reply. She just looked down at the abrasions on her arms. They were only minor scrapes, the aftermath of flying glass, but she stared at them with what looked like quiet despair.

So that's it, thought Helena, horrified. *She thinks they're trying to kill her. Why doesn't she strike back? Why doesn't she fight?*

But Marie hadn't the will. One could see that, just by the slump of her shoulders.

My poor, dear friend, thought Helena, gazing at Marie with pity, *how very much alike we are. And yet, how very different.*

* * *

A man sat on the bench across from him, silently eyeing Jordan's clothes, his shoes, his watch. A well-pickled fellow by the smell of him, thought Jordan with distaste. Or did that delightful odor, that unmistakable perfume of cheap wine and ripe underarms, emanate from the other occupant of the jail cell? Jordan glanced at the man snoring blissfully in the far corner. Yes, there was the likely source.

The man on the bench was still staring at him. Jordan tried to ignore him, but the man's gaze was so intrusive that Jordan finally snapped, "What are you looking at?"

"C'est en or?" the man asked.

"Pardon?"

"La montre. C'est en or?" The man pointed at Jordan's watch.

"Yes, of course it's gold!" said Jordan.

The man grinned, revealing a mouthful of rotted teeth. He rose and shuffled across the cell to sit beside Jordan. Right beside him. His gaze dropped speculatively to Jordan's shoes. *"C'est italienne?"*

Jordan sighed. "Yes, they're Italian."

The man reached over and fingered Jordan's linen jacket sleeve.

"All right, that's it," said Jordan. "Hands to yourself, chap! *Laissez-moi tranquille!*"

The man simply grinned wider and pointed to his own shoes, a pair of cardboard and plastic creations. "You like?"

"Very nice," groaned Jordan.

The sound of footsteps and clinking keys approached. The man sleeping in the corner suddenly woke up and began to yell, *"Je suis innocent! Je suis innocent!"*

"M. Tavistock?" called the guard.

Jordan jumped at once to his feet. "Yes?"

"You are to come with me."

"Where are we going?"

"You have visitors."

The guard led him down a hall, past holding cells jammed full with prisoners. Good grief, thought Jordan, and he'd thought his cell was bad. He followed the guard through a locked door into the booking area. At once his ears were assaulted with the sounds of bedlam. Everywhere phones seemed to be ringing, voices arguing. A ragtag line of prisoners waited to be processed, and one woman kept yelling that it was a mistake, all a mistake. Through the babble of French, Jordan heard his name called.

"Beryl?" he said in relief.

She ran to him, practically knocking him over with the force of her embrace. "Jordie! Oh, my poor Jordie, are you all right?"

"I'm fine, darling."

"You're really all right?"

"Never better, now that you're here." Glancing over her shoulder, he saw Richard and Daumier standing behind her. The cavalry had arrived. Now this terrible business could be cleared up.

Beryl pulled away and frowned at his face. "You look ghastly."

"I probably smell even worse." Turning to Daumier, he said, "Have they found out anything about Colette?"

Daumier shook his head. "A single bullet, nine millimeters, in the temple. Plainly an execution, with no witnesses."

"What about the gun?" asked Jordan. "How can they accuse me without having a murder weapon?"

"They do have one," said Daumier. "It was found in the storm drain, very near the car."

"And no witnesses?" said Beryl. "In broad daylight?"

"It is a side street. Not many passersby."

"But someone must have seen something."

Daumier gave an unhappy nod. "A woman did report seeing a man force his way into Colette's car. But it was on Boulevard Saint-Germain."

Jordan groaned. "Oh, great. That would've been me."

Beryl frowned. "You?"

"I talked her into giving me a ride back to the hotel. My fingerprints will be all over the inside of that car."

"What happened after you got into the car?" Richard asked.

"She let me off at the Ritz. I went up to the room for a few minutes, then came back down to talk to her. That's when I found…" Groaning, he clutched his head. "Lord, this can't be happening."

"Did you see anything?" Richard pressed him.

"Not a thing. But…" Jordan's head slowly lifted. "Colette may have."

"You're not sure?"

"While we were driving to the hotel, she kept frowning at the mirror. Said something about imagining things. I looked, but all I saw was traffic." Miserable, he turned to Daumier. "I blame myself, really. I keep thinking, if only I'd paid more attention, if I hadn't been so wrapped up—"

"She knew how to protect herself," interrupted Daumier. "She should have been prepared."

"That's what I don't understand," said Jordan. "That she was caught so off guard." He glanced at his watch. "There's still plenty of daylight. We could go back to

Boulevard Saint-Germain. Retrace my steps. Something might come back to me."

His suggestion was met with dead silence.

"Jordie," said Beryl, softly, "you can't."

"What do you mean, I can't?"

"They won't release you."

"But they have to release me! I didn't do it!" He looked at Daumier. To his dismay, the Frenchman regretfully shook his head.

Richard said, "We'll do whatever it takes, Jordan. Somehow we'll get you out of here."

"Has anyone called Uncle Hugh?"

"He's not at Chetwynd," said Beryl. "No one knows where he is. It seems he left last night without telling anyone. So we're going to see Reggie and Helena. They've friends in the embassy. Maybe they can pull some strings."

Dismayed by the news, Jordan could only stand there, surrounded by the chaos of milling prisoners and policemen. *I'm in prison and Uncle Hugh's vanished,* he thought. *This nightmare is getting worse by the second.*

"The police think I'm guilty?" he ventured.

"I am afraid so," said Daumier.

"And you, Claude? What do you think?"

"Of course he knows you're innocent!" declared Beryl. "We all do. Just give me time to clear things up."

Jordan turned to his sister, his beautiful, stubborn sister. The one person he cared most about in the world. He took off his watch and firmly pressed it into her hand.

She frowned. "Why are you giving me this?"

"Safekeeping. I may be in here a rather long time. Now, I want you to go home, Beryl. The next plane to London. Do you understand?"

"But I'm not going anywhere."

"Yes, you are. And Richard is damn well going to see to it."

"How?" she retorted. "By dragging me off by the hair?"

"If that's what it takes."

"You need me here!"

"Beryl." He took her by the shoulders and spoke quietly. Sensibly. "A woman's been killed. And she was trained to defend herself."

"It doesn't mean I'm next."

"It means they're frightened. Ready to strike back. You have to go home."

"And leave you in this place?"

"Claude will be here. And Reggie—"

"So I fly home and leave you to rot in prison?" She shook her head in disagreement. "Do you really think I'd do that?"

"If you love me, you will."

Her chin came up. "If I love you," she said, "I'll do no such thing." She threw her arms around him in a fierce, uncompromising embrace. Then, brushing away tears, she turned to Richard. "Let's go. The sooner we talk to Reggie, the sooner we'll clear up this mess."

Jordan watched his sister walk away. It was just like her, he thought, to steer her own straight and stubborn course through that unruly crowd of pickpockets and prostitutes. "Beryl!" he yelled. "Go home! Don't be a bloody idiot!"

She stopped and looked back at him. "But I can't help it, Jordie. It runs in the family." Then she turned and walked out the door.

Chapter 6

"Your brother's right," said Richard. "You should go home."

"Don't *you* start now," she snapped over her shoulder.

"I'll drive you to the hotel to pack. Then I'm taking you to the airport."

"You and what regiment?"

"For once will you take some advice?" he yelled.

She spun around on the crowded sidewalk and turned to confront him. "Advice, yes. Orders, no."

"Okay, then just listen for a minute. Your coming to Paris was a crazy move to begin with. Sure, I understand why you did it. I understand that you'd want to know the truth about your parents. But things have changed, Beryl. A woman's been killed. It's a whole new ball game now."

"What am I supposed to do about Jordan? Just leave him there?"

"I'll take care of it. I'll talk to Reggie. We'll get him the best lawyer there is—"

"And I run home? Wash my hands of the whole mess?" She looked down at the watch she was holding. Jordan's watch. Quietly she said, "He's my family. Did you see how wretched he looked? It would kill him to stay in that place. If I left him there, I'd never forgive myself."

"And if something happened to you, Jordan would never forgive himself. And neither would I."

"I'm not your responsibility."

"But you are."

"And who decided that?"

He reached for her then, trapping her face in his hands. "I did," he whispered, and pressed his lips to hers. She was so stunned by the ferocity of his kiss that at first she couldn't react; too many glorious sensations were assaulting her at once. She heard his murmurings of need, felt the hot surge of his tongue into her mouth. Her own body responded, every nerve singing with desire. She was oblivious to the traffic, the passersby on the sidewalk. There were only the two of them and the way their bodies and mouths melted together. All day they'd been fighting this, she thought. And all day she knew it was hopeless. She knew it would come to this—one kiss on a Paris street, and she was lost.

Gently he pulled away and gazed down at her. "*That's* why you have to leave Paris," he murmured.

"Because you command it?"

"No. Because it makes sense."

She stepped back, desperate to put space between them, to regain some control—any control—over her emotions. "Sense to you, perhaps," she said softly. "But not to me." Then she turned and climbed into his car.

He slid in beside her and shut the door. Though they sat in silence, she could feel his frustration radiating throughout the car.

"What can I say that would make you change your mind?" he asked.

"*My* mind?" She looked at him and managed a tight, uncompromising smile. "Absolutely nothing."

"It's rather a sticky situation," said Reggie Vane. "If the charges weren't so serious—theft, perhaps, or even assault—then the embassy might be able to do something. But murder? I'm afraid that's beyond diplomatic intervention."

They were talking in Reggie's private study, a masculine, dark-paneled room very much like her uncle Hugh's at Chetwynd. The bookshelves were lined with English classics, the walls hung with hunting scenes of foxes and hounds and gentlemen on horseback. The stone fireplace was an exact copy, Reggie had told them, of the hearth in his childhood home in Cornwall. Even the smell of Reggie's pipe tobacco reminded Beryl of home. How comforting to discover that here, on the outskirts of Paris, was a familiar world transplanted straight from England.

"Surely the ambassador can do something?" said Beryl. "This is Jordan we're talking about, not some soccer-club hooligan. Besides, he's innocent."

"Of course he's innocent," said Reggie. "Believe me, if there was anything I could do about it, our Jordan wouldn't stay in that cell a moment longer." He sat down on the couch beside her and clasped her hands, the whole time focusing his mild blue eyes on her face. "Beryl, darling, you have to understand. Even the ambassador himself can't work miracles. I've spoken to him, and he's not optimistic."

"Then there's nothing you or he can do?" Beryl asked miserably.

"I'll arrange for a lawyer—one our embassy recommends. He's an excellent fellow, someone they call in for just this sort of thing. Specializes in English clients."

"And that's all we can hope for? A good attorney?"

Reggie's answer was a regretful nod.

In her disappointment, Beryl didn't hear Richard move to stand close behind her, but she did feel his hands coming to rest protectively on her shoulders. *How I've come to rely on him,* she thought. *A man I shouldn't trust. And yet I do.*

Reggie looked at Richard. "What about the Intelligence angle?" he asked. "Any evidence forthcoming?"

"French Intelligence is working with the police. They'll be running ballistic tests on the gun. No fingerprints were found on it. The fact that he's Lord Lovat's nephew will get him some special consideration. But in the end, it's still a murder charge. And the victim's a Frenchwoman. Once the local papers get hold of the story, it will sound like some spoiled English brat trying to slither out of criminal charges."

"And there's enough ill will toward us British as it is," said Reggie. "After thirty years in this country, I should know. I tell you, as soon as my year's up at the bank, I'm going home." His gaze wandered longingly to the painting over the mantelpiece. It was of a country home, its walls festooned with blue wisteria blossoms. "Helena hated it in Cornwall—thought the house was far too primitive. But it suited my parents. And it suits me." He looked at Beryl. "It's a frightening thing, getting into trouble so far from home. One is always aware that one is vulnerable. And neither class nor money can make things right."

"I've told Beryl she should fly home," said Richard.

Reggie nodded. "My feelings exactly."

"I can't," said Beryl. "I'd feel like a rat jumping ship."

"At least you'd be a live rat," said Richard.

Angrily she shrugged off his touch. "But a rat all the same."

Reggie reached for her hand. "Beryl," he said quietly, "listen to me. I was your mother's oldest friend—we grew up together. So I feel a special responsibility. And you have no idea how painful it is for me to see one of Madeline's children in such a fix. It's awful enough that Jordan's in trouble, but to worry about you, as well..." He gave her hand a squeeze. "Listen to your Mr. Wolf here. He's a sensible fellow. Someone you can trust."

Someone I can trust. Beryl felt Richard's gaze on her back, felt it as acutely as a touch, and her spine stiffened. She focused firmly on Reggie. Dear Reggie, whose shared past with Madeline made him part of her family.

She said, "I know you mean only the best, Reggie, but I can't leave Paris."

The two men looked at each other, exchanging shared expressions of frustration, but not surprise. After all, they had both known Madeline; they could expect nothing less than stubbornness from her daughter.

There was a knock on the study door. Helena poked her head in. "All right for me to come in?"

"Of course," said Beryl.

Helena entered, carrying a tray of tea and biscuits, which she set down on the end table. "I'm always careful to ask first," she said with a smile as she poured out four cups, "before I trespass in Reggie's private abode." She handed Beryl a cup. "Have we made any headway, then?"

From the silence that greeted her question, Helena knew the answer. She looked at once apologetic. "Oh, Beryl. I'm so sorry. Isn't there *something* you can do, Reggie?"

"I'm already doing it," said Reggie, with more than a hint of impatience. Turning his back to her, he took a pipe down from the mantelpiece and lit it. For a moment, there was only the sound of the teacups clinking on saucers and the soft put-put-put of Reggie's lips on the pipe stem.

"Reggie?" ventured Helena again. "It seems to me that calling an attorney is merely being reactive. Isn't there something, well, *active* that could be done?"

"Such as?" asked Richard.

"For instance, the crime itself. We all know Jordan couldn't have done it. So who did?"

Reggie grunted. "You're hardly qualified as a detective."

"Still, it's a question that will have to be answered. That young woman was killed while watching over Jordan. So this may all stem from the reason Jordan's in Paris to begin with. Though I can't quite see how a twenty-year-old case of murder could be so dangerous to someone."

"It was more than murder," Beryl observed. "Espionage was involved."

"That business with the NATO mole," Reggie said to Helena. "You remember. Hugh told us about it."

"Oh, yes. Delphi." Helena glanced at Richard. "MI6 never actually identified him, did they?"

"They had their suspicions," said Richard.

"I myself always wondered," said Helena, reaching for a biscuit, "about Ambassador Sutherland. And why he committed suicide so soon after Madeline and Bernard died."

Richard nodded. "You and I think along the same lines, Lady Helena."

"Though I can't say he didn't have other reasons to jump off that bridge. If I were a man married to Nina, I'd have killed myself long ago." Helena bit sharply into the biscuit; it was a reminder that even mousy women have teeth.

Reggie tapped his pipe and said, "It's not right for us to speculate."

"Still, one can't help it, can one?"

By the time Reggie walked his guests to the front door, darkness had fallen and the night had taken on a damp, unseasonable chill. Even the high walls surrounding the Vanes' private courtyard couldn't seem to shut out the sense of danger that hung in the air that night.

"I promise you," said Reggie, "I'll do everything I can."

"I don't know how to thank you," Beryl murmured.

"Just give me a smile, dear. Yes, that's it." Reggie took her by the shoulders and planted a kiss on her forehead. "You look more and more like your mother every day. And from me, there is no higher compliment." He turned to Richard. "You'll look out for the girl?"

"I promise," said Richard.

"Good. Because she's all we have left." Sadly he touched Beryl's cheek. "All we have left of Madeline."

"Were they always that way together?" asked Beryl. "Reggie and Helena?"

Richard kept his eyes on the road as he drove. "What do you mean?"

"The sniping at each other. The put-downs."

He chuckled. "I'm so used to hearing it, I hardly notice it anymore. Yes, I guess it was that way when I met them twenty years ago. I'm sure part of it's due to his resentment of Helena's money. No man likes to feel, well, kept."

"No," she said quietly, looking straight ahead. "I suppose no man would." *Is that how it would be between us?* she wondered. *Would he hold my money against me? Would his resentment build up over the years, until we ended up like Reggie and Helena, sharing a lifetime of hell together?*

"Part of it, too," said Richard, "is the fact that Reggie never really liked being in Paris, and he never liked being a banker. Helena talked him into taking the post."

"She doesn't seem to like it here much, either."

"No. And so there they are, always sniping at each other. I'd see them at parties with your parents, and I was always struck by the contrast. Bernard and Madeline seemed so much in love. Then again, every man who met your mother couldn't help but fall in love, just a little."

"What was it about her?" asked Beryl. "You said once that she was…enchanting."

"When I met her, she was about forty. Oh, she had

a gray hair here and there. A few laugh lines. But she was more fascinating than any twenty-year-old woman I'd ever met. I was surprised to hear that she wasn't born to nobility."

"She was from Cornwall. Old Spanish blood. Dad met her one summer while on holiday." Beryl smiled. "He said she beat him in a footrace. In her bare feet. And that's when he knew she was the one for him."

"They were well matched, in every way. I suppose that's what fascinated me—their happiness. My parents were divorced. It was a pretty nasty split, and it soured me on the whole idea of marriage. But your parents made it look so easy." He shook his head. "I was more shocked than anyone about their deaths. I couldn't believe that Bernard would—"

"He didn't do it. I know he didn't."

After a pause, Richard said, "So do I."

They drove for a moment without speaking, the lights of passing traffic flashing at them through the windshield.

"Is that why you never married?" she asked. "Because of your parents' divorce?"

"It was one reason. The other is that I've never found the right woman." He glanced at her. "Why didn't you marry?"

She shrugged. "Never the right man."

"There must have been someone in your life."

"There was. For a while." She hugged herself and stared out at the darkness rushing past.

"Didn't work out?"

She managed a laugh. "I'm lucky it didn't."

"Do I detect a trace of bitterness?"

"Disillusionment, really. When we first met, I

thought he was quite extraordinary. He was a surgeon about to leave on a mercy mission to Nigeria. It's so rare to find a man who really cares about humanity. I visited him, twice, in Africa. He was in his element out there."

"And what happened?"

"We were lovers for a while. And then I came to realize how he saw himself. The great white savior. He'd swoop into a primitive hospital, save a few lives, then fly home to England for a bracing dose of adulation. Which, it turned out, he could never get enough of. One adoring woman wasn't sufficient. He had to have a dozen." Softly she added, "And I wanted to be the only one." She leaned back against the car seat and stared out at the glow of Paris. The City of Light, she thought. Still, there were those shadows, those dark alleys and even darker secrets.

Back at the Place Vendôme, they sat for a moment in the parked car, not speaking, just sitting side by side in the gloom. *We're both exhausted,* she thought. *And the night isn't over yet. I'll have to pack Jordan's things. A toothbrush, a change of clothes. Bring them back to the prison...*

"Then I can't talk you into leaving," he said.

She looked out at the plaza, at the silhouette of two lovers strolling arm in arm through the darkness. "No. Not until he's free. Not until we see this through to the end."

"I was afraid you'd say that. But I'm not surprised. Just the other day you told me you had a hard head."

She looked at his face, saw the gleam of his smile in the shadows. "This isn't hardheadedness, Richard. This is loyalty. To Jordan. To my parents. We're Tavistocks, you see, and we stand by each other."

"Standing by Jordan, I can see. But your parents are dead."

"It's a matter of honor."

He shook his head. "Bernard and Madeline aren't around to care about honor. It's a medieval concept, to march into battle for something as abstract as the family name."

She climbed out of the car. "Obviously the Wolf family name means nothing to you," she said coldly.

He was out of the car and moving right beside her as she walked through the hotel lobby and stepped into the elevator. "Maybe it's my peculiarly American point of view, but my name is what *I* make of it. I don't wear the family crest tattooed on my forehead."

"You couldn't possibly understand."

"Of course not," he retorted as they stepped out of the elevator. "I'm just a dumb Yank."

"I never called you any such thing!"

He followed her into the suite and shut the door with a thud. "Still, it's clear I'm not up to her Ladyship's standards."

She whirled around and faced him in anger. "You're holding it against me, aren't you? My name. My wealth."

"What's bothering me has nothing to do with your being a Tavistock."

"What *is* bothering you, then?"

"The fact that you won't listen to reason."

"Ah. My hard head."

"Yes, your hard head. And your dumb sense of honor. And your…your…"

She moved right up to him. Tilting up her chin, she stared him straight in the eye. "My what?"

He took her face in his hands and planted a kiss on

her mouth, a kiss so long and hard that she had difficulty catching her breath. When at last he pulled back, her legs were wobbly and her pulse was roaring in her ears.

"*That's* what's bothering me," he said. "I can't think straight when you're around. Can't concentrate long enough to tie my own shoelaces. You brush past me, or just look at me, and my mind goes off on certain tangents I'd rather not specify. It's the kind of situation that leads to mistakes. And I don't like to make mistakes."

"You're the one who can't concentrate. And I'm the one who has to fly home?" She turned and started across the room toward the connecting door to Jordan's suite. "Sorry, Richard," she said, moving past the window, "but you'll just have to keep those lusty male hormones under—"

Her words were cut off by the crack of the shattering window.

Reflexes made her pivot away from the sting of flying glass. In the next instant, Richard lunged at her and sent her sprawling to the shard-littered floor.

Another bullet zinged through the window and thudded into the far wall.

"The light!" shouted Richard. "Got to kill the light!" He began to crawl toward the bedside lamp and had almost reached it when the second window shattered. Broken glass rained on top of him.

"Richard!" screamed Beryl.

"Stay down!" He took a deep breath, then rolled across the floor. He grabbed the lamp cord and yanked the plug from the outlet. Instantly the room was plunged into darkness. The only light came through the windows, shining dimly in from the Place Vendôme. An eerie silence fell over the room, broken only by the hammering of Beryl's heartbeat in her ears.

She started to rise to her knees.

"Don't move!" warned Richard.

"He can't see us."

"He might have an infrared scope. Stay down."

Beryl dropped back to the floor and felt the bite of broken glass through her sleeves. "Where's it coming from?"

"Has to be one of the buildings across the plaza. Long-range rifle."

"What do we do now?"

"We call for reinforcements." She heard him crawling in the darkness, then heard the clang of the telephone hitting the floor. An instant later, he muttered an oath. "Line's dead! Someone's cut the wire."

New panic shot through Beryl. "You mean they've been in the room?"

"Which means—" Suddenly he fell silent.

"Richard?"

"Shh. Listen."

Over her pounding heartbeat, she heard the faint whine of the hotel elevator as it came to a stop at their floor.

"I think we're in trouble," said Richard.

Chapter 7

"He can't get in," said Beryl. "The door's locked."

"They'll have a passkey. If they managed to get in here earlier…"

"What do we do?"

"Jordan's room. Move!"

At once she was on her knees and crawling toward the connecting door. Only when she'd reached it did she realize Richard wasn't following her.

"Come on!" she whispered.

"You go. I'll hold them off."

She glanced back in disbelief. "What?"

"They'll check this room first to see if we've been hit. I'll slow them down. You get out through Jordan's suite. Head for the stairwell and don't stop running."

Beryl crouched frozen in the connecting doorway. *This is suicide. He has no gun, no weapon at all.* Already he was slipping through the shadows. She could just make out his figure, poised by the door. Waiting for the attack.

The knock on the door made her jerk in panic. "Mlle Tavistock?" called a man's voice. Beryl didn't answer; she didn't dare to. *"Mademoiselle?"* the voice called again.

Richard was gesturing frantically at her through the darkness. *Get out! Now.*

I can't leave him, she thought. *I can't let him fight this alone.*

A key grated in the lock.

There was no time to consider the risks. Beryl grabbed the bedside lamp, scrambled toward Richard, and planted herself right beside him.

"What the hell are you doing?" he whispered.

"Shut up," she hissed back.

They both flattened against the wall as the door swung open in front of them. There was a pause, the span of just a few heartbeats, and then they heard footsteps cross the threshold into the room. The door slowly swung closed, revealing the silhouettes of the intruders—two men, standing in the darkness. Beryl could feel Richard coil up beside her, could almost hear his silent one-two-three countdown. Suddenly he was flying at the nearest man; the force of the impact sent both men slamming to the floor.

Beryl raised the lamp and brought it crashing down on the head of the second intruder. He collapsed at her feet, facedown and groaning. She dropped beside him and began patting his clothes for a gun. Through his jacket, she felt a hard lump under his arm. A holster? She rolled him over onto his back. Only then, as a crack of light through the partially closed door spilled across his face, did she realize their mistake.

"Oh, my God," she said. She glanced at Richard, who'd just grabbed his opponent by the collar and was about to shove him against the wall. "Richard, don't!" she yelled. "Don't hurt him!"

He paused, still clutching the other man's collar in his fists. "Why the hell not?" he muttered.

"Because these are the wrong men, that's why!" She went to the wall switch and flicked on the overhead light.

Richard blinked in the sudden brightness. He stared at the hotel manager, cowering in his grip. Then he turned and looked at the man who lay groaning by the door. It was Claude Daumier.

At once Richard released the manager, who promptly shrank away in terror. "Sorry," said Richard. "My mistake."

"If I'd known it was you," said Beryl, pressing a bag of ice to Daumier's head, "I wouldn't have whacked you so hard."

"If you had known it was me," muttered Daumier, "I would hope you wouldn't have whacked me at all." He sat up on the couch and caught the bag of ice before it could slide off. "*Zut alors,* what did you use, *chérie?* A brick?"

"A lamp. And not a very big one, either." She glanced at Richard and the hotel manager. Both men were looking slightly the worse for wear—especially the manager. That black eye of his was colorful testimony to the damaging potential of Richard's fist. Now that the crisis was over, and they were safely barricaded in the manager's office, the situation struck Beryl as more than a little hilarious. A senior French Intelligence agent, beaned by a lamp? Richard, still nursing his bruised knuckles. And the poor hotel manager, assiduously maintaining a safe distance from those same knuckles. She could have laughed—if the whole affair hadn't been so frightening.

There was a knock on the door. Instantly Beryl tensed, only to relax again when she saw that it was a policeman. *I'm still high on adrenaline,* she thought as she watched Daumier and the cop converse in French. *Still expecting the worst.*

The policeman withdrew, closing the door behind him.

"What did he say?" Beryl asked.

"The shots were fired from across the plaza," said Daumier. "They have found bullet casings on the rooftop."

"And the gunman?" asked Richard.

Regretfully Daumier shook his head. "Vanished."

"Then he's still on the loose," said Richard. "And we don't know when he'll strike again." He looked at the manager. "What about that telephone wire? Who could've cut it?"

The man shrank back a step, as though expecting another blow. "I do not know, *monsieur!* One of the maids, she says her passkey was misplaced for a few hours today."

"So anyone could have gotten in."

"No one from our staff! They are thoroughly checked. You see, we have many important guests."

"I want your employees revetted. Every last one of them."

The manager nodded meekly. Then, still wincing in pain from the black eye, he left the office.

Richard began to pace, carelessly yanking his tie loose as he moved. "We have an intruder who cuts the phone line. A marksman stationed across the plaza. A high-powered rifle positioned for a shot straight into Beryl's room. Claude, this is sounding worse by the minute."

"Why would they try to kill me?" asked Beryl. "What have I done?"

"You've asked too many questions, that's what." Richard turned to Daumier. "You had it right, Claude. The matter's not dead, not by a long shot."

"We were both in that room, Richard," said Beryl. "How do you know he was aiming at me?"

"I wasn't the one walking past that window."

"You're the one who's CIA."

"The qualifying prefix is *ex,* as in, no longer with the Company. I'm not a threat to anyone."

"And I am?"

"Yes. By virtue of your name—not to mention your curiosity." He glanced at Daumier. "We need a safe house, Claude. Can you arrange it?"

"We keep a flat in Passy for protection of witnesses. It will serve your purpose."

"Who else knows about it?"

"My people. A few ministry officials."

"That's too many."

"It is the best I can offer. It has an alarm system. And I will assign guards."

Richard paused, thinking, weighing the risks. At last he nodded. "It will have to do for tonight. Tomorrow, we'll come up with something else. Maybe a plane ticket." He looked at Beryl.

This time she didn't protest. Already she could feel the adrenaline fading away. A moment ago, every nerve felt wired for action; now a plane home was beginning to sound sensible. All it took was a short flight across the Channel, and she'd be safe in the refuge of Chetwynd. It was all so easy, so tempting.

And she was so very, very tired.

With a numb sense of detachment, Beryl listened as Daumier made the necessary phone calls. He hung up and said, "I will have a car and escort brought around. Beryl's clothes will be delivered to the flat later. Oh, and Richard, you will no doubt want this." He reached under his suit jacket and withdrew a semiautomatic pistol from his shoulder holster. He handed it to Richard. "A loan. Just between us, of course."

"Are you sure you want to part with it?"

"I have another." Daumier slid off his holster, which he also gave to Richard. "You remember how to use one?"

Richard checked the ammunition clip and nodded grimly. "I think it'll come back."

A policeman knocked on the door. The car was waiting.

Richard took Beryl's arm and helped her to her feet. "Time to drop out of sight for a while. Are you ready?"

She looked at the gun he was holding, noted how easily he handled it, how comfortably he slid it into the holster. A professional, she thought. The transformation was almost frightening. *How well do I really know you, Richard Wolf?*

For now, the question was irrelevant. He was the one man she could count on, the one man she had to trust.

She followed him out the door.

"We should be safe here. For tonight, at least." Richard double-bolted the apartment door and turned to look at her.

She was standing in the center of the living room, her arms wrapped around her shoulders, a dazed look in her eyes. This was not the brash and stubborn Beryl he knew, he thought. This was a woman who'd faced sheer terror and knew the worst wasn't over yet. He wanted to go to her, to take her in his arms and promise her that nothing would ever hurt her while he was around, but they both knew it was a promise he might not be able to keep. In silence, he circled the flat, checking to see that the windows were secure, the drapes closed. A glance outside told him there were two guards watching the building, one at the front entrance, one at the rear. A safety net, he thought. For when I let my attention slip. And it *would* slip. Sooner or later, he would have to sleep.

Satisfied that all was locked up tight, he went back to the living room. He found Beryl sitting on the couch, very quiet, very still. Almost…defeated.

"Are you all right?" he asked.

She gave a shrug, as though the question was irrelevant—as though they had far more important things to consider.

He took off his jacket and tossed it over a chair. "You haven't eaten. There's some food in the kitchen."

Her gaze focused on his shoulder holster. "Why did you quit the business?" she asked.

"You mean the Company?"

She nodded. "When I saw you holding that gun, it… it suddenly struck me. What you used to be."

He sat down beside her. "I've never killed anyone. If that makes a difference."

"But you're trained to do it."

"Only in self-defense. That's not the same thing as murder."

She nodded, as though trying very hard to agree with him.

He took the Glock from the holster and held it out to her. She regarded it with undisguised abhorrence.

"Yes, I understand how you feel," he said. "This gun's a semiautomatic. Nine millimeter bullets, sixteen cartridges to the magazine. Some people consider it a work of art. I think of it as a tool of last resort. Something I hope to God I never have to use." He set it on the coffee table, where it lay like an evil reminder of violence. "Pick it up if you want to. It's not very heavy."

"I'd rather not." She shuddered and looked away. "I'm not afraid of guns. I mean, I've handled rifles before. I used to go shooting with Uncle Hugh. But those were only clay pigeons."

"Not quite the same thing."

"No. Not quite."

"You asked why I quit the Company." He pointed to the Glock. "That was one of the reasons. I've never killed anyone, and I'm not itching to. For me, the intelligence business was a game. A challenge. The enemy was well-defined—the Russians, the East Germans. But now…" He picked up the gun and held it thoughtfully in his palm. "The world's turned into a crazy place. I can't tell who the enemy is anymore. And I knew that sooner or later, I'd lose my edge. I could already feel it happening."

"Your edge?"

"It's my age, you know. You hit forty and you don't react the way you did as a twenty-year-old. I like to think I've grown smarter, instead, but what I really am is more cautious. And a lot less willing to take risks." He looked at her. "With anyone's life."

She met his gaze. Looking into her eyes, he suddenly found himself wanting to babble all sorts of crazy things. To tell her that the one life he didn't want to risk was hers. When had this stopped being a mere babysitting job? he wondered. When had it become something much more? A mission. An obsession.

"You frighten me, Richard," she said.

"It's the gun."

"No, it's you. All the things I don't know about you. All the secrets you're keeping from me."

"From now on, I promise I'll be absolutely honest with you."

"But it started out as half truths. Not telling me you knew my parents. Or how they died. Don't you see, it's my childhood all over again! Uncle Hugh with his head full of classified secrets." She let out a breath of frustration and looked away. "Then I see you with that… thing."

He touched her face and gently turned it toward him. "It's just a temporary evil," he murmured. "Until this is over." She kept looking at him, her eyes bright and moist, her hair tumbling about her shoulders. *She wants to trust me,* he thought. *But she's afraid.*

He couldn't help himself. He kissed her. Once. Twice. The second time, he felt her lips yield under his, felt her whole body seem to turn liquid at his touch. He kissed her a third time and found his hands sliding through her hair, his fingers hopelessly becoming tangled in all that raven silk. She sighed, a delicious sound of surrender, invitation, and she sagged backward onto the couch.

Suddenly he, too, was falling, tumbling on top of her. Their lips met in a touch that instantly turned electric. She reached around his neck and pulled him down hard against her—

And flinched. That blasted gun again. The holster had pushed into her breast, had served as an ugly reminder of all the things that had happened today. All the things that could still happen.

He looked at her face, at her hair flung across the cushions, at the mingling of fear and desire he saw in her eyes. *Not now,* he thought. *Not this way.*

Slowly he pulled away and they both sat up. For a moment, they remained side by side on the couch, not touching, not speaking.

She said, "I'm not ready for this. I'll put my life in your hands, Richard. But my heart, that's a different matter."

"I understand."

"Then you'll also understand that I'm not a fan of James Bond, or anyone remotely like him. I'm not impressed by guns, or by the men who use them." She rose to her feet and moved pointedly away from the couch. Away from him.

"So what does impress you?" he asked. "If not a man's gun?"

She turned to him and he saw a flicker of humor cross her face. *The old Beryl,* he thought. *Thank God she's still there, somewhere.*

"Straight talk," she said. "That's what impresses me."

"Then that's what you'll get. I promise."

She turned and walked to the bedroom. "We'll see."

Jordan was not impressed by this lawyer, no, he was not impressed at all.

The man had greasy hair and a greasy little mustache, and he spoke English with the exaggerated accent of a second-rate actor playing a stereotypical Frenchman. All those "eets" and "zees" and *"Mon Dieus."* Still, Jordan reasoned, since Beryl had hired the man, he must be one of the best attorneys in Paris.

You could have fooled me, thought Jordan, gazing across the prison interview table at the smarmy M. Jarre.

"Not to worry," said the man. "Everything will be taken care of. I am reviewing the papers now, and I believe we will soon reach an agreement to have you released."

"What about the investigation?" asked Jordan. "Any progress?"

"Very slow. You know how it is, M. Tavistock. In a city as large as Paris, the police, they are overworked. You cannot be impatient."

"And my uncle? Have you been able to reach him?"

"He is in complete agreement with my planned course of action."

"Is he coming to Paris?"

"He is detained. Business keeps him at home, I am afraid."

"At home? But I thought…" Jordan paused. Didn't Beryl say Uncle Hugh had left Chetwynd?

M. Jarre rose from the table. "Rest assured that all

that can be done, will be done. I have instructed the police to transfer you to a more comfortable cell."

"Thank you," said Jordan, still puzzling over the reference to Uncle Hugh. As the attorney was leaving the room, Jordan called out, "M. Jarre? Did my uncle happen to mention how his…negotiations went in London?"

The attorney glanced back. "They are still in progress, I understand. But I am sure he will tell you himself." He gave a nod of farewell. "Good evening, M. Tavistock. I hope you find your new cell more agreeable." He walked out.

What the dickens is going on? thought Jordan. He wondered about this all the way to his cell—his new cell. One look at the pair of shady characters seated inside and his suspicions about M. Jarre deepened. *This* was more agreeable quarters?

Reluctantly Jordan stepped inside and flinched at the clang of the door shutting behind him. The jailer walked away, his footsteps echoing down the hall.

The two prisoners were staring at his fine Italian shoes, which contrasted dreadfully with the regulation prison garb he was wearing.

"Hello," said Jordan, for want of anything else to say.

"Anglais?" asked one of the men.

Jordan swallowed. *"Oui. Anglais."*

The man grunted and pointed to an empty bunk. "Yours."

Jordan went to the bunk, set his bundle of street clothes on the foot of the bed, and stretched out on the mattress. As the two prisoners babbled away in French, Jordan kept wondering about that greasy attorney and why he had lied about Uncle Hugh. If only he could get in touch with Beryl, ask her what was going on…

He sat up at the sound of footsteps approaching the cell. It was the guard, escorting yet another prisoner—this one a balding, round-cheeked man with a definite waddle and a pleasant enough face. The sort of fellow you'd expect to see standing behind a bakery counter. *Not your typical criminal,* thought Jordan. *But then, neither am I.*

The man entered the cell and was directed to the fourth and last bunk. He sat down, looking stunned by the circumstances in which he found himself. François was his name, and from what Jordan could gather using his elementary command of French, the man's crime had something to do with the fair sex. Solicitation, perhaps? François was not eager to talk about it. He simply sat on his bed and stared at the floor. *We're both new to this,* thought Jordan.

The other two cellmates were still watching him. Sullen young men, obviously sociopathic. He'd have to keep his eye on them.

Supper came—an atrocious goulash accompanied by French bread. Jordan stared at the muddy brown gravy and thought wistfully of his supper the night before—poached salmon and roast duckling. Ah, well. One had to eat regardless of one's circumstances. What a shame there wasn't a bottle of wine to wash down the meal. A nice Beaujolais, perhaps, or just a common Burgundy. He took a bite of goulash and decided that even a bad bottle of wine would be welcome—anything to dull the taste of this gravy. He forced himself to eat it and made a silent vow that when he got out of here—*if* he got out of here—the first place he'd head for was a decent restaurant.

At midnight, the lights were turned off. Jordan

stretched out on the blanket and made every effort to sleep, but found he couldn't. For one thing, his cellmates were snoring to wake the dead. For another, the day's events kept playing and replaying in his mind. That drive with Colette from Boulevard Saint-Germain. The way she had glanced at the rearview mirror. If only he had paid more attention to who might be following them back to the hotel. And then, against his will, he remembered the horror of finding her body in the car, remembered the stickiness of her blood on his hands.

Rage bubbled up inside him—an impotent sense of fury about her death. *It's my fault,* he thought. If she hadn't been watching over him, protecting him.

But that's not why she died, Jordan thought suddenly. He was nowhere nearby when it happened. So why did they kill her? Did she know something, see something…

…or someone?

His thoughts veered in a new direction. Colette must have spotted a face in her rearview mirror, a face in the car that was following them. After she'd dropped Jordan off at the Ritz, maybe she'd seen that someone again. Or he'd seen her and knew she could identify him.

Which made the killer someone Colette knew. Someone she recognized.

He was so intent on piecing together the puzzle, he didn't pay much attention to the creak of the bunk springs somewhere in the cell. Only when he heard the soft rustle of movement did he realize that one of his cellmates was approaching his bed.

It was dark; he could make out only faintly a shadowy figure moving toward him. One of those young hoods, he thought, come to rifle his jacket.

Jordan lay perfectly still and willed his breathing to

remain deep and even. *Let the coward think I'm still asleep. When he moves close enough, I'll surprise him.*

The shadow slipped quietly through the darkness. Six feet away, now five. Jordan's heart was pounding, his muscles already tensed for action. *Just a little closer. A little closer. He'll be reaching for the jacket hanging at the foot of the bed...*

But the man moved instead to Jordan's head. There was a faint arc of shadow—an arm being raised to deliver a blow. Jordan's hand shot out just as his assailant attacked.

He caught the other man's wrist and heard a grunt of surprise. His attacker came at him with his free hand. Jordan deflected the blow and scrambled off the bunk. Still gripping his attacker's wrist, he gave it a vicious twist, eliciting a yelp of pain. The man was thrashing to get free now, but Jordan held on. He was not going to get away. Not without learning a lesson. He shoved the man backward and heard the satisfying thud of his opponent's body hitting the cinder-block wall. The man groaned and tried to pull free. Again, Jordan shoved. This time they both toppled over onto a cot, landing on its sleeping occupant. The man in Jordan's grasp began to writhe, to jerk. At once Jordan realized this was no longer a man fighting to free himself. This was a man in the throes of a convulsion.

He heard the sound of footsteps and then the cell lights flashed on. A guard yelled at him in French.

Jordan released his assailant and backed away in surprise. It was the moon-faced François. The man lay sprawled on the bed, his limbs twitching, his eyes rolled back. The young hood on whom François had landed frantically rolled away from beneath the body and stared in horror at the bizarre display.

François gave a last grunt of agony and fell still.

For a few seconds, everyone watched him, expecting him to move again. He didn't.

The guard gave a shout for assistance. Another guard came running. Yelling at the prisoners to stand back, they rushed into the cell and examined the motionless François. Slowly they straightened and looked at Jordan.

"Est mort," one of them murmured.

"That—that's impossible!" said Jordan. "How can he be dead? I didn't hit him that hard!"

The guards merely stared at him. The other two prisoners regarded Jordan with new respect and backed away to the far side of the cell.

"Let me look at him!" demanded Jordan. He pushed past the guards and knelt by François. One glance at the body and he knew they were right. François was dead.

Jordan shook his head. "I don't understand..."

"*Monsieur,* you come with us," said one of the guards.

"I couldn't have killed him!"

"But you see for yourself he is dead."

Jordan suddenly focused on a fine line of blood trickling down François's cheek. He bent closer. Only then did he spot the needle-thin dart impaled in the dead man's scalp. It was almost invisible among the salt-and-pepper hairs of his temple.

"What in blazes...?" muttered Jordan. Swiftly he glanced around the floor for a syringe, a dart gun—whatever might have injected that needle point. He saw nothing on the floor or on the bed. Then he looked down at the dead man's hand and saw something clutched in his left fist. He pried open the frozen fingers and the object slid out and landed on the bedcovers.

A ballpoint pen.

At once he was hauled back and shoved toward the cell door. "Go," said the guard. "Walk!"

"Where?"

"Where you can hurt no one." The guard directed Jordan into the corridor and locked the cell door. Jordan caught a fleeting glimpse of his cellmates, watching him in awe, and then he was hustled down the hallway and into a private cell, this one obviously reserved for the most dangerous prisoners. Double-barred, no windows, no furniture, only a concrete slab on which to lie. And a light blazing down relentlessly from the ceiling.

Jordan sank onto the slab and waited. For what? he wondered. Another attack? Another crisis? How could this nightmare possibly get any worse?

An hour passed. He couldn't sleep, not with that light shining overhead. Footsteps and the clank of keys alerted him to a visitor. He looked up to see a guard and a well-dressed gentleman with a briefcase.

"M. Tavistock?" said the gentleman.

"Since there's no one else here," muttered Jordan, rising to his feet, "I'm afraid that must be me."

The door was unlocked, and the man with the briefcase entered. He glanced around in dismay at the Spartan cell. "These conditions… Outrageous," he said.

"Yes. And I owe it all to my wonderful attorney," said Jordan.

"But *I* am your attorney." The man held out his hand in greeting. "Henri Laurent. I would have come sooner, but I was attending the opera. I received M. Vane's message only an hour ago. He said it was an emergency."

Jordan shook his head in confusion. “Vane? Reggie Vane sent you?”

“Yes. Your sister requested my immediate services. And M. Vane—”

“Beryl hired you? Then who the hell was…” Jordan paused as the bizarre events suddenly made sense. Horrifying sense. “M. Laurent,” said Jordan, “a few hours ago, there was a lawyer here to see me. A M. Jarre.”

Laurent frowned. “But I was not told of another attorney.”

“He claimed my sister hired him.”

“But I spoke to M. Vane. He told me Mlle Tavistock requested *my* services. What did you say was the other attorney’s name?”

“Jarre.”

Laurent shook his head. “I am not familiar with any such criminal attorney.”

Jordan sat for a moment in stunned silence. Slowly he raised his head and looked at Laurent. “I think you’d better contact Reggie Vane. At once.”

“But why?”

“They’ve already tried to kill me once tonight.” Jordan shook his head. “If this keeps up, M. Laurent, by morning I may be quite dead.”

Chapter 8

They were following her again. Black hounds, trotting across the dead leaves of the forest. She heard them rustle through the underbrush and knew they were moving closer.

She gripped Froggie's bridle, struggled to calm her, but the mare panicked. Suddenly Froggie yanked free of Beryl's grasp and reared up.

The hounds attacked.

Instantly they were at the horse's throat, ripping, tearing with their razor teeth. Froggie screamed, a human scream, shrill with terror. *Have to save her,* thought Beryl. *Have to beat them away.* But her feet seemed rooted to the ground. She could only stand and watch in horror as Froggie dropped to her knees and collapsed to the forest floor.

The hounds, mouths bloodied, turned and looked at Beryl.

She awakened, gasping for breath, her hands clawing at the darkness. Only as her panic faded did she hear Richard calling her name.

She turned and saw him standing in the doorway. A lamp was shining in the room behind him, and the light gleamed faintly on his bare shoulders.

"Beryl?" he said again.

She took a deep breath, still trying to shake off the last threads of the nightmare. "I'm awake," she said.

"I think you'd better get up."

"What time is it?"

"Four a.m. Claude just phoned."

"Why?"

"He wants us to meet him at the police station. As soon as possible."

"The police station?" She sat up sharply as a terrible thought came to mind. "Is it Jordan? Has something happened to him?"

Through the shadows, she saw Richard nod. "Someone tried to kill him."

"An ingenious device," said Claude Daumier, gingerly laying the ballpoint pen on the table. "A hypodermic needle, a pressurized syringe. One stab, and the drug would be injected into the victim."

"Which drug?" asked Beryl.

"It is still being analyzed. The autopsy will be performed in the morning. But it seems clear that this drug, whatever it was, was the cause of death. There is not enough trauma on the body to explain otherwise."

"Then Jordan won't be blamed for this?" said Beryl in relief.

"Hardly. He will be placed in isolation, no other prisoners, a double guard. There should be no further incidents."

The conference room door opened. Jordan appeared, escorted by two guards. *Dear Lord, he looks terrible,* thought Beryl as she rose from her chair and went to hug him. Never had she seen her brother so disheveled. The beginnings of a thick blond beard had sprouted on his jaw, and his prison clothes were mapped with wrinkles. But as they pulled apart, she gazed in his eyes and saw that the old Jordan was still there, good-humored and ironic as ever.

"You're not hurt?" she asked.

"Not a scratch," he answered. "Well, perhaps a few," he amended, frowning down at his bruised fist. "It's murder on the old manicure."

"Jordan, I swear I never hired any lawyer named Jarre. The man was a fraud."

"I suspected as much."

"The man I did hire, M. Laurent, Reggie swears he's the best there is."

"I'm afraid even the best won't get me out of this fix," Jordan observed disconsolately. "I seem destined to be a long-term resident of this fine establishment. Unless the food kills me first."

"Will you be serious for once?"

"Oh, but you haven't tasted the goulash."

Beryl turned in exasperation to Daumier. "What about the dead man? Who was he?"

"According to the arrest record," said Daumier, "his name was François Parmentier, a janitor. He was charged with disorderly conduct."

"How did he end up in Jordan's cell?" asked Richard.

"It seems that his attorney, Jarre, made a special request for both his clients to be housed in the same cell."

"Not just a request," amended Richard. "It must've been a bribe. Jarre and the dead man were a team."

"Working on whose behalf?" asked Jordan.

"The same party who tried to kill Beryl," said Richard.

"What?"

"A few hours ago. It was a high-powered rifle, fired at her hotel window."

"And she's still in Paris?" Jordan turned to his sister. "That's it. You're going home, Beryl. And you're leaving at once."

"I've been trying to tell her the same thing," said Richard. "She won't listen."

"Of course she won't. My darling little sister never does!" Jordan scowled at Beryl. "This time, though, you don't have a choice."

"You're right, Jordie," said Beryl. "I don't have a choice. That's why I'm staying."

"You could get yourself killed."

"So could you."

They stood facing each other, neither one willing to give ground. *Deadlock,* thought Beryl. *He's worried about me, and I'm worried about him. And we're both Tavistocks, which means neither of us will ever concede defeat.*

But I have the upper hand on this one. He's in jail. I'm not.

In disgust, Jordan turned and flopped into a chair. "For Pete's sake, work on her, Wolf!" he muttered.

"I'm trying to," said Richard. "Meanwhile, we still

haven't answered a basic question—who wants you both dead?"

They fell silent for a moment. Through a cloud of fatigue, Beryl looked at her brother, thinking that he was supposed to be the clever one in the family. If he couldn't figure it out, who could?

"The key to all this," said Jordan, "is François, the dead man." He looked at Daumier. "What else do you know about him? Friends, family?"

"Only a sister," said Daumier. "Living in Paris."

"Have your people spoken to her yet?"

"There is no point to it."

"Why not?"

"She is, how do you say…?" Daumier tapped his forehead. "*Retardataire.* She lives at the Sacred Heart Nursing Home. The nuns say she cannot speak, and she is in very poor health."

"What about his job?" said Richard. "You said he worked as a janitor."

"At Galerie Annika. An art gallery, in Auteuil. It is a reputable establishment. Known for its collection of works by contemporary artists."

"What does the gallery say about him?"

"I spoke only briefly to Annika. She says he was a quiet man, very reliable. She will be in later this morning to answer questions." He glanced at his watch. "In the meantime, I suggest we all try to catch some sleep. For a few hours, at least."

"What about Jordan?" asked Beryl. "How do I know he'll be safe here?"

"As I said, he will be kept in a private cell. Strict isolation—"

"That might be a mistake," said Richard. "There'd be no witnesses."

If anything happens to him... Beryl shivered.

Jordan nodded. "Wolf's right. I'd feel a whole lot safer sharing a cell with someone."

"But they could lock you up with another hired killer," said Beryl.

"I know just the fellows to share my cell," said Jordan. "A pair of harmless enough chaps. I hope."

Daumier nodded. "I will arrange it."

It was wrenching to see Jordan marched away. In the doorway, he paused and gave her a farewell wave. That's when Beryl realized she was taking this far harder than he was. But that's old Jordie for you, she mused. Never one to lose his good humor.

Outside, the first streaks of daylight had appeared in the sky, and the sound of traffic had already begun its morning crescendo. Beryl, Richard and Daumier stood on the sidewalk, all of them tottering on the edge of collapse.

"Jordan will be safe," said Daumier. "I will see to it."

"I want him to be more than safe," said Beryl. "I want him out of there."

"For that, we must prove him innocent."

"Then that's exactly what we'll do," she said.

Daumier looked at her with bloodshot eyes. He seemed far older tonight, this kindly Frenchman in whose face the years had etched deep furrows. He said, "What you must do, *chérie,* is stay alert. And out of sight." He turned toward his car. "Tonight, we talk again."

By the time Beryl and Richard had returned to the flat in Passy, Beryl could feel herself nodding off. The latest jolt of tension had worn off, and her energy was on a fast downhill slide. Thank God Richard still seemed to be operating on all cylinders, she thought as they climbed out of the car. If she collapsed, he could drag her up those steps.

He practically did. He put his arm around her and walked her through the door, up the hall and into the bedroom. There, he sat her down on the bed.

"Sleep," he said, "as long as you need to."

"A week should about do it," she murmured.

He smiled. And though sleep was blurring her vision, she saw his face clearly enough to register, once again, that flicker of attraction between them. It was always there, ready to leap into full flame. Even now, exhausted as she was, images of desire were weaving into shape in her mind. She remembered how he'd stood, shirtless, in the bedroom doorway, the lamplight gleaming on his shoulders. She thought how easy it would be to invite him into her bed, to ask for a hug, a kiss. And then, much, much more. *Too much bloody chemistry between us,* she pondered. *It addles my brain, keeps me from concentrating on the important issues. I take one look at him, I inhale one whiff of his scent, and all I can think about is pulling him down on top of me.*

Gently he kissed her forehead. "I'll be right next door," he said, and left the room.

Too tired to undress, she lay down fully clothed on the bed. Daylight brightened outside the window, and the sounds of traffic drifted up from the street. If this nightmare was ever over, she thought, she'd have to stay away from him for a while. Just to get her bearings again. Yes, that's what she'd do. She'd hide out at Chetwynd. Wait for that crazy attraction between them to fade.

But as she closed her eyes, the images returned, more vivid and tempting than ever. They pursued her, right into her dreams.

Richard slept five hours and rose just before noon. A shower, a quick meal of eggs and toast, and he felt the old engines fire up again. There were too few hours in the day, too many matters to attend to; sleep would have to assume a lower priority.

He peeked in on Beryl and saw that she was still asleep. Good. By the time she woke up, he should be back from making his rounds. Just in case he wasn't, though, he left a note on the nightstand. "Gone out. Back around three. R." Then, as an afterthought, he laid the gun beside the note. If she needed it, he figured, it'd be there for her.

After confirming that the two guards were still on duty, he left the flat, locking the door behind him.

His first stop was 66 Rue Myrha, the building where Madeline and Bernard died.

He had gone over the Paris police report again, had read and reread the landlord's statement. M. Rideau claimed he'd discovered the bodies on the afternoon of July 15, 1973, and had at once notified the police. Upon being questioned, he'd told them that the attic was rented to a Mlle Scarlatti, who used the place only infrequently and paid her rent in cash. On occasion, he had heard moans, whimpers, and a man's voice emanating from the flat. But the only person he ever saw face-to-face was Mlle Scarlatti, whose head scarves and sunglasses made it difficult for him to be specific about her appearance. Nevertheless, M. Rideau was certain that the dead woman in the flat was indeed the lusty Scarlatti woman. And the dead man? The landlord had never seen him before.

Three months after this testimony, M. Rideau had sold the building, packed up his family, and left the country.

That last detail had garnered only a footnote in the police report: "Landlord no longer available for statements. Has left France."

Richard had a hunch that the landlord's departure from the country just might be the most important clue they had. If he could locate Rideau's current whereabouts and question him about those events of twenty years before…

He knocked at each flat in the building, but came up with no leads. Twenty years was a long time; people moved in, moved out. No one remembered any M. Rideau.

Richard went outside and stood for a moment on the sidewalk. A ball hurtled past, pursued by a pack of scruffy kids. The endless soccer match, he mused, watching the tangle of dirty arms and legs.

Over the children's heads, he spotted an elderly woman sitting on her stoop. At least seventy years old, he guessed. Perhaps she'd lived here long enough to know the former residents of this street.

He went over to the woman and spoke to her in French. "Good afternoon."

She smiled a sweet, toothless grin.

"I am trying to find someone who remembers M. Jacques Rideau. The man who used to own that building over there." He pointed to number 66.

Also in French, she answered: "He moved away."

"You knew him, then?"

"His son was all the time visiting in my house."

"I understand the whole family left France."

She nodded. "They went to Greece. And how do you suppose he managed that, eh? Him, with that old car! And the clothes their children wore! But off they go to their villa." She sighed. "And I am here, where I'll always be."

Richard frowned. "Villa?"

"I hear they have a villa, near the sea. Of course, it may not be true—the boy was always making up stories. Why should he start telling the truth? But he claimed it was a villa, with flowers growing up the posts." She laughed. "They must all be dead by now."

"The family?"

"The flowers. They could not even remember to water their pots of geraniums."

"Do you know where in Greece they moved to?"

The woman shrugged. "Somewhere near the sea. But then, isn't all of Greece near the sea?"

"The name of the village?"

"Why should I remember these things? He was not *my* boyfriend."

Frustrated, Richard was about to turn away when he suddenly registered what the woman had just said. "You mean, the landlord's son—he was your daughter's boyfriend?"

"My granddaughter."

"Did he call her? Write her any letters?"

"A few. Then he stopped." She shook her head. "That is how it is with young people. No devotion."

"Did she keep any of those letters?"

The woman laughed. "All of them. To remind her husband what a fine catch he made."

It took a bit of persuasion for Richard to be invited inside the old woman's apartment. It was a dark, cramped flat. Two small children sat at the kitchen table, gnawing fistfuls of bread. Another woman—most likely in her mid-thirties, but with much older eyes—sat spooning cereal into an infant's mouth.

"He wants to see your letters from Gerard," said the grandmother.

The younger woman eyed Richard with suspicion.

"It's important I speak with his father," explained Richard.

"His father doesn't want to be found," she said, and resumed feeding the baby.

"Why not?"

"How should I know? Gerard didn't tell me."

"Does it have to do with the murders? The two English people?"

She paused, the spoon halfway to the baby's mouth. "You are English?"

"No, American." He sat down across from her. "Do you remember the murders?"

"It was a long time ago." She wiped the baby's face. "I was only fifteen."

"Gerard wrote you letters, then stopped. Why?"

The woman gave a bitter laugh. "He lost interest. Men always do."

"Or something could have happened to him. Maybe he couldn't write to you. And he wanted to, very much."

Again, she paused.

"If I go to Greece, I can inquire on your behalf. I only need to know the name of the village."

She sat for a moment, thinking. Wiping up the baby's mess. She looked at her two children, both of them runny nosed and whining. *She's longing to escape,* he imagined. *Wishing her life had turned out some other way. Any other way. And she's thinking about this long-lost boyfriend, and how things might have been, for the two of them, in a villa by the sea...*

She stood up and went into another room. A moment later, she returned and laid a thin bundle of letters down on the table.

There were only four—not exactly a record of devotion. All were still tucked in their envelopes. Richard skimmed their contents, noting an outpouring of adolescent yearnings. "I will come back for you. I will love you always. Do not forget me…" By the fourth letter, the passion was clearly cooling.

There was no return address, either on the letters or on the envelopes. The family's whereabouts were obviously meant to be kept secret. But on one of the envelopes, a postmark was clearly printed: Paros, Greece.

Richard handed the letters back to the woman. She cradled them for a moment, as though savoring the memories. *So many years ago, a lifetime ago, and see what has become of me...*

"If you find Gerard…if he is still alive," she said, "ask him…"

"Yes?" Richard said gently.

She sighed. "Ask him if he remembers me."

"I will."

She held the letters a moment longer. And then, with a sigh, she laid them aside and picked up the spoon. In silence, she began to feed the baby.

He made one more stop before returning to the flat, this time at the Sacred Heart Nursing Home.

It was a far grimmer institution than the one Richard had visited the day before. No private rooms here, no sweet-faced nuns gliding down the halls. This was one step above a prison, and a crowded one at that, with three or four patients to a room, many of them restrained in their beds. Julee Parmentier, François's retarded sister, occupied one of the grimmest rooms of all. Barely clothed, she lay on top of a plastic-lined mattress. Protective mitts covered her hands; around her waist was a wide belt, its ends secured to the bed with just enough slack for her to shift from side to side, but not sit up. She barely seemed to register Richard's presence; instead she moaned and stared relentlessly at the ceiling.

"She has been like this for many years," said the nurse. "An accident, when she was twelve. She fell from a tree and hit her head on some stones."

"She can't speak at all? Can't communicate?"

"When her brother François would visit, he said she would smile. He insisted he saw it. But…" The nurse shrugged. "I saw nothing."

"Did he visit often?"

"Every day. The same time, nine o'clock in the morning. He would stay until lunch, then he would go to his work at the gallery."

"He did this every day?"

"Yes. And on Sunday he would stay later—until four o'clock."

Richard gazed at the woman in the bed and tried to imagine what it must have been like for François to sit for hours in this room with its noise and its smells. To devote every free hour of his life to a sister who could not even recognize his face.

"It is a tragedy," said the nurse. "He was a good man, François."

They left the room and walked away from the sight of that pitiful creature lying on her plastic sheet.

"What will happen to her now?" asked Richard. "Will someone see that she's cared for?"

"It hardly matters now."

"Why do you say that?"

"Her kidneys are failing." The nurse glanced up the hall, toward Julee Parmentier's room, and shook her head sadly. "Another month, two months, and she will be dead."

"But you must know where he went," insisted Beryl.

The French agent merely shrugged. "He did not say, *Mademoiselle.* He only instructed me to watch over the flat. And see that you came to no harm."

"And that's all he said? And then he drove off?"

The man nodded.

In frustration, Beryl turned and went back into the flat, where she reread Richard's note: "Gone out. Back around three." No explanations, no apologies. She crumpled it up and threw it at the rubbish can. And what was she supposed to do now? Wait around all day for him to return? What about Jordan? What about the investigation?

What about lunch?

Her hunger pangs could no longer be ignored. She went to the kitchen and opened the refrigerator. She stared in dismay at the contents: a carton of eggs, a loaf of bread and a shriveled sausage. No fruit, no vegetables, not even a puny carrot. Stocked, no doubt, by a man.

I'm not going to eat that, she determined, closing the refrigerator door. *But I'm not going to starve, either. I'm going to have a proper meal—with or without him.*

Daumier's men had delivered her belongings to the flat the night before. From the closet, she chose her most nondescript black dress, pinned up her hair under a wide-brimmed hat, and slid on a pair of dark glasses. *Not too hideous,* she decided, glancing at herself in the mirror.

She walked out of the flat into the sunshine.

The guard stationed at the front door confronted her at once. "*Mademoiselle,* you are not allowed to leave."

"But you let *him* leave," she countered.

"Mr. Wolf specifically instructed—"

"I'm hungry," she said. "I get quite cranky when I'm hungry. And I'm not about to live on eggs and toast. So if you can just direct me to the nearest Métro station..."

"You are going *alone?*" he asked in horror.

"Unless you'd care to escort me."

The man glanced uneasily up and down the street. "I have no instructions in this matter."

"Then I'll go alone," she said, and breezily started to walk away.

"Come back!"

She kept walking.

"Mademoiselle!" he called. "I will get the car!"

She turned and flashed him her most brilliant smile. "My treat."

Both guards accompanied her to a restaurant in the nearby neighborhood of Auteuil. She suspected they chose the place not for the quality of its food, but for the intimate dining room and the easily surveyed front entrance. The meal itself was just a shade above mediocre: bland vichyssoise and a cut of lamb that could have doubled for leather. But Beryl was hungry enough to savor every morsel and still have an appetite for the *tarte aux pommes.*

By the time the meal was over, her two companions were in a much more jovial mood. Perhaps this bodyguard business was not such a bad thing, if the lady was willing to spring for a meal every day. They even relented when Beryl asked them to make a stop on the drive back to the flat. It would only take a minute, she said, to look over the latest art exhibit. After all, she might find something to strike her fancy.

And so the men accompanied her to Galerie Annika.

The exhibit area was one vast, soaring gallery—three stories, connected by open walkways and spiral staircases. Sunlight shone down through a skylit dome, illuminating a collection of bronze sculptures displayed on the first floor.

A young woman, her spiky hair a startling shade of red, came forward to greet them. Was there something in particular *Mademoiselle* wished to see?

"May I just look around a bit?" asked Beryl. "Or perhaps you could direct me to some paintings. Nothing too modern—I prefer classical artists."

"But of course," said the woman, and guided Beryl and her escorts up the spiral stairs.

Most of what she saw hanging on the walls was hideous. Landscapes populated by deformed animals. Birds with dog heads. City scenes with starkly cubist buildings. The young woman stopped at one painting and said, "Perhaps this is to your liking?"

Beryl took one look at the nude huntress holding

aloft a dead rabbit and said, "I don't think so." She moved on, taking in the eccentric collection of paintings, fabric hangings and clay masks. "Who chooses the work to be displayed here?" she asked.

"Annika does. The gallery owner."

Beryl stopped at a particularly grotesque mask—a man with a forked tongue. "She has a…unique eye for art."

"Quite daring, don't you think? She prefers artists who take risks."

"Is she here today? I'd very much like to meet her."

"Not at the moment." The woman shook her head sadly. "One of our employees died last night, you see. Annika had to speak to the police."

"I'm sorry to hear that."

"Our janitor." The woman sighed. "It was quite unexpected."

They returned to the first-floor gallery. Only then did Beryl spot a work she'd consider purchasing. It was one of the bronze sculptures, a variation on the Madonna-and-child theme. But as she moved closer to inspect it, she realized it wasn't a human infant nursing at the woman's breast. It was a jackal.

"Quite intriguing, don't you think?"

Beryl shuddered and looked at her spiky-haired guide. "What brilliant mind dreamed *this* one up?"

"A new artist. A young man, just building his reputation here in Paris. We are hosting a reception in his honor tonight. Perhaps you will attend?"

"If I can."

The woman reached into a basket and plucked out

an elegantly embossed invitation. This she handed to Beryl. “If you are free tonight, please drop in.”

Beryl was about to slip the card carelessly into her purse when she suddenly focused on the artist’s name. A name she recognized.

Galerie Annika presente:
Les sculptures de Anthony Sutherland
17 juillet 7-9 du soir.

Chapter 9

"This is crazy," said Richard. "An unacceptable risk."

To his annoyance, Beryl simply waltzed over to the closet and stood surveying her wardrobe. "What do you think would be appropriate tonight? Formal or semi?"

"You'll be out in the open," said Richard. "An art reception! I can't think of a more public place."

Beryl took out a black silk sheath, turned to the mirror, and calmly held the dress to her body. "A public place is the safest place to be," she observed.

"You were supposed to stay here! Instead you go running around town—"

"So did you."

"I had business…"

She turned and walked into the bedroom. "I did, too," she called back cheerfully.

He started to follow her, but halted in the doorway when he saw that she was undressing. At once he turned around and stood with his back pressed against the doorjamb. “A craving for a three-star meal doesn’t constitute necessity!” he snapped over his shoulder.

“It wasn’t a three-star meal. It wasn’t even a half star. But it was better than eggs and moldy bread.”

“You’re like some finicky kitten, you know that? You’d rather starve than deign to eat canned food like every other cat.”

“You’re quite right. I’m a spoiled Persian and I want my cream and chicken livers.”

“I would’ve brought you back a meal. Catnip included.”

“You weren’t here.”

And that was his mistake, he realized. He couldn’t leave this woman alone for a second. She was too damn unpredictable.

No, actually she *was* predictable. She’d do whatever he *didn’t* want her to do.

And what he didn’t want her to do was leave the flat tonight.

But he could already hear her stepping into the black dress, could hear the whisper of silk sliding over stockings, the hiss of the zipper closing over her back. He fought to suppress the images those sounds brought to mind—the long legs, the curve of her hips… He found himself clenching his jaw in frustration, at her, at himself, at the way events and passions were spinning out of his control.

“Do me up, will you?” she asked.

He turned and saw that she’d moved right beside him. Her back was turned and the nape of her neck was practically within kissing distance.

"The hook," she said, tossing her hair over one shoulder. He inhaled the flowery scent of shampoo. "I can't seem to fasten it."

He attached the hook and eye and found his gaze lingering on her bare shoulders. "Where did you get that dress?" he asked.

"I brought it from Chetwynd." She breezed over to the dresser and began to slip on earrings. The silk sheath seemed to mold itself to every luscious curve of her body. "Why do you ask?"

"It's Madeline's dress. Isn't it?"

She turned to look at him. "Yes, it is," she said quietly. "Does that bother you?"

"It's just—" he let out a breath "—it's a perfect fit. Curve for curve."

"And you think you're seeing a ghost."

"I remember that dress. I saw her wear it at an embassy reception." He paused. "God, it's really eerie, how that dress seems made for you."

Slowly she moved toward him, her gaze never wavering from his face. "I'm not her, Richard."

"I know."

"No matter how much you may want her back—"

"Her?" He took her wrists and pulled her close to him. "When I look at you, I see only Beryl. Of course, I notice the resemblance. The hair, the eyes. But *you're* the one I'm looking at. The one I want." He bent toward her and gently grazed her lips with a kiss. "That's why I want you to stay here tonight."

"Your prisoner?" she murmured.

"If need be." He kissed her again and heard an answering purr of contentment from her throat. She tilted her head back, and his lips slid to her neck, so smooth, so deliciously perfumed.

"Then you'll have to tie me up…" she whispered.

"Whatever you want."

"…because there's no other way you're going to keep me here tonight." With a maddening laugh, she wriggled free and walked into the bathroom.

Richard suppressed a groan of frustration. From the doorway, he watched as she pinned up her hair. "Exactly what do you expect to get out of this event, anyway?" he demanded.

"One never knows. That's the joy of intelligence gathering, isn't it? Keep your ears and eyes open and see what turns up. I think we've learned quite a lot already about François. We know he has a sister who's ill. Which means François needed money. Working as a janitor in an art gallery couldn't possibly pay for all the care she needed. Perhaps he was desperate, willing to do anything for money. Even work as a hired assassin."

"Your logic is unassailable."

"Thank you."

"But your plan of action is insane. You don't need to take this risk—"

"But I do." She turned to him, her hair now regally swept into a chignon. "Someone wants me and Jordan dead. And there I'll be tonight. A perfectly convenient target."

What a magnificent creature she is, he thought. *It's that unbeatable bloodline, those Bernard and Madeline genes. She thinks she's invincible.*

"That's the plan, is it?" he said. "Tempt the killer into making a move?"

"If that's what it takes to save Jordan."

"And what's to stop the killer from carrying it out?"

"My two bodyguards. And you."

"I'm not infallible, Beryl."

"You're close enough."

"I could make a mistake. Let my attention slip."

"I trust you."

"But I don't trust myself!" Agitated, he began to pace the bedroom floor. "I've been out of the business for years. I'm out of practice, out of condition. I'm forty-two, Beryl, and my reflexes aren't what they used to be."

"Last night they seemed quick enough to me."

"Walk out that door, Beryl, and I can't guarantee your safety."

She came toward him, looking him coolly in the eye. "The fact is, Richard, you can't guarantee my safety anywhere. In here, out on the streets, at an artist's reception. Wherever I am, there's a chance things could go wrong. If I stay in this flat, if I stare at these walls any longer, thinking of all the things that could happen, I'll go insane. It's better to be out *there.* Doing something. Jordan isn't able to, so I have to be the one."

"The one to set yourself up as bait?"

"Our only lead is a dead man—François. Someone hired him, Richard. Someone who may have connections to Galerie Annika."

For a moment Richard stood gazing at her, thinking, *She's right, of course. It's the same conclusion I came to. She's clever enough to know exactly what needs to be done. And reckless enough to do it.*

He went to the nightstand and picked up the Glock. A pound and a half of steel and plastic, that's all he had to protect her with. It felt flimsy, insubstantial, against all the dangers lurking beyond the front door.

"You're coming with me?" she said.

He turned and looked at her. "You think I'd let you go alone?"

She smiled, so full of confidence it frightened him. It was Madeline's old smile. Madeline, who'd been every bit as confident.

He slid the Glock into his shoulder holster. "I'll be right beside you, Beryl," he said. "Every step of the way."

Anthony Sutherland stood posing like a little emperor beside his bronze cast of the Madonna with jackal. He was wearing a pirate shirt of purple silk, black leather pants and snakeskin boots, and he seemed not in the least bit fazed by all the photographers' flashbulbs that kept popping around him. The art critics were in vapors over the show. "Frightening." "Disturbing." "Images that twist convention." These were some of the comments Beryl overheard being murmured as she wandered through the gallery.

She and Richard stopped to look at another of Anthony's bronzes. At first glance, it had looked like two nude figures entwined in a loving embrace. Closer inspection, however, revealed it to be a man and woman in the process of devouring each other alive.

"Do you suppose that's an allegory for marriage?" said a familiar voice. It was Reggie Vane, balancing a glass of champagne in one hand and two dainty plates of canapés in the other.

He bent forward and gave Beryl an affectionate kiss on the cheek. "You're absolutely stunning tonight, dear. Your mother would be proud of you."

"Reggie, I had no idea you were interested in modern art," said Beryl.

"I'm not. Helena dragged me here." In disgust, he glanced around at the crowd. "Lord, I hate these things. But the St. Pierres were coming, and of course Marie always insists Helena show up as well, just to keep her company." He set his empty champagne glass on top of the bronze couple and laughed at the whimsical effect. "An improvement, wouldn't you say? As long as these two are going to eat each other, they might as well have some bubbly to wash each other down."

An elegantly attired woman swooped in and snatched away the glass. "Please, be more respectful of the work, Mr. Vane," she scolded.

"Oh, I wasn't being disrespectful, Annika," said Reggie. "I just thought it needed a touch of humor."

"It is absolutely perfect as it is." Annika gave the bronze heads a swipe of her napkin and stood back to admire the interwoven figures. "Whimsy would ruin its message."

"What message is that?" asked Richard.

The woman turned to look at him, and her head of boyishly cropped hair suddenly tilted up with interest. "The message," she said, gazing intently at Richard, "is that monogamy is a destructive institution."

"That's marriage, all right," grunted Reggie.

"But free love," the woman continued, "love that has no constraints and is open to all pleasures—that is a positive force."

"Is that Anthony's interpretation of this piece?" asked Beryl.

"It's how *I* interpret it." Annika shifted her gaze to Beryl. "You are a friend of Anthony's?"

"An acquaintance. I know his mother, Nina."

"Where is Nina, by the way?" asked Reggie. "You'd

think she'd be front-and-center stage for *darling* Anthony's night of *glory.*"

Beryl had to laugh at Reggie's imitation of Nina. Yes, when Queen Nina wanted an audience, all she had to do was throw one of these stylish bashes, and an audience would invariably turn up. Even poor Marie St. Pierre, just out of the hospital, had put in an appearance. Marie stood off in a corner with Helena Vane, the two women huddled together like sparrows in a gathering of peacocks. It was easy to see why they'd be such close friends; both of them were painfully plain, neither one was happily married. That their marriages were not happy was only too clear tonight. The Vanes were avoiding each other, Helena off in her corner darting irritated looks, Reggie standing as far away as possible. And as for Marie St. Pierre—her husband wasn't even in the room at the moment.

"So this is in praise of free love, is it?" said Reggie, eyeing the bronze with new appreciation.

"That is how I see it," said Annika. "How a man and a woman should love."

"I quite agree," said Reggie with a sudden burst of enthusiasm. "Banish marriage entirely."

The woman looked provocatively at Richard. "What do you think, Mr...?"

"Wolf," said Richard. "I'm afraid I don't agree." He took Beryl's arm. "Excuse us, will you? We still have to see the rest of the collection."

As he led Beryl away toward the spiral staircase, she whispered, "There's nothing to see upstairs."

"I want to check out the upper floors."

"Anthony's work is all on the first floor."

"I saw Nina slink up the stairs a few minutes ago. I want to see what she's up to."

They climbed the stairs to the second-floor gallery. From the open walkway, they paused to look over the railing at the crowd on the first floor. It was a flashy gathering, a sea of well-coiffed heads and multicolored silks. Annika had moved into the limelight with Anthony, and as a new round of flashbulbs went off, they embraced and kissed to the sound of applause.

"Ah, free love," sighed Beryl. "She obviously has samples to pass around."

"So I can see."

Beryl gave him a sly smile. "Poor Richard. On duty tonight and can't indulge."

"*Afraid* to indulge. She'd eat me up alive. Like that bronze statue."

"Aren't you tempted? Just a little?"

He looked at her with amusement. "You're baiting me, Beryl."

"Am I?"

"Yes, you are. I know exactly what you're up to. Putting me to the test. Making me prove I'm not like your friend the surgeon. Who, as you implied, also believed in free love."

Beryl's smile faded. "Is that what I'm doing?" she asked softly.

"You have a right to." He gave her hand a squeeze and glanced down again at the crowd.

He's always alert, always watching out for me, she thought. *I'd trust him with my life. But my heart? I still don't know...*

In the downstairs gallery, a pair of musicians began to play. As the sweet sounds of flute and guitar floated through the building, Beryl suddenly sensed a pair of eyes watching her. She looked down at the cluster of bronze statues and spotted Anthony Sutherland, standing by his Madonna with jackal. He was gazing right at her. And the expression in his eyes was one of cold calculation.

Instinctively she shrank away from the railing.

"What is it?" asked Richard.

"Anthony. It's the way he looks at me."

But by then Anthony had already turned away and was shaking Reggie Vane's hand. An odd young man, thought Beryl. What sort of mind dreams up these nightmarish visions? Women nursing jackals. Couples devouring each other. Had it been so difficult, growing up as Nina Sutherland's son?

She and Richard wandered through the second-floor gallery, but found no sign of Nina.

"Why are you so interested in finding her?" asked Beryl.

"It's not her so much as the way she went up those stairs. Obviously trying not to be noticed."

"And you noticed her."

"It was the dress. Those trademark bugle beads of hers."

They finished their circuit of the second floor and headed up the staircase to the third. Again, no sign of Nina. But as they moved along the walkway, the musicians in the first-floor gallery suddenly ceased playing. In the abrupt silence that followed, Beryl heard Nina's voice—a few loud syllables—just before it dropped to a whisper. Another voice answered—a man's, speaking softly in reply.

The voices came from an alcove, just ahead.

"It's not as if I haven't been patient," said Nina. "Not as if I haven't *tried* to be understanding."

"I know. I know—"

"Do you know what it's been *like* for me? For Anthony? Have you any *idea?* All those years, waiting for you to make up your mind."

"I never let you want for anything."

"Oh, how *fortunate* for us! My goodness, how generous of you!"

"The boy has had the best—everything he's ever wanted. Now he's twenty-one. My responsibility ends."

"Your responsibility," said Nina, "has only just *begun*."

Richard yanked Beryl around the corner just as Nina emerged from the alcove. She stormed right past them, too angry to notice her audience. They could hear her high heels tapping down the staircase to the lower galleries.

A moment later, a second figure emerged from the alcove, moving like an old man.

It was Philippe St. Pierre.

He went over to the railing and stared down at the crowd in the gallery below. He seemed to be considering the temptation of that two-story drop. Then, sighing deeply, he walked away and followed Nina down the stairs.

Down in the first-floor gallery, the crowd was starting to thin out. Anthony had already left; so had the Vanes. But Marie St. Pierre was still standing in her corner, the abandoned wife waiting to be reclaimed. A full room's length away stood her husband Philippe, nursing a glass of champagne. And standing between them was that macabre sculpture, the bronze man and woman devouring each other alive.

Beryl thought that perhaps Anthony had hit upon the truth with his art. That if people weren't careful, love would consume them, destroy them. As it had destroyed Marie.

The image of Marie St. Pierre, standing alone and forlorn in the corner, stayed with Beryl all the way back to the flat. She thought how hard it must be to play the politician's wife—forever poised and pleasant, always supportive, never the shrew. And all the time knowing that your husband was in love with another woman.

"She must have known about it. For years," said Beryl softly.

Richard kept his gaze on the road as he navigated the streets back to Passy. "Who?" he asked.

"Marie St. Pierre. She must have known about her husband and Nina. Every time she looks at young Anthony, she'd see the resemblance. And how it must hurt her. Yet all these years, she's put up with him."

"And with Nina," said Richard.

Beryl sat back, puzzled. *Yes, she does put up with Nina. And that's the part I don't understand. How she can be so civil, so gracious, to her husband's mistress. To her husband's bastard son...*

"You think Philippe is Anthony's father?"

"That's what Nina meant, of course. All that talk about Philippe's responsibilities. She meant Anthony." She paused. "Art school must be very expensive."

"And Philippe must've paid a pretty bundle over the years, supporting the boy. Not to mention Nina, whose tastes are extravagant, to say the least. Her widow's pension couldn't have been enough to—"

"What is it?" asked Beryl.

"I just had a flash of insight about her husband, Stephen Sutherland. He committed suicide a month after your parents died—jumped off a bridge."

"Yes, you told me that."

"All these years, I've thought his death was related to the Delphi case. I suspected he was the mole, that he killed himself when he thought he was about to be discovered. But what if his reasons for jumping off that bridge were entirely personal?"

"His marriage."

"And young Anthony. The boy he discovered wasn't his son at all."

"But if Stephen Sutherland wasn't Delphi..."

"Then we're back to a person or persons unknown."

Persons unknown. Meaning someone who could still be alive. And afraid of discovery.

Instinctively she glanced over her shoulder, checking to see if they were being followed. Just behind them was the Peugeot with the two French agents; beyond that she saw only a stream of anonymous headlights. Richard was right, she thought. She should have stayed in the flat. She should have kept her head low, her face out of sight. Anyone could have spotted her this afternoon. Or they could be following her right this moment, could be watching her from somewhere in that sea of headlights.

Suddenly she longed to be back in the flat, safely surrounded by four walls. It began to seem endless, this drive to Passy, a journey through a darkness full of perils.

When at last they pulled up in front of the building, she was so anxious to get inside that she quickly started to climb out of the car. Richard pulled her back in.

"Don't get out yet," he said. "Let the men check it first."

"You don't really think—"

"It's a precaution. Standard operating procedure."

Beryl watched the two French agents climb the steps and unlock the front door. While one man stood watch on the steps, the other vanished inside.

"But how could anyone find out about the flat?" she asked.

"Payoffs. Leaks."

"You don't think Claude Daumier—"

"I'm not trying to scare you, Beryl. I just believe in being careful."

She watched as the lights came on inside the flat. First the living room, then the bedroom. At last, the man on the steps gave them the all-clear signal.

"Okay, it must be clean," said Richard, climbing out of the car. "Let's go."

Beryl stepped out onto the curb. She turned toward the building and took one step up the sidewalk—

—and was slammed backward against the car as an explosion rocked the earth. Shattered glass flew from the building and rained onto the street. Seconds later, the sky lit up with the hellish glow of flames shooting through the broken windows. Beryl sank to the ground, her ears still ringing from the blast. She stared numbly as tongues of flame slashed the darkness.

She couldn't hear Richard's shouts, didn't realize he was crouched right beside her until she felt his hands on her face. "Are you all right?" he cried. "Beryl, look at me!"

Weakly she nodded. Then her gaze traveled to the

front walkway, to the body of the French agent lying sprawled near the steps.

"Stay put!" yelled Richard as he pivoted away from her. He dashed over to the fallen man and knelt beside him just long enough to feel for a pulse. At once he was back at Beryl's side. "Get in the car," he said.

"But what about the men?"

"That one's dead. The other one didn't stand a chance."

"You don't know that!"

"Just get in the car!" ordered Richard. He opened the door and practically shoved her inside. Then he scrambled around to the driver's side and slid behind the wheel.

"We can't just leave them there!" cried Beryl.

"We'll have to." He started the engine and sent the car screeching away from the curb.

Beryl watched as a succession of streets blurred past. Richard drove like a madman, but she was too stunned to feel afraid, too bewildered to focus on anything but the river of red taillights stretching ahead of them.

"Jordan," she whispered. "What about Jordan?"

"Right now I have to think about you."

"They found the flat. They can get to him!"

"I'll take care of it later. First we get you to a safe place."

"Where?"

He swerved across two lanes and shot onto an off ramp. "I'll come up with one. Somewhere."

Somewhere. She stared out at the night glow of Paris. A sprawling city, an ocean of light. A million different places to hide.

To die.

She shivered and shrank deep into the seat. "And then what?" she whispered. "What happens next?"

He looked at her. "We get out of Paris. Out of the country."

"You mean—go home?"

"No. It won't be safe in England, either." He turned his gaze back to the road. The car seemed to leap through the darkness. "We're going to Greece."

Daumier answered the phone on the second ring. "Allô?"

A familiar voice growled at him from the receiver. *"What the hell is going on?"*

"Richard?" said Daumier. "Where are you?"

"A safe place. You'll understand if I don't reveal it to you."

"And Beryl?"

"She's unhurt. Though I can't say the same for your two men. Who knew about the flat, Claude?"

"Only my people."

"Who else?"

"I told no one else. It should have been a safe enough place."

"Apparently you were wrong. Someone found out."

"You were both out of the flat earlier today. One of you could have been followed."

"It wasn't me."

"Beryl, then. You should not have allowed her out of the building. She could've been spotted at Galerie Annika this afternoon and followed back to the flat."

"My mistake. You're right, I shouldn't have left her alone. I can't afford to make any more mistakes."

Daumier sighed. "You and I, Richard, we have

known each other too long. This is not the time to stop trusting each other."

There was a brief silence on the other end. Then Richard said, "I'm sorry, but I have no choice, Claude. We're going under."

"Then I will not be able to help you."

"We'll go it alone. Without your help."

"Wait, Richard—"

But the line had already gone dead. Daumier stared at the receiver, then slowly laid it back in the cradle. There was no point in trying to trace the call; Richard would have used a pay phone—and it would be in a different neighborhood from where he'd be staying. The man was once a professional; he knew the tricks of the trade.

Maybe—just maybe—it would keep them both alive.

"Good luck, my friend," murmured Daumier. "I am afraid you will need it."

Richard risked one more call from the pay phone, this one to Washington, D.C.

His business partner answered with his usual charmless growl. "Sakaroff here."

"Niki, it's me."

"Richard? How is beautiful Paris? Having a good time?"

"A lousy time. Look, I can't talk long. I'm in trouble."

Niki sighed. "Why am I not surprised?"

"It's the old Delphi case. You remember? Paris, '73. The NATO mole."

"Ah, yes."

"Delphi's come back to life. I need your help to identify him."

"I was KGB, Richard. Not Stasi."

"But you had connections to the East Germans."

"Not directly. I had little contact with Stasi agents. The East Germans, you know...they preferred to operate independently."

"Then who *would* know about Delphi? There must be some old contact you can pump for information."

There was a pause. "Perhaps..."

"Yes?"

"Heinrich Leitner," said Sakaroff. "He is the one who could tell you. He oversaw Stasi's Paris operations. Not a field man—he never left East Berlin. But he would be familiar with Delphi's work."

"Okay, he's the man I'll talk to. So how do I get to him?"

"That is the difficult part. He is in Berlin—"

"No problem. We'll go there."

"—in a high-security prison."

Richard groaned. "That *is* a problem." In frustration, he turned and stared through the phone-booth door at the subway platform. "I've got to get in to see him, Niki."

"You'll need approval. That will take days. Papers, signatures..."

"Then that's what I'll have to get. If you could make a few calls, speed things up."

"No guarantees."

"Understood. Oh, and one more thing," said Richard. "We've been trying to get ahold of Hugh Tavistock. It seems he's vanished. Have you heard anything about it?"

"No. But I will check my sources. Anything else?"

"I'll let you know."

Sakaroff grunted. “I was afraid you would say that.”

Richard hung up. Stepping away from the pay phone, he glanced around at the subway platform. He saw nothing suspicious, only the usual stream of night-time commuters—couples holding hands, students with backpacks.

The train for Creteil-Préfecture rolled into the station. Richard stepped onto it, rode it for three stops, then got off. He lingered on the next platform for a few minutes, surveying the faces. No one looked familiar. Satisfied that he hadn’t been followed, he boarded the Bobigny-Picasso train and rode it to Gare de l’Est. There he stepped off, walked out of the station, and headed briskly back to the *pension.*

He found Beryl still awake and sitting in an armchair by the window. She’d turned off all the lights, and in the darkness she was little more than a silhouette against the glow of the night sky. He shut and bolted the door. “Beryl?” he said. “Everything all right?”

He thought he saw her nod. Or was it just the quivering of her chin as she took a breath and let out a soft, slow sigh?

“We’ll be safe here,” he said. “For tonight, at least.”

“And tomorrow?” came the murmured question.

“We’ll worry about that when the time comes.”

She leaned back against the chair cushions and stared straight ahead. “Is this how it was for you, Richard? Working for Intelligence? Living day to day, not daring to think about tomorrows?”

He moved slowly to her chair. “Sometimes it was like this. Sometimes I wasn’t sure there’d be a tomorrow for me.”

"Do you miss that life?" She looked at him. He couldn't see her face, but he felt her watching him.

"I left that life behind."

"But do you miss it? The excitement? That lovely promise of violence?"

"Beryl. Beryl, please." He reached for her hand; it was like a lump of ice in his grasp.

"Didn't you enjoy it, just a little?"

"No." He paused. Then softly he said, "Yes. For a short time. When I was very young. Before it turned all too real."

"The way it did tonight. Tonight, it was real for me. When I saw that man lying there…" She swallowed. "This afternoon, you see, we had lunch together, the three of us. They had the veal. And a bottle of wine, and ice cream. And I got them to laugh…" She looked away.

"It seems like a game, at first," said Richard. "A make-believe war. But then you realize that the bullets are real. So are the people." He held her hand in his and wished he could warm it, warm her. "That's what happened to me. All of a sudden, it got too real. And there was a woman…"

She sat very still, waiting, listening. "Someone you loved?" she asked softly.

"No, not someone I loved. But someone I liked, very much. It was in Berlin, before the Wall came down. We were trying to bring over a defector to the West. And my partner, she got trapped on the wrong side. The guard spotted her. Fired." He lifted Beryl's hand to his lips and kissed it, held it.

"She…didn't make it?"

He shook his head. "And it wasn't a game of make-believe any longer. I could see her body lying in the no-man's-zone. And I couldn't reach her. So I had to leave her there, for the other side..." He released her hand. He moved to the window and looked out at the lights twinkling over Paris. "That's when I left the business. I didn't want another death on my conscience. I didn't want to feel...responsible." He turned to her. In the faint glow from the city, her face looked pale, almost luminous. "That's what makes this so hard for me, Beryl. Knowing what could happen if I make a mistake. Knowing that your life depends on what I do next."

For a long time, Beryl sat very still, watching him. Feeling his gaze through the darkness. That spark of attraction crackled like fire between them as it always did. But tonight there was something more, something that went beyond desire.

She rose from the chair. Though he didn't move, she could feel the fever of his gaze as she glided toward him, could hear the sharp intake of his breath as she reached up and touched his beard-roughened face. "Richard," she whispered, "I want you."

At once she was swept into his arms. No other embrace, no other kiss, had ever stolen her breath the way this one did. *We are like that couple in bronze,* she thought. *Starved for each other. Devouring each other.*

But this was a feast of love, not destruction.

She whimpered and her head fell back as his mouth slid to her throat. She could feel every stroke of his hands through the silky fabric of her dress. Oh Lord, if he could do this to her with her clothes on, what lovely torment would he unleash on her naked flesh? Already her breasts were tingling under his touch, her nipples turned to tight buds.

He unzipped her dress and slowly eased it off her shoulders.

It hissed past her hips and slid into a silken ripple on the floor. He, too, traced the length of her torso, his lips moving slowly down her throat, her breasts, her belly. Shuddering with pleasure, she gripped his hair and moaned, "No fair…"

"All's fair," he murmured, easing her stockings down her thighs. "In love and war…"

By the time he had her fully undressed, by the time he'd shed his own clothes, she was beyond words, beyond protest. She'd lost all sense of time and space; there was only the darkness, and the warmth of his touch, and the hunger shuddering deep inside her. She scarcely realized how they found their way to the bed. Eagerly she sank backward onto the mattress, and heard the squeak of the springs, the quickening duet of their breathing. Then she pulled him down against her, drew him onto and into her.

Starved for each other, she thought as he captured her mouth under his, invaded it, explored it. *Devouring each other.*

And like two who were famished, they feasted.

He reached for her hands, and their fingers entwined in a tighter and tighter knot as their bodies joined, thrusted, exulted. Even as her last shudders of desire faded away, he was still gripping her hands.

Slowly he released them and cradled her face instead. He pressed gentle kisses to her lips, her eyelids. "Next time," he whispered, "we'll take it slower. I won't be in such a hurry, I promise."

She smiled at him. "I have no complaints."

"None?"

"None at all. But next time…"

"Yes?"

She twisted her body beneath him, and they tumbled across the sheets until her body was lying atop his. "Next time," she murmured, lowering her lips to his chest, "it's my turn to do the tormenting."

He groaned as her mouth slid hotly down to his belly. "We're taking turns?"

"You're the one who said it. All's fair…"

"…in love and war." He laughed. And he buried his hands in her hair.

They met in the usual place, the warehouse behind Galerie Annika. Against the walls were stacked dozens of crates containing the paintings and sculptures of would-be artists, most of them no doubt talentless amateurs hoping for a spot on a gallery wall. But who can really say which is art and which is rubbish? thought Amiel Foch, gazing around at the room full of crated dreams. To me, it is all the same. Pigment and canvas.

Foch turned as the warehouse door swung open. "The bomb went off as planned," he said. "The job is done."

"The job is *not* done," came the reply. Anthony Sutherland emerged from the night and stepped into the warehouse. The thud of the door shutting behind him echoed across the bare concrete floor. "I wanted the woman neutralized. She is still alive. So is Richard Wolf."

Foch stared at Anthony. "It was a delayed fuse, set off two minutes after entry! It could not have ignited on its own."

"Nevertheless, they are still alive. Thus far, your

record of success is abysmal. You could not finish off even that stupid creature, Marie St. Pierre."

"I will see to Mme St. Pierre—"

"Forget her! It's the Tavistocks I want dead! Lord, they're like cats! Nine bloody lives."

"Jordan Tavistock is still in custody. I can arrange—"

"Jordan will keep for a while. He's harmless where he is. But Beryl has to be taken care of soon. My guess is that she and Wolf are leaving Paris. Find them."

"How?"

"You're the professional."

"So is Richard Wolf," said Foch. "He will be difficult to trace. I cannot perform miracles."

There was a long silence. Foch watched the other man pace among the crates, and he thought, *This boy is nothing like his mother. This one has the ruthlessness to see things through. And the nerve not to flinch at the consequences.*

"I cannot search blindly," said Foch. "I must have a lead. Will they go to England, perhaps?"

"No, not England." Anthony suddenly stopped pacing. "Greece. The island of Paros."

"You mean…the Rideau family?"

"Wolf will try to contact him. I'm sure of it." Anthony let out a snort of disgust. "My mother should have taken care of Rideau years ago. Well, there's still time to do it."

Foch nodded. "I leave for Paros."

After Foch had left, Anthony Sutherland stood alone in the warehouse, gazing about at the crates. So many hopes and dreams locked away in here, he reflected. But not mine. Mine are on display for all to see and admire.

The work of these poor slobs may molder into eternity. But I am the toast of Paris.

It took more than talent, more than luck. It took the help of Philippe St. Pierre's cold hard cash. Cash that would instantly dry up if his mother was ever exposed.

My father Philippe, thought Anthony with a laugh. *Still unsuspecting after all these years. I have to hand it to my lovely mother—she knows how to keep them under her spell.*

But feminine wiles could take one only so far.

If only Nina had cleaned up this matter years ago. Instead, she'd left a live witness, had even paid the man to leave the country. And as long as that witness lived, he was like a time bomb, ticking away on some lonely Greek island.

Anthony left the warehouse, walked down the alley, and climbed into his car. It was time to go home. Mustn't keep his mother awake; Nina did worry about him so. He tried never to distress her. She was, after all, the only person in this world who really loved him. Understood him.

Like peas in a pod, Mother and I, he thought with a smile. He started his car and roared off into the night.

They came to escort him from his cell at 9:00 a.m. No explanations, just the clink of keys in the door, and a gruff command in French.

Now what? wondered Jordan as he followed the guard up the corridor to the visitation room. He stepped inside, blinking at the glare of overhead fluorescent lights.

Reggie Vane was waiting in the room. At once he

waved Jordan to a chair. "Sit down. You look bloody awful, my boy."

"I feel bloody awful," said Jordan, and sank into the chair.

Reggie sat down, too. Leaning forward, he whispered conspiratorially, "I brought what you asked for. There's a nice little *charcuterie* around the corner. Lovely duckling terrine. And a few *baguettes.*" He shoved a paper bag under the table. *"Bon appétit."*

Jordan glanced in the bag and gave a sigh of pleasure. "Reggie, old man, you're a saint."

"Had some nice leek tarts to go with it, but the cop at the front desk insisted on helping himself."

"What about wine? Did you manage a decent bottle or two?"

Reggie shoved a second bag under the table, eliciting a musical clink from the contents. "But of course. A Beaujolais and a rather nice Pinot noir. Screw-top caps, I'm afraid—they wouldn't allow a corkscrew. And you'll have to hand over the bottles as soon as they're empty. Glass, you know."

Jordan regarded the Beaujolais with a look of sheer contentment. "How on earth did you manage it, Reggie?"

"Just scratched a few itchy palms. Oh, and those books you wanted—Helena will bring them by this afternoon."

"Capital!" Jordan folded the bag over the bottles. "If one must be in prison, one might as well make it a civilized experience." He looked up at Reggie. "Now, what's the latest news? I've had no word from Beryl since yesterday."

Reggie sighed. "I was dreading that question."

"What's happened?"

"I think she and Wolf have left Paris. After the explosion last night—"

"What?"

"I heard it from Daumier this morning. The flat where Beryl was staying was bombed last night. Two French agents killed. Wolf and your sister are fine, but they're dropping out for a while, leaving the country."

Jordan gave a sigh of relief. Thank God Beryl was out of the picture. It was one less problem to worry about. "What about the explosion?" he asked. "What does Daumier say about it?"

"His people feel there are similarities."

"To what?"

"The bombing of the St. Pierre residence."

Jordan stared at him. "But that was a terrorist attack. Cosmic Solidarity or some crazy group—"

"Apparently bombs are sort of like fingerprints. The way they're put together identifies their maker. And both bombs had identical wiring patterns. Something like that."

Jordan shook his head. "Why would terrorists attack Beryl? Or me? We're civilians."

"Perhaps they think otherwise."

"Or perhaps it wasn't terrorists in the first place," said Jordan, suddenly pushing out of his chair. He paced the room, pumping fresh blood to his legs, his brain. Too many hours in that cell had turned his body to mush; he needed a stiff walk, a slap of fresh air. "What if," he suggested, "that bombing of the St. Pierre place wasn't a terrorist attack at all? What if that Cosmic Solidarity nonsense was just a cover story to hide the real motive?"

"You mean it wasn't a political attack?"

"No."

"But who would want to kill Philippe St. Pierre?"

Jordan suddenly stopped dead as the realization hit him. "Not Philippe," he said softly. "His wife. Marie."

"*Marie* planted the bomb?"

"No! Marie was the *target!* She was the only one home when the bomb went off. Everyone assumes it was a mistake, an error in timing. But the bomber knew exactly what he was doing. He was trying to kill Marie, not her husband." Jordan looked at Reggie with new urgency. "You have to reach Wolf. Tell him what I just said."

"I don't know where he is."

"Ask Daumier."

"He doesn't know, either."

"Then find out where my uncle's gone off to. If ever I needed a family connection, it's right now."

After Reggie had left, the guard escorted Jordan back to his cell. The instant he stepped inside, the familiar smells assaulted him—the odor of sour wine and ripe bodies. Back with old friends, he thought, looking at the two Frenchmen snoring in their cots, the same two men whose cell he'd shared when he was first arrested. A drunk, a thief and him. What a happy little trio they made. He went to his cot and set down the two paper bags with the food and wine. At least he wouldn't have to gag on any more goulash.

Lying down, he stared at the cobwebs in the corner. So many leads to follow, to run down. *A killer's on the loose and here I am, locked up and useless. Unable to test my theories. If I could just get the help of someone I trust, someone I know beyond a doubt is on my side...*

Where the hell is Beryl?

* * *

The Greek tavern keeper slid two glasses of retsina onto their table. "Summertime, we have many tourists," he said with a shrug. "I cannot keep track of foreigners."

"But this man, Rideau, isn't a tourist," said Richard. "He's been living on this island twenty years. A Frenchman."

The tavern keeper laughed. "Frenchmen, Dutchmen, they are all the same to me," he grunted and went back into the kitchen.

"Another dead end," muttered Beryl. She took a sip of retsina and grimaced. "People actually *drink* this brew?"

"And some of them even enjoy it," said Richard. "It's an acquired taste."

"Then perhaps I'll acquire it another time." She pushed the glass away and looked around the gloomy taverna. It was midday, and passengers from the latest cruise ship had started trickling in from the heat, their shopping bags filled with the usual tourist purchases: Grecian urns, fishermen's caps, peasant dresses. Immersed in the babble of half a dozen languages, it was easy for Beryl to understand why the locals might not bother to distinguish a Frenchman from any other outsider. Foreigners came, they spent money, they left. What more did one need to know about them?

The tavern keeper reemerged from the kitchen carrying a sizzling platter of calamari. He set it on a table occupied by a German family and was about to head back to the kitchen when Richard asked, "Who might know about this Frenchman?"

"You waste your time," said the tavern keeper. "I tell you, there is no one on this island named Rideau."

"He brought his family with him," said Richard. "A wife and a son. The boy would be in his thirties now. His name is Gerard."

A dish suddenly clattered to the floor behind the counter of the bar. The dark-eyed young woman standing at the tap was frowning at Richard. "Gerard?" she said.

"Gerard Rideau," said Richard. "Do you know him?"

"She doesn't know anything," the tavern keeper insisted, and waved the young woman toward the kitchen.

"But I can see she does," said Richard.

The woman stood staring at him, as though not certain what to do, what to say.

"We've come from Paris," said Beryl. "It's very important we speak to Gerard's father."

"You are not French," said the woman.

"No, I'm English." Beryl nodded toward Richard. "He's American."

"He said…he said it was a Frenchman I should be careful of."

"Who did?"

"Gerard."

"He's right to be careful," said Richard. "But he should know things have gotten even more dangerous. There may be others coming to Paros, looking for his family. He has to talk to us, *now*." He pointed to the tavern keeper. "He'll be your witness. If anything goes wrong."

The woman hesitated, then went into the kitchen. A moment later, she reemerged. "He does not answer the telephone," she said. "I will have to drive you there."

It was a bumpy ride down a lonely stretch of road to Logaras beach. Clouds of dust flew in the open window and coated the jet black hair of their driver. Sofia was her name, and she had been born on the island. Her father managed the hotel near the harbor; now her three brothers ran the business. She could do a better job of it, she thought, but of course no one valued a woman's opinion, so she worked instead at Theo's tavern, frying calamari, rolling dolmas. She spoke four languages; one must, she explained, if one wished to live off the tourist trade.

"How do you know Gerard?" asked Beryl.

"We are friends" was the answer.

Lovers, guessed Beryl, seeing the other woman's cheeks redden.

"His family is French," said Sofia. "His mother died five years ago, but his father is still alive. But their name is not Rideau. Perhaps—" she looked at them hopefully "—it is a different family you are looking for?"

"They might have changed their name," said Beryl.

They parked near the beach and strode out across the rocks and sand. "There," said Sofia, pointing to a distant sailboard skimming the water. "That is Gerard." She waved and called to him in Greek.

At once the board spun around, the multicolored sail snapping about in a neat jibe. With the wind at his back, Gerard surfed to the beach like a bronzed Adonis and dragged the board onto the sand.

"Gerard," said Sofia, "these people are looking for a man named Rideau. Is that your father?"

Instantly Gerard dropped his sailboard. "Our name is not Rideau," he said curtly. Then he turned and walked away.

"Gerard?" called Sofia.

"Let me talk to him," said Richard, and he followed the other man up the beach.

Beryl stood by Sofia and watched the two men confront each other. Gerard was shaking his head, denying any knowledge of any Rideau family. Through the whistle of the wind, Beryl heard Richard's voice and the words "bomb" and "murder." She saw Gerard glance around nervously and knew that he was afraid.

"I hope I have done the right thing," murmured Sofia. "He is worried."

"He should be worried."

"What has his father done?"

"It's not what he's done. It's what he knows."

At the other end of the beach, Gerard was looking more and more agitated. Abruptly he turned and walked back to Sofia. Richard was right behind him.

"What is it?" asked Sofia.

"We go," snapped Gerard. "My father's house."

This time the drive took them along the coast, past groves of struggling olive trees on their left, and the gray-green Aegean on their right. The smell of Gerard's suntan lotion permeated the car. Such a dry and barren land, Beryl observed, looking out across the scrub grass. But to a man from a French slum, this would have seemed like a paradise.

"My father," said Gerard as he drove, "speaks no English. I will have to explain to him what you are asking. He may not remember."

"I'm sure he does remember," said Richard. "It's the reason you left Paris."

"That was twenty years ago. A long time..."

"Do *you* remember anything?" asked Beryl from the back seat. "You were...what? Fifteen, sixteen?"

"Fifteen," said Gerard.

"Then you must remember 66 Rue Myrha. The building where you lived."

Gerard gripped the steering wheel tightly as they

bounced onto a dirt road. "I remember the police coming to see the attic. Asking my father questions. Every day, for a week."

"What about the woman who rented the attic?" asked Richard. "Her name was Scarlatti. Do you remember her?"

"Yes. She had a man," said Gerard. "I used to listen to them through the door. Every Wednesday. All the sounds they made!" Gerard shook his head in amusement. "Very exciting for a boy my age."

"So this Mlle Scarlatti, she used the attic only as a love nest?" asked Beryl.

"She was never there except to make love."

"What did they look like, these two lovers?"

"The man was tall—that's all I remember. The woman, she had dark hair. Always wore a scarf and sunglasses. I do not remember her face very well, but I remember she was quite beautiful."

Like her mother, thought Beryl. Could she be wrong? Had it really been her, meeting her lover in that rundown flat in Pigalle?

She asked softly, "Was the woman English?"

Gerard paused. "She could have been."

"Meaning you're not certain."

"I was young. I thought she was foreign, but I did not know from where. Then, after the murders, I heard she was English."

"Did you see their bodies?"

Gerard shook his head. "My father, he would not allow it."

"So your father was the first to see them?" asked Richard.

"No. It was the man."

Richard glanced at Gerard in surprise. "Which man?"

"Mlle Scarlatti's lover. We saw him climb the steps to the attic. Then he came running back down, quite frantic. That's when we knew something was wrong and called the police."

"What happened to that man?"

"He drove away. I never saw him again. I assumed he was afraid of being accused. And that was why he sent us the money."

"The payoff," said Richard. "I guessed as much."

"For silence?" asked Beryl.

"Or false testimony." He asked Gerard, "How was the money delivered?"

"A man came with a briefcase only hours after the bodies were found. I'd never seen him before—a short, rather stocky Frenchman. He came to our flat, took my father into a back room. I did not hear what they said. Then the short man left."

"Your father never spoke to you about it?"

"No. And he told us we were not to speak of it to the police."

"You're certain that the briefcase contained money?"

"It must have."

"How do you know?"

"Because suddenly we had things. New clothes, a television. And then, soon afterward, we came to Greece. And we bought the house. There, you see?" He pointed. In the distance was a sprawling villa with a red-tiled roof. As they drove closer, Beryl saw bougainvillea trailing up the whitewashed walls and spilling over a covered veranda. Just below the house, waves lapped at a lonely beach.

They parked next to a dusty Citroën and climbed out.

The wind whistled in from the sea, stinging their faces with sand. There was no other house in sight, only this solitary building, tucked into the crags of a barren hill.

"Papa?" called Gerard, climbing the stone steps. He swung open the wrought-iron gate. "Papa?"

No one answered.

Gerard pushed through the front door and stepped across the threshold, Beryl and Richard right behind him. Their footsteps echoed through silent rooms.

"I called here from the tavern," said Sofia. "There was no answer."

"His car is outside," said Gerard. "He must be here." He crossed the living room and started toward the dining room. "Papa?" he said, and halted in the doorway. An anguished cry was suddenly wrenched from his throat. He took a step forward and seemed to stumble to his knees. Over his shoulder, Beryl caught a view into the formal dining room beyond.

A wood table stretched the length of the room. At the far end of the table, a gray-haired man had slumped onto his dinner plate, scattering chick-peas and rice across the table's surface.

Richard pushed past Gerard and went to the fallen man. Gently he grasped the head and lifted the face from its pillow of mashed rice.

In the man's forehead was punched a single bullet hole.

Chapter 10

Amiel Foch sat at an outdoor café table, sipping espresso and watching the tourists stroll past. Not the usual dentures-and-bifocals crowd, he observed as a shapely redhead wandered by. This must be the week for honeymooners. It was five o'clock, and the last public ferry to Piraeus would be sailing in half an hour. If the Tavistock woman planned to leave the island tonight, she'd have to board that ferry. He'd keep an eye on the gangplank.

He polished off his snack of stuffed grape leaves and started in on dessert, a walnut pastry steeped in syrup. Curious, how the completion of a job always left him ravenous. For other men, the spilling of blood resulted in a surge of libido, a sudden craving for hot, fast sex. Amiel Foch craved food instead; no wonder his weight was such a problem.

Dispatching the old Frenchman Rideau had been easy; killing Wolf and the woman would not be so simple. Earlier today he had considered an ambush, but Rideau's house stood on an empty stretch of shoreline, the only access a five-mile-long dirt road, and there was nowhere to conceal his car. Nowhere to lie in wait without being detected. Foch had a rule he never broke: always leave an escape route. The Rideau house, set in the midst of barren scrub, was too exposed for any such retreat. Richard Wolf was armed and would be watching for danger signs.

Amiel Foch was not a coward. But he was not a fool, either.

Far wiser to wait for another opportunity—perhaps in Piraeus, with its crowded streets and chaotic traffic. Pedestrians were killed all the time. An accident, two dead tourists—it would raise hardly a stir of interest.

Foch's gaze sharpened as the afternoon ferry pulled into port. There was only a brief unloading of passengers; the island of Paros was not, after all, on the usual Mykonos-Rhodes-Crete circuit made by tourists. At the bottom of the gangplank, a few dozen people had already gathered to board. Quickly Foch surveyed the crowd. To his consternation, he saw neither the woman nor Wolf. He knew they'd been on the island today; his contact had spotted the pair in a tavern this morning. Had they slipped away by some other route?

Then he noticed the man in the tattered windbreaker and black fisherman's cap. Though his shoulders were hunched, there was no disguising the man's height—six feet tall, at least, with a tautly athletic build. The man turned sideways, and Foch caught a glimpse of his face, partly obscured by a few days' worth of stubble. It was, indeed, Richard Wolf. But he appeared to be traveling alone. Where was the woman?

Foch paid his café bill and wandered over to the landing. He mingled with the waiting passengers and studied their faces. There were a number of women, tanned tourists, Greek housewives clad modestly in black, a few hippies in blue jeans. Beryl Tavistock was not among them.

He felt a brief spurt of panic. Had the woman and Wolf separated? If so, he might never find her. He was tempted to stay on the island, to search her out…

The passengers were moving up the gangplank.

He weighed his choices and decided to follow Wolf. Better to stick with a flesh-and-blood quarry. Sooner or later, Wolf would reunite with the woman. Until then, Foch would have to bide his time, make no moves.

The man in the fisherman's cap walked up the gangplank and into the cabin. After a moment, Foch followed him inside and took a seat two rows behind him, next to an old man with a box of salted fish. It wasn't long before the engines growled to life and the ferry slid away from the dock.

Foch settled back for the ride, his gaze focused on the back of Wolf's head. The smell of fuel and dried fish soon became nauseating. The ferry pitched and heaved on the water, and his lunch of dolmas and espresso was threatening to come back up. Foch rose from his seat and scrambled outside. Standing at the rail, he gulped in a few breaths of fresh air and waited for the nausea to pass. At last it eased, and he reluctantly turned to go back into the cabin. He headed up the aisle, past Wolf—

Or the man he'd *thought* was Wolf.

He was wearing the same ratty windbreaker, the same black fisherman's cap. But this man was clean shaven, younger. Definitely not the same man!

Foch glanced around the cabin. No Wolf. He hurried outside to the deck. No Wolf. He climbed the stairs to the upper level. Again, no Wolf.

He turned and saw the island of Paros receding behind them, and he let out a strangled curse. It was all a feint! They were still on the island—they had to be.

And I'm trapped on this boat to Piraeus.

Foch slapped the railing and cursed himself for his own stupidity. Wolf had outsmarted him—again. The old professional using his bag of tricks. There was no point interrogating the man in the cabin; he was probably just some local dupe hired to switch places with Wolf for the ferry ride.

He looked at his watch and calculated how many hours it would take him to get back to the island via a hired boat. With any luck, he could be stalking them tonight. If they were still there. He'd find them, he vowed. Wolf might be a professional. But then, so was he.

From inside a nearby café, Richard watched the ferry glide out of the harbor and heaved a sigh of relief. The old bait and switch had worked; no one had followed him off the boat. He'd been suspicious of one man in particular—a balding fellow in nondescript tourist clothes. Richard had noticed how the man had scanned the boarding passengers, how his gaze had paused momentarily on Richard's face.

Yes, he was the one. The bait was laid out for him.

The switch was a snap.

Once inside the ferry cabin, Richard had tossed his cap and jacket on a seat, walked up the aisle, and exited out the other door. By prior arrangement, Sofia's brother—six foot one and with black hair—had slid into that same seat, donned the cap and jacket, and promptly cradled his face in his arms, as though to sleep.

Richard had waited behind some crates on deck just long enough for all the passengers to board. Then he'd simply walked off the boat.

No one had followed him.

He left the café and climbed into Sofia's car.

It was a six-mile drive to the cove. Sofia and her brothers had *Melina,* the family fishing boat, ready to go, her engine running, her anchor line set to hoist. Richard scrambled out of the rowboat and up the rope ladder to *Melina*'s deck.

Beryl was waiting for him. He took her in his arms, hugged her, kissed her. "It's all right," he murmured. "I lost him."

"I was afraid I'd lose *you.*"

"Not a chance." He pulled back and smiled at her. With her black hair whipping in the wind, and her eyes the same crystalline green as the Aegean, she reminded him of some Greek goddess. Circe, Aphrodite. A woman who could hold a man forever bewitched.

The anchor thudded on deck. Sofia's brothers guided *Melina*'s bow around to face the open sea.

It started out a rough passage, the summer winds fierce and constant, the sea a rolling carpet of swells. But at sunset, as the sky deepened to a glorious shade of red, the wind suddenly died and the water turned glassy. Beryl and Richard stood on deck and gazed at the darkening silhouettes of the islands.

Sofia said, "We arrive late tonight."

"Piraeus?" asked Richard.

"No. Too busy. We pull in at Monemvassia where no one will see us."

"And then?"

"You go your way. We go ours. It is safer, for all of us." Sofia glanced toward the stern at her two brothers, who were laughing and clapping each other on the back. "Look at them! They think this is a nice little adventure! If they had seen Gerard's father…"

"Will you be all right?" asked Beryl.

Sofia looked at her. "I worry more about Gerard. They may be looking for him."

"I don't think so," said Richard. "He was only a boy when he left Paris. His testimony can't hurt them."

"He remembered enough to tell *you,*" countered Sofia.

Richard shook his head. "But I'm not sure what any of it meant."

"Perhaps the killer knows. And he will be looking for Gerard next." Sofia glanced back across the stern, toward the island. Toward Gerard, who had refused to flee. "His stubbornness. It will get him killed," she muttered, and wandered away into the cabin.

"What do you think it meant?" asked Beryl. "That business about the short man with the briefcase? Was it just a payoff to Rideau, to keep him silent?"

"Partly."

"You think there was something else in that briefcase," she said. "Something besides money."

He turned and saw the glow of the sunset on her face, the intensity of her gaze. *She's quick,* he thought. *She knows exactly what I'm thinking.* He said, "I'm sure there was. I think the lover of our mysterious Mlle Scarlatti found himself in a very sticky situation. Two dead bodies in his garret, the police certain to be notified. He sees a way to extricate himself from two crises at once. He sends his man to pay off Rideau, asks him not to identify him to police."

"And the second crisis?"

"His status as a mole."

"Delphi?"

"Maybe he knew Intelligence was about to close in. So he places the NATO documents in a briefcase…"

"And has his hired man plant the briefcase in the garret," finished Beryl. "Near my father's body."

Richard nodded. "*That's* what Inspector Broussard was trying to tell us—something about a briefcase. Remember that police photo of the murder scene? He kept pointing to an empty spot near the door. What if the briefcase was planted *after* that initial crime photo was taken? The inspector would have realized it was done postmortem."

"But he couldn't pursue the matter, because French Intelligence confiscated the briefcase."

"Exactly."

"They assumed my father was the one who brought the documents into the garret." She looked at him, her eyes glittering with determination. "How do we prove it? Any of it?"

"We identify Mlle Scarlatti's lover."

"But our only witness was Rideau. And Gerard was just a boy. He scarcely remembers what the man looked like."

"So we go to another source. A man who would know Delphi's true identity—his East German spymaster. Heinrich Leitner."

She stared at him in surprise. "Do you know how to reach him?"

"He's in a high-security prison in Berlin. Trouble is,

German Intelligence won't exactly allow us free access to their prisoners."

"As a diplomatic favor?"

His laugh was plainly skeptical. "An ex-CIA agent isn't exactly on their most-favored list. Besides, Leitner might not want to see me. Still, it's a chance we'll take." He turned to gaze over the bow at the darkening sea.

He felt her move close beside him, felt her nearness as acutely as the warmth of the setting sun. It was enough to drive him crazy, having her so close and being unable to make love to her. He found himself counting the hours until they would be alone again, until he could undress her, make love to her. *And I once considered her too rich for my blood. Maybe she is. Maybe this is just a fever that'll burn itself out, leaving us both sadder and wiser. But for now she's all I think about, all I crave.*

"So that's where we're headed next," she whispered. "Berlin."

"There'll be risks." Their gazes met through the velvet dusk. "Things could go wrong…"

"Not while you're around," she said softly.

I hope you're right, he thought as he pulled her into his arms. *I hope to God you're right.*

The dice clattered against the cell wall and came to rest with a five and a six showing.

"Ah-hah!" crowed Jordan, raising a fist in triumph. "What does that make it? Ten thousand francs? *Dix mille?*"

His cellmates, Leroi and Fofo, nodded resignedly.

Jordan held out his hand. "Pay up, gentlemen." Two grubby slips of paper were slapped into his palm. On each was written the number ten thousand. Jordan grinned. “Another round?”

Fofo shook the dice, threw them against the wall, and groaned. A three and a five. Leroi threw a pair of twos.

Jordan threw another five and six. His cellmates handed over two more grubby slips of paper. *Why, I’ll be a millionaire by tomorrow,* Jordan rejoiced, looking down at the growing pile of IOUs. On paper, anyway. He picked up the dice and was about to make another toss when he heard footsteps approach.

Reggie Vane was standing outside the cell, holding a basket of smoked salmon and crackers. “Helena sent these over,” he said as he slid the basket through the small opening at the bottom of the cell door. “Oh, and there’s fresh linen, napkins and such. One can’t dine properly on paper, can one?”

“Certainly not,” agreed Jordan, gratefully accepting the basket of goodies. “You are a true friend, indeed, Reggie.”

“Yes, well…” Reggie grinned and cleared his throat. “Anything for a child of Madeline’s.”

“Any word from Uncle Hugh?”

“Still unreachable, according to your people at Chetwynd.”

Jordan set the basket down in frustration. “This is most bizarre! I’m in prison. Beryl’s vanished. And Uncle Hugh’s probably off on some classified mission for MI6.” He began to pace the cell, oblivious to the fact that Fofo and Leroi were hungrily raiding the contents of the basket. “What about that bomb investigation? Anything new?”

“The two bombings are definitely linked. The devices were manufactured by the same hand. It appears someone's targeted both Beryl and the St. Pierres."

"I think the target was Marie St. Pierre, in particular." Jordan stopped and looked at Reggie. "Let's say Marie *was* the target. What's the motive?"

Reggie shrugged. "She's not the sort of woman to pick up enemies."

"You should be able to come up with an answer. She and your wife are best chums, after all. Helena must know who'd want to kill Marie."

Reggie gave him a troubled look. "It's not as if there's any, well…proof."

Jordan moved toward him. "What are you thinking?"

"Just rumors. Things Helena might have mentioned."

"Was it about Philippe?"

Reggie looked down. "I feel a bit…well, ungentlemanly, bringing it up. You see, it happened years ago."

"What did?"

"The affair. Between Philippe and Nina."

Jordan stared at him through the bars. *There it is,* he thought. *There's the motive.* "How long have you known about this?" he asked.

"I heard about it fifteen, twenty years ago. You see, I couldn't understand why Helena disliked Nina so much. It was almost a…a hatred. You know how it is sometimes with females, all those catty looks. I assumed it was jealousy. My Helena's never been comfortable with more…well, attractive women. As a matter of fact, if I so much as glance at a pretty face, she gets downright nasty about it."

"How did she learn about Philippe and Nina?"

"Marie told her."

"Who else knew about it?"

"I doubt there were many. Poor Marie's not one to advertise her humiliation. To have one's husband dallying with a…a piece of baggage like Nina!"

"Yet she stayed married to Philippe all these years."

"Yes, she's loyal that way. And what good would it do to make a public stink of it? Ruin his career? Now he's finance minister. Chances are, he'll go to the top. And Marie will be with him. So in the long run, it was worth it."

"If she lives to see it."

"You're not saying Philippe would kill his own wife? And why now, at this late date?"

"Perhaps she issued an ultimatum. Think about it, Reggie! Here he is, inches away from being prime minister. And Marie says, 'It's your mistress or me. Choose.'"

Reggie looked thoughtful. "If he chooses Nina, he'd have to get rid of his wife."

"Ah, but what if he chooses Marie? And Nina's the one left out in the cold?"

They frowned at each other through the bars.

"Call Daumier," said Jordan. "Tell him what you just told me, about the affair. And ask him to put a tail on Nina."

"You don't really think—"

"I think," said Jordan, "that we've been looking at this from the wrong angle entirely. The bombing wasn't a political act. All that Cosmic Solidarity rubbish was merely a smoke screen, to cover up the real reason for the attack."

"You mean it was personal?"

Jordan nodded. "Murder usually is."

The flight to Berlin was half-empty, so the only logical reason that disheveled pair of passengers in row two should be sitting in first class was that they must have actually paid the fare, a fact the flight attendant found difficult to believe, considering their appearance. Both wore dark sunglasses, wrinkled clothes and unmistakable expressions of exhaustion. The man had a week's worth of dark stubble on his jaw. The woman was deeply sunburned and her black hair was tangled and powdered with dust. Their only carry-on was the woman's purse, a battered straw affair coated with sand. The attendant glanced at the couple's ticket stubs. Athens—Rome—Berlin. With a forced smile, she asked them if they wished to order cocktails.

"Bloody Mary," said the woman in the Queen's perfect English.

"A Rob Roy," said the man. "Hold the bitters."

The woman went to fetch their drinks. When she returned, the man and woman were holding hands and looking at each other with the weary smiles of fellow survivors. They took their drinks from the tray.

"To our health?" the man asked.

"Definitely," the woman answered.

And, grinning, they both tipped back their glasses in a toast.

The meal cart was wheeled out and on it were lobster patties, crown roast of lamb, wild rice and mushroom caps. The couple ate double servings of everything and topped their dinner off with a split of wine. Then, like a pair of exhausted puppies, they curled up against each other and fell asleep.

They slept all the way to Berlin. Only when the plane rolled to a stop at the terminal did they jerk awake, both of them instantly alert and on guard. As the passengers filed out, the flight attendant kept her gaze on that rumpled pair from Athens. There was no telling who they were or what they might be up to. First-class passengers did not usually travel the world dressed like bums.

The couple was the last to disembark.

The attendant followed the pair onto the passenger ramp and stood watching as they walked toward a small crowd of greeters. They made it as far as the waiting area.

Two men stepped into their path. At once the couple halted and pivoted as though to flee back toward the plane. Three more men magically appeared, blocking off their escape. The couple was trapped.

The attendant caught a glimpse of the woman's panicked face, the man's grim expression of defeat. She had been sure there was something wrong about them. They were terrorists, perhaps, or international thieves. And there were the police to make the arrest. She watched as the pair was led away through the murmuring crowd. Definitely not first class, she thought with a sniff of satisfaction. Oh, yes, one could always tell.

Richard and Beryl were shoved forward into a windowless room. "Stay here!" came the barked command, then the door was slammed shut behind them.

"They were waiting for us," said Beryl. "How did they know?"

Richard went to the door and tested the knob. "Dead bolt," he muttered. "We're locked in tight." In frustration, he began to circle the room, searching for another way out. "Somehow they knew we were coming to Berlin..."

"We paid for the tickets in cash. There was no way they could have known. And those were airport guards, Richard. If they want us dead, why bother to arrest us?"

"To keep you from getting your heads shot off," said a familiar voice. "That's why."

Beryl wheeled around in astonishment at the portly man who'd just opened the door. "Uncle *Hugh?*"

Lord Lovat scowled at his niece's wrinkled clothes and tangled hair. "You're a fine mess. Since when did you adopt the gypsy look?"

"Since we hitchhiked halfway across Greece. Credit cards, by the way, are *not* the preferred method of payment in small Greek towns."

"Well, you made it to Berlin." He glanced at Richard. "Good work, Wolf."

"I could've used some assistance," growled Richard.

"And we would've happily provided it. But we had no idea where to find you, until I spoke with your man, Sakaroff. He said you'd be headed for Berlin. We only just found out you'd gone via Athens."

"What are *you* doing in Berlin, Uncle Hugh?" demanded Beryl. "I thought you were off on another one of your secret missions."

"I'm fishing."

"Not for fish, obviously."

"For answers. Which I'm hoping Heinrich Leitner will provide." He took another look at Beryl's clothes and sighed. "Let's get to the hotel and clean you both up. Then we'll pay a visit to Herr Leitner's prison cell."

"You have clearance to speak to him?" said Richard in surprise.

"What do you think I've been doing here these last few days? Wining and dining the necessary officials." He waved them out of the room. "The car's waiting."

In Uncle Hugh's hotel suite, they showered off three days' worth of Greek dust and sand. A fresh set of clothes was delivered to the room, courtesy of the concierge—sober business attire, outfits appropriate for a visit to a high-security prison.

"How do we know Leitner will tell us the truth?" asked Richard as they rode in the limousine to the prison.

"We don't," said Hugh. "We don't even know how much he *can* tell us. He oversaw Paris operations from East Berlin, so he'd be acquainted with code names, but not faces."

"Then we may come away with nothing."

"As I said, Wolf, it's a fishing expedition. Sometimes you reel in an old tire. Sometimes a salmon."

"Or, in this case, a mole."

"If he's cooperative."

"Are you prepared to hear the truth?" asked Richard. The question was directed at Hugh, but his gaze was on Beryl. Delphi could still be Bernard or Madeline, his eyes said.

"Right now, I'd say ignorance is far more dangerous," Hugh observed. "And there's Jordan to consider. I have people watching out for him. But there's always the chance things could go wrong."

Things have already gone wrong, thought Beryl, looking out the car window at the drab and dreary buildings of East Berlin.

The prison was even more forbidding—a massive concrete fortress surrounded by electrified fences. The very best of security, she noted, as they moved through the gauntlet of checkpoints and metal detectors. Uncle Hugh had obviously been expected, and he was greeted with the chilling disdain of an old Cold War enemy. Only when they'd arrived at the commandant's office was any courtesy extended to them. Glasses of hot tea were passed around, cigars offered to the men. Hugh accepted; Richard declined.

"Up until recently, Leitner was most uncooperative," said the commandant, lighting a cigar. "At first, he denied his role entirely. But our files on him are proof positive. He *was* in charge of Paris operations."

"Has Leitner provided any names?" asked Richard.

The commandant peered at Richard through the drifting cloud of cigar smoke. "You were CIA, were you not, Mr. Wolf?"

Richard gave only the briefest nod of acknowledgment. "It was years ago. I've left the business."

"But you understand how it is, to be dogged by one's past associations."

"Yes, I understand."

The commandant rose and went to look out his window at the barbed-wire fence enclosing his prison kingdom. "Berlin is filled with people running from their shadows. Their old lives. Whether it was for money or for ideology, they served a master. And now the master is dead and they hide from the past."

"Leitner's already in prison. He has nothing to lose by talking to us."

"But the people who worked for him—the ones not yet exposed—they have everything to lose. Now the East German files are open. And every day, some curious citizen opens one of those files and discovers the truth. Realizes that a friend or husband or lover was working for the enemy." The commandant turned, his pale blue eyes focused on Richard. "That's why Leitner has been reluctant to give names—to protect his old agents."

"But you say he's more cooperative these days?"

"In recent weeks, yes."

"Why?"

The commandant paused. "A bad heart, the doctors say. It fails, little by little. In two months, three…" He shrugged. "Leitner sees the end coming. And in exchange for a few last comforts, he's sometimes willing to talk."

"Then he may give us answers."

"If he is in the mood." The commandant turned to the door. "So, let us see what sort of mood Herr Leitner is in today."

They followed him down secured corridors, past mounted cameras and grim-faced guards, into the very core of the complex. Here there were no windows; the air itself seemed hermetically sealed from the outside world. *From here there is no escape,* thought Beryl. *Except through death.*

They stopped at cell number five. Two guards, each with his own key, opened separate locks. The door swung open.

Inside, on a wooden chair, sat an old man. Oxygen tubing snaked from his nostrils. His regulation prison garb—tan shirt and pants, no belt—hung loosely on his shrunken frame. The fluorescent lights gave his face a yellowish cast. Beside the man's chair stood an oxygen tank; except for the hiss of the gas flowing through his nasal prongs, the room was silent.

The commandant said, "*Guten Tag,* Heinrich."

Leitner said nothing. Only by a brief flicker of his eyes did he acknowledge the greeting.

"I have brought with me today, Lord Lovat, from England. You are familiar with the name?"

Again, a flicker in the old man's blue eyes. And a whisper, barely audible, "MI6."

"That's right," said Hugh. "Since retired."

"So am I," was the reply, not without a trace of humor. Leitner's gaze shifted to Beryl and Richard.

"My niece," said Hugh. "And a former associate. Richard Wolf."

"CIA?" said Leitner.

Richard nodded. "Also retired."

Leitner managed a faint smile. "How differently we enjoy our retirements." He looked once again at Hugh. "A social call on an old enemy? How thoughtful."

"Not a social call, exactly," said Hugh.

Leitner began to cough, and the effort seemed almost too much for him; when at last he settled back into his chair, his face had a distinctly blue tinge. "What is it you wish to know?"

"The identity of your double agent in Paris. Code name Delphi."

Leitner didn't speak.

"Surely the name is familiar, Herr Leitner. Over the years, Delphi must have passed on invaluable documents. He was your link to NATO operations. Don't you remember?"

"That was twenty years ago," murmured Leitner. "The world has changed."

"We want only his name. That's all."

"So you may put Delphi in a cage like this? Shut away from the sun and air?"

"So we can stop the killing," said Richard.

Leitner frowned. "What killing?"

"It's going on right now. A French agent, murdered

in Paris. A man, shot to death in Greece. It's all linked to Delphi."

"That cannot be possible," said Leitner.

"Why?"

"Delphi has been put to sleep."

Hugh frowned at him. "Are you saying he's dead?"

"But that makes no sense," said Richard. "If Delphi's dead, why is the killing still going on?"

"Perhaps," said Leitner, "it has nothing at all to do with Delphi."

"Perhaps you are lying," said Richard.

Leitner smiled. "Always a possibility." Suddenly he began to cough again; it had the gurgling sound of a man drowning in his own secretions. When at last he could speak, it was only between gasps for oxygen. "Delphi was a paid recruit," he said. "Not a true believer. We preferred the believers, you see. They did not cost as much."

"So he did it for money?" asked Richard.

"A rather generous sum, over the years."

"When did it stop?"

"When it became a risk to all involved. So Delphi ended the association. Covered all tracks before your counterintelligence could close in."

"Is that why my parents were killed?" asked Beryl. "Because Delphi had to cover his tracks?"

Leitner frowned. "Your parents?"

"Bernard and Madeline Tavistock. They were shot to death in a garret in Pigalle."

"But that was a murder and suicide. I saw the report."

"Or were they both murdered? By Delphi?"

Leitner looked at Hugh. "I gave no such order. And that is the truth."

"Meaning some of what you told us is *not* the truth?" Richard probed.

Leitner took a deep breath of oxygen and painfully wheezed it out. "Truth, lies," he whispered. "What does it matter now?" He sank back in his chair and looked at the commandant. "I wish to rest. Take these people away."

"Herr Leitner," said Richard, "I'll ask this one last time. Is Delphi really dead?"

Leitner met his gaze with one so steady, so unflinching, it seemed that surely he was about to tell the truth. But the answer he gave was puzzling at best.

"Dormant," he said. "That is the word I would use."

"So he's not dead."

"For your purposes," Leitner said with a smile, "he is."

Chapter 11

"A sleeper. That's what Delphi must be," said Richard. They had not dared discuss the matter in the limousine—no telling whom their driver really worked for. But here, in a noisy restaurant, with waiters whisking back and forth, Richard could finally spell out his theories. "I'm sure that's what he meant."

"A sleeper?" asked Beryl.

"Someone they recruit years in advance," said her uncle. "As a young adult. The person may be kept inactive for years. They live a normal life, try to gain influence in some trusted position. And then the signal's sent. And the sleeper's activated."

"So that's what he meant by dormant," said Beryl. "Not dead. But not active, either."

"Precisely."

"For this sleeper to be of any use to them, he'd have

to be in a position of influence. Or close to it," said Beryl thoughtfully.

"Which describes Stephen Sutherland to a T," said Richard. "American ambassador. Access to all security data."

"It also describes Philippe St. Pierre," said Hugh. "Minister of Finance. In line for French prime minister—"

"And extremely vulnerable to blackmail," added Beryl, thinking of Nina and Philippe. And of Anthony, the son born of their illicit affair.

"I'll contact Daumier," said Hugh. "Have St. Pierre vetted again."

"While he's at it," said Richard, "ask him to vet Nina."

"Nina?"

"Talk about positions of influence! An ambassador's wife. Mistress to St. Pierre. She could've heard secrets from both sides of the bed."

Hugh shook his head. "Considering her double digit IQ, Nina Sutherland's the last person I'd expect to work for Intelligence."

"And the one person who'd get away with it."

Hugh glanced around impatiently for the waiter. "We have to leave for Paris at once," he said, and slapped enough marks on the table to pay for their coffees. "There's no telling what's happening to Jordan."

"If it is Nina, do you think she could get at Jordan?" asked Beryl.

"All these years, I've overlooked Nina Sutherland," said Hugh. "I'm not about to make the same mistake now."

Daumier met them at Orly Airport. "I have reexamined the security files on Philippe and Nina," he said as they rode together in his limousine. "St. Pierre is clean. His record is unblemished. If he is the sleeper, we have no evidence of it."

"And Nina?"

Daumier gave a deep sigh. "Our dear Nina presents a problem. There was an item that was not addressed in her earlier vetting. She was eighteen when she first appeared on the London stage. A small part, quite insignificant, but it launched her acting career. At that time, she had an affair with one of her fellow actors—an East German by the name of Berte Klausner. He claimed he was a defector. But three years later, he vanished from England and was never heard from again."

"A recruiter?" asked Richard.

"Possibly."

"How on earth did this little affair make it past Nina's vetting?" asked Beryl.

Daumier shrugged. "It was noted when Nina and Sutherland were married. By then she'd retired from the theater to become a diplomat's wife. She didn't serve in any official capacity. As a rule, security checks on wives—especially if they are American—are not as demanding. So Nina slipped through."

"Then you have evidence of possible recruitment," said Beryl. "And she could have had access to NATO secrets by way of her husband. But you can't prove she's Delphi. Nor can you prove she's a murderer."

"True," admitted Daumier.

"I doubt you'll get her to confess, either," said Richard. "Nina was once an actress. She could probably brazen her way through anything."

"That is why I suggest the following action," said Daumier. "A trap. Tempt her into making a move."

"With what bait?" asked Richard.

"Jordan."

"That's out of the question!" said Beryl.

"He has already agreed to it. This afternoon, he will be released from prison. We move him to a hotel where he will attempt to be conspicuous."

Hugh laughed. "Not much of a stretch for our Jordan."

"My men will be stationed at strategic points in the hotel. If—and when—an attack occurs, we will be prepared."

"Things could go wrong," said Beryl. "He could be hurt—"

"He could be hurt in prison, as well," said Daumier. "At least this may provide us with answers."

"And possibly a dead body."

"Have you a better suggestion?"

Beryl glanced at Richard, then at her uncle. They were both silent. *I can't believe they're agreeing to this,* she thought.

She looked at Daumier. "What do you want *me* to do?"

"You'd complicate things, Beryl," said Hugh. "It's better for you to stay out of the picture."

"The Vanes' house has excellent security," said Daumier. "Reggie and Helena have already agreed that you should stay with them."

"But I haven't agreed," said Beryl.

"Beryl." It was Richard. He spoke quietly. Unbendingly. "Jordan will be protected from all angles. They'll be ready for the attack. This time, nothing will go wrong."

"Can you guarantee it? Can any of you?"

There was silence.

"Nothing can be guaranteed, Beryl," said Daumier quietly. "We have to take this chance. It may be the only way to catch Delphi."

In frustration, she looked out the window, thinking of the options. Realizing there were none—not if any of this was to be resolved—she said softly, "I'll agree to it on one condition."

"What's that?"

She looked at Richard. "I want you to be with him. I trust you, Richard. If you're watching Jordan, I know he'll be all right."

Richard nodded. "I'll be right by his side."

"Who else knows about this plan?" asked Hugh.

"Just a few of my people," said Daumier. "I was careful not to let any of this leak out to Philippe St. Pierre."

"What do Reggie and Helena know?" asked Beryl.

"Only that you need a safe place to stay. They are doing this as a favor to old friends."

As an old friend was exactly the way Beryl was greeted upon arrival at the Vanes' residence. As soon as the gates closed behind the limousine, and they were inside the high walls of the compound, she was swept into the comfort of their home. It all seemed so safe, so familiar: the English wallpaper, the tray of tea and biscuits on the end table, the vases of flowers perfuming the rooms. Surely nothing could hurt her here...

There was scarcely time to say goodbye to Richard. While Daumier and Hugh waited outside in the car, Richard pulled Beryl into his arms. They shared a last embrace, a last kiss.

"You'll be perfectly safe here," he whispered. "Don't leave the compound for any reason."

"*You're* the one I worry about. You and Jordan."

"I won't let anything happen to him." He tipped up her chin and pressed his lips to hers. "And that," he murmured, "is a promise." He touched her face and grinned, a confident grin that made her believe anything was possible.

Then he walked away.

She stood on the doorstep and watched the car drive out of the compound, saw the iron gates close shut behind it. *I'm with you,* she thought. *Whatever happens, Richard, I'm right there beside you.*

"Come, Beryl," said Reggie, affectionately draping his arm around her shoulders. "I have an instinct about these things. And I'm positive everything will turn out just fine."

She looked up at Reggie's smiling face. *Thank God for old friends,* she thought. And she let him lead her back into the house.

Jordon was down on all fours in his jail cell, rattling a pair of dice in his hand. His cellmates, the two shaggy, ripe-smelling ruffians—or could that odor be Jordan's?—hovered behind him, stamping their feet and yelling. Jordan threw the dice; they tumbled across the floor and clattered against the wall. Two fives.

"Zut alors!" groaned the cellmates.

Jordan raised his fist in triumph. *"Oh, là là!"* Only then did he see his visitors staring at him through the bars. "Uncle Hugh!" he said, jumping to his feet. "Am I glad to see you!"

Hugh's disbelieving gaze scanned the interior of the cell. Over the cot was draped a red-checked tablecloth, laid out with platters of sliced beef, poached salmon, a bowl of grapes. A bottle of wine sat chilling in a plastic bucket. And on a chair beside the bed was neatly stacked a half dozen leather-bound books and a vase of roses. "This is a prison?" quipped Hugh.

"Oh, I've spruced it up a bit," said Jordan. "The food was wretched, so I had some delivered. Brought in the reading material, as well. But," he said with a sigh, "I'm afraid it's still very much a prison." He tapped the bars. "As you can see." He looked at Daumier. "So, are we ready?"

"If you are still willing."

"Haven't much of a choice, have I? Considering the alternative."

The guard unlocked the door and Jordan stepped out, carrying his bundle of street clothes. But he couldn't walk away without a proper goodbye to his cellmates. He turned and found Fofo and Leroi staring at him mournfully. "Afraid this is it, fellows," he said. "It's been—" he thought a moment, struggling to come up with the right adjective "—a uniquely fragrant experience." On impulse, he tossed his tailored linen jacket to the disbelieving Fofo. "I think that might fit you," he said. "Wear it in good health." Then, with a farewell wave, he followed his companions out of the building and into Daumier's limousine.

They drove him to the Ritz—same floor, different room. A fashionably appropriate place for an assassination, he thought wryly as he came out of the shower and dressed in a fresh suit.

"Bulletproof windows," said Daumier. "Microphones in the front room. And there'll be two men, stationed across the hall. Also, you should have this." Daumier reached into his briefcase and pulled out an automatic pistol. He handed it to Jordan, who regarded the weapon with a raised eyebrow.

"Worst-case scenario? I'll actually have to defend myself?"

"A precaution. You know how to use one?"

"I suppose I can muddle through," said Jordan, expertly sliding in the ammunition clip. He looked at Richard. "Now what happens?"

"Have a meal in the restaurant downstairs," said Richard. "Take your time, make sure you're seen by as many employees as possible. Leave a big tip, be conspicuous. And return to your room."

"And then?"

"We wait and see who comes knocking."

"What if no one does?"

"They will," said Daumier grimly. "I guarantee it."

Amiel Foch received the call a mere thirty minutes later. It was the hotel maid—the same woman who'd been so useful a week before, when he'd needed access to the Tavistocks' suites.

"He is back," she said. "The Englishman."

"Jordan Tavistock? But he's in prison—"

"I have just seen him in the hotel. Room 315. He seems to be alone."

Foch grimaced in amazement. Perhaps those Tavistock family connections had come through. Now he was a free man—and a vulnerable target. "I need to get into his room," said Foch. "Tonight."

"I cannot do it."

"You did it before. I'll pay double."

The maid gave a snort of disgust. "It's still not enough. I could lose my job."

"I'll pay more than enough. Just get me the passkey again."

There was a silence. Then the woman said, "First, you leave the envelope. Then, I get you the key."

"Agreed," said Foch, and hung up.

He immediately made a call to Anthony Sutherland. "Jordan Tavistock is out of prison," he said. "He's taken a room at the Ritz. Do you still wish me to proceed?"

"This time, I want it done right. Even if I have to supervise it myself. When do we move?"

"I do not think it is wise—"

"When do we move?"

Foch swallowed his angry response. It was a mistake letting Sutherland take part. The boy was just a voyeur, eager to experience the ultimate power—the taking of a life. Foch had sensed it years ago, from the day they'd first met. He'd known just by looking at him that he'd be addicted to thrills, to intensity, be it sexual or otherwise.

Now the young man wished to experience something novel. Murder. This was a mistake, surely, a mistake…

"Remember who's paying your fees, M. Foch," said Sutherland. "And outrageous fees, too. I'm the one who makes the decisions, not you."

Even if they are stupid, dangerous decisions? wondered Foch. At last he said, "It will be tonight. We wait for him to sleep."

"Tonight," agreed Sutherland. "I'll be there."

At eleven-thirty, Jordon turned off the lights in his hotel room, stuffed three pillows under the bedspread, and fluffed it all up so that it vaguely resembled a human shape. Then he took his position by the door, next to Richard. In the darkness they sat and waited for something to happen. Anything to happen. So far, the evening had been a screaming bore. Daumier had made him a prisoner of his own hotel room. He'd watched two hours of telly, glanced through *Paris Match,* and completed five crossword puzzles. What must I do to attract this assassin? he wondered. Send him an engraved invitation?

Sighing, he leaned back against the wall. "Is this the sort of thing you used to do, Wolf?" he murmured.

"A lot of waiting around. A lot of boredom," said Richard. "And every so often, a moment of abject terror."

"What made you leave the business? The boredom or the terror?"

Richard paused. "The rootlessness."

"Ah. The man longs for home and hearth." Jordan smiled. "So tell me, does my sister figure into the equation?"

"Beryl is…one of a kind."

"You didn't answer the question."

"The answer is, I don't know," Richard admitted. He squared his shoulders to ease the tension in his muscles. "Sometimes, it seems like the world's worst possible match. Sure, I can put on a tuxedo, stand around swirling a snifter of brandy. But I don't fool anyone, least of all myself. And certainly not Beryl."

"You really think that's what she needs? A fop in black tie?"

"I don't know what she needs. Or what she wants. I know she probably thinks she's in love. But how the devil can anyone know for certain, when things are so crazy?"

"You wait till things *aren't* so crazy. Then you decide."

"And live with the consequences."

"You're already lovers, aren't you?"

Richard looked at him in surprise. "Are you always so inquisitive about your sister's love life?"

"I'm her closest male relative. And therefore responsible for defending her honor." Jordan laughed softly. "Someday, Wolf, I may have to shoot you. That is, if I survive the night."

They both laughed. And they settled back to wait.

At 1:00 a.m., they heard the faint click of a door closing in the hallway. Had someone just stepped out of the stairwell? Instantly Jordan snapped fully alert, his adrenaline kicking into overdrive. He whispered, "Did you hear—"

Richard was already rising to a crouch. Through the darkness, Jordan could sense the other man tensing for action. Where were Daumier's agents? he wondered frantically. Were the two of them on their own?

A key grated slowly in the lock. Jordan froze, heart thundering, the sweat breaking out on his palms. The gun felt slippery in his grasp.

The door swung open; two figures slowly edged into the room. The first took aim at the bed. A single bullet was all the gunman managed to squeeze off before Richard flew at him sideways. The force of his assault sent both men thudding to the floor.

Jordan shoved his gun into the ribs of the second intruder and barked, "Freeze!"

To Jordan's astonishment, the man didn't freeze, but turned and fled from the room.

Jordan dashed after him into the hall, just in time

to see the two French agents tackle the fugitive to the floor. They yanked him, kicking and squirming, back to his feet. In amazement, Jordan stared at the man. *"Anthony?"*

"I'm bleeding!" spat Anthony Sutherland. "They broke my nose! I think they broke my nose!"

"Keep squealing, and they'll break a lot more," growled Richard.

Jordan turned and saw Richard haul the gunman out of the room. He yanked his head back, so Jordan could see his face. "Take a good look. Recognize him?"

"Why, it's my bogus attorney," said Jordan. "M. Jarre."

Richard nodded and forced the balding Frenchman to the floor. "Now let's find out his real name."

"It's extraordinary," mused Reggie, "how very much you look like your mother."

The butler had long since cleared away the coffee cups, and Helena had vanished upstairs to see to the guest room. Beryl and Reggie sat alone together, enjoying a nip of brandy in his wood-paneled library. A fire crackled in the hearth—not for warmth on this July night, but for reassurance, the ancestral comfort of flames against the night, against the world's evils.

Beryl cradled the brandy snifter in her hands and watched the reflection of firelight in the golden liquid. She said, "When I remember her, it's from a child's point of view. So I remember only the things a child finds important. Her smile. The softness of her hands."

"Yes, yes. That was Madeline."

"I've been told she was quite enchanting."

"She was," said Reggie softly. "She was the loveliest, most extraordinary woman I've ever known..."

Beryl looked up and saw that he was staring at the fire as though seeing, in its flames, the faces of old ghosts. She gave him a fond look. "Mother told me once that you were her oldest and dearest friend."

"Did she?" Reggie smiled. "Yes, I suppose that's true. Did you know we played together, as children. In Cornwall..." He blinked and she thought she saw the faint gleam of tears on his lashes. "I was the first, you know," he murmured. "Before Bernard. Before..." Sighing, he sank back in his chair. "But that was a long time ago."

"You still think of her a great deal."

"It's difficult not to." He drained his brandy glass. Unsteadily he poured another—his third. "Every time I look at you, I think, 'There's Madeline, come back to life.' And I remember how much, how very much I miss her—" Suddenly he stiffened and glanced at the doorway. Helena was standing there, wearily shaking her head.

"You've had more than enough for tonight, Reggie."

"It's only my third."

"And how many more will come after that one?"

"Bloody few, if you have your way."

Helena came into the room and took his arm. "Come, darling. You've kept Beryl up long enough. It's time for bed."

"It's only one o'clock."

"Beryl's tired. And you should be considerate."

Reggie looked at their guest. "Oh. Oh, yes, perhaps you're right." He rose to his feet and moved on unsteady legs toward Beryl. She turned her face as he bent over to plant a kiss on her cheek. It was a wet, sloppy kiss, heavy with the smell of brandy, and she had to suppress the urge to pull away. He straightened, and once again she saw the sheen of tears in his eyes. "Good night, dear," he murmured. "You'll be perfectly safe with us."

With a sense of pity, Beryl watched the old man shuffle out of the library.

"He's simply not able to tolerate spirits the way he used to," said Helena, sighing. "The years pass, you know, and he forgets that things change. Including his capacity for liquor." She gave Beryl a rueful smile. "I do hope he didn't bore you too much."

"Not at all. We talked about Mother. He said I remind him of her."

Helena nodded. "Yes, you do resemble her. Of course, I didn't know her nearly as well as Reggie did." She sat down on the armrest of a chair. "I remember the first time I met her. It was at my wedding. Madeline and Bernard were there, practically newlyweds themselves. You could see it, just by the way they looked at each other. Quite a lovely couple..." Helena picked up Reggie's brandy snifter, tidied the table. "When we met again in Paris, it was fifteen years later, and she hadn't aged a bit. It was eerie how unchanged she was. When all the rest of us felt so acutely the passage of time."

There was a long pause. Then Beryl asked, "Did she have a lover?" The question was asked softly, so softly it was almost swallowed in the gloom of that library.

The silence that followed stretched on so long, she thought perhaps her words had gone unnoticed. But then Helena said, "It shouldn't surprise you, should it? Madeline had that magic about her. That certain something the rest of us seem to lack. It's a matter of luck, you know. It's not something one achieves through effort or study. It's in one's genes. An inheritance, like a silver spoon in one's mouth."

"My mother wasn't born with a silver spoon."

"She didn't need one. She had that magic, instead." Abruptly Helena turned to leave. But in the doorway she caught herself and looked back at Beryl with a smile. "I'll see you in the morning. Good night."

Beryl nodded. "Good night, Helena."

For a long time, Beryl frowned at the empty doorway and listened to Helena ascend the stairs. She went to the hearth and stared at the dying embers. She thought of her mother, wondered if Madeline had ever stood here, in this library, in this house. Yes, of course she would have. Reggie was her oldest friend. They would have visited back and forth, the two couples, as they had in England years before…

Before Helena had insisted Reggie accept the Paris post.

The question suddenly came to her: *Why?* Was there some unspoken reason the Vanes had suddenly left England? Helena had grown up in Buckinghamshire; her ancestral home was a mere two miles from Chetwynd. Surely it must have been difficult to pack up her household, to leave behind all that was familiar, and move to a city where she couldn't even speak the language. One didn't blithely make such a move.

Unless one was fleeing *from* something.

Beryl's head lifted. She found herself staring at a ridiculous statuette on the mantelpiece—a fat little man holding a rifle. It had the inscription: "Reggie Vane—most likely to shoot his own foot. Tremont Gun Club." Lined up beside it were various knickknacks from Reggie's past—a soccer medal, an old photo of a cricket team, a petrified frog. Judging by the items on display, this must be Reggie's private abode, the room to which he retreated from the world. The room that would hold his secrets.

She scanned the photos, and nowhere did she see a picture of Helena. Nor was there one on the desk or on the bookshelves—a fact she thought odd, for she remembered her father's library and all the snapshots of Madeline he kept so conspicuously in view. She moved to Reggie's cherry desk and quietly began to open the drawers. The first revealed the expected clutter of pens and paper clips. She opened the second and saw only a sheaf of cream-colored stationery and an address book. She closed the drawers and began to circle the room, thinking, *This is where you keep your most private treasures. The memories you hide, even from your wife...*

Her gaze came to rest on the leather footstool. It appeared to be a matched set with the easy chair, but it had been moved out of position, and instead sat at the side of the chair where it served no purpose...except to stand on.

She glanced directly up at the mahogany breakfront that stood against the wall. The shelves were filled with antique books, protected behind glass doors. The cabinet was at least eight feet tall, and on top was a matched pair of china bowls.

Beryl pushed the footstool over to the breakfront, climbed onto the stool, and reached up to retrieve the first bowl. It was empty and coated in dust. So was the second bowl. But as she slid the bowl back onto the cabinet, she met resistance. She reached back as far as she could, and her fingers met something flat and leathery. She grasped the edge and pulled it off the cabinet.

It was a photo album.

She took it over to the hearth and sat down by the dying fire. There she opened the cover to the first picture in the album. It was of a laughing, black-haired girl. The girl was twelve years old perhaps, and sitting on a swing, her skirt bunched up hoydenishly around her thighs, her bare legs dangling. On the next page was another photo—the same girl, a bit older now, dressed in May Day finery, flowers woven into her tangled hair. More photos, all of the black-haired girl: clad in waders and fishing in a stream, waving from a car, hanging upside down from a tree branch. And last—a wedding photo. It had been torn jaggedly in two, so that the groom was missing, and only the bride remained.

For an eternity, Beryl stared at the face she knew from her childhood—the face so very much like her own. She touched the smiling lips, traced the upswept tendrils of black hair. She thought about how it must be for a man to so desperately love a woman. To lose her to another man. To flee from those memories of her to a foreign city, only to have her reappear in that same city. And to find that, even fifteen years later, the feelings remain, and there is nothing you can do to ease your anguish, nothing at all…so long as she is alive.

Beryl shut the album and went to the telephone. She didn't know how to reach Richard, so she dialed Daumier's number instead and was greeted by a recorded message, intoned in businesslike French.

After the beep, she said, "Claude, it's Beryl. I have to speak to you at once. I think I've found some new evidence. Please, come get me! As soon as you—" She stopped, her hand suddenly frozen on the receiver. What was that click on the line?

She listened for other sounds, but heard only the pounding of her own heart—and silence. She hung up. The extension, she thought. Someone had been listening on the extension.

Quickly she rose to her feet. *I can't stay here, not in this house. Not under this roof. Not when I know he could have been the one.*

Clutching the album firmly in her arms, she left Reggie's library and hurried across the foyer. After disarming the security system, she stepped out the front door.

Outside, it was a cool night, the sky clear, the stars faintly twinkling against the distant haze of city light. She looked across the stone courtyard and saw that the iron gates were closed—no doubt locked, as well. As a bank executive in Paris, Reggie was a prime target for terrorists; he would install the very best security for his home.

I have to get out of here, she determined. *Without anyone knowing.*

And then what? Thumb a ride to the nearest police station? Daumier's flat? *Anywhere but here.*

She traced the perimeter of the courtyard, searching the high wall for a doorway, an exit. She spotted another gate, but it, too, was locked. No way around it, she thought. She'd have to climb over. Quickly she scanned the trees and spotted an apple tree with a branch overhanging the wall. Clutching the photo album in one hand, she scrambled up onto the lowest branch. It was an easy climb to the next branch, and the next, but every movement made the tree sway and sent apples thudding noisily to the ground. At the top of the wall, she tossed the album down on the other side and dropped to the ground beside it. At once she scooped up the album and turned toward the road.

The blinding beam of a flashlight made her freeze.

"So it's not a burglar after all," said a voice. "What on earth are you doing, Beryl?"

Squinting against the light, Beryl could barely make out Helena's silhouette standing before her. "I… I wanted to take a walk. But the gate was locked."

"I would have opened it for you."

"I didn't want to wake you." She turned her gaze from the flashlight. "Please, could you drop the torch? It hurts my eyes."

The beam slowly fell, and stopped at the photo album in Beryl's arms. Beryl had clasped the album to her chest, hoping Helena hadn't recognized it, but it was too late. She had already seen it.

"Where was it?" asked Helena softly. "Where did you find it?"

"The library," said Beryl. No point in lying now; the evidence was there, plainly in her grasp.

"All these years," murmured Helena. "He kept it all these years. And he swore to me—"

"What, Helena? What did he swear to?"

There was silence. "That he no longer loved her," came the whispered answer. Then a laugh, full of self-mockery. "I've lost out to a ghost. It was hopeless enough when she was alive. But now she's dead, and I can't fight back. The dead, you see, don't grow old. They stay young and beautiful. And perfect."

Beryl took a step forward, her arms extended in sympathy. "They weren't lovers, Helena. I know they weren't."

"I was never perfect enough."

"But he married you. There must have been love involved—"

Helena stepped away, angrily brushing off Beryl's offer of comfort. "Not love! It was spite. Some stupid, masculine gesture to show her he couldn't be hurt. We were married a month after she was. I was his consolation prize, you see. I gave him all the right connections. And the money. He happily accepted those. But he never really wanted my love."

Again, Beryl tried to reach out to her; again, Helena rebuffed the gesture. Beryl said softly, "It's time to move on, Helena. Make your own life, without him. While you're still young…"

"He *is* my life."

"But all these years, you must have known! You must have suspected that Reggie was the one who—"

"Not Reggie."

"Helena, please think about it!"

"Not Reggie."

"He was obsessed, unable to let her go! To let another man have her—"

"It was me."

Those three words, uttered so quietly, chilled Beryl's blood to ice. She stared at the silhouette standing before her, her thoughts instantly shifting to ones of escape. She could flee down the road, pound at the nearest door… She shifted onto the balls of her feet and was about to make a dash past Helena, when she heard the click of the pistol hammer.

"You look so very much like her," whispered Helena. "When I first saw you, years ago at Chetwynd, it was almost as if she'd come back. And now, I have to kill her all over again."

"But I'm not Madeline—"

"It makes no difference now who you are. Because you know." Helena raised her arm and Beryl saw, through the shadows, the faint gleam of the gun in her hand. "The garage, Beryl," she said. "We're going for a drive."

Chapter 12

"Amiel Foch," said Daumier, flipping through a file folder. "Age forty-six, formerly with French Intelligence. Presumed dead three years ago, after a helicopter crash off Cyprus—"

"He faked his own death?" asked Richard.

Daumier nodded. "It is not an easy matter to resign from Intelligence and simply start work as a mercenary. One would be subject to constraints."

"But if one is declared dead—"

"Precisely." Daumier skimmed the next page and stopped. "Here it is," he said. "The link we have been searching for. In 1972, M. Foch served as our liaison to the American mission. It seems there was a telephone threat against Ambassador Sutherland's family. For several years, Amiel Foch remained in contact with the Sutherland household. He was later reassigned to other duties, until his…death."

"When he became available for private clients. To perform any service," said Hugh.

"Including assassination." Daumier closed the folder and said to his assistant, "Bring in Mrs. Sutherland."

The woman who walked through the door was the same brash and confident Nina Sutherland that Richard had always known. She swept into the room, glanced around with disdain at her audience, then gracefully settled into a chair. "A bit late in the day for a command performance, don't you think?" she asked.

And a performance was just what they were going to get, thought Richard. Unless they shook her up. He pulled up a chair and sat down, facing her. "You know that Anthony's been taken into custody?"

A flicker of fear—just a flicker—rippled through her eyes. "It's a mistake, of course. He's never done anything wrong in his life."

"Murder through hire? Contracts with assassins?" Richard raised an eyebrow. "Ironclad charges, multiple witnesses. I'd say this is serious enough to warrant a very long stay behind bars."

"But he's only a boy and not—"

"He's of age. And fully responsible for his crimes." Richard glanced at Daumier. "Claude and I were just discussing what a shame it was. To be locked up so young. He'll be, how old when he's released, Claude? Fifty, do you think?"

"I would guess closer to sixty," said Daumier.

"Sixty." Richard shook his head and sighed. "His whole life behind him. No wife. No children." Richard looked Nina sympathetically in the eyes. "No grandchildren..."

Nina's face had turned ashen. She said in a whisper, "What do you want from me?"

"Cooperation."

"And what's my payback?"

"We can be lenient," said Daumier. "After all, he *is* just a boy."

Swallowing hard, Nina looked away. "It's not his fault. He doesn't deserve to be—"

"He's responsible for the deaths of two French agents. And the attempted murders of Marie St. Pierre and Jordan."

"He didn't do anything!"

"But he hired Amiel Foch to do his dirty work. What kind of a monster did you raise, Nina?"

"He was only trying to protect *me!*"

"From what?"

Nina's head drooped. "The past," she whispered. "It never goes away. Everything else changes, but the past…"

The past, thought Richard, remembering Heinrich Leitner's words. *We're always in its shadow.* "You were Delphi," he said. "Weren't you?"

Nina said nothing.

He leaned forward, and his voice dropped to a quiet, almost intimate murmur. "Perhaps it started out as a bit of a lark," he suggested. "An amusing game of spies and counterspies. Perhaps you liked the excitement. Or was it the money that tempted you? Whatever the reason, you passed a secret or two to the other side. Then it was classified documents. And suddenly you were in their pocket."

"It was only for a short time!"

"But by then it was too late. NATO intelligence got

wind of it. And they were closing in. So you worked out a way to shift the blame. Somehow you lured Bernard and Madeline to your little love nest in Rue Myrha. There you shot them both."

"No."

"You planted the documents near Bernard's body."

"No."

Richard grabbed Nina by the shoulders and forced her to look at him. "And then you walked away and went on with your merry life. Isn't that how it went?"

Nina gave a pitiful sob. "I didn't kill them!"

"Isn't it?"

"I swear I didn't kill them! They were already dead!"

Richard released her. Nina sank back into the chair, her whole body shuddering with sobs.

"Who killed them?" demanded Richard. "Amiel Foch?"

"No, I never asked him to."

"Philippe?"

She looked up sharply. "No! He was the one who *found* them. He was frantic when he called me. Afraid he'd be accused of it. That's when I called in Foch. Asked him to make arrangements with Rideau, the landlord. A cash payment to change his testimony."

"And the documents? Who planted them?"

"Foch did. By then, the police had already been called. Foch had to slip the briefcase into the garret."

Jordan cut in, "She's just admitted she's Delphi. Now we're supposed to believe some other mysterious culprit did the killing?"

"It's the truth!" insisted Nina.

"Oh, right!" sneered Jordan. "And the killer just happened to choose the very flat where you and Philippe met every week?"

Nina shook her head in bewilderment. "I don't know why he chose our flat."

"It had to be you. Or Philippe," said Jordan.

"I would never…he would never…"

"Who else knew about the garret?" asked Richard.

"No one."

"Marie St. Pierre?"

"No." She paused, then whispered, "Yes, perhaps…"

"So Philippe's wife knew."

Nina nodded miserably. "But no one else."

"Wait," Jordan suddenly interjected. "Someone else *did* know about it."

Everyone looked at him.

"What?" said Richard.

"I heard it from Reggie. Helena knew about the affair—Marie told her. And if Marie knew about the garret on Rue Myrha, then—"

"So did Helena." Richard stared at Jordan. With that one look, they both knew what the other was thinking.

Beryl.

Instantly they both turned to leave. "Get us some backup!" Richard snapped to Daumier. "Have them meet us there!"

"The Vanes' residence?"

Richard didn't answer; he was already running out the door.

"Get in the car," said Helena.

Beryl halted, her hand frozen on the door handle of the Mercedes. "There'll be questions, Helena."

"And I'll have the answers. I was asleep, you see. I

slept all night. And when I woke up, you were gone. Left the compound on your own, never to be seen again."

"Reggie will remember—"

"Reggie won't remember a thing. He's stone drunk. As far as he knows, I never left the bed."

"They'll suspect you—"

"It's been twenty years, Beryl. And they still don't suspect." She raised the gun. "Get in. The driver's seat. Or do I have to change my story? Tell them I thought I was shooting a burglar?"

Beryl stared at the gun barrel pointed squarely at her chest. She had no choice. Helena really would shoot her. She climbed into the car.

Helena slid in beside her and tossed the keys into Beryl's lap. "Start the engine."

Beryl turned the key; the Mercedes purred to life like a contented cat. "My mother never meant to hurt you," said Beryl softly. "She was never interested in Reggie. She never wanted him."

"But he wanted *her.* Oh, I saw how he used to look at her! Do you know, he used to say her name in his sleep. There I'd be, lying next to him, and he'd be thinking of her. I never knew, I never really knew, if they were..." She swallowed. "Drive."

"Where?"

"Just go out the gate. Go!"

Beryl eased the Mercedes out of the garage and across the cobblestoned courtyard. Helena pressed a remote control and the iron gate automatically swung open. It closed again behind them as they drove through. Ahead stretched the tree-lined road. No other cars, no other witnesses.

The steering wheel felt slick with her sweat. Beryl

gripped it tightly, just to keep her hands from shaking. "My father never hurt you," she whispered. "Why did you have to kill him?"

"Someone had to be blamed. Why not make it a dead man? And the fact it was Nina's secret flat—that made it all the more convenient." She laughed. "You should have seen how Nina and Philippe scrambled to cover things up."

"And Delphi?"

Helena shook her head in bewilderment. "What about Delphi?"

So she knows nothing about it, thought Beryl. *All this time, we've been chasing the wrong clues. Richard will never know—will never suspect—what really happened.*

The road began to curve and wind through the trees. They were headed into the depths of the Bois de Boulogne. *Is this where they'll find me?* she wondered, dismayed. *In some lonely copse of trees? At the muddy bottom of a pond?*

She peered ahead to the road beyond their headlights. They were approaching another curve.

It may be my only chance. I can let her shoot me. Or I can go down fighting. She pointed the car on a straight course. Then she hit the accelerator pedal. The engine roared and tires screamed. Beryl was thrust back against the seat as the Mercedes lurched forward.

Helena cried out, "No!" and clawed for control of the wheel. A split-second before they hit the trees, Helena managed to swerve them sideways. Suddenly they were tumbling like helpless riders in an out-of-control carnival ride. The Mercedes toppled over and over, windows shattered, and the two passengers were flung against the dashboard.

The car came to rest on its roof.

It was the blare of the horn that dragged Beryl back to consciousness. And the pain. Excruciating pain, tearing at her leg. She tried to move and realized that her chest was wedged against the steering wheel, and that her head was somehow cradled in the small space between the windshield and the upside-down dashboard. She pushed away from the steering wheel. The effort made her cry out in pain, but she managed to slide her body a few precious inches across the crumpled roof. For a moment, she rested, gasping for breath, waiting for the pain in her leg to ease. Then, gritting her teeth, she pushed again and managed to slide through into a larger pocket of space. The front seat? Everything seemed so mangled, so confusing in the darkness. The tumble had left her disoriented.

But she was not so dazed that she didn't smell the odor of gasoline growing stronger every second. *I have to get to a window—have to squeeze through before it explodes.* Blindly she reached out to feel her surroundings, and her hand shoved up against something warm. Something wet. She twisted her head around and came face-to-face with Helena's corpse.

Beryl screamed. Suddenly frantic to get out, to escape those sightless eyes, she squirmed away, clawing for the window. New pain, even more excruciating, ripped through her shattered leg and flooded her eyes with tears. She touched window frame, bits of glass and then...a branch! *I'm almost there. Almost there.*

Half crawling, half dragging herself, she managed to squeeze through the opening. Just as her body rolled onto the ground, the dirt beneath her seemed to give way and she began to slide down a leafy embankment. She landed in a ditch near some trees.

A burst of light suddenly shot into the sky. Through eyes blurred with agony, she looked up and saw the first flicker of the inferno. Seconds later, she heard the popping of glass, then a terrifying whoosh as a fountain of flames engulfed the vehicle.

Why, Helena? Why? The flames blurred, faded into a gathering darkness. She closed her eyes and shivered among the fallen leaves.

Three miles from the Vanes' residence, they spotted the fire. It was a car, upended, stretched diagonally across the road. A Mercedes.

"It's Helena's," shouted Richard. "My God, it's Helena's!" He leaped out and ran toward the burning car. He almost tripped over a shoe lying in the road. To his horror he saw it was a woman's pump. *"Beryl!"* he screamed. He was about to make a desperate lunge for the car door when the flames suddenly shot higher. A window burst out, scattering glass across the pavement. The searing heat sent him stumbling backward, his nostrils stinging with the stench of his own singed hair. He recovered his balance and was about to make another lunge through the flames when Jordan grabbed his arm.

"Wait!" cried Jordan.

Richard wrenched away. "Have to get her out!"

"No, *listen!*"

That's when he heard it—a moan, almost inaudible. It came not from the car, but from somewhere in the trees.

At once he and Jordan were scrambling along the roadside, yelling Beryl's name. Again, Richard heard the moan, closer now, coming from the shadows just below the road. He clambered down the dirt bank and stumbled into a drainage ditch.

That's where he found her, sprawled among the leaves. Barely conscious.

He gathered her up and was terrified by how limp, how cold her body felt in his arms. *She's in shock,* he realized. *We have precious little time...*

"Have to get her to a hospital!" he yelled.

Jordan ran ahead and yanked open the car door. Richard, clutching Beryl in his arms, slid into the back seat.

"Go!" he barked.

"Hang on," muttered Jordan, scrambling into the driver's seat. "It's going to be a wild ride."

With a screech of tires, their car shot off down the road. *Stay with me, Beryl,* Richard begged silently as he cradled her body in his arms. *Please, darling. Stay with me...*

But as the car sped through the darkness, she seemed to grow ever colder to his touch.

Through the haze of anesthesia, she heard him call her name, but the sound of his voice seemed so very far away, seemed to come from a distant place she could not possibly reach. Then she felt his hand close tightly over hers, and she knew he was right beside her. She could not see his face; she could not muster enough strength to open her eyes. Yet she knew he was there, that he would still be there when she awoke the next morning.

But it was Jordan whom she saw sitting by her bed. The late-morning sunlight streamed over his fair hair and a leather-bound book of poetry lay in his lap. He was reading Milton. *Dear Jordan,* she thought. *Ever reliable, ever serene. If only I had inherited such peace of mind.*

Jordan glanced up from the page and saw that she was awake. "Welcome back to the world, little sister," he said with a smile.

She groaned. "I'm not so sure I want to be back."

"The leg?"

"Killing me."

He reached for the call button. "Time to indulge in the miracle of morphine."

But even miracles take time. After the nurse delivered the injection, Beryl closed her eyes and waited for the pain to ease, for the blessed numbness to descend.

"Better?" asked Jordan.

"Not yet." She took a deep breath. "God, I hate being an invalid. Talk to me. Please."

"About what?"

Richard, she thought. *Please tell me about Richard. Why he isn't here. Why he's not the one sitting in that chair...*

Jordan said, quietly, "You know, he was here. Earlier this morning. But then Daumier called."

She lay still, not speaking. Waiting to hear more.

"He cares about you, Beryl. I'm sure he does." Jordan closed his book and set it on the bedside table. "Really, he seems an agreeable fellow. Quite capable."

"Capable," she murmured. "Yes, he is that."

"He didn't turn tail and run. He did look after you."

"As a favor," she amended. "To Uncle Hugh."

He didn't answer. And she thought that Jordie, too, had his doubts about their odds for happiness. And so did she. From the very beginning.

The morphine began to take effect. Little by little, she felt herself drift toward sleep. Only vaguely did she hear Richard enter the room and speak softly to Jordan. They murmured something about Helena and her body being burned beyond recognition. As the drug swept her brain toward unconsciousness, a memory suddenly flashed with horrifying vividness into her mind—the flames engulfing the car, engulfing Helena.

For loving too deeply, too fiercely, this was Helena's punishment.

She felt Richard take her hand and press it to his lips.

And what punishment, she wondered, would be hers?

Epilogue

Buckinghamshire, England
Six weeks later

Froggie was restless, stamping about in her stall, whinnying for escape.

"Look at her, the poor thing," Beryl said and sighed. "She hasn't been run nearly enough, and I think she's going quite insane. You'll have to exercise her for me."

"Me? On the back of that…that maniac?" Jordan snorted. "I'm much too fond of my own neck."

Beryl hobbled over to the stall on her crutches. At once Froggie poked her head over the door and gave Beryl an insistent want-to-go-running nudge. "Oh, but she's such a pussycat."

"A pussycat with a foul temper."

"And she so badly needs a good, hard gallop."

Jordan looked at his sister, who was wobbling unsteadily on leg cast and crutches. She seemed so pale and thin these days. As if those long weeks in the hospital had drained something vital from her spirit. A bit of pallor was to be expected, of course, considering all the blood she'd lost, all the days of pain she'd suffered after the operation to pin her shattered femur. Now the leg was healing well, and the pain was only a memory, but she still seemed only a ghost of herself.

It was Richard Wolf's fault.

At least the fellow had been decent enough to hang around during Beryl's hospitalization. In fact, he'd practically haunted her room, spending every daylight hour by her bed. And all the flowers! Every morning, a fresh bouquet.

Then, one day, he was gone. Jordan hadn't heard the explanation. He'd walked into his sister's hospital room that morning and found her staring out the window, all packed and ready to go home to Chetwynd.

Three weeks ago, they'd flown back. And she's been brooding ever since, he thought, looking at her wan face.

"Go on, Jordie," she said. "Give her a bit of a run. It'll be another month before I can ride her again."

Resignedly, Jordan swung open the stall door and led Froggie out to be saddled. "You'd better behave, young lady," he muttered to the beast. "No rearing. No bucking. And definitely no trampling your poor, defenseless rider."

Froggie gave him a look that could only be interpreted as the equine equivalent of *we'll see about that.*

Jordan mounted and gave Beryl a wave.

"Take care of her!" Beryl called out. "See she doesn't hurt herself!"

"Your concern is most touching!" he managed to blurt out just before Froggie took off at a mad gallop for the fields. Jordan managed a last backward glance at Beryl standing forlornly by the stable. How small she looked, how fragile. Not at all the Beryl he knew. Would she ever be herself again?

Froggie was bearing him toward the woods. He concentrated on hanging on for dear life as the beast made a beeline for the stone wall. "You just have to take that bloody hurdle, don't you?" he muttered as Froggie's mane whipped his face. "Which means *I* have to take the bloody hurdle—"

Together they flew over the wall, clearing it neatly. *Still in the saddle,* thought Jordan with a grin of triumph. *Not so easy to get rid of me, is it?*

It was the last thought in his head before Froggie tossed him off her back.

Jordan landed, fortunately enough, on a large clump of moss. As he sprawled beneath the wildly spinning treetops, he was vaguely aware of the sound of tires grinding across the dirt road, and then he heard someone call his name. Groggily he sat up.

Froggie was standing over him, looking not in the least bit apologetic. And behind her, climbing out of a red MG, was Richard Wolf.

"Are you all right?" Richard called out, running toward him.

"Tell me, Wolf," Jordan groaned. "Are you out to kill all the Tavistocks? Or are you after one of us in particular?"

Laughing, Richard helped him to his feet. "I'd lay the blame where it belongs. On the horse."

Both men looked at Froggie. She answered with what sounded suspiciously like a laugh.

Richard asked quietly, "How's Beryl doing these days?"

Jordan began to clap the dirt from his trousers. "Her leg's healing fine."

"Besides the leg?"

"Not so fine." Jordan straightened and looked the other man in the eye. "Why did you walk out?"

Sighing, Richard looked off in the direction of Chetwynd. "She asked me to."

"What?" Jordan stared at him in bewilderment. "She never told me—"

"She's a Tavistock, like you. Doesn't believe in whining or complaining. Or losing face. It's that pride of hers."

"Ah, so it was like that, was it?" Jordan said. "An argument?"

"Not even that. It just seemed, with all those differences between us…" He shook his head and laughed. "Face it, Jordan. She's tea and crumpets, I'm coffee and doughnuts. She'd hate it in Washington. And I'm not sure I could adjust to…this." He gestured to the rolling fields of Chetwynd.

But you will adjust, foresaw Jordan. *And so will she. Because it's plain for any idiot to see that you two belong together.*

"Anyway," said Richard, "when Niki called and reminded me we had a job in New Delhi, Beryl told me to go. She thought it would be a good test for us to be apart for a while. Said the Royal Family does it that way.

To see if absence makes the heart—and hormones—forget."

"And does it?"

Richard grinned. "Not a chance," he said, and climbed back into his car. "I may be signing up with your wild and crazy family, after all. Any objections?"

"None," said Jordan. "But I *will* offer a bit of advice. That is, if you two expect to share a long and healthy life together."

"What's the advice?"

"Shoot the horse."

Laughing, Richard let out the brake and sped away toward Chetwynd.

Toward Beryl.

As Jordan watched the MG vanish around the bend, he thought, *Good luck to you, little sister. I'm glad one of us has finally found someone to love. Now if only I could be so fortunate...*

He turned to Froggie. "And as for you," he said aloud, "I am about to teach you exactly who's boss around here."

Froggie gave a snort. Then, with a triumphant toss of her mane, she turned and galloped away, riderless, toward Chetwynd.

"It's quite unlike you to be brooding this way," said Uncle Hugh as he picked another tomato and set it in his basket. He looked faintly ridiculous in his floppy gardening hat. More like the groundskeeper than the lord of the manor. Crouching on his knees, he uncovered another bright red globe and carefully plucked the treasure. "Don't know why you're so gloomy these days. After all, the leg's almost healed."

"It's not the leg," said Beryl.

"One would think you were permanently crippled."

"It's not the leg."

"Well, what is it, then?" asked Hugh, moving on to the row of pole beans. Suddenly he stopped and glanced back at her. "Oh, it's him, isn't it?"

Sighing, Beryl reached for her crutches and rose from the garden bench. "I don't wish to discuss it."

"You never do."

"I still don't," she said, and stubbornly headed down the brick path toward the maze. She brushed past the edging of lavender, stirring the scents of the late summer garden. Once they'd walked this path together, she thought. And now she was walking it alone.

She entered the maze and, using her crutches, maneuvered around all the secret twists and turns. At last she emerged at the center and sat down on the stone bench. *Yes, I'm brooding again,* she realized. *Uncle Hugh's right. Have to stop this and get on with my life.*

But first, she would have to stop thinking of him. Had he stopped thinking of her? All the doubts, the fears, came back to assail her. She'd put him to the test, she thought. And he'd failed it.

From a distance, she heard someone call her name. It was so faint at first, she thought she might have imagined it. But there it was again—moving closer now!

She lurched to her feet, wobbling on the crutches. *"Richard?"*

"Beryl?" came the answering shout. "Where are you?"

"In the maze!"

His footsteps moved closer along the path. "Where?"

"The center!"

Through the high hedge walls, she heard his sheepish laughter. "And now I'm expected to find my way to the cheese?"

"Just think of it," she challenged him, "as a test of true love."

"Or true insanity," he muttered, rustling into the maze.

"I'm quite annoyed with you, you know," she called.

"I think I've noticed."

"You didn't write. You didn't call, not once!"

"I was too busy trying to catch planes back to London. And besides, I wanted you to miss me. Did you?"

"No, I didn't."

"You didn't?"

"Not at all." She bit her lip. "Oh, perhaps a bit…"

"Ah, so you *did* miss me—"

"But not much."

"I missed *you.*"

She paused. "Did you?" she asked softly.

"So much, in fact, that if I don't find the bloody center of this bloody maze pretty damn quick, I'm going to—"

"Going to what?" she asked breathlessly.

A rustle of branches made her turn. Suddenly he was there beside her, pulling her into his arms, covering her mouth with a kiss so deep, so insistent, she felt herself swaying dizzily. The crutches slipped away and fell to the ground. She didn't need them—not when he was there to hold her.

He drew away and smiled at her. "Hello again, Miss Tavistock," he whispered.

"You came back," she murmured. "You really came back."

"Did you think I wouldn't?"

"Does that mean you've thought about it? About us?"

He laughed. "I could scarcely concentrate on anything else. On the job, the client. Finally I had to call in Niki to pinch-hit for me, while I straighten out this mess with you."

She asked softly, "You think it *can* be straightened out?"

Gently he framed her face with his hands. "I don't know. Some folks would probably call us a long shot."

"And they'd be right. There are so many things that could pull us apart..."

"And just as many things that will keep us together." He lowered his face to hers, gently brushed her lips with his. "I confess, I'll never make a proper gentleman. Cricket's not my bag. And you'll have to put a gun to my head to get me up on a horse. But if you're willing to overlook those terrible flaws..."

She threw her arms around his neck. "What flaws?" she whispered, and their lips met again.

From the distance came the peal of the ancient church bells. Six o'clock. The coming of twilight and shadows, sweetly scented. *And love,* thought Beryl as he pulled her, laughing, into his arms.

Quite definitely, love.

* * * * *

USA TODAY bestselling author **Rita Herron** wrote her first book when she was twelve but didn't think real people grew up to be writers. Now she writes so she doesn't have to get a real job. A former kindergarten teacher and workshop leader, she traded storytelling to kids for writing romance, and now she writes romantic comedies and romantic suspense. Rita lives in Georgia with her family. She loves to hear from readers, so please visit her website, ritaherron.com.

Books by Rita Herron

Harlequin Intrigue

A Badge of Honor Mystery

Mysterious Abduction
Left to Die
Protective Order
Suspicious Circumstances

The Heroes of Horseshoe Creek

Lock, Stock and McCullen
McCullen's Secret Son
Roping Ray McCullen
Warrior Son
The Missing McCullen
The Last McCullen

Visit the Author Profile page at Harlequin.com for more titles.

JUSTICE FOR A RANGER

Rita Herron

To Mallory Kane and Delores Fossen for birthing this fabulous story line and letting me be a part of it. Here's to more Rangers stories in the future...

Chapter 1

Hell must have finally frozen over in Justice, Texas.

That was the only explanation for the phone call requesting his services from his half brothers, Lieutenant Zane McKinney and Sergeant Sloan McKinney, both Texas Rangers.

As was Cole, but they had never met or asked for his help on a case before.

Not him—the bastard, bad-boy brother they all hated.

Cole traced a proud finger over the silver star he'd earned through his own blood, sweat and tears. He was a sergeant now himself. He'd made the grade with no help. No financial support or fancy education. No loving, doting parents.

Not like Zane and Sloan.

A bitter laugh rumbled from deep within his gut as

he threw his clothes into a duffel bag, stepped into the hot sunshine and climbed on his Harley. Dammit. He'd been ordered to leave his current case behind, come straight out of the trenches where he'd been working a lead on a smuggling ring along the border, to assist in Justice.

Of course, his half brothers must be desperate to exonerate their father, to finally free him of the murder charges that had hung around his neck like an albatross the past sixteen years. A murder investigation that had been revived because Sarah Wallace, daughter of Lou Anne Wallace, the woman his father had slept with and had been accused of strangling with her own designer purse, had just been murdered in the same hotel room, in the same manner.

And most likely by the same person who'd killed her mother.

Bitterness swelled inside Cole as choking as the insufferable summer heat. Did his brothers actually think he gave a damn about the outcome? That he'd come running to team up with them to save their father because he wanted to see Jim McKinney's good name restored?

Jim McKinney—the father who'd abandoned him and his mother. The father who'd never acknowledged his existence. The father who had been nothing more than a sperm donor on his behalf.

The man who'd broken his mother's heart.

Barb Tyler had never married after her short affair with Jim McKinney. She'd claimed Jim had ruined her for another man. And she'd taken that love with her to her grave no more than a year after Jim McKinney's arrest. If Cole hadn't known better, he'd have thought she'd died of grief for the man's lost reputation herself.

He hated Jim for it.

Still, he was a Texas Ranger. Part of the most revered, effective investigative law enforcement agency in the world. And he was damn proud to be a lawman. God knows he'd been on a crash course to jail himself when Clete McHaven, the rancher his mother had cooked for, had caught him trying to steal from his ranch and had made him work off the debt or go to the pen.

He scrubbed a hand over his three days' growth of beard stubble, knowing he looked like hell as he strapped on his biker's helmet, cranked up the Harley's engine and tore down the driveway. Dust and pebbles spewed from his tires as he careened onto the highway. Anger and determination had him pushing the speed limit.

Not that he was in a hurry to see the long-lost family that had cast him aside as if he was a leper.

But he had a chance to prove that a real Texas Ranger didn't need book education or to be a good ole boy. That his tracking skills had earned him a spot as a top-notch lawman.

He had no intention of begging for accolades from the McKinneys, of trying to worm his way into their snotty huddle. Hell, he didn't need them or their approval.

And he would not play favorites in the investigation.

Jim McKinney had been a bastard who couldn't keep his pants zipped. And although he'd never been convicted of murder, if he had killed Lou Anne Wallace and her daughter, Cole would find out. Then he would snap the handcuffs around his wrists and haul him to jail where he belonged.

And he wouldn't think twice about who suffered when he did.

* * *

To some people going home meant reuniting with loved ones. Reliving warm memories and seeing friends. Safety.

To Joey Hendricks it meant pain and anxiety. Opening wounds that had never healed. Dealing with her own guilt over her two-year-old brother's disappearance sixteen years ago. And facing a mother and father she hadn't spoken to in years. A mother and father who hated each other.

But she did work for the governor as a special investigator and when the infamous governor of the great state of Texas said jump, she jumped.

The sign for Justice, Texas, appeared, and she grimaced. At first sight, it looked like a cozy small town in which to raise a family. A place where everyone knew his neighbor, no one ever met a stranger and they would welcome her back with loving arms.

But secrets and hatred had festered in the town like sores that wouldn't heal. And someone wanted to keep those secrets hidden. They'd murdered Sarah Wallace to do so and had tried to kill her sister Anna and the sheriff, Carley Matheson, when they'd searched for the truth.

Her heart turned over as she passed Main Street Diner. She'd been shocked when her mother, whose total culinary skills when Joey had been growing up constituted throwing together a plate of cheese and crackers to accompany her cocktail dinner, had bought the establishment. She'd been shocked even further to learn that Donna had given up the booze and pills.

Not shocked enough to want to see her just yet, though.

Oh, it was inevitable that she face both her dysfunctional parents, but first she wanted to learn more about the investigation. Just how much and what kind of evidence did the sheriff have against Leland and Donna Hendricks?

Late evening shadows cast gray lines across the street and storefront awnings as she spotted the Matheson Inn, where she'd reserved a room. She tightened her fingers around the steering wheel and veered into a parking spot, then stared at the burned-down ruins of the Justice jail. The sign for the police department had turned to black soot. Ashes, charred black wood, burned metal all lay in rubble. Only the metal bars of the jail cell remained standing, empty and exposed, as if still waiting for a prisoner. A stark reminder that the original killer had never been incarcerated. And now he'd murdered again.

Poor Sarah Wallace… Memories of her troubled teenage years haunted her. When Lou Anne and Leland had married, Lou Anne's daughters, Sarah and Anna, had moved in with them for a short time. But they hadn't been any happier about the union than Joey, so they'd moved out shortly after. She hadn't been close to either of them, but she hated to think that Sarah had been murdered.

The stench of the fire and charred remains still filled the air, wafting in the suffocating heat as she climbed out. In front, a media crew and several locals had gathered, a camera rolling.

The very reason she was here. To control the media circus. More than one investigation had been blown because of some dim-witted or too-aggressive reporter.

Innocent people had been tried and convicted in the process.

Other times the guilty had gone free.

The governor was adamant that the past not repeat itself. Lou Anne Wallace's murderer had escaped sixteen years ago, as had the person who'd kidnapped Justin, Joey's own baby brother. The town of Justice had never gotten over either event. Jim McKinney's impeccable Texas Ranger reputation had been ruined because of his affair with Lou Anne and his subsequent arrest, his family shattered because of it.

And it had destroyed what was left of Joey's already crumbling family, as well.

The governor had worked with the D.A.'s office at the time of Lou Anne's murder. Ironically Joey had been afraid that her family name would hinder her career, but the governor had given her a chance to prove herself. And she had. In fact, Governor Grange had been more of a father figure to her the past four years than her own dad had.

And he'd trusted her enough to send her here now, trusted her to be objective about the McKinneys. After all, Jim McKinney's sons were in charge of the case. Rangers investigating one of their own, especially a family member—definitely a conflict of interest.

Tucking a strand of her unruly blond hair behind one ear, she buttoned her suit jacket and headed toward the media. Harold Dennison, a reporter who had a reputation for causing trouble, stood in front of the dilapidated ruins recounting the events of the night of the fire.

"Local sheriff Carley Matheson and Texas Ranger, former sheriff of Justice and hometown boy Sergeant Sloan McKinney were inside the jail when an explosion rocked the walls and caused the building to catch fire. Both Sheriff Matheson and Sergeant McKinney barely escaped with their lives." The camera panned across the site, capturing the destruction and violence. "Sheriff Matheson has been taken to a safe house but continues to work in conjunction with the Texas Rangers to solve the current homicide, which appears to be connected to the murder of Lou Anne Wallace sixteen years ago."

"Do they have any leads yet?" an elderly man asked from the crowd.

A woman in the front row hugged her children to her side protectively. "When will there be an arrest?"

"Did Jim McKinney kill Sarah Wallace and her mother?" someone else shouted.

Dennison caught sight of Joey, and a predatory gleam appeared in his eyes. "Good question. I see someone here who might have the answer."

Joey braced herself for a confrontation. Dennison was like a snake coiled to attack anyone even remotely related to the crime.

And she was definitely related.

"Miss Hendricks is from the governor's office and, I believe, one of your own homegrown girls." He offered a challenging look that sent alarm bells clanging in her head. His comment had been a direct hit to irk her.

She'd heard his ugly insinuations before. As if she was unworthy of working with the esteemed governor. The daughter of a small-town drunk and a rich oil baron father who might have sold his own baby's life for a dollar.

Well, a hundred thousand to be exact, but same difference.

"Would you like to address the citizens?" Dennison

extended the microphone to her as if they were working together.

Not on his life, they weren't.

But Joey had learned how to play the game with the big guns. And she'd be damned if she'd let this pigheaded moron intimidate her.

She pasted on a professional smile and accepted the mike. "Joey Hendricks here. I am a special investigator with the governor's office. I want to assure the residents that the governor is aware of the situation in Justice. The Department of Public Safety and the Texas Rangers are working diligently to solve the recent homicide as well as the murder of Lou Anne Wallace, and the attempted murders of Anna Wallace, Sheriff Matheson and Sergeant McKinney. We intend to restore a sense of peace and order to Justice as soon as possible." She smiled, injecting confidence into each word. "It's imperative that you folks remain calm. If you have any information pertaining to these crimes, no matter how insignificant, please step forward. Together, we can end the terror seizing the town."

Dennison arched a brow. "So that means that you're prepared to own up to your family's possible involvement in the murders?"

Heat caused rivulets of perspiration to collect on her nape. "I trust the Texas Rangers and Justice Police Department to find the truth." She gestured toward the black-sooted police department building. "In spite of the recent demise of our local facility, the law enforcement agents are working 24/7. When information becomes available, I will see that it is dispensed to facilitate an arrest." She leveled a warning look at Dennison. "After all, we don't want the investigation ruined by false reporting or irresponsible press coverage."

Dennison moved like a true viper. "Is it true that the police are focusing the investigation on your parents, Miss Hendricks? That your father tampered with his own surveillance tapes to hide his part in your brother's kidnapping and murder? That he killed his wife, Lou Anne, because she intended to disclose his scheme?"

Joey's insides clenched, a tremor running through her, although she tried desperately to mask any reaction. "As I said before, I will disclose information as soon as the facts become available. To speculate about unsubstantiated allegations would be detrimental to the investigation."

He opened his mouth to continue his interrogation, but she cut him off with a withering look. "Thank you in advance for your cooperation." She shoved the microphone back in Dennison's hand and walked away.

Head high, shoulders rigid, she passed the inn, then the Main Street Diner and headed to the one spot in town that held a few precious good memories. Although there were bad ones there, as well.

The Last Call. She'd dragged her mother from the bar more times than she could count. Had driven her home and helped her to bed, listening to her vent her anger at Leland for his infidelities and her anguish over her missing toddler son.

But Joey had had her first taste of hard liquor in the establishment, too. And lost her virginity afterward.

A sardonic laugh escaped her. Sex was out of the question tonight.

But a drink was definitely in the picture.

Something strong to help her forget that her parents

were once again smack-dab in the middle of a homicide investigation. That she blamed them for her brother's disappearance.

That her own guilt was unbearable.

Suddenly a low roar rent the night air, and tires screeched. A lone headlight blared in her eyes. She froze momentarily, then realized it wasn't a car, but a motorcycle careening toward her. A Harley with a leather-clad man all in black.

His tires screeched and sparks flew from the asphalt. He obviously didn't see her.

And if she didn't move fast, he was going to plow right into her.

Chapter 2

Cole gripped the handlebars with a white-knuckled grip as he skidded sideways. Sparks flew from the asphalt, and his tires ground against the gravel, sending small rocks scattering in a dozen directions. Instead of having the good sense to move, the leggy blonde froze in place, making the blood rush to his head and sending a shard of panic through his chest.

He had to miss her, but damn—he didn't want to tear up the expensive machine below him, either.

Okay, she was much more important than his Harley, but still…

He caught the bulk of the bike's weight with his muscled strength, tilted his body sideways to compensate for the spin and to keep the Hog from rolling, then roared past her and skidded to a stop near the rail hitching post in front of the Last Call. She jumped into the shadows of the awning just as he cut the engine.

Hissing a sigh of relief and frustration, he shot off the bike, whirled around and glared at her. Adrenaline fired his veins and sent a furious round of curse words sailing past his lips. He wanted to wrap his hands around her delectable little throat. "What the...didn't your mother teach you not to stand in the street?"

"You moron!" she shouted back at the same moment. "You nearly killed me."

Moron? "*You're* questioning *my* intelligence?" He ripped off his helmet, then slung his hair out of his face. "Dammit, sugar, you're the one who needs to watch where you're going!"

"I could say the same thing to you." She jabbed a sharp red fingernail at his chest. "I don't know what kind of hole you crawled out of, but pedestrians have the right-of-way in this town, and the speed limit is... well, you were way over it."

Her scathing words reminded him too quickly what he'd already known—that he shouldn't expect a warm welcome in Justice. That some people here thought he was a low-life slime just because he was the bastard son of Jim McKinney.

The very reason he'd headed to the bar first thing.

Before he faced his half brothers the next morning, he intended to have a cold one, unwind and cool off. And where better to get the local scoop than the town's pub?

Loose lips liked to talk...

A sliver of moonlight caught her blond hair and sassy eyes, and his gut did an odd flip-flop. She was the hottest woman he'd ever laid eyes on. Her bare legs came up to her neck, the suit jacket she wore had popped the top button and a generous amount of cleavage spilled over the top of a black lacy camisole beneath. Damn.

He'd never met a drink or a woman he didn't like, or at least wanted to taste. And this was one tall drink of water that tempted his thirst, badly.

"You give every man you meet this much trouble?"

She gave him a scathing look. "Men are nothing but cheaters and liars. They use women, then walk away when they're finished."

"Ouch." She'd been hurt badly by someone. He swallowed against the sudden dryness of his throat. He felt as if he'd eaten dust. Or maybe her comment hit too close to home. "What if I said I'm sorry?"

She tossed a silky-looking strand of hair over her shoulder. "For yourself or for the sorriness of all those with the Y chromosome?"

His mouth twitched. "Both."

Her lips finally quirked. "All right. I… I…guess you're forgiven."

She glanced back at the jail cell standing like a monument in the center of town across the street, and he realized she might have just come from that media circus. She didn't look happy about it, either.

He'd sped past it, irritated at the thought of facing the mangy reporters. He imagined the headlines with a snarl.

Poor little illegitimate son shows up in town to help exonerate his father.

So what was her problem with them?

Not that he cared, but looking at her was a nice diversion. "Let me buy you a cold one. You look like you need it as much as I do."

"You can't imagine." She rolled her shoulders, and a whispery sigh escaped her that made his chest tighten.

Man, he did like women. All their softness. The way they smelled. The feel of their skin against his.

And hers looked soft and creamy. And her voice, now she'd stopped screaming at him, sounded low and throaty.

Sultry.

Oblivious to the train of his lustful thoughts, she sashayed ahead of him and reached for the door. His gaze latched on to the rounded curve of her hips in that short, tight skirt, and his hands itched to reach out and wrap themselves around her tush.

He shoved them into his pockets instead. Women were trouble, and he was here on business, not to get laid or involved with a local.

A sea of smoke and noise engulfed him as they entered the bar. Willie Nelson's voice droned out from the jukebox, peanut shells littered the scarred wooden floor, and the scent of beer and cigarette smoke clouded the room.

Ahh, pure heaven to a man's senses.

She hesitated slightly, though, and he noticed the men in the back stop their pool game to gape at her. At the same time, two old-timers sharing a pitcher turned to ogle her, and the bartender, a fortysomething bald man with a thick neck, raised an appreciative brow. This girl would not be paying for her own drinks. No sirree.

But what would the jerks expect in return?

Cole's protective instincts surged to life. "How about a booth?"

She plunked into a corner one, and he claimed the seat across from her, then shot the other men a warning look as if to say she was off-limits. Outside the shadows of night and the awning had shielded her face, but although the lights were dim now, he saw her face clearly.

He'd thought he'd sweated outside in his leathers with the summer heat beating down on him on the ride into Justice, but his temperature skyrocketed toward the hundreds as he realized who this sexy bombshell was.

Joey Hendricks—he'd seen her several times on television beside the governor. Holy hell. She was a hotshot special investigator with the state.

And she was also the daughter of the oil baron Leland Hendricks, who'd been accused of the kidnapping and murder of his own child. Hendricks and his ex-wife, Donna, had been major suspects in the murder of Lou Anne Wallace.

The reason she was here hit him like a fist in his gut. She had come for the same reason he had.

Because of the Wallace homicide investigation.

And if he guessed right, her parents were probably suspects in this new murder as well as the first one.

Joey struggled to steady her breathing. Her adrenaline was still racing from the confrontation with Denison and then nearly getting mowed down in the street. And the sight of this biker dude…wow.

All that black leather, dark black scraggly hair down to his shoulders, scruffy bearded face, sweat beading on his forehead gave him a threatening look.

But not in a way that said he might physically hurt her. In a way that screamed raw, primal sexuality. Like a man who'd just returned from a long, heated battle against a beast in the wilderness, a battle he'd no doubt won.

As he would win over any woman he met. All it took was one look into those enigmatic, brooding eyes and the sound of that husky deep voice, and she'd forgotten the fact that he'd nearly killed her.

The moron.

Then again, on closer inspection, his eyes did hold a level of intelligence. Street-smart, not all book-bred. This guy had been around and knew the ropes.

And heaven help her, that incredibly fit body conjured wicked fantasies. He had wide broad shoulders. Pecs to die for. Muscular thighs that could pin a woman beneath him while he tortured her with his tongue.

He gestured toward the bartender, and she took advantage of the moment to assess him in more detail. Even his hands were large, broad. His blunt, strong fingers were sprinkled with dark hair that made her wonder what they would feel like on her. Touching her. Stroking her sensitive skin.

A jagged scar jutted out from the neckline of his black T-shirt, and she imagined the rest of his body beneath. A chest sprinkled with the same dark hair, another scar maybe. And a tattoo or two hidden somewhere on his bronzed skin.

What was she doing? He wasn't her type. She liked sophisticated, educated men. Men with jobs. Men who shaved and bathed regularly.

"What'll you have, sugar?" he drawled.

You. She gaped at his mouth, then realized that she was acting like a fool. And Joey Hendricks, professional investigator for the governor, was not a fool. Never had been. Not over a man.

She'd taken notes from her parents' disastrous divorce and her father's infidelities, and decided relationships just weren't worth the trouble. Although a one-nighter, especially with a hunk like this guy, might be fun. A stress release. Maybe even mind-altering. Certainly hotter than any night she'd experienced in years.

Then she remembered her reason for coming to Justice and vetoed the idea.

The drink would have to suffice. "A shot of tequila."

He arched a thick brow, and she raised her own in challenge. "What? You don't think I can handle it?"

"Honey, I think you can handle anything that comes your way."

With one flick of his hand, he waved the waitress over—a twentysomething girl who turned eyes of adoration toward him—then ordered Joey a shot and a Stella for himself.

He would order a beer with a woman's name. "You don't like tequila?" she asked.

He leaned back against the booth edge, stretched his long legs out so one of them brushed hers beneath the table. "On the contrary. José and I have been best friends for years."

She couldn't help herself. She grinned at his statement. He looked like a tequila-drinking hellion straight from a biker's fest. She imagined him stuffing dollars into the bras of women as they bared their chests for him, and her senses hummed with awareness.

What was wrong with her?

For all she knew he might be a freeloader who had women in ten different cities, and kids to go with each one. Kids he'd never claimed.

Or he could be a criminal.

He turned his dark eyes on her just as the waitress delivered their drinks.

"Thanks." He grabbed the beer and moved the shot in front of Joey.

The girl stood beside him for a moment as if waiting for him to address her again. Annoyed when he didn't pay her more attention, she gave Joey a decidedly unfriendly stare as if they were schoolkids fighting over the only boy in town.

Pickings must be slim in Justice. She should warn the waitress to steer clear of men like him—untrustworthy men in titillating packages that screamed with sex appeal—then decided to heed the warning herself.

She didn't intend to be in Justice long. Then again, she'd have to stay until this case was solved.

And deal with her parents…

What if one of them was arrested? What if they were guilty?

Her lungs tightened at the thought, and she sprinkled salt on her hand, licked it, tossed down the shot, sucked the lime, then dropped the shot glass onto the table with a smile. As she swiped her hand across her mouth, an intense, hungry look flared in his deep-set eyes.

"You want another one, Joey?"

Her breath caught. How did he know her name?

The newscast…he must have seen it.

"In a minute. But I'm afraid you have me at a disadvantage." She straightened, reminding herself that her image counted. Especially if she intended to counteract the negative one she'd been saddled with thanks to her mother and father's tawdry actions. "You know who I am, but you haven't introduced yourself."

His cocky smile faltered slightly. As if stalling, he took a long pull of his beer, set it down and scraped his hair off his forehead. Then finally he leaned forward, his dark eyes trained on her. "Sergeant Cole McKinney, Texas Ranger."

Joey licked her lips in stunned silence.

This hot-as-all-get-out biker bad boy was Cole McKinney? The Cole McKinney, illegitimate child of Jim

McKinney? The boy who'd been shunned by the McKinney family?

And he was a Texas Ranger? A law enforcement agent?

Not a freeloading biker or a criminal.

"I see the wheels turning in your head, Joey Hendricks." His husky voice skated over her raw nerve endings. "And yeah, I'm that Cole McKinney, a sum of all those rotten things you were thinking. And a few more you don't even know about."

"I...what are you doing here?" she whispered.

A bitter laugh followed, husky and filled with emotions she was certain he hadn't meant to reveal. Then quiet acceptance registered in his intense eyes as if he expected skepticism. Even disdain.

And he probably did. He'd been an outcast from the town all his life.

"Believe it nor not," he said quietly, "the Texas Rangers requested my services as a tracker to help find Sarah Wallace's killer."

Suddenly at a loss for words, she didn't protest when Cole raised his hand and ordered her another shot. Instead she accepted it graciously, then studied him with a different eye. If the Texas Rangers had requested his assistance, he must be damn good at his job.

What did he know about the investigation? Something the Rangers hadn't revealed to the press?

Her hand trembled as she turned up the second shot glass.

Was he here to arrest one or both of her parents?

Cole took another long pull of the beer, hoping the cold liquid would chill the fire burning his body. A heat caused both from his temper at her reaction to his name and his body reacting with lust to her every movement.

"So, Cole, how did you get to be a Ranger?"

A smile quirked his mouth. If he didn't know better, he'd think he'd just made the woman nervous.

Then again, knowing what he did about her family, he figured the Rangers were probably the last people she wanted to see.

And his brothers probably would resent her interference, as well. Since the Rangers were part of the state agency, they'd think the governor sent her to spy on them. Hell, he probably had.

"I joined the Army at seventeen," he said with a shrug. Unlike Zane, who'd gone to college, earned a degree in criminal justice and worked in criminal investigation. Or Sloan, who had been sheriff of Justice.

"Then I spent some time in the Middle East, got into military security." Sniper training to be exact, but he didn't have to spill his guts. Like how many kills he had under his belt. "When I got out, I joined the DPS and became a motorcycle state trooper for a couple of years."

She cocked a brow at that, and he grinned. "The way you handled that bike, you must have grown up on a Harley."

He laughed, then sobered as he remembered how hard he'd worked to earn his first bike. Just the way he'd scraped for everything in his life. "Naw, on a ranch, but I was a bull rider." And he wanted to ride her.

The thought made him tighten his fingers around the long neck of the beer bottle. He could not get involved with Joey Hendricks. Even though he'd earned the college credits necessary for the Rangers, he was rough around the edges. He'd hunted down the worst dregs of society, worked undercover in operations that would make her head spin. He'd killed and not looked back.

She was sophisticated. Educated. Out of his league.

And although she worked for the governor and might not admit it, she was tied to this town and her family. Had a vested interest in protecting her parents, whereas he was tied to no one. Didn't care who was arrested as long as justice was served. In fact, he wouldn't be in town long enough to let the dust settle on his seat. And if he had to lock up one of his blood kin, so be it.

"So, you haven't seen your brothers yet?" she asked.

"You mean half brothers?" He finished his beer, then grunted. "Nope. I'll have that pleasure in the morning."

She nodded, and drummed her fingernails on the table, then glanced around the bar, looking restless again. Or was she looking for someone in particular?

"What about you? Visited your family yet?"

Pain tightened her features. "No. Haven't spoken to Mommy and Daddy dearest in years."

Now, that surprised him. On second thought, he didn't know why. From what he'd read about the homicide investigation into the case of Lou Anne Wallace, about Joey's brother's kidnapping and her mother's past drinking problem, her family was as dysfunctional as the McKinneys. But still, family ties ran thick and deep.

Was she here in an official capacity, or had she come because of her own secret agenda—to see that her mother and father weren't arrested for the crimes?

Chapter 3

Cole finally dragged his butt into the shower at dawn. He hadn't slept worth a flip for thinking about the investigation and wondering how his brothers would react to the sight of him. Not that he cared...

And then there had been the fantasies about a certain sexpot blonde that had plagued him all night long.

After their drink, he'd walked her to the inn where they both were staying. Adding more fuel to the flames of his imagination, he learned she was in the room right next door to him, so they'd shared an awkward but titillating moment in the hallway as they'd said good night. Awkward because he'd damn near forgotten his head and kissed her. Titillating because he'd sensed she'd wanted it as much as he had, and that she would have let him.

Then they would have ended up in bed for some mind-blowing sex—at least that's where the kiss had led in his fertile fantasy—and he would have at least felt sated, if not rested.

Now he just felt irritable and restless.

Because nothing had happened.

He showered and managed to find a razor, wishing he'd had time for a haircut, then cursed himself for worrying about his appearance. He didn't give a damn what his brothers thought—or anyone else in town.

Grimacing, he dressed in his normal Ranger wear: clean jeans, a white Western shirt, boots, belt and tie. Determined to prove he was a top-notch Ranger himself, he pinned on his badge and grabbed his Stetson and the folder of notes he had collected on the first investigation of Lou Anne Wallace's murder sixteen years ago. Then he headed to that diner he'd seen last night, to pick up some breakfast before he met the McKinney brothers and the local deputies for a briefing. If he was here to track evidence in the woods, he needed food and coffee, and lots of it.

After all, he had a big advantage over his half brothers. He wasn't personally attached to Jim McKinney or anyone else in town.

A bloodcurdling scream pierced the air and forced thirteen-year-old Joey from her peaceful sleep.

Her mother.

She threw the covers aside, jumped up and ran to the door. But when she swung it open, a thick plume of smoke curled through the hallway. The scent of charred wood and fabric hit her. Oh God, the house was on fire!

Her father...no, daddy was at his house.

She had to get to her mother...but where was she?

And little Justin?

His room was downstairs next to her mother's.

Joey ran through the fog of smoke, feeling for the banister to help guide her, coughing and choking as she made her way to the door of the nursery. Flames licked the walls in the kitchen and crawled along the floor in the den. The curtains erupted into a ball of fire and sparks flew from the ceiling. Wood crackled and popped, splintering as the table collapsed into flames.

Her mother was already awake, standing at the crib.

Joey's eyes stung from the smoke. "We have to get out of here!"

Her mother spun around, eyes wild with terror, a crazed expression on her face. "Where's my baby? What did you do with him? You were supposed to watch him for me!"

Joey's heart pounded as she rushed forward to check the crib. Little Justin was not inside. Panic stabbed at her chest, robbing her of air. Where was her baby brother? Had he crawled out? Could he be somewhere in the house?

No, please no, the fire...it might have gotten him already. Or he might have inhaled too much smoke...

Her mother jerked her by her pajama shirt and shook her. "Where is he, Joey? Where's my baby? What did you do with him?"

"Mom! I don't know. Let me go." She yanked her mother's fingers away. "I'll look for him."

The scent of liquor permeated her mother's breath. "Tell me what you did with him!"

Joey's heart wrenched. "I put him to bed...he was here." A sob racked her, and heat scalded her face. The fire was slipping toward the hall. They had to get out.

"Please, Mom, call the fire department. I'll hunt for Justin!"

Her mother threw her hands in the air. "No! He's gone—he's not here! Someone took him, I know it!"

"Mother, call the fire department. We need help! And get Rosa!" Joey frantically searched the room and closet to see if Justin might have hidden inside. But no Justin.

Outside, a siren wailed, indicating that someone had phoned the firemen. Probably Rosa. Thank heavens. Now, if she could just find her little brother...

But she couldn't search with her mother in hysterics, so she dragged her into the hallway. The kitchen was engulfed in flames. She couldn't go that way. The front door was smoky, the flames licking at the wall casing and rippling a path of fire in front of it. Her heart racing, she glanced around the room for her baby brother, but didn't see him. Maybe he was in the playroom upstairs.

Suddenly Rosa raced into the hallway, a stricken look on her face. "Hurry! Out the window in my room!"

"We can't, we have to find Justin!" Joey screamed. "Take Mom outside. I'll look for him!"

She shoved her mother toward Rosa, and her mother crumbled in Rosa's arms. Joey lurched toward the steps to search upstairs, but firemen crashed through the front, spraying water. Chaos erupted. One of the firemen grabbed Rosa and her mother, and another one ran toward her.

"Come on, this house is going down!" he yelled. "You can't go upstairs! No time to save your things!"

"My baby brother...we can't find him!" Joey cried.

The fireman gently coaxed her toward the other man. "Get out of here now! We'll find the boy!"

* * *

Joey jerked awake and sat up, sweating and shaking. Tears rained down her face, the familiar guilt and terror gripping her full force.

The chaos. The firemen hacking away the window, breaking glass. Pushing her mother, Rosa, then her outside. Them collapsing on the lawn and watching in abject shock as the flames engulfed room after room and the house collapsed in front of them.

The firemen eventually appearing through the haze of smoke and debris, looking dazed, frustrated, sorrowful.

Their arms empty. They hadn't found Justin.

Then her father had driven up, frantic and acting like a madman as he discovered the horror.

For the next forty-eight hours, she and her mother had moved on autopilot. Her mother had had to be sedated. Her father had stalked the police for a report.

Joey had blamed herself. And in every waking or sleeping moment she'd heard her little brother's cry.

Then finally a small amount of relief. The reports proved that Justin had not been in the fire.

He had disappeared instead.

The theory was that he'd been kidnapped. The fire had been a ruse to distract them.

And then a new kind of terror had seized them. Fear that a monster had Justin. A sexual predator. A child killer. They'd imagined the worst. And then the horrible wait. Hoping and praying for a phone call. A ransom note.

But the note and call had never come.

Which had made them all suspect that something had gone wrong with the kidnapping.

And that Justin was dead after all.

The nightmare had magnified tenfold after that. The police had turned on the family. Questioned them all. Donna. Her father. Even Joey and Rosa.

And eventually they'd accused her father of planning the kidnapping/murder for the insurance money.

Joey swiped tears from her eyes and headed to the shower. Although it had been sixteen years since that day, she still smelled the smoke and sweat on her skin. Still felt the flames singeing her skin, heard her mother's cries of terror and the accusations she'd hurled. And the image of her father breaking down had been etched in her mind.

Had his tears been real? Or had he planned the disappearance of her brother and his grief had been an act?

Had her brother not disappeared, would her parents ever have reconciled? Not with Lou Anne in the picture…

The very motive the police had attached to her mother years ago.

Donna had cloaked herself in bitterness after the divorce. Mentally Joey recognized the fact that the problems between her parents had driven the family apart long before the kidnapping/murder. But Justin's disappearance had ended any chance they'd had of reclaiming a normal, civilized relationship.

She would never be free of the guilt.

Her stomach twisted into a knot. She was here to help find the answers.

But heaven help her, she was afraid of what the grand jury might find.

It hadn't occurred to Cole when he'd entered the café that the owner of the Main Street Diner was Joey's mother. But with her flaming red hair, he'd recognized her instantly from old news photos. Dressed in an immaculate pantsuit with pearls around her neck, she greeted the customers while an Hispanic woman she called Rosa bustled around filling coffee mugs and serving breakfast.

Donna had given him the once-over when he'd first entered, as if she thought she should recognize him but didn't. And she'd glanced at him with hooded eyes a dozen times since, trying to figure him out.

He hadn't offered up his identity. Right now his anonymity might play in his favor.

"More coffee?" Rosa asked.

He nodded and thanked her for topping up his cup. "Those biscuits were the best I've ever tasted."

"Gracias, señor." She strode away with a smile of pride, although when she joined Donna, they disappeared into the back room speaking in hushed voices.

He reread the notes on the kidnapping/murder investigation while he polished off his steak and eggs. Donna Hendricks's drinking problem, coupled with her husband's affairs, had led to a bitter divorce and custody battle. Both Joey, thirteen at the time, and Donna's toddler son, Justin, were caught in the war, but Leland had won custody. Then one night, when Joey and Justin were at Donna's, a horrible fire had broken out. Rosa Ramirez had been the caretaker/nanny and housekeeper for Donna when Justin had been kidnapped.

Cole had been a teenager himself, but news of the fire and kidnapping/murder of the toddler had been all over TV.

In the police reports, he skimmed Donna's statement. Then Leland's. Donna had been despondent over her son's disappearance and the possibility of his death. She'd nearly had a breakdown and had been treated for depression. Leland had appeared to be distraught, had vowed to find his son and pay for his return, no matter the cost. Both had vehemently denied allegations that they were involved in a kidnapping/murder scheme.

Joey's interview had been the tale of a traumatized teenager. A kid who'd tried to save her drunken mother and find her baby brother in the midst of a blazing fire. A kid who probably still had nightmares of that night.

Then the speculations had started. Leland, the big oil baron, had been broke. He'd allegedly concocted a fake kidnapping/murder in order to collect on a life insurance policy. Donna had testified against her ex.

Leland had blamed Donna, and claimed that if she'd been sober, she might have heard someone break in and take their toddler.

They'd waited on a ransom note, one that hadn't arrived. The police had grown suspicious, then finally they'd decided the fake kidnapping/murder had turned sour.

More details on the family dynamics had been disclosed. Lou Anne Wallace, Leland's second wife, had been spoiled and supposedly married Leland for his money. She had her own kids, Anna and Sarah, and didn't want custody of Joey or Justin. She especially hadn't wanted a screaming two-year-old. And she'd never given up her affairs.

Cole grimaced. He imagined how miserable Joey must have felt, then clenched his jaw—he had to stop thinking about Joey Hendricks.

But her mother, Donna, was another story. She'd hated Lou Anne Wallace for marrying Leland. Donna had speculated that since Lou Anne hadn't wanted the kids around, she had helped Leland with his scheme.

Others suspected Leland murdered Lou Anne because she intended to go to the police about his illegal plan.

But no one knew the truth.

Then Sarah Wallace had come to town a few days ago, supposedly with new evidence, but she'd been murdered before revealing the details.

All roads led back to the kidnapping/murder of Justin Hendricks. If they found out the truth about that night, they'd find the answers to the Wallace women's murders.

The door creaked open, and he froze with his coffee cup midway to his mouth as Joey walked in. She looked gorgeous and sexy as hell. Her long blond hair was pulled back in a clip at her nape, and she wore jeans that outlined those long legs and her tight butt, and a soft, feminine blouse that gaped above her cleavage. His mouth watered.

Last night she had admitted she hadn't spoken to her parents in years. He wondered what kind of fireworks would fly this morning between her and Donna.

What exactly did Donna Hendricks know about her son's disappearance and the murders of the Wallace women?

Joey had braced herself to see her mother, but the sight of Donna holding a coffeepot, looking so domestic, nearly bowled her over.

She didn't know this woman at all.

Her mother had been a sloppy drunk. Joey had rescued her from brawls, helped her stagger inside the house when she'd passed out on the lawn, cleaned up her messes and put her to bed.

She'd also dragged her away from the nasty fights

with her father, Donna screaming that her father was a lying, cheating bastard, Leland shouting back that Donna was a drunken whore.

Her mother glanced up at the door, then saw her and visibly paled.

Joey's throat constricted. What had she expected? For her mother to race toward her with open arms and a welcoming hug? For forgiveness for not taking better care of Justin? For the unconditional love she'd never offered?

The room grew quiet, tension vibrating through the diner that smelled of hot sausages, coffee and cinnamon rolls. Her stomach roiled. Steeling herself against the small-town gossip and whispers, she glanced across the room, searching. For what she didn't know. A familiar face? An old friend?

Not that she had any here.

Then she spotted Cole McKinney. In a sea of strangers, he looked like the least vicious of the sharks.

Heaven help her, but she headed straight for his table. Her legs felt shaky, and she clutched the table edge, then slid into the chair across from him without waiting for an invitation. He cocked one dark brow, then offered her a sideways smile of understanding. Her heart fluttered wildly, and she felt like kissing him.

Ridiculous.

Then again, she'd struggled with that same feeling the night before. A temptation she had resisted.

For good reason, too. She had no time for a fling or romantic entanglement, especially with Cole McKinney.

Although the first part of the night she'd spent fantasizing about what might have happened if she had relented. One hot kiss would have led to another. Then tawdry, naked, wild sex.

"Good mornin'," he said in a sexy drawl.

Was it? She wanted to growl. She'd heard him next door tossing and turning and pacing the floor the night before, as well.

She had to inform the Mathesons that the inn walls needed better insulation against the noise.

She nodded anyway, though, unable to speak. Her voice was lost somewhere in between fantasies of Cole, the tremors remaining from her nightmare this morning and the stunned look on her mother's face.

Donna slowly walked toward her.

Joey swallowed, then noticed the files that Cole shoved into a folder. Files about the murders. Files about her missing brother. An old photo of her and her parents at the police station being questioned after Justin's disappearance.

His solemn look told her he understood her discomfort.

He had no idea. She was behaving irrationally. Running to him as if he was her friend. As if he could save her from herself and her family when he'd come here to investigate every last one of them.

Cole McKinney had no real connections to the town or her family. If he found any dirty secrets hiding in the closet, he would have no qualms about exposing them.

No, he wasn't her friend. Couldn't help her.

No one could.

Chapter 4

Donna Hendricks's heels clicked ominously in the sudden stillness of the room. Cole watched, scrutinizing every movement. The other patrons craned their necks and their conversations quieted. Apparently they were as interested in the unfolding drama between mother and daughter as he was.

Although Joey tried to camouflage her nervous reaction, her breath rattled in the quiet tension as Donna paused beside the table.

"Joey…when did you get to town?"

Joey turned a steady, unemotional gaze on her mother. "Last night."

Donna placed a coffee mug on the table, filled it for her daughter and glanced at Cole in question as if to ask if they were together. "Where are you staying?"

"I reserved a room at the Matheson Inn."

Donna wet her ruby-red lips with her tongue. "And who's your friend here?"

A small smile curved Joey's mouth as if she was taking some perverse pleasure in watching her mother squirm. Or maybe in being seen with him in a town that lived for the rumor mill.

"This is Cole McKinney," Joey said. "*Sergeant* Cole McKinney, Texas Rangers."

Donna's mouth widened into a shocked O, then she narrowed her penciled eyebrows. "You're Jim McKinney's *other* son?"

Cole gritted his teeth at her condescending tone and gave a clipped nod. He would never call the man his father.

Donna pressed a shaky hand to her throat. "Then you're here about the investigation into Sarah Wallace's murder?"

"Yes, ma'am."

Donna angled her head toward her daughter. "And what about you, Joey? Did you come to see me or your father?"

Joey cradled the coffee mug between her hands. "The governor sent me to oversee the case, and handle the media."

Disappointment mingled with some other troubled emotion on Donna's face. Pain? Guilt? Fear of being exposed? "I see. Have you talked to Leland yet?"

Joey's look turned more strained. "No, but I'm sure I will. The Rangers will undoubtedly question him again. And I plan to sit in on all the interrogations."

Donna studied her daughter for a full minute without a reply. Then as if disappointed in Joey's comment, she gestured toward the menu. "Rosa will come and take your order."

With a blistering look, she strode back to the breakfast counter, then disappeared behind the doors leading to the back. Rosa frowned and rushed toward Joey, although when she reached the table, she hesitated as if she wasn't sure how Joey would accept her overture.

But Joey stood, sporting the first sincere smile he'd seen on her face. "Rosa…it's nice to see you."

Sadness tinged Rosa's eyes as she hugged Joey.

"Let me get you some breakfast." Rosa patted Joey's shoulder like a doting mother. "How about one of Rosa's famous Mexican omelets, the ones you loved when you were a little *niña, sí?*"

Joey shook her head. "No, thanks, Rosa. I…don't have time."

Cole removed some bills from his wallet and laid them on the table, uncomfortable with the private moment. Time to meet his brothers and get to work. "I have to go now. Breakfast was great, Rosa."

She nodded and whispered, *"Gracias, señor."* But her dark eyes also reflected a wariness that made him wonder if she was hiding something, as well.

He would find out sooner or later. A second later Joey caught up with him. "You're on your way to the briefing?"

"Yes."

"I'm going with you. I need to catch up on the details of the investigation."

He frowned, held the door open for her, and they walked across the street to the courthouse in silence. As soon as they entered the conference room, which had been designated as a temporary office for the sheriff, the room quieted. Zane occupied the chair behind the desk as if he'd self-appointed himself head of command while Sloan was propped on the edge, looking like a relaxed hometown boy. A deputy stood by the window staring outside as if he'd been watching for Cole to warn his half brothers of his arrival.

Cole had seen pictures of both of them in the paper, had kept abreast of their careers, their commendations and awards. Both had been popular in high school. Zane, the valedictorian, Mr. JHS—Justice High School—and a quarterback on the football team. And Sloan had been a baseball star and won the state championship. They'd also been noted for their work in solving various high-profile cases.

But he had never met them face-to-face.

He was surprised at the way his stomach clenched. Both men resembled Jim to a degree, although there were subtle differences.

Judging from their solemn expressions they weren't happy about meeting him. Fine, he was a necessary evil. Here to do a job, not make friends with his siblings.

Zane gave him a clipped nod of acknowledgment. "Glad you finally made it."

Sloan's look wasn't as hospitable. "We've been waiting."

Cole returned their greeting with a scowl. Then Joey entered the room, and the tension intensified to a deafening roar.

"What the hell is she doing here?" Zane asked.

Cole wasn't surprised at their reaction.

Next to him, the last thing the Rangers wanted was a special investigator for the governor—and the daughter of a prime suspect—breathing down their necks as if the governor didn't trust them to do their jobs.

But the governor obviously recognized that each of the participants had a personal interest in the outcome of the case. His half brothers and Joey included.

And the verdict was still out over whether or not any of them were on the same side.

Joey plastered her professional, detached face in place. No doubt her position here threw a kink in their family-run operations. The fact that she'd arrived with their illegitimate half brother hadn't ingratiated her with the McKinney men, either.

But she refused to let these men intimidate her with their macho, own-the-town attitudes. She'd told the governor the McKinneys wouldn't welcome her nosing into what they considered *their* investigation, but the case had drawn statewide attention, and the Rangers investigating one of their own, especially their father, meant lines could be crossed.

She smiled smoothly and claimed a seat at the conference table with the local deputies. "You know why I'm here. You're too close to the people involved."

"And you're not?" Zane said sarcastically.

She shrugged. "My parents and I aren't exactly tight. Besides, I'm a professional. The governor wants this case solved, and he's the boss."

"We're professionals, too, and can handle the case just fine without you," Zane said.

Joey folded her hands in front of her on the table. "Listen, I'm not going home until we've ended this investigation and someone is arrested for Sarah Wallace's murder. So you'll have to put up with me, boys."

She gave them a saccharine grin. "Besides, look on the bright side. I can run interference with the media. You don't want a circus in town creating panic and trying your suspects before you make an arrest."

Cole claimed the chair beside her, enjoying her spunky side. "All right, now that our happy little party is assembled, why don't you fill us in on what you have so far? If I'm tracking in the woods today, I'd like to get started."

Zane huffed and Sloan made a disgusted sound, but gestured toward the whiteboard on the wall, which held various facts, including the TOD for Lou Anne's and Sarah Wallace's murders.

"All right," Zane began. "Sarah Wallace came to town to meet her sister, Anna, and share evidence she'd uncovered about their mother's death. She used a prepaid cell phone, which we haven't recovered yet, to phone Anna, but when Anna arrived, she found Sarah's body in the hotel room. She was already dead, had been strangled like her mother. Later someone tried to kill Anna in the same way."

"Why kill Anna?" Joey asked.

"Apparently the killer thought Anna knew something to incriminate him. Or her."

Cole nodded. "Did she?"

"No. But later, Anna remembered a false bottom in one of their mother's suitcases. Sarah had it with her," Zane explained. "We examined it and found papers Sarah had hidden inside. The notes and papers indicated that Donna Hendricks might have intended to pay off Lou Anne for providing her with information about Leland's alleged plans to fake the kidnapping and murder of his son. We're getting a search warrant now to access Donna's financial records, along with Rosa's."

"So you believe Lou Anne blackmailed Donna?" Cole asked.

Sloan nodded. "Lou Anne didn't want more kids, so when she discovered Leland's plan, she phoned Donna to tell her. She tried to blackmail Donna into paying her for the tip. We think Donna probably agreed, but Donna wanted Lou Anne to report Leland to the FBI."

"Why wouldn't Donna just go to the police herself?" Cole asked.

"Because she was bitter over losing the custody battle," Sloan supplied. "Without evidence, Leland could have accused her of conspiring with him to pull off the kidnapping/murder. Or he could have accused her of orchestrating the entire plan herself and she'd lose any visitation rights with her children."

"And no one would believe my mother because she was a drunk back then." Joey understood the implied assumption. It was possible that when Lou Anne refused to go to the FBI, Donna had killed her.

"What about Rosa?" Joey drummed her nails on the table. "Why are you looking at her records?"

"She bought liquor and drugs for Donna," Zane interjected. "If Donna wanted to hide money to pay off a blackmailer, she might have enlisted Rosa's help."

"Has Donna confessed to any of this?" Cole asked.

Zane grimaced. "No, not yet."

"While Zane's been handling the grand jury, I stepped in to help Sheriff Matheson," Sloan said. "We were studying the papers Sarah left when the fire broke out in the jail. Then someone tried to shoot Carley." Anger hardened Sloan's face. "She's in a safe house now, but she's searching Donna's financial records for more details."

"So you're focusing on my parents now?" Joey asked. Could one of them be a murderer? Had her mother or father killed Lou Anne, and now Sarah? Had one of them really shot the sheriff to keep her from finding out the truth?

Her stomach knotted again. "I thought Leland had an alibi for the night of Lou Anne's murder?"

Zane's boots hit the floor with a thud. "We discovered that he tampered with the surveillance cameras, so his alibi is shot."

"What about your father, Jim McKinney?" Joey asked. "He was seen leaving the inn that night."

The men traded an odd look.

"What are you not saying?" Cole asked.

Sloan twisted sideways and Zane clenched his jaw. "We haven't ruled out Jim yet."

"And Stella?" Joey asked. "She hated Lou Anne for her affair with Jim."

Pain flashed into both men's eyes. "Stella had a breakdown," Zane said. "She's in the hospital, despondent. I'm not sure how much more information we'll get from her."

"Dad..." Sloan paused, then continued, "Jim agreed to see a psychiatrist to try to jog his memory of the events of that night, but Stella got upset and told him no. Then she broke down. The stress has been unbearable for her."

"She was always fragile," Zane said in a low voice.

Joey frowned and steepled her hands. They seemed completely focused on making her parents out to be the villains. And Zane and Sloan were keeping secrets. Something about Stella and their father.

Her cell phone rang, and she checked the number. Governor Grange.

"Excuse me, guys. I have to take this." She stepped away from them and answered the call.

"Joey, how's it going in Justice?"

"The Rangers are conferencing now," Joey said. "No definitive leads yet. They've brought in Sergeant Cole McKinney to track evidence in the woods near the inn."

A long sigh filled with tension followed. "I hope they tie this up soon and put the guy responsible for these murders away. How is Dennison?"

"I can handle him," Joey said.

"Good. Keep me posted."

Joey agreed and pocketed her phone, contemplating Zane's and Sloan's summary of the investigation.

What were the McKinney brothers hiding?

If her parents were guilty...well, she'd have to find a way to accept it. But if they were innocent, she didn't want them railroaded to jail for a crime they hadn't committed. After all, they had suffered terribly over Justin's death.

Perhaps Stella had suffered a breakdown out of guilt. Maybe she had killed Lou Anne and had hidden behind a weak woman's facade all these years to deflect suspicion from herself.

Cole tried to ignore the quick flash of worry in Joey's eyes. He'd just met the woman. He could not let himself care about her or how the outcome of this investigation might affect her personally.

"So, what exactly am I looking for?" Cole asked.

"We need an expert to search the woods by the inn," Sloan said. "The night Sarah Wallace was murdered, Sheriff Matheson saw a figure in dark clothing. She chased the culprit into the woods, but he shot her in the ribs. Actually cracked one. We'd like to recover any bullet casing or other evidence that you might find."

Cole stood. "I assume you have a horse available, along with the standard crime scene kit and supplies."

Zane stood, as well. "At your disposal."

"Meanwhile, I'm going to get that search warrant for Donna's records," Sloan said.

Cole nodded, anxious to get outside. He loved the fresh air, the scents of nature, the sunshine beating on his face. Fieldwork was his specialty, not digging through files, although he did plenty of that, too.

Twenty minutes later, he saddled a beautiful quarter horse named Apache, strapped on the supplies he'd need in the saddlebags and rode into the woods. Sloan and Zane had searched the edge, so he needed to go deeper. Find out how the killer had escaped. Locate that bullet.

Although it had rained recently, and some evidence might have washed away, he slowed Apache to a walk and studied each section of the forest, each patch of weeds and each tree for signs that someone had recently been through. A broken branch. Trampled bramble. An indentation in the bark not made by an animal. Each detail provided a clue and indicated he was on the right track.

He noticed a footpath along with muddy prints, although dead leaves and debris created problems in lifting a print. Still, he tied Apache to a tree and combed the area on foot, kneeling to inspect the markings and the ground. He photographed each patchy section and collected dirt for trace in hopes that they might be able to match it to a suspect's shoes and make an arrest.

Working diligently, he took a partial molding of the footprint, as well. It would give them a general clue as to the size of their suspect. A fiber from a piece of clothing was caught in a branch, and he removed an evidence bag and tweezers, snagged the fiber and bagged it to send to forensics. The next few hours he combed each mile of the woods, then finally traced his way back toward the inn and his horse. He found two other fibers, along with more footprints—muddied and misshapen, different from the first ones—so he took the best print he could lift.

Not for the first time, he considered the fact that they might be dealing with more than one perp here. What if the killer had an accomplice? Donna and Leland could have worked together. Or one of them could have hired help to do their dirty work.

About seventy-five feet to the right of where he'd tied Apache, he noticed a shattered piece of bark on a live oak. He removed the magnifying glass from his bag and examined it, then decided a bullet had scraped past. He collected the sample, bagged it, then turned and assessed the area. The bullet had grazed Carley, then bounced off the tree, which had slowed its descent. Noting the location where Sloan said the sheriff had been running, and had been shot, he estimated the trajectory of the bullet and where the shooter might have been standing when he'd fired. Zeroing in on the angle, he calculated the speed and scrutinized the other foliage until he located the shell. With gloved fingers, he picked it up and studied it. A .38.

Hell, half the town probably owned guns, and half of

those were probably .38s. But modern science could do wonders. If they had a suspect and his gun, they would be able to match it.

He searched for other bullets and evidence, but found nothing. A few feet away, though, something shiny glinted through a patch of bramble. Sweat beaded on his forehead and trickled down his neck as he recognized the item.

The silver star of Texas—a Ranger's badge.

The badges were handmade from Mexican silver coins, making each one unique, and easily identifiable to its recipient. Some badges still had coin lines on the outer rim of the circle, and you could see the peso on the back of the badge. The coin on the back wasn't always at a perfect upright angle, either, and had distortions caused from being handmade.

He swallowed against the sudden dryness in his throat as he lifted it to the sun. When Jim McKinney's badge had been reported missing years ago, right after Lou Anne Wallace's murder, a description had been posted. The badge had three coin marks on the lower right star point.

He flipped the badge over and grimaced as he scrutinized the point.

If he was right, this star had belonged to Jim McKinney, his bastard father. According to police reports, Jim had claimed he'd lost it the night Lou Anne Wallace was murdered.

Chapter 5

Joey rubbed her temple where a headache throbbed. There had been enough charged electricity in that meeting between the McKinney brothers to start a brushfire. Outside, she breathed in the fresh air, hoping to calm her nerves, but she spotted her mother approaching and her anxiety rose another notch. The reporter from hell, Harold Dennison, trailed behind her like a fox chasing a rabbit.

Which one would be the lesser of two evils?

"Joey, please wait. I'd like to talk to you," Donna called.

Joey halted, knowing the confrontation was inevitable. Besides, she'd be lying to herself if she said she'd come here only because of the governor's request. She was secretly afraid the grand jury would indict one or both of her parents, and she wanted answers. Running wouldn't help her get to the truth.

Donna's eyes flitted nervously across the street, then behind Joey. Instantly recognizing the press, she stopped and her mouth flattened into a thin line. "Let's step into my office so we can talk in private."

Joey nodded, her shoulders tense as she followed Donna through the back door of the restaurant and into an office. She was surprised by the minimalist furnishings. Simple oak desk, leather chair, a love seat in the corner beside a potted plant. The room almost looked homey. Much more domestic than the mother she remembered.

Still, Donna didn't have a hair out of place. Joey felt like an awkward teenager beside her with her linen pantsuit, manicured nails and skillfully applied makeup.

In fact, she'd never quite fitted the mold of what her parents envisioned as the perfect daughter. Donna would have liked a petite ballerina or cheerleader. Leland had wanted a boy—the reason he'd nicknamed her Joey instead of Josie or called her by her full name. Then he'd had Justin, and for a while she'd thought he might be happy.

But her mother's drinking and her father's financial problems had torn them apart. Then came the nightmare of the custody battle, her brother's disappearance and the allegations against her father.

Joey had felt betrayed by them all. And what about Justin? Had he died when he was two? Where had the killer left his small body? It had never been recovered. The image of his trusting cherub face still haunted her.

And what if he was still alive? If so, where had he been all these years? Had a family adopted him? Did he remember that he had a big sister?

Even that hope was tainted with worry, though. If

he had survived, someone abusive, even a deviant child molester, might have taken him in. Or he could have been sold into slavery of some kind or taken across the border. He might not even know his real name.

The harsh possibilities threatened to consume her, but oblivious to her daughter's pain as always, Donna turned and smiled. "It's so good to see you, Josephine."

Joey braced herself. "Is it, Mother? I didn't think you really cared."

Donna gasped, then forced another tight smile on her face, recovering quickly. "Yes, it is. I realize that the last time we saw each other things were unpleasant. But I've changed, sweetheart. I don't drink anymore."

Joey twined her fingers together.

"And I've no need for pills, either, so you see, I'm clean. I have been for a long time." She gestured around the office. "This is my life. The business, this café. It may not seem like much to you now that you work for the governor, but it's mine and I'm proud of it."

Sincerity and wariness underscored Donna's words, at odds with the bitterness that Donna wore as a second skin. "That's good, Mother. I'm glad to see you're… happy now."

Her mother's false smile faded slightly. "Well, that happiness and peace may not last. Not if the sheriff and those McKinney men keep nosing around."

"A woman was murdered, Mother," Joey pointed out. "They have to investigate her death. You don't want a killer running free here in town again, do you?"

Donna's face paled, and she glanced down at her hands. "No, but neither do I want my name dragged through the mud." She gave Joey an imploring look. "It's taken years for me to recover from your father's…

behavior, and the shame. And now those Rangers want to dredge up the past. All the painful memories of losing your brother."

Joey winced. Her mother had suffered—they all had.

"You have power now, Joey," Donna continued. "You have to convince them to stop looking into your brother's old case."

Joey's blood ran cold. Donna knew she was in charge of the press, that she was working on the investigation. Would Donna use her to find out what the police had on her?

"And why should I do that, Mother?" Joey sighed. "I'd think you of all people would want to know the truth about what happened to Justin." God knew, *she* did.

Donna glanced sideways, an odd look on her face, and Joey saw her gaze land on a photograph on the desk.

A brass frame held a picture of her and Justin standing beside the Christmas tree the holiday before he'd been abducted. The warm memory washed over Joey in a wave of nostalgia. Justin had been awestruck by the shiny twinkling lights, had babbled that he wanted a red fire truck for Christmas, and a train set and a pony. She had lifted him on her shoulders to help him hang his stocking on the mantel. She remembered his gleeful cry the next morning when he'd found the toys beneath the tree. And the Shetland pony out in the backyard…

"There's not a day that goes by that I don't think about Justin and wish we had him back," Donna said in a thick voice. She hitched in a breath, then resolve hardened her tone. "But opening up old wounds will do nothing but tear us apart again, Joey. Please, do what you can to get those Rangers off our backs. We barely survived the first time. I'm not sure any of us can live through a second go around."

Joey studied her mother's intense expression with unease. Was her mother's grief the real reason she didn't want the Rangers probing into the kidnapping/murder now? Or was it because she and Leland had gotten away scot-free years ago, and she was afraid they'd find evidence to convict them? If they did, would she expect Joey to cover for them?

Leland Hendricks had been shocked the night before when he'd seen Joey on the TV with that slimeball reporter Dennison, and disappointed that she hadn't shown up at his house later that evening.

Emotions pummeled him as he watched her exit Donna's diner. Anger. Hurt. Betrayal. And a deep disappointment that she had chosen to see her mother before him.

Donna was probably gloating right now.

Then again, Joey hadn't spoken to him in years, so what did he expect?

That she'd realize he wasn't the villain everyone had painted him to be? That even though he had made terrible mistakes years ago—marrying Donna for one, marrying Lou Anne for another—that he had suffered every day since?

Dammit, he had provided a home for her when her mother had been too drunk and incapacitated on pills to stand upright. And in spite of the allegations against him, he had loved her and had never wanted Justin harmed.

Guilt weighed heavily on his soul as he headed toward the back of the diner. The past rose from the shadows like a dragon breathing a fiery trail down his neck. His life had been such a mess back then. His finances in ruins. His responsibilities to his business a pressure cooker ready to explode, problems attacking him from all sides. Then his family troubles. Donna's insatiable drinking and the drugs. And then Lou Anne—the woman had turned into a minefield of trouble herself. She hadn't been able to give up her lovers. Jim McKinney for one. She'd practically flaunted her affairs in his face. And she hadn't wanted his kids. Not Joey or Justin.

Especially not Justin.

He had to talk to Donna. Find out what new lies she might have planted in Joey's head.

A ripple of anxiety clawed at his throat. All these years Joey had hated him. He had to wonder why.

Did Joey know more about Justin's disappearance than she'd admitted?

Something that would make him look guilty?

Late afternoon shadows slanted across the land as Cole rode Apache up to the stables. Zane and Sloan stood by an official Rangers's car waiting for him as if they'd been there for hours. He tightened his jaw, glad he'd found some evidence to prove his worth, but also irritated that they hadn't waited at the makeshift sheriff's office for him. Didn't they trust him to keep the evidence intact?

He pulled on the reins and slowed Apache to a walk, patting his side and mumbling his thanks to the horse as the beast loped into the fenced corral and headed for a drink of water.

Cole threw his leg over the animal and climbed down. He enjoyed the feel of the horse beneath him, the power of the animal just as he did his Harley. The only thing sweeter was a woman beneath him. An image of Joey flashed into his mind, and he imagined her spread on the grassy slope of the hill, naked and ready to be ridden.

The brief image played havoc with his concentration. Sexual fantasies didn't belong in the middle of this case.

He stroked Apache's mane then began to unfasten his saddlebags as his half brothers approached. "Thanks, buddy, you did good today." While he'd prefer to stay and brush down the horse himself, he turned him over to the stable hand so he could deal with the Rangers.

"Did you have any luck?" Zane asked.

He wasn't lucky, he was a damn good tracker. But he refused to get into a pissing contest with the McKinneys. "I found the bullet, and collected a few other fibers that might help. Also took some footprints. They're partials but you might get something from them."

"Great." Sloan smiled, and Cole realized he resembled Jim McKinney. He wondered if Sloan was as smooth with the women.

"With that bullet, maybe we can determine who shot Carley and make an arrest," Sloan said. "That SOB needs to pay."

"Right," Zane said. "Cole, give me everything you found, and I'll send it to the crime lab."

Cole frowned. "I could have brought it over. No need for you to have wasted time waiting around." *Unless you didn't trust me.*

"You did your job," Zane said. "We can take it from here."

Cole narrowed his eyes as he handed over the evidence bags. "Excuse me?"

"We can handle the investigation," Sloan said. "We just needed some help in tracking this down."

"You mean you're dismissing me from the case now?" Cole asked in a hard voice. "But I just got here."

His brothers exchanged an odd look that raised Cole's suspicions.

"Why do you want me gone? Is there something you guys are covering up? Something about Jim McKinney?"

"No," Zane said a little too quickly.

Cole didn't believe them. "You have new evidence against him, don't you? What is it? Did Stella tell you something? Is that why she had a breakdown? She finally admitted the truth, that he killed Lou Anne Wallace?"

A muscle ticked in Zane's jaw, and Cole realized he'd hit the nail on the head.

"No," Sloan barked. "But you'd probably like to see him fry, wouldn't you? You've hated him all these years, and you want to see him suffer."

A knot of fury balled in Cole's stomach. He hadn't expected anything but animosity from his brothers. Yet he had hoped they'd be fair.

"I'm a Ranger, same as you," he said harshly. "Jim McKinney means nothing to me, one way or the other. So you're wrong. I don't want to see him locked up. Nor do I want him to walk away if he's guilty." He grabbed his saddlebags and slung them over his shoulder. "You see, McKinneys, I'm not caught up in your family drama the way you are. And as far as *our* father goes, frankly I don't give a damn what happens to him."

Furious, he stalked toward his Harley, hung the bags across the back, grabbed his helmet and yanked it on.

Then he tore down the graveled driveway, spitting dust and rocks behind his wheels.

Still, the silver star of Texas he'd found, the one he thought belonged to Jim McKinney, burned his pocket, taunting him with doubt as he headed back into town.

"No justice in Justice—that seems to be the recurring theme the local residents are complaining about here in Tarrant County, Texas." Dennison lowered the mike to a white-haired lady in a purple knit pantsuit. "Do you agree, ma'am?"

She fluttered an age-spotted hand to her throat. "It seems that way. Poor Sarah Wallace strangled with her own purse strap."

The lady beside her clutched her handbag under her arm as if she feared the killer might do the same thing to her. "We just want to be safe again," the little woman said.

"The worst part is knowing that it's the same man who killed Lou Anne Wallace sixteen years ago." They both darted furtive looks across the street. "What if he's been here all this time, acting like he's one of us, and we never knew it!"

"I thought that Jim McKinney probably killed Lou Anne," the first woman interjected. "Or maybe his wife did out of jealousy. He sure did shame poor Stella."

"I just hope Jim's boys can be fair and do the right thing if they have to arrest their father," the second woman said. "Such a scandal."

"Do you ladies believe this case is connected to the Hendricks baby kidnapping and murder?" Dennison asked.

"Oh, my word, yes." They both sputtered.

"Leland Hendricks has more money than God now,"

the second woman chirped. "He'll probably pay his way out of it this time just like he did back then."

Joey clenched her jaw. She understood the women's concerns. Hadn't she thought the same thing herself?

But hearing her father slandered again hurt more than she wanted to admit.

Still, if she confronted Dennison now, it would appear as if she was defending her father. The best defense would be to find out the truth.

Spotting the bar nearby, she dashed inside. Maybe someone here might offer insight into the past.

A little early for hard liquor, she ordered a beer and claimed a seat at the bar. A few locals played pool in the back while the jukebox blared out country tunes. The waitress who'd flirted with Cole frowned at her, while a middle-aged man in a suit took a chair beside her, and a man in jeans and a cowboy shirt and hat took the other.

"Bud, I'm Joey Hendricks," she said to the bartender.

"I know who you are, honey. I saw you on the news."

She grimaced at the pet name. But she wanted answers and honey caught more flies than vinegar so she smiled. "How long have you been in Justice?"

"I grew up here," Bud said as he wiped the counter. "Owned this bar for the last twenty years."

"So you must know everyone in town?"

"Pretty much." He gestured around the smoky room and dark corners. "People come here to let down and relax."

"And hook up," Joey said with a smile.

He shrugged. "Nothing wrong in that."

"Not if you're single."

Bud leaned forward, propping himself on his elbows. "I mind my own business. If I don't, I lose customers."

Joey nodded. "Did Jim McKinney meet Lou Anne Wallace here sixteen years ago?"

He poured a scotch for the suited man and a glass of merlot for the lady who'd joined him, then turned back to her. "They didn't exactly keep their affair a secret. Jim liked women. Period."

"So Lou Anne wasn't his only lover?"

"Just the last."

Joey stewed over that comment. She'd always wondered if Stella might have killed Lou Anne out of jealousy or revenge for screwing her husband. But if Jim had another woman on the side, that lady might not have liked the competition.

Bud's tone grew hushed. "Lou Anne's marriage to Leland didn't stop her from giving up men."

"Jim wasn't the only man she fooled around with?"

He grunted sarcastically, then turned away to handle an order from the waitress.

Joey pondered this information. Maybe Jim's lover wanted to get rid of Lou Anne. Or what if one of Lou Anne's lovers or their wives knocked her off? Had the police explored that theory?

But who else had slept with Jim McKinney? And what about Lou Anne? Who else had she taken to her bed?

Would her father know?

Her head throbbed at the thought of asking him. But she had to follow through on the possibility. She'd question him tomorrow.

Exhausted, she thanked Bud, paid for her beer, then crossed the street to the inn. Cole's Harley sat in front of the building, and she contemplated knocking on his door to see if he'd found anything new. But it was late, and if she did, she'd suffer the same dilemma as the night before.

Better to confront him in the morning when she wasn't feeling so vulnerable. And when the sight or smell of him wouldn't keep her awake all night again with longing.

She entered the inn, and veered into the stairwell to go to the second floor. Darkness bathed the hallway, and behind her, she thought she detected a footstep. The floor creaked, and she spun around, searching the darkness.

"Who's there?"

Silence stretched for a heartbeat, the whisper of someone's breathing tainting the quiet. Joey clutched her purse, wishing she had brought her gun with her instead of leaving it in the room. Bracing herself for an attack, she hurried up the steps. The footsteps sounded behind her, picking up their pace, grating on her nerves. Finally she burst through the door to the hallway, jammed the key into her room and vaulted inside. Her breath caught as she slammed the door and leaned against it. The room was pitch-dark, the air hot and sticky.

A shadow caught her eye, and she realized she wasn't alone.

She opened her mouth to scream, and reached for the doorknob, but the intruder grabbed her around the neck, cutting off her air with the heel of his hand. He clamped his other hand over her mouth and dragged her against him. "Stop nosing around, or your mother is going to get hurt."

Chapter 6

Cole swore as he threw his saddlebags on the floor of the inn room. How dare Zane and Sloan McKinney dismiss him as if he was some lackey they didn't want to be bothered with any longer. He'd come a long way to help them and that was the thanks he got.

Not that he expected a dinner invitation at the family table, but they obviously couldn't wait to see him ride out of town. Of course, then they could go about their business as always and pretend that he didn't exist the way they'd done all his life.

The way Jim McKinney had.

His throat thickened with emotions as he ran his thumb over his pocket where he'd stored the badge he'd found in the woods. Heat emanated from the metal, reminding him that he was crossing the line not turning over evidence. Was the man really worth him risking his own reputation as a Ranger? He could argue that he'd been concerned about what Sloan and Zane would do with the badge, that they might cover for their father.

But was that true? Or did some small part of him want to exonerate Jim McKinney himself?

No. He didn't give a damn about the man who'd abandoned him and his mother.

If he were guilty, he'd arrest him and see that he fried for his wrongdoings.

Bitterness knocked at the shell of apathy he'd carved around his heart, but he tamped it down. Not caring was the best defense against them all. Becoming emotional would only make him weak. Make them think he wanted to be part of the McKinneys. That he actually missed being a member of their family.

How the hell could he miss something he'd never had?

His family consisted of his mother. That was all he needed. All he ever would.

Being alone suited him fine. He had no one to answer to. No one to take care of. No one to worry about when he was on the job.

No one to warm his bed.

An image of Joey Hendricks and those mile-long legs came to mind, and he turned toward the door. Maybe he'd pay her a visit tonight before he left. See what she'd found out today.

Ask her if she'd like to share a drink before bedtime. And then…what?

Sleep with him before he hit the road?

A smile curved his mouth, and he opened the door and stepped into the hall. But just as he raised his hand to knock, he heard a noise from inside her room. A table being bumped. Something crashed. Scuffling. Then a scream.

His heart hammered into overdrive.

"Joey!" He jiggled the doorknob but it was locked. Another scream rent the air and a loud *thunk.* Someone was definitely in the room.

Joey was in trouble.

He slid his gun from his ankle holster, then slammed his shoulder against the door with all his force.

Joey swung her elbow backward into the man's stomach. He grunted, then shoved her to the floor on her knees. She twisted and tried to see his face, but he kicked her in the back, and she doubled over in pain. God, if she could only reach her gun.

"Joey!" Cole's voice reverberated through the haze, and she heard his body slam against the door, jarring the wood and echoing off the walls.

Her attacker yanked her head backward by her hair and pushed a gun to the base of her skull. "Move and you die."

She froze, breathing hard, her mind racing. "Who are you? Why are you doing this?"

"If you care about your mother, steer the Rangers away from her."

Her mind raced. She couldn't believe she'd let this creep get the best of her. If she grabbed his ankle and tripped him, she might have a chance. But he might press the trigger, and she'd be dead.

Dying was not in her plans tonight.

"Do you understand?" He lifted his foot, and stomped her back again with his boot. Pain split her lower extremities, and she cried out, sucking in air to breathe through the agony. "Yes..."

Growling something in Spanish, he kicked her shoulder so hard that tears trickled down her cheeks, and she slumped to the floor, fighting nausea.

Hugging her arms around her middle, she dragged in deep breaths, battling against the need to pass out as he leaped out the window.

Cole slammed the door again, and it swung open with a vicious *whoosh.* His boots pounded on the floor as he ran inside. She glanced sideways, crawled to her hands and knees, but the room was still spinning. "Go get him!" she snarled between clenched teeth.

"Dammit!" Cole checked the window, then ran back and knelt beside her. "Joey, are you all right?"

"Yes, I said go after him!"

"Let me call 911 and get security!"

"No, I'll call security. Go after the bastard!"

Cole glared at her, but jumped up and vaulted toward the door to give chase. She struggled to drag herself upright while he disappeared out the door.

Weapon drawn, Cole searched the shadows near the inn for signs of Joey's attacker, but didn't see him on the street or in the bushes flanking the property. With the rising panic in town, most people had obviously chosen to stay home or turn in before dark so the streets were nearly deserted. Still, a few stragglers moved along the storefronts and town square, but no one was running or acting suspicious. A teenage couple making out beneath the awning of the drugstore. Two cowboys exiting the Last Call. An old-timer walking his dog.

Frustration clawed at Cole. The guy had slithered

through town to a getaway vehicle or slunk off into the neighboring woods. His guess would be the woods.

He ventured into the thicket of trees nearest the inn, watching for movement. Animals scurried through the brush, a dog howled somewhere in the distance, and mosquitoes swarmed around his face. Storm clouds crawled above, turning the sky a more ominous black and robbing any light the moon might have offered.

Sweat trickled down his jaw as he slipped through the forest, padding slowly so as not to disturb the brush and alert the man as to his presence should he be hiding nearby. He spent a half hour searching, pausing at each turn, looking in the shadows, but came up empty.

Resigned the guy had escaped, Cole walked back through the thick woods, taking a different route in case he'd missed something. But when he reached the inn, he still hadn't spotted the man. Worried about Joey, he hurried inside the inn. A young guy who looked like he was barely twenty glanced up from the front desk with a frown.

"Where in the hell is your security guard?" Cole barked.

The boy gestured toward a gray-haired man hobbling toward them. "Miss Hendricks called. I checked her floor and the main one, but didn't find anyone."

Cole rolled his eyes. The old geezer looked as if he was half-blind himself, and was moving like a turtle.

"Call the sheriff's office. Tell dispatch to put you through to Lieutenant Zane McKinney and Sergeant Sloan McKinney there immediately!"

"Right." The man fumbled with his flashlight, then reached for his cell phone. "I'm all over it."

Cole did not feel comforted by the thought. But he

ran up the stairwell toward Joey's room anyway. He had to see her and make sure she was really all right.

When he rounded the corner, the door still stood ajar. Dammit, she should have locked it. What was she thinking?

Ready to ream into her, he barreled inside. She was sitting on the bed in a crouched position as if she was in pain. But she held a .38 in her shaky hands, and it was aimed at him.

Joey's hands trembled as she fixed the gun on the silhouette in the doorway. She'd heard the footsteps and hoped it was Cole, but she refused to be caught off guard again.

"Joey?" The shadow slowly held up a hand. "It's me, Cole. Put down the gun slowly."

Her breath tumbled from her mouth, full of relief, and she finally allowed herself to relax. Still, her hand jerked as she lowered the weapon. "Did you catch him?"

Cole shook his head, his expression stony as he moved into the room. "I searched the neighboring streets and woods, but he disappeared. Are you all right?"

No, she was a mess, but she hated to admit it. As tough as she'd always perceived herself to be, and although she had taken self-defense classes, a real attack was different from a staged one in a practice setting.

"Did you call for an ambulance?"

"I don't need a doctor, Cole. I'm fine."

"I don't believe you." Cole slid down onto the bed beside her, checked the safety on the gun, then placed it inside the nightstand drawer. Then he tilted her chin up with his thumb. "Where did he hurt you?"

Concern tinged his gruff voice, bringing unwanted tears to her eyes. She blinked them away, hoping he hadn't seen them, furious with herself.

"Ahh, Joey."

A sob escaped her as Cole pulled her into his arms. She collapsed against his chest, grateful not to be alone with the memories of the man who'd attacked her.

He crushed her into his arms, and stroked her hair gently as he rocked her back and forth. "Are you really all right? You don't need a doctor?"

"No..." She clutched his arms, savoring his strength and the scent of his raw masculinity.

He brushed a hand across her cheek and forced her to look at him. "Tell me what happened."

Her throat ached with the effort to hold back more tears. "I thought someone was behind me on the stairwell, so I rushed into the room and slammed the door shut. He grabbed me as soon as I came inside."

"He was inside the room when you entered?"

She nodded and leaned her head against his chest again, remembering the feel of the man's hand at her throat. Then his voice in her ear. "He told me to stop nosing around or Donna would end up hurt."

"He threatened your mother?"

"Yes."

He trailed his hand down her back, and she winced. "He did hurt you?"

"I'm just bruised."

"Let me see." His fingers went to the bottom of her shirt, but she pushed his hands away.

"Stop it, Cole. I'm fine."

"Then show me." His dark eyes dared her to prove her statement.

She ground her teeth together, and shook her head.

He reached for his cell phone. "Then I'm calling the paramedics."

"No." She rested her hand on his, waiting for him to rescind his threat, but he didn't back down. Instead he reached for her shirt again. She sucked in a sharp breath and closed her eyes, trembling as he slowly unbuttoned her shirt, and parted the fabric. Cool air kissed her skin as his fingers trailed over her body. In spite of the fact that he only meant to check her injuries, her nipples beaded beneath the flaming red lace of her bra. His own hiss told her that he noticed her reaction.

"He kicked me in the back," she said in a low voice. "And my shoulders."

"Turn around."

"Cole?"

"Do it, Joey."

His harsh voice reeked of anger. She huffed in frustration and pivoted while he examined her back. His fingers gently traced a path over the sore tissue, trailing from her shoulder blades down to her waist. Then he turned her in his arms, and she felt raw, vulnerable. Exposed.

One look down at his hands and she itched to have them stroking her other places. Quivering with need, she glanced at his eyes and saw a mixture of emotions. Desire flickered in the depths along with fury.

"I'm going to kill the SOB," he muttered.

"Cole…" He hushed her with a finger to her lips, then lowered his head and replaced his fingers with his mouth. She clung to his arms, and parted her lips for him.

* * *

Cole had no idea what had possessed him, but one minute he was examining the bruises on Joey's beautiful body, his anger rising like a beast within him, and he'd wanted to kill the man, then the next minute he'd dragged her into his arms and fused his mouth with hers.

She tasted like beer and sin and temptation, a heady combination. Yet she'd been attacked, and needed comfort. Not to be mauled by another man. Behind him, the sound of footsteps registered. A man's voice followed.

"Excuse me. I thought this was an emergency."

Cole pulled away from Joey, and yanked her shirt together, angling himself to shield her as Zane McKinney's stern voice registered.

Hellfire and damnation. He'd come here to prove he was a professional and now his half brothers had caught him behaving anything but professionally. Joey's expression morphed somewhere between the pale shock of her attack, pain from the physical wounds and crimson from embarrassment. He stood, giving her time to rebutton her shirt while he blocked the door.

"I did ask the security guard to call you," Cole said. "Miss Hendricks was attacked in her room. I was just checking her injuries."

Zane's left eyebrow rose a fraction as a small smile played on his mouth. "Is that what you were doing?"

"Yes." Although the kiss had shaken him to the core. Coupled with the fact that she might have died tonight, his emotions flew into a tailspin. Pure animal lust mixed with white-hot fury rallied through him.

Joey stood and approached Zane. "A man broke into

my room and threatened me, Lieutenant McKinney. Cole showed up and tried to catch him, but he managed to escape."

"Are you all right? Should I call a doctor?"

"No, I'm just bruised," Joey insisted.

"Did you see the assailant?" Zane asked.

Joey shook her head. "No, it was too dark, and he grabbed me from behind."

"Did he say anything?"

She gave Cole a wary look but nodded. "He told me to drop the investigation or my mother would get hurt."

Cole chewed the inside of his cheek. For some reason he sensed Joey was holding something back. Had her attacker threatened her in another way?

Sloan appeared and frowned at him as he poked his head in the room. "I thought you were leaving town, Cole."

"I'm not going," he announced. "Not until we find out what's going on around here."

His brothers' reactions were exactly what he expected. Both glared at him as if the subject wasn't open for discussion. They had dismissed him, and he was supposed to comply.

But Cole had never been a compliant child. And he certainly wasn't as an adult. Like it or not, he didn't intend to leave Joey now. Not after that cataclysmic kiss. And not with the killer breathing down her neck with threats.

Chapter 7

Joey sensed the tension between Cole and the McKinney brothers. Tension born from their parent's mistakes, a fact that had automatically set the men against each other just as the investigation put them all on opposite sides.

The next two hours whizzed by in a chaotic nightmare. Lieutenant Zane McKinney took charge, ordered a crime scene unit to search the room for trace evidence, check the security tapes and insisted that a doctor evaluate her and photograph and record her injuries. Obviously feeling displaced, Cole volunteered to drive her to the hospital and waited while she was X-rayed and processed to the letter of the law.

True, she wanted to catch her assailant, but she also knew he was probably a hired hand, not the top dog behind the crimes. And she vacillated between various interpretations of his threat. Had he meant that he would hurt Donna if she didn't steer the investigation away from her, or that exposing the truth would hurt Donna?

Both terrified her in different ways. The first that Donna might be physically harmed. The latter that Donna had actually been involved in the murders.

Anxiety hit her full force—did she believe her mother was innocent or guilty?

She wanted to think that she had been a victim…but Donna had been drinking years ago when Lou Anne had been killed, and had hated Lou Anne. She'd had motive, opportunity and the capabilities to pull it off. She was physically fit, could shoot a gun and she'd been desperate to regain custody of her son. Getting rid of Lou Anne and framing Leland for the crime would have been her ticket to reverse the court decision.

A dull ache settled in her chest at the thought. She didn't want to believe that her mother had committed murder or tried to cover up by shooting the sheriff and burning down the jail.

Tears pricked at her eyelids, and she blinked them away as she walked to the waiting room to meet Cole. She'd never admitted her feelings to anyone, not even herself. But for years, she had craved Donna's affection and love.

Joey's childhood haunted her. She'd wondered why Donna had preferred booze to tucking her children in at night. Why at thirteen, when she'd been struggling with adolescence, with being a tomboy and a gangly too-tall teenager, Donna had fallen into depression and alcohol.

And Joey and Justin had been caught in a tug-of-war that followed. Pawns in the vindictive battle Donna and Leland had waged against one another.

But Justin had lost the most.

Cole stood by the waiting room door with a cup of coffee in hand, his expression solemn. "Everything all right?"

How could it be when one or both of her parents might be killers?

She nodded, though, determined to see this investigation through. "I'm free to go now."

"Good. I told the doc to send the trace to our lab. Maybe we'll get evidence to nail this guy."

Joey remained silent as they walked out to the car. The summer heat was oppressive, making her clothes stick to her skin. The smell of her attacker still clung to her, or maybe it was the scent of her own fear. She desperately wanted a shower and some rest. But when she closed her eyes, she knew she would see that shadow lunge for her. She'd feel his hands tightening around her throat, and the gun pressed at the base of her skull.

A shudder tore through her as she climbed in the car Cole had borrowed from the Rangers. "Did you think of anything else about your attacker?" Cole asked.

Joey massaged her temple and closed her eyes, reliving the assault. "He had an Hispanic accent." She jerked her eyes open. "I didn't think about that at the time."

"Probably a hired hand. Maybe an illegal."

Which meant he'd be impossible to find. But she'd been right—he was working for someone else. But whom?

"Unfortunately he ducked the security cameras." Cole's lips curled into a snarl. "What about earlier tonight? Did you talk to anyone who might have followed you?"

She tried to remember if she'd seen anyone watching her at the bar. "I had a beer at the Last Call and talked to Bud for a while."

Cole veered onto the street to the inn. "Learn anything new?"

"He suggested that both Jim McKinney and Lou Anne Wallace had other affairs."

Cole grunted. "I'm not surprised."

"Then it's possible that one of their lovers might have killed Lou Anne."

"It sounds feasible. Of course Stella had reason to want Lou Anne dead, too."

"I think we should talk to both of them," Joey said.

Cole chuckled sarcastically. "I'm sure she'll welcome seeing me."

"I can question her if you want, Cole."

He shrugged. "I don't need coddling, Joey. Hell, maybe I'll pay Jim McKinney a visit. It's time I met the man."

Joey squeezed his hand. In spite of the unbearable heat, the chill that had pervaded her earlier grew in intensity. They both had to face their fathers with difficult questions.

Lou Anne's affair with Jim had been hard on Leland's ego. And if she'd threatened to report his plan to the police or Donna, he had motive to kill Lou Anne. Another affair would rub salt into his wounds and might have sent him over the edge.

But would her own father hire someone to attack her to protect himself or Donna?

She had to know the truth. She only hoped she could live with whatever she discovered.

When Cole escorted Joey back into the inn, the crime scene unit was finishing processing the room.

"Get your things and we'll move you," Cole said.

Joey nodded and hurried to repack her suitcase while Cole arranged for a room, then conferred with Zane and Sloan in the hall. “Did you find anything?”

Zane shrugged. “Sorry. No prints. He must have worn gloves.”

“We received word about the bullet you found in the woods,” Sloan said. “Forensics lifted a partial and is running it now. If we’re lucky, the print is in the system. If not, at least when we catch this guy, we’ll have something to use as a comparison.”

“Let me know if you get a hit or a name,” Cole said. He thought about the silver star he’d found in the woods. If Jim was guilty of two murders, had he hired someone to kill Joey? Or maybe to scare her away?

Zane cleared his throat. “Look, Cole, we appreciate your help, but we can handle the situation now.”

“I’m not leaving town,” Cole said. “Not while Joey is in danger.”

“I didn’t know you two were that close,” Zane said.

Cole narrowed his eyes. “We’re not. But it looks like she might need protection. That comes with our job title, doesn’t it, Lieutenant?”

Zane grunted, but Cole thought he detected a small smile on Sloan’s mouth. They might not respect him because he was their illegitimate half brother, but he had proven his worth today. In fact, if he hadn’t been around, Joey might have ended up dead.

Not a thought that settled well with him at all. The world needed more long-legged, spunky blondes.

Joey appeared at the door, ducked beneath the crime scene tape and halted.

“How are you now, Miss Hendricks?” Zane asked.

“I’m fine, just exhausted.”

"Do you want me to post one of the deputies outside your door?" Zane asked.

Joey's eyes widened. "I don't think that will be necessary. I'll lock the room and be fine."

"By the way, that gun we found in the nightstand—I'm assuming you have a license to carry, and that you know how to use it?" Sloan asked.

"Yes, I do." Joey's mouth tightened. "And if I could have gotten to it, that guy wouldn't have escaped."

"Where'd you learn to shoot?" Zane asked.

Joey stiffened.

"Never mind," Zane said with a small smile. "I'm sure Donna taught you."

"As a matter of fact, she did," Joey said. "And I'm a damn good shot, too."

"I'm sure you are," Zane said. "But in light of tonight's events, perhaps you should leave town."

"Good try, Lieutenant McKinney, but I'm here at the governor's request," Joey said. "And I don't intend to leave until this investigation is complete."

Zane ran a hand through his hair. "Well, then, it seems we all want the same thing."

Cole grunted. He doubted it. Zane and Sloan wanted to see their father exonerated, and Joey's father or mother or both convicted for the crime. They were working with the grand jury now to try to get an indictment against Leland.

"Call me if there are any more problems," Zane said.

Cole hooked his thumbs in his belt loops. "Let me know what you find out from forensics."

Zane nodded, then he and Sloan left. Cole turned to Joey, his gaze zeroing in on the red bruise marks around her neck. Anger ripped through him.

Cole unlocked the door to the room on the opposite side of his, then checked the interior, making certain the locks on the windows were secure. Joey stowed her suitcase on the floor and a small toiletry bag inside the bathroom.

The antique furniture and braided rug made the room look more like a guest room in someone's home than a hotel. And that bed looked damn inviting…

It was big enough for two, easily.

Joey tugged a strand of her blond hair behind her ear and sank onto the quilt, obviously exhausted.

"You could stay in my room with me," Cole offered.

Joey nearly choked on a laugh. "You are smooth, Cole McKinney."

Not smooth enough or he would already have bedded her.

Which would have made him the bastard everyone assumed him to be. Maybe he was more like Jim McKinney than he wanted to believe.

Still, she appeared so vulnerable and…sweet that he walked toward her, leaned over and threaded his fingers into the soft tresses of her hair. It felt like silk and satin and every man's wildest dreams. He imagined it draped across his bare belly, his hands sliding down to cup her breasts and suck on her lips, and his sex hardened.

She parted her mouth and licked the rosy petaled outline of her lips, taunting him with a memory of that earlier kiss.

"Cole?"

Her sultry whisper echoed with need. Desire. Hunger.

"I should go now," he said, struggling to resist her.

"Yes, you probably should."

He nodded but his feet refused to move.

Her chest rose and fell with her breathing, drawing his eye to the soft swell of her cleavage. Underneath that shirt there were bruises.

But also a beautiful body. And melon-sized globes encased in red lace.

Puckered nipples he wanted to taste and suckle.

Hell.

He leaned over and captured her mouth with his. She made a small throaty sound like a whimper, then opened to him as if in invitation. He teased her lips apart with his tongue, then delved inside and explored her mouth again. She tasted hot and passionate, and erotic sensations exploded in the tiny tongue thrusts that met his lips.

Instantly unsettled by the strength of his reaction, he pulled back and stared at her eyes. They were slitted, sleepy looking, sensual. Aroused.

"Why did you do that?" she whispered.

He murmured the only thing he could. The truth. "Because I had to."

Shaken even more by that thought, he stalked out the door, his declaration reverberating in his ears.

Cole had always loved women. Had been a player.

But he had never actually loved any woman over another, or let a female get to him. He'd never felt this protective or…needy.

And he couldn't now.

Especially not with Joey Hendricks. Hell, she was the daughter of not just one, but two prime suspects in the mystery he'd come here to unravel. She was the last damn woman he needed to get involved with.

His detective instincts surged to life, raising suspicions. Dammit. Joey was a smart woman. Maybe she was here to distract him and his half brothers from looking at her parents as suspects. She'd obviously prefer Jim McKinney be arrested instead.

He had to watch her. Gain access to any information she uncovered. And staying close to her was the only way to do that.

Jim McKinney stared at his wife's frail body as she slept. The hospital bed swallowed her ninety pounds of bones, and her pallor was as white as the pristine sheets she lay upon. The scent of antiseptic and medicine and the clinking of hospital machinery and nurses' voices echoed in the sterile halls, reminding him that Stella was sick.

And that he was to blame for her illness.

He dropped his head into his splayed hands, guilt weighing on him. He hated what their marriage and life had become. When they'd first wed, Stella had been a beautiful girl. He'd thought he loved her. Yet he'd quickly realized that he was flawed, that she wasn't enough. He didn't intend to make excuses for his behavior, but she had been spoiled, stubborn and had insisted on having everything her way. In and out of the bedroom.

The second part he could take, but the first—her bossiness as well as her lack of interest in sex had been enough to send him looking for satisfaction elsewhere. At least that was how he'd justified his indiscretions.

But then he'd hooked up with Lou Anne, she had been murdered, and his life had gone downhill fast.

Stella mumbled something, her eyelids fluttering as

she wrestled with the covers. He adjusted the blanket, trying to soothe her from whatever demons dogged her.

Her eyes opened momentarily, but her gaze looked clouded as if she had no idea where she was or what was happening to her.

"Rest now, Stella."

She muttered something incoherent, then mumbled the word "bastard." She meant both him and Cole. She'd never forgiven him for having another child, and when she heard that Cole was coming to town, she was certain he intended to rub his father's indiscretions in her face. To Stella, appearance meant everything.

For that reason, he'd wondered why she'd stayed with him all these years. He'd lost his job, his respect and friends over the murder charges and he'd never regained them.

Of course, staying with him was her way of punishing him. Each day her anger and bitterness ate at her. She'd used it to hold onto him.

He scrubbed a hand over his face, walked to the window and looked out at the mottled storm clouds. Sweat rolled down his neck and collar as he wondered what his boys had found when they'd searched the woods.

All three of his boys—Rangers.

He couldn't believe he'd shamed them by losing his position, yet they'd all joined the Rangers anyway. God, he'd failed at his job. Failed his wife. His boys. Especially Cole…

He'd heard that Sarah had evidence that might help them find Lou Anne's killer.

Why had she called him that night? To tell him that she knew he had killed her mother? Or had she discovered something to prove his innocence?

If only he could remember what happened the night Lou Anne died…

All he recalled was his argument with Stella, her vicious put-downs. And his plans to assuage his ego with Lou Anne's luscious body. And then the booze…

If he had killed Lou Anne, it was time he learned the truth. Half the town, including his wife, had tried and convicted him in their minds anyway. And he'd resigned from the Rangers before they'd forced him out. Now he spent his days stacking groceries in a little store. And staring at a shell of a woman who no longer loved him. How much worse could prison be?

Still, guilt drew him to Stella. She had lied about her whereabouts that night—she hadn't had an alibi. Sometimes he wondered if he'd repressed the memory because he'd witnessed her kill Lou Anne.

When he'd mentioned using a psychiatrist to jog his memory, Stella had become violently upset, then broken down. Was she afraid of what he would remember because it might implicate her as the killer?

Chapter 8

Sleep eluded Joey for hours after Cole said good night. Long into the hot, sultry evening, she lay awake, tossing, turning in the big double bed. The image of her attacker approaching tormented her. The feel of his hands on her throat, his breath against her ear…

The fear that he might return and kill her this time.

Shivering, she rolled to her side and stared at the blank wall. The ceiling fan whirled above, stirring the tepid air. Outside, the soft sound of cicadas and crickets chirped in the night. She listened for any indication that Cole might still be awake and swore she could almost hear his breathing through the paper-thin walls.

She imagined his hands touching her instead of the other man's vile grip, and erotic sensations splintered through her. Only that thin piece of plywood and insulation separated her from the sexiest man she'd ever met. That and her own resolve to stay professional and not sleep with him. Cole was too masculine, too hot, too damn sexy for his own good. He'd be a dynamite lover in bed. Would soothe her fears for the night. Ignite her senses. Make her forget all about that man who'd tried to choke her and that her parents might be guilty of murder.

But then he'd go his way and she'd be all alone again.

Not that Joey Hendricks needed anyone. She'd been alone for years. Ever since she was a kid really. Donna had been too absorbed in her drinking to notice anything she did. And Leland…he'd been as addicted to women as Donna had been to booze.

She closed her eyes, and pressed her fingers to her lips. Her mouth still tingled from the feel of Cole McKinney's lips on her skin.

She was starting to understand addiction—she couldn't stop thinking about the big handsome man. His kisses teased her to forget her ethics. To accept one night if that was all he could offer.

She shoved away the covers. Heavens, the room was hot. Was Cole sweating next door, too? Was he already asleep, alone in the bed?

Naked with the sheets kicked off?

She hissed, irritated and aroused at the sensual picture that image painted in her mind's eye. He was so tall that she imagined his arms sprawled above his head. His bronzed skin slick with perspiration. His long legs dangling over the side of the bed. His sex thick and swollen, jutting out as if needing to be stroked.

What would he do if she knocked on his door? Would he tell her to go away? Or would he pull her into his arms? Take her to bed and kiss away her anxiety?

Stroke her with those wide, masculine hands? Crawl on top of her and love her until she didn't remember her own name?

Mercy. One night with him would be more exciting than all the nights she'd spent with other men combined. She'd been pretty socially inept at flirting when she was young and the men she'd finally connected with later on in life hadn't exactly been stellar lovers. Of course, maybe she hadn't excited them all that much.

Or maybe they were the wrong men.

But Cole…she had no doubt in her mind that he would please her in bed. She closed her eyes, imagined him sliding beneath the covers. She could almost feel his body brushing hers, his heat radiating her skin, him pulsing inside her…

Cole listened for sounds of trouble next door, and knew that *he* was in the one in trouble. All he could think about was Joey Hendricks. How much he wanted her body. How it would feel beneath him. How her breasts would fit inside his hands.

How he would fit inside her.

His sex hardened and thickened, and sweat broke out on his skin. He should take a cold shower. Or maybe go for a run. A long, exhausting one that would tire his muscles, his wandering mind and his aching libido.

But then Joey would be alone.

And although the feisty, independent smart woman would balk at the idea of a bodyguard, he'd assigned himself the job. And her body was a damn fine one to have to watch.

Hmm, might not be a bad job at all.

He'd been undercover near the border and in some

god-awful places the last year. Being inside *her* would prove to be a tempting reprieve and would feel like heaven to a man who'd come from hell.

Dammit. He had to stop thinking like that. Like Jim McKinney would think.

Was he no better than the bastard man who'd sired him?

His brothers didn't want him or Joey on the case. Granted, her story about handling the media had credit, but it was also an excuse. She was going to dig into the investigation here, and he would be right by her side. Helping her question the locals. Finding answers. Protecting her. Making sure she didn't cover up the truth.

And taking her to bed.

His feet hit the floor and he forced himself to do some push-ups.

He would *not* take her to bed.

But he would guard her delectable body with his life.

He pumped himself through two hundred push-ups, then flicked on a light and sat down to study the files. Jim McKinney had been a major suspect in the original murder.

And Cole had assumed he was guilty. After all, a man who cheated on his wife, impregnated another woman and never acknowledged his third son didn't exactly merit trust or respect.

Had his mother believed in Jim's innocence? Or had she stayed away and not encouraged a relationship between him and Cole because she'd thought that Jim might possess a violent streak? That he was dangerous?

But what was Jim's motive? Had Lou Anne wanted Jim to leave Stella and marry her? That didn't make sense. Then again, Lou Anne might have married Leland Hendricks for his money, then discovered the man was tapped out to the nines, and decided Jim was a better catch. But according to the files, Lou Anne had her own money, money she'd kept secret from Leland. Or had he discovered the funds and killed her hoping to gain access to her accounts?

He'd follow up when he interrogated Leland. And he'd ask his father about his affairs when he finally met him. If Lou Anne had wanted more than he was willing to give.

Willing—or capable?

His own panicked reaction to commitment made guilt tug at his chest. A small part of him understood Jim's wandering eye, his love for women. The very reason Cole had never married. If he ever did, it would be for life. He would not cheat on a woman or knock up some girl and leave her in the wind, or a child without a father. Not to bear the shame and feelings of unworthiness that got tangled in a child's mind when he was unwanted.

And what about other lovers that Jim, Leland or Lou Anne might have had? Joey had mentioned the possibility. Who else had Lou Anne slept with? Had Jim been keeping another woman on the side? Had Leland decided that taking another woman to his bed might be ample payback for his wife's indiscretions?

He heard the bed squeak next door and realized Joey might still be awake. His body twitched with arousal at the mere thought of her lying in the bed. In spite of the air conditioner, he was so damn hot. Would she be wearing a skimpy, transparent gown? Something silky and flimsy?

Or maybe nothing at all?

He moaned in frustration, then dropped to the floor again, and lapsed into another fit of push-ups. No way would he get any sleep tonight.

Joey hugged her arms around her and finally dozed into a fitful sleep. But in her sleep, once again the past rose to haunt her.

Joey hated being a teenager.

In fact she hated everything about her life. She was thirteen and flat-chested. Her feet were too big for her gangly body. And she was a big klutz, especially in front of the boys.

Todd Johnson had belly laughed at her tonight. And she'd been trying so hard to impress him.

Tears dribbled down her face as she ran up the driveway to her father's new house. She hated the cold monstrosity. Hated the fact that her mother wouldn't be there, and that she and Justin had been forced to move in with her father. The lying, cheating bastard.

All she wanted to do was crawl into bed and hide for the rest of her miserable existence. She couldn't go back to school.

Or to the ranch where Todd worked.

Which meant she had to give up Chance, the palomino she loved with all her heart.

But Todd had seen her feeble attempt in the teenage rodeo competition, and she'd never live it down. She hadn't made it past the first rounds. No, she'd fallen flat on her face in the dusty ground while the mare she'd been paired with had kicked and bucked. She'd rejected her immediately just as the boys did.

Why couldn't she have been more like her mother?

Donna had been a rodeo star when she was young. Agile, confident, elegant, a champion rider. Joey had seen all the trophies and admired her mother's athleticism and skill.

And Donna had most likely been a charmer, too. She was still beautiful.

Except when she was slurring her words and slit-eyed drunk.

She swiped at the tears on her face, hoping that her father wasn't in the study as she let herself in the dark, tomblike house. She didn't want to face him tonight.

The lights were off downstairs. He was probably already in bed with Lou Anne. She shuddered at the thought of what the two of them might be doing. He was so enamored with his new wife that he probably didn't even realize Joey had missed her curfew. Sometimes she wondered why he'd fought for custody when he didn't seem to know she existed. He didn't pay attention to her brother, Justin, either.

He just wanted to hurt Donna. He didn't care about his daughter, not really. Just his new whore.

She removed her boots and placed them by the door to the mudroom, then stepped in her socked feet across the marble floor to sneak upstairs. The house seemed eerily silent. No home-cooked meal scenting the kitchen. No bustling Rosa. No laughter.

Not that her parents had laughed the last few years.

Sadness welled in her chest. At first she'd been heartbroken tonight that neither he nor Donna had shown up to cheer her performance, but now she was glad they hadn't seen her disastrous fall. Of course, she hadn't really expected them to come to the event.

Ever since the bitter divorce, it was as if she was in-

visible. Once the marriage ended, they'd written her out of their lives. She was just a problem to deal with, a piece of rope to pull back and forth between them.

From her baby brother's room, she heard a soft cry. She paused on the back staircase, waiting to see if her father roused. But his room was on the opposite end from the nursery. The housekeeper would probably go to him.

Guilt pressed against her chest. Justin hated the new housekeeper.

The wail grew louder, and she rushed to the nursery and eased the door open. Justin stood in the crib, jerking with sobs. With the moon glinting through the window shade, she saw his chubby fists curled around the edge of the crib. Saw the tears streaming down his little face. Her heart squeezed.

"Mommy...." he whimpered. "Want Mommy."

Joey's stomach knotted. Poor little Justin. He missed their mother. At least she'd had a few good years with Donna when she was young, before the drinking and fighting with Leland had begun. Not that she blamed her mother. If her husband cheated on her like her father cheated on Donna, she'd probably be depressed, too.

No, she'd kill his sorry ass instead.

"Mommy!" Justin cried. "Want Mommy!"

"Shh, Justin, Joey's here." She forced her voice to a whisper, then carried him to the rocking chair in the corner. Justin wrestled for a minute, fussing, but she stroked his round head, smiling at the fine baby hair on his scalp, and began to sing his favorite lullaby.

Justin clutched his blue blanket in his fists. "Want Mommy..."

"I know," Joey whispered with tears in her eyes. She wanted her, too. But the judge said they had to live with Leland and his whore. So she and Justin had to stick together. She cradled him closer. She'd take care of him, always...

Joey jerked awake, heaving with tears and rocking herself back and forth. She'd never stop missing her brother, wondering if he was dead. And if her parents had arranged Justin's kidnapping and were responsible for his death, she would help send them to jail.

What if they were overlooking a suspect? Maybe another one of her father's lovers. Or Lou Anne's.

Would he share their names with her if she asked?

Her phone jangled and she checked the number. The governor. Tempted to ignore the call, she pushed the hair from her face, but she couldn't avoid her boss. Not the governor of Texas.

She picked up the handset, not surprised to hear him rant her name.

"What in the world is going on, Joey? I saw the news. You were attacked last night?"

Hell. Dennison again. How had he found out? Was he tapped into the police scanner? "I'm fine, Governor Grange. I guess my being here is making someone nervous."

"Maybe you should come back then," he said in a concerned voice. "I'll send someone else to handle the press."

A man. No, she'd worked too darn long and hard to get this post to run with her tail tucked between her legs. "No, I can handle things. Besides, I've connected with Sergeant Cole McKinney."

"Connected?"

She swallowed, not wanting to elaborate. "Yes, he and his half brothers are estranged, so I think he may be a good source for us."

"Ahh, the bastard son with vengeance on his mind. Wonderful. He's ready to put Jim McKinney away then?"

Joey stiffened at his referral to Cole being a bastard. "Yes. And I think that Lou Anne might have been having an affair with someone else. I'm going to look into that angle today."

A long pause. Then the governor cleared his throat. "Are you sure that's smart? The evidence has pointed to Jim McKinney all along."

"And to my father," Joey said. "The other McKinney brothers are trying to get the grand jury to indict him."

"So you believe your father is innocent?"

The governor had asked her the same question before she'd left and she hadn't known how to answer. She still didn't. "I don't know. But I want the truth once and for all."

"All right." He made a noise in his throat, then Joey heard his wife's soft voice in the background. "Let me know what you find out. But be careful, Joey."

Joey agreed, then hung up and headed to the shower. She had work to do, and she desperately wanted to prove herself to the governor.

Even if it meant exposing all the dirty little secrets in Justice. Including her own family's.

By dawn Cole had showered and dressed. He paced the small room, anxious to confront Stella and his father.

But he didn't want to leave Joey alone.

He heard the shower water kick on in her room and

groaned. The next half hour was brutally torturous as images of a naked and soaking wet Joey traipsed through his mind. Joey's perky breasts slick with soap, her nipples distended from the water's sensation, bubbles sliding down her belly, legs and thighs.

Finally he'd had enough. With his badge pinned in place to remind him of his purpose in Justice, he strode next door and knocked. Had he given her time to dress or would he find her wearing a towel, naked beneath?

Much to his disappointment, when she opened the door, she was dressed. But the short denim skirt looked feminine as hell, with a tank top that outlined her voluptuous shape. God, even clothed, she was a tempting siren, and it was only 6:00 a.m.

"What are your plans today?" he asked.

She tilted her head sideways and studied him, a sparkle of interest in her eyes that did nothing but send fire to his belly. "I'm going to eat breakfast at Donna's. Then I thought I'd visit my old man."

He nodded. "Why don't we stop by the hospital and see Stella on the way? We'll go from there to question Jim."

"You want us to go together?" Surprise tinged Joey's voice.

"After what happened last night, I'm not letting you out of my sight."

Wariness and something else flashed in her eyes—a frisson of sexual arousal? "You're going to be my bodyguard, Cole?"

"Yep. I plan to guard your body with my life," he said, allowing a teasing note to enter his voice.

Her eyes lit up. "Why doesn't that make me feel safe?"

He chuckled and leaned forward, then took her arm. "Because you know I want you," he said bluntly.

Laughter erupted from her, but she didn't back away. Instead she walked down the hall, her hips swaying as if to confirm that she liked his flirting.

He liked her, too. Which complicated the situation even more. He'd wanted women before, but he'd never actually *liked* one.

Thankfully breakfast at Donna's sobered them both from their banter. Tension thrummed through the room as soon as they entered. The locals seemed nervous, darting furtive glances around as if expecting a killer to emerge from their booth and suddenly strike.

The reporter, Harold Dennison, approached. "I heard you were assaulted last night. Care to comment, Miss Hendricks?"

Joey shrugged. "No."

He tapped his pad impatiently. "Come on, Joey. You work for the governor. An attack on you is newsworthy and you know it. Especially since your family is involved in the investigation of both the Wallace murders."

"You've already got your story," Joey said emphatically. "So buzz off, Dennison."

Anger flared in the man's beady eyes, and for a moment, Cole thought he was going to pounce on Joey. He stood abruptly, jarring the condiments on the table as his leg knocked the table edge. "You heard the lady. Now get lost or you deal with me."

"Are you threatening me?" Dennison's eye twitched.

Cole jerked him by the collar, smiling as the man's chicken neck bobbed red. "I'm an officer of the law, mister. I can arrest you for interfering with an investigation, and make sure you get buried in some cell where you'll wish I had hurt you."

"This is not over. I will get the *whole* story." Dennison slanted a furious look at Cole but stalked off.

Cole saw Donna watching him from the corner. An odd expression flared on Rosa's face. Almost a smile as if she was pleased that he'd defended Joey.

He threw some money on the table. "Come on, Joey. We have work to do."

She took a last sip of her coffee and headed to the door. Outside, the morning air already felt stifling. Joey lifted her hair off her neck and fanned it, making him itch to kiss that soft area behind her earlobe.

But he ignored his instincts, climbed in the Rangers-issued vehicle and drove straight to the hospital. He wanted to talk to Jim, but first he'd hear Stella's side of the story. His gut tightened. Or maybe he was just stalling seeing his old man.

Joey clenched the dashboard as he parked. "Do you want me to question her?"

He shook his head. "I'm not running like my mother did," he said. "Let everyone here deal with it."

She nodded, and climbed out and they walked up to the entrance. Inside he checked with the nurses' station and asked for Stella's room number.

"I'm sorry, but only family members are allowed visitation," the nurse said.

"It's imperative that I speak with her." Cole flashed his badge. "Sergeant Cole McKinney."

The woman glanced nervously at an older nurse who shook her head. "The doctor's orders were very specific."

A man's voice echoed from the hall, and Cole froze. Zane's. Sloan's voice followed.

Ignoring the nurse's scowl, he strode down the hall. Joey followed on his heel, silent but supportive.

He spotted his half brothers standing outside a closed door and met them with a stony look.

"What in the hell are you doing here?" Zane asked.

"I came on official business to talk to Stella."

Sloan stepped forward, arms crossed. "Our mother is not up for visitors. She's fragile and needs rest."

"As a Ranger, I have every right to question her," Cole said.

"I'm in charge of this investigation," Zane stated in a commanding voice. "And I say that you don't."

Joey cleared her throat. "As a representative of the governor's staff, I say Cole is entitled to question Stella."

Both men glared at Joey.

"Tell the governor that our mother is ill, and that she cannot be interrogated." Zane's deep voice boomed with authority as he addressed Joey. Then he hooked a thumb toward Cole. "Especially by *him*."

"That's right," Sloan interjected. "You will only upset her, Cole. She can't handle seeing you right now."

Cole gritted his teeth so hard his jaw ached. "But Stella might know something to help solve this case. And you two are covering for her."

"She's heavily medicated and incoherent," Sloan muttered.

Suddenly the door swung open, and Stella's frail form appeared. Her face looked gaunt, thin, and dark circles shadowed her large eyes. She clung to the doorway as if she might slide right down to the floor if she let go.

"Good grief, boys, what's all this shouting about?" She spotted Cole and swayed. "Why are you here? To rub my nose in my husband's indiscretions?"

The pain and tears in her voice sparked guilt to flare in Cole's chest. This woman hated his mother and him, but his mom had been a victim of Jim's wandering libido.

"No, Mrs. McKinney. I want to know if your husband killed Sarah Wallace and her mother," Cole said matter-of-factly.

Zane reached for his mother to hold her upright. "Leave us alone!" Stella whispered harshly. "Go back to your heathen mother."

Grief seared Cole. "My mother is dead. She has been for years."

"So now you want to intrude on our family?" Stella shrieked. "I won't let that happen. We already have enough trouble!" She clutched both her sons as if they were anchors. "Make him leave now, please, make him go away."

Cole felt Joey's hand on his arm, but he eased away from her touch. "I'm sorry, Mrs. McKinney—"

Suddenly Harold Dennison appeared as if he'd emerged from the woodwork, and a camera flash blinded Cole. Dennison snapped more pictures in rapid succession, capturing Stella's frantic screams. Sloan tried to coax his mother into the room while Zane snarled at Dennison. "Get the hell out of here!"

"You can't stop me from reporting the news," Dennison said with a smirk on his face.

"You have no right to follow Texas Rangers or spy on my family," Zane barked.

Joey reached for Dennison's arm. "Harold, you can't print those photos—"

Dennison shook his finger at them. "You may be Rangers, but your family is dead center in the middle of these murders, and if you're covering for them, you'll be exposed."

Zane shoved Dennison toward the door. "We do not have to answer to you. We're the law here."

"Yes, you do answer to me," Dennison wailed. "The public has a right to the truth. The citizens of Justice are terrified."

"Get out!" Zane yelled.

Stella sobbed against Sloan, while he tried to soothe her pitiful cries.

Behind them footfalls pounded the floor. Boots. Then a commanding voice. "What in the Lord's name is going on?"

Zane hauled Dennison toward the exit.

Cole's stomach clenched. Jim McKinney stalked toward him wearing a pearl-gray Stetson, jeans, a white shirt and tie—dressed like a Ranger. Except his badge was missing.

A tail of a rattler dangled from the silver rope hatband. His hair was slightly graying and his back slightly bowed, but he still seemed formidable, a stranger who obviously didn't want Dennison or him around.

A cold, shocked look settled on Jim's face as his blue eyes met Cole's.

Cole forced steel to his backbone and tried to ignore Stella's shrieking. After all these years, it was time to introduce himself to the man who'd sired him and treated him as if he was a piece of garbage.

Chapter 9

Joey tried to remain calm as the tension escalated between the McKinneys. Stella looked as if she might faint any minute, and when Zane returned, a vein bulged in his neck. He would tear Cole apart if he upset her further.

Compassion for Cole stirred her own anger at the circumstances. He had been an innocent baby born from an affair and had been cast away from his rightful father. It wasn't fair. He deserved the same love and benefits Zane and Sloan had received, but instead had suffered their disdain, as well as ridicule from others.

"You need to leave, Cole," Zane said. "You've caused enough damage as it is."

"He's right." Sloan tried to coax an hysterical Stella back inside the room.

A flash of pain mixed with anger on Cole's face. Joey felt the injustice of his brothers' words and wanted to defend him, but also understood Zane and Sloan's predicament. They were simply protecting their ill mother.

Still, Cole wasn't the villain.

His expression changed from anger to sympathy as Stella leaned against Sloan and nearly passed out, raising Joey's admiration for him more.

"Put your mother back to bed." Jim gestured toward Sloan and Zane, then turned a harsh look on Cole. "You shouldn't have come here, Cole."

"I realize none of you want me around. But I'm a Texas Ranger, too." He tapped his badge. "I'm sworn to uphold the law with this badge, and I intend to get to the truth."

Jim's mouth flattened into a thin line. "Then let's go somewhere and talk."

Zane reached for his father's arm as Sloan ushered his mother inside the room and shut the door. "Dad, you don't have to do this."

Jim tipped his Stetson back and absentmindedly rubbed a hand over his shirt where his badge would have been. Joey had seen Cole make the same gesture more than once. Sloan and Zane did the same thing.

Maybe the men were more alike than they realized.

"Fine," Cole said. "Lead the way."

"There's a coffee shop around the corner." Jim glanced at Joey, his graying eyebrows arched. "I heard the governor sent you."

"Yes, and she's coming with us," Cole said in a voice that invited no argument.

"Cole, if you want time alone, I'll meet you later," Joey offered.

Cole shook his head. "No, there's nothing we have to say that you shouldn't hear. After all, you're overseeing the investigation."

Jim shifted on the balls of his feet, looking nervous, but nodded abruptly and led the way down the stairs to a coffee shop adjoining the hospital. When they all had steaming cups of coffee in hand, they claimed a booth.

"All right, Cole, what do you want to ask?" Jim said.

Emotions tinged his eyes, telling Joey more about Jim McKinney than he wanted to reveal. He was sizing up Cole, soaking in details about him as a parent would a long-lost child. He was glad to finally meet his third son. That he had regrets, not just about the investigation, but about his illegitimate child. He wanted to know more about him, to reach out and touch him.

He wanted to say things that he'd never say, especially in front of her. Maybe never.

Because he didn't think he had a right.

And he didn't. Not after he'd abandoned Cole all his life.

And Cole—she sensed he wanted more, too, but he wouldn't allow himself to ask for it.

The reasons came to her with undying clarity. Cole had built walls of steel around his heart to protect himself just as she had. He was afraid of being rejected. Of being hurt. Of not being wanted.

She sipped her coffee, and blinked back tears. Or maybe she was projecting her feelings and needs onto Cole because she was thinking about her impending reunion with her own estranged father.

Either way, Cole McKinney touched something deep inside her, something she hadn't expected to feel.

Cole hated himself for caring what Jim McKinney thought of him, but he'd imagined this meeting for so long that he needed time to absorb the moment as they settled into their seats. He wanted his father to see that he'd achieved professional status and was on the same level as Sloan and Zane, Jim's *real* sons.

But of course, his mere presence had rocked the tight little family unit. And the fact that he'd upset the fragile Stella McKinney had not won him favors.

Dammit, he even felt sorry for Stella himself. She was pitiful.

But she also might be a murderer. Or hiding one—her own husband.

Hell, had any one of them considered how his own mother had dealt with raising a child alone? Granted, having an affair with a married man wasn't exactly something to admire, but it took two to tango, and she'd been left holding the responsibility on her lonesome.

Had Jim ever wondered what had happened to him after his mother's death? When he'd been all alone…

Jim could have at least sent flowers to his mother's grave.

Jim cleared his throat. "All right, Cole. Why did you really come?"

"To help track down Sarah Wallace's killer."

Jim's blue eyes narrowed.

"You didn't know that your two sons requested my help?"

Jim shook his head. "Things have been crazy around here with the fire and the sheriff being shot."

"Exactly." He glanced at Joey and saw her watching him. Maybe he should have left her at the inn so she wouldn't have witnessed his humiliation, but he'd run from Justice and his family long enough. He refused to be ignored anymore.

"I suppose you've read all the reports on the investigation," Jim said in a low voice.

Cole nodded. "Did you kill Sarah Wallace?"

Jim gave him a sharp look. "You don't pull any punches, do you?"

"No. Someone also attacked Miss Hendricks last night. They either wanted to kill her or scare her off. Did you hire someone to do that?"

"No."

"Did you kill Sarah Wallace?" he asked again.

Jim shook his head. "No."

"What about Lou Anne?"

Silence registered, full of tension. Jim removed his Stetson and ran a hand over his thick, graying hair, avoiding eye contact. "You read the report. I was inebriated that night. I don't remember what happened."

"You could undergo hypnosis to recover your memory."

"Actually I've discussed it with Sloan and Zane. Stella was against it. Then she had the breakdown..."

Maybe she was too afraid of the answers they'd find. Either that he killed Lou Anne or *she* had.

"What about Stella? Do you think she might have killed Lou Anne?"

"Absolutely not." Jim shifted restlessly, toying with the snake braid on his hatband. "Stella has always been weak, fragile. She wouldn't have the guts to murder anyone."

"Not even a woman who might steal her husband from her?" Cole's voice resonated with anger. "After all, Lou Anne wasn't your first indiscretion. Maybe she was just the one who sent Stella over the edge."

Jim shoved his hat back on his head. "I told you, she's not capable of murder."

"Anyone is capable of killing another person," Joey cut in. "Especially if they're driven to it."

Jim blasted Joey with an angry look, then started to stand.

"We're not finished, Mr. McKinney," Joey said.

He grunted. "I am."

Cole thumped his hand on the table. "One more question."

Turmoil registered in Jim's eyes. Did he think Cole was going to ask him something personal? Like why he'd never tried to see him, not even once during all the years he'd been so nearby?

"Whom else did you sleep with at the time?" Cole asked.

Jim's expression registered surprise, then confusion. "Why is that relevant?"

"I'm just trying to be thorough. If you, Stella, Leland or Donna didn't kill Lou Anne, perhaps one of your other lovers did? Maybe some woman who saw Lou Anne as a problem between the two of you?"

"If that's true, then why not kill Stella? She was my wife."

Cole nodded. "Maybe she thought she could convince you to leave your wife."

Jim stared at him for a long moment, emotions warring on his face. "I would never have left her," he said in a gravelly voice. "Every woman I slept with knew that."

Jim turned and walked away, leaving Cole's heart racing with fury and his message ringing in his head. Cole's mother had slept with him knowing he'd never leave his wife, but she'd loved him anyway.

* * *

Cole's mouth tightened as he balled his hands into fists. Joey sensed he was at the end of his restraint, that he was about to chase down his father and punch him. She couldn't say that she blamed him.

The man had made no personal acknowledgment of his third son, no apology, no I-love-you declarations.

Then again, she and Cole had been interrogating him on possible murder charges. And she supposed she had to admire the fact that he had some decency and hadn't left his wife, especially since Stella seemed so fragile and needy.

"I need to get out of here," Cole said.

She reached out to comfort him, but he shook his head. Pain radiated from his features, making her heart swell with unwanted emotions. She wanted to soothe him and ease the pain.

Instead she started toward the exit. "I guess we meet my father now."

He gave her an understanding look, then his cell phone jangled. He answered it as they stepped into the heat and walked to the sedan.

"Sergeant McKinney speaking."

She climbed in and fastened her seat belt while he spoke in a low voice. When he hung up, he started the car and the air conditioner, then shifted into gear and drove from the parking lot.

"That was Deputy Burns. He's been reviewing Sarah Wallace's phone records."

"Did he find anything?"

"Just that Sarah called Jim McKinney before she died. Apparently Jim told him about the call, but he didn't speak to Sarah. He was gone and Stella took the call."

Joey tapped her nails on her thigh. "What if Stella thought Sarah wanted to pick up with Jim where her mother left off?"

"It's possible." Cole paused, twisting his mouth in thought. "Or Stella might have been worried that Sarah had the evidence to send either her or Jim to jail so she killed her."

Joey hesitated to bring up the painful subject, but they couldn't skirt it. "You're not buying Jim's story that Stella is too weak to commit murder?"

Cole shook his head. "I agree with you. Anyone is capable if they're pushed far enough. And Stella...had her reasons," he said tightly.

"Was there anything else?" Joey asked.

"They checked Donna's and Rosa's phone records as well. It seems Rosa was on the phone with her mother while Anna was strangled so that rules her out."

Joey's heart fluttered with shock. "You suspected Rosa of killing Sarah?"

He shrugged. "They've been looking into every conceivable angle, Joey. Apparently Donna has a bank account Sloan and Sheriff Matheson are investigating, so they examined all their phone records and are reviewing their financial statements."

Joey thumbed her fingers through her hair, raking the mass away from her cheek with a frown. She'd have to ask her mother about that account.

And Rosa was close to Donna and had been dedicated to her over the years. But Rosa had loved Justin more than life itself. She would have never been involved in a plot that might endanger him. Not loving, sweet Rosa who'd made sure Joey's clothes were clean and pressed for school, who'd made her enchiladas and baked chocolate fudge cookies for Justin. Rosa who had been a mother to Joey and Justin when Donna had her own affair with the bottle.

Nerves tightened every cell in her body as Cole drove up the oak-lined driveway to her father's estate. Looking at his magnificent spread now, it was difficult to believe that Leland had ever been financially strapped.

But even if he had, it wouldn't have justified kidnapping his own son.

Cole parked, killed the engine, then turned to look at her. "Are you sure you're ready for this?"

"No." A nervous laugh escaped her, and Cole's mouth tilted into a smile.

"I like your honesty, Joey. That's rare these days."

She tensed. If she was totally honest, she'd admit to him how terrified she was that her parents might be guilty. That she wanted Jim McKinney to be the culprit.

Oddly Cole might understand. He must have mixed feelings about his father just as she had about her own.

They were very much alike in that manner. Both ignored, abandoned in some ways, yet putting up a tough front as if they didn't care about the outcome. But living with the stigma of being a murderer's child would only add to the pain they'd already been saddled with.

"We can come back later if you want."

How chivalrous of him to offer her a way out. "No, let's get this over with." Besides, she didn't intend to let him question Leland alone.

He opened the door and met her by the passenger side before she could climb out. As she led him up the brick walkway, he placed a hand to the small of her back, a gesture that felt comforting and intimate at the same time. She rang the doorbell, and he gave her a questioning look. This was supposed to be her home, but she had never felt at home here. Not like she had in the tiny house she remembered as a child, the one where her parents had still been happy.

A servant she didn't recognize answered the door. "Miss Hendricks, welcome. My name is Broderick, so let me know if you need anything. We've been wondering when you'd stop by."

"Is my father home?"

The balding, thin man dressed in a butler's uniform glanced suspiciously at Cole. "Yes. Who shall I say is here to visit?"

"Sergeant Cole McKinney, Texas Rangers."

Broderick nodded curtly, then gestured for them to follow him to her father's study, a massive room filled with leather couches, sleek cherry furniture, volumes of collector's books and journals and magazines filled with information for entrepreneurs and oil barons.

Broderick excused himself to retrieve her father, and Joey paced the office, feeling caged, and aching to run and escape the confrontation destined to ensue. Cole claimed a seat in one of the wing chairs, stretching his long legs out and looking at ease as he studied the room.

Five minutes later, an aproned woman appeared with a tray of cakes, tea and coffee. Joey's stomach revolted, but Cole accepted coffee. Her father strode in seconds later, wearing an expensive suit, his shoulders rigid, his gaze traveling from her to Cole in a condescending manner. He looked older and grayer, Joey noted, although he still dominated a room with his presence.

"Well, this is interesting," Leland said. "I didn't expect my first contact with you in years to be in the eyes of the Texas Rangers. Especially the bastard son of Jim McKinney."

Cole set his coffee cup down on the tray, the only indication that her father's comment angered him. But Joey knew differently. She was beginning to read the man and hated for him to have to endure such ridicule.

"Father, rudeness doesn't become you."

Her father snapped his head her way with a flare of indignation in his eyes. "I only spoke the truth."

"So, if you're into telling the truth these days, why don't you start with your part in the Wallace murders?" Cole asked in a voice steeped with barely controlled rage.

Leland picked up a cigar and rolled it between his fingers and thumb. "I've already given my statement to the sheriff and to the other Texas Rangers."

"We've read it," Joey said. "And you claim that you didn't have anything to do with Justin's kidnapping or murder?"

The agony that flashed into her father's eyes seemed so real and heart wrenching that Joey's throat closed. Her own guilt surfaced, causing pain to ricochet through her in waves that nearly made her double over.

Cole gave her an odd look, then piped up. "Did you?"

Leland sank into his desk chair and wiped at perspiration on his forehead. "I would never have hurt a child. There's not a day that goes by that I don't wish Justin had been found."

Missing his son didn't mean he hadn't orchestrated a plan that had gone awry. And he probably wanted Justin to be found to take suspicion off of himself.

Joey's resolve hardened. She remembered how convincing her father had been in court when he'd ruthlessly taken her and Justin from Donna. How he'd lied to have his affair.

"Dad, did you set up the kidnapping to get the insurance money?"

He shook his head. "How can you even ask me that, Joey?"

"How can I not?"

"Mr. Hendricks," Cole cut in. "Did you know about your wife's secret account?"

"No. If I had, I would have asked for help."

"Maybe you did and she refused you," Cole suggested.

Leland bristled. "That's ridiculous. I said I didn't know, and that's the truth."

Cole didn't look convinced. "We're aware that Lou Anne Wallace had an affair with Jim McKinney. Was he the only man she was seeing before her death?"

The question seemed to take him off guard. He rolled the cigar between his fingers again, then tapped it on the desk as if he wanted to light up but was trying to give up the habit.

"Dad?" Joey asked. "Was there another man…or men in Lou Anne's life?"

Confusion, anger, then hope sparkled on Leland's face as if he just realized the implication of the question. "Obviously there were, since there were two semen samples in her body when she died. But I don't know any names. And the police never pursued it. They just came after me."

Joey hadn't known about the second semen sample. She wondered if Cole had, if he'd intentionally kept the information from her.

Cole's phone jangled and he frowned, checked the number, then stood. "It's Zane. I'd better take it."

Joey nodded, and her father watched Cole leave the room. Leland moved to the wall behind his desk, revealed a safe, methodically keyed in the combination, then opened the door. With a sigh, he removed a small, black worn book and handed it to Joey. "This belonged to Lou Anne. It was private. I…never showed it to the police."

"What is it?" Joey asked.

"Lou Anne's date book where she kept an account of all her…meetings. It might prove helpful."

Excitement raced through her veins. "Why didn't you show this to the police?"

"I didn't want all of Lou Anne's indiscretions plastered over the papers. Her affair with McKinney was humiliating enough."

Cole's boots pounded on the marble floor, and she jammed the date book in her purse. She'd check it out first and see if it offered any information. Then she'd decide whether or not to show it to Cole. After all, it might prove to be nothing…

Then again, it might lead to Lou Anne and Sarah Wallace's killer.

And what about Justin—did the book contain information about her brother's kidnapping and murder?

Irritation crawled through Cole as he drove Joey back to the Matheson Inn. Zane had phoned to inform him that the doctors had sedated Stella and were worried that she might permanently slip into a catatonic state. He had warned Cole not to visit her again.

Hell, he was sorry that Stella was so weak and ill.

But she had made her choices years ago. And she might have killed Lou Anne or covered for her husband.

Jim had chosen her over Cole's mother who had loved him with all her heart. Barb Tyler had been a strong gutsy woman who'd deserved better.

His stomach rumbled, reminding him that they had missed lunch altogether. Storm clouds darkened the sky as they neared town, a town filled with secrets and deception.

A town where a murderer still lurked, probably gloating over the fact that he—or she—had gotten away all this time.

He cut his gaze toward Joey. She had been quiet since climbing in the car and kept worrying her purse strap with her fingers. He knew the meeting with her father hadn't gone as she'd probably hoped.

"Do you want to stop for a late lunch, or early dinner?"

She bit down on her lip, and he reached up and touched her chin. "Joey?"

Behind him, a car raced up on his tail, and he jerked his gaze from Joey to the rearview mirror. He'd been mentally distracted and hadn't noticed the traffic, much less this car approaching so quickly.

He sped up slightly. The car sped up as well, then suddenly zoomed up close to his tail and swerved sideways. Seconds later, a loud popping sound echoed through the air, then a bullet pinged off the side of the car.

"Dammit. Hang on!"

Joey clenched the dashboard as he jerked the car sideways. "What was that?"

"Someone's shooting at us!"

He pressed the gas, and the sedan vaulted forward. Joey turned to look at the car, but he swerved the opposite way and the sudden movement flung her against the car door. The gunfire pinged again, and he pulled to the left, but the right front tire popped. Damn. They were hit. Then the car raced up on his tail and slammed into them, sending them into a spin. Tires squealed and the scent of smoke spewed from the wheels. He cursed again. The shooter must have hit the gas tank.

A small hill sloped downward to a wooded area. He tried to maintain control, but lost it as the car spun and rolled toward the woods. Joey screamed, and he threw out his arm to shield her as glass exploded and the air bags deployed. The car rolled over, bounced, skidded, then slammed into a tree. Immediately the front of the car erupted into flames.

He yelled Joey's name. They had to get out before the car blew up completely!

Chapter 10

Panic shot through Joey as the car skidded into the tree and fire burst from the hood. The air bag trapped her, and she was hanging upside down between it and the seat. The scent of smoke and gas permeated the air, raising her fear another notch. Her chest ached from the impact of the bag, and her arm from being thrown against the door, but she was alive.

Next to her, Cole grunted and swiped at the air bag. "Joey, are you all right?"

"Yeah. You?"

"Yes. But we have to get out of here fast. The car's going to blow any second."

"I know." She jiggled her seat belt trying to free it. "Cole, my seat belt is stuck!"

Cole ripped the air bag open with a pocketknife and shoved it away from her face, jerked off his own seat belt, then split the seat belt with the sharp blade, freeing her. She gripped the door handle and pushed her hand up to brace herself as her body slid down and her head hit the roof.

He hit the automatic button to roll down the windows but they didn't budge. "Dammit." Cole slammed his elbow into the window and the glass shattered. He chipped away the remaining jagged edges with the knife, then turned to her. "Come on. We have to crawl out."

He shoved his broad shoulders through, and dove onto the ground while Joey crawled to the driver's side. She grabbed her purse and he pulled her through the opening headfirst. Her heart pounded at the sight of the flames shooting from the front of the car. Heat suffused her face, and the smell of gasoline filled her nostrils as she landed on top of Cole. He caught her, and they rolled sideways on the ground, then he dragged her toward a clearing away from the sedan. A fraction of a second later, the car exploded with a thunderous roar and bright orange flames colored the gray sky, smoke billowing in a thick cloud.

Joey heaved for a breath as Cole leaned against a tree. She searched the road and woods for the shooter or another car, and saw Cole doing the same, but the driver had left them to die.

The thought sent another shudder through her, and she realized how close they'd come to death.

Cole turned her to face him. "Are you hurt?"

She shook her head, but her shoulder and chest ached. She might have cracked a rib or two and she'd have more bruises. His hand was bleeding from the broken glass, his face covered with sweat and dusted with soot.

Their gazes met, anger and fear pumping adrenaline

through her. She saw the same emotions mirrored in his eyes as he yanked her into his arms and held her.

"God, Joey," Cole said in a gruff voice. "That was close."

"I know." She leaned into his strength, unable to remember the last time she'd let someone support her. But she couldn't resist now.

"Did you see anything?" she whispered.

He rested his head on top of hers. "No, just a dark car. I couldn't even get the make."

Joey clung to his arms and pressed her face into his warmth. Today they had confronted Stella, Jim McKinney and her father. Had one of their own family members tried to have them killed? It was hard to believe they might be so evil…

The date book in her purse felt heavy, reminding her that it might hold a clue as to Lou Anne's killer. She had to study it tonight and see if it offered answers.

Cole stroked her back while the car continued to burn. Fire hissed and popped, crackling. Heat seared her skin, the flames painting lines of orange and red across Cole's strong face.

Cole removed his cell phone and punched in a number. "Zane, it's Cole. Someone just tried to kill me and Joey." He paused. "A dark car. Gunshots fired at us. The car sideswiped us and sent us into a spin. We need a fire truck and crime team out here now."

Joey closed her eyes. All she wanted to do was retreat to the inn and bury herself in Cole's arms. Kiss him and have him hold her all night and help her forget that her own family might be out to destroy her.

Within minutes, sirens wailed and bright lights flickered through the sky as the fire truck screeched to a stop.

Zane raced up on the heels of the fire truck, a crime scene unit van following, one of the deputies vaulting out with him. Unfortunately Dennison was in tow as well, shooting photos as he approached.

"Get the crime scene area roped off immediately!" Zane ordered. "And keep Dennison out!"

The deputy jumped into motion, as did the crime unit and firemen.

Zane took one look at the inferno that had been Cole's Rangers-issued car and anger blazed in his eyes. "Are you guys all right?"

"Just bruised and scratched," Cole said. "I can't believe the guy escaped."

Zane spun on Dennison. "Get the hell out of here!"

"You'd be better off cooperating," Dennison sputtered as he snapped a shot of Zane. "Your antagonism only makes you look guilty of conspiracy to cover up a crime."

Zane froze, a lethal look in his eyes. Cole felt the same rage burn within him, and grappled for control.

Joey stepped forward, irritation on her face, but her voice remained calm. "I'll take care of him." She pulled Dennison to the side, gave him a short version of what had happened, then they spoke in hushed tones.

"What did you see?" Zane asked.

Cole kept an eye on them while he spoke to Zane. He didn't like the fact that Dennison was one step behind them.

"Nothing much. The car raced up behind me, but I couldn't get the model or see the driver."

"I'll have the crime techs look for tire marks," Zane said.

"Dammit, you won't be able to retrieve paint samples from where the other car hit us off of that charred mess," Cole said in disgust.

Zane went to confer with the crime unit while Dennison headed to his van, looking vaguely satisfied.

"How'd you manage that?" Cole asked.

"I promised to share the crime report when the guys are finished."

Cole grunted, still battling the rage inside him as the firemen extinguished the blaze, and the paramedics bandaged his wrist and examined Joey for injuries. She admitted to bruised ribs from the air bag's force and a sore arm, and the paramedic insisted on taking her to the hospital for X-rays. She protested but Cole spoke up.

"Please, Joey. We want to document any injuries so when we catch this SOB we can use it in court to nail him."

Her face looked strained but she conceded. She obviously wanted the shooter to pay for what he'd done as much as he did.

"Once I finish here, I'll meet up with you at the hospital," he said.

Joey nodded and climbed into the ambulance with a frown. An odd pang hit him at seeing her in the ambulance, and he realized that he had the urge to go with her.

Just a protective instinct, he assured himself. Nothing more. He wasn't going to *miss* her. He was simply worried about her safety.

For the next hour and a half, he worked with Zane to oversee the crime unit and search for any signs of tire marks or that the car might have stopped and the shooter might have climbed out, but they found nothing. They had to wait until the fire died and cooled to search for the bullet casings, or see if one had lodged in the tire.

"Where did you go after you left the hospital?" Zane asked.

Cole shrugged. "We paid Leland Hendricks a visit."

Zane's brows shot up at that. "And?"

"He denied killing Lou Anne and Sarah Wallace just as he did before."

"Did he offer any new information?"

Cole shook his head. "No. If he's guilty, he's not going to confess." Not unless they found some hard evidence against him. "But he confirmed that Lou Anne had an affair with another man. Someone besides Jim. He didn't give us a name, though."

Zane rammed a hand through his hair. "That's right. There were two semen samples. That's one of the points the lawyer used to get Dad off back then."

"Joey and I will see if we can find out who it was."

Zane nodded. "Let me know if you do. By the way, Leland drives a dark Cadillac. Do you think he could have followed you and Joey?"

Cole's stomach twitched. He didn't want to think Leland would hurt his own daughter, but he didn't trust the man. "I don't know. It seems too risky a move for a hotshot like him to do himself."

"You're probably right. Leland's style would be to hire someone."

"Like the guy who attacked Joey in her room?"

Zane nodded.

Cole cleared his throat as Zane started to walk off. "Zane, I… I'm sorry about your mother."

Zane's gaze bore into his as if searching for an underlying meaning. Finally he seemed to realize Cole's sincerity, and gave a curt nod. “Thanks. Come on and I’ll give you a ride to the hospital to pick up Joey.”

Cole followed him, an odd feeling settling in his gut. He had no idea why he’d apologized about Stella McKinney. He’d hated the entire family for years. Had known that Stella hated him. And her reaction proved that she blamed him for her problems, that he was an embarrassment to the entire family. That she’d never accept him.

And Jim McKinney seemed cowed by her so he would never accept Cole, either.

But he’d seen the pain in Zane’s and Sloan’s eyes when Stella had collapsed, and remembered taking care of his own mother when she’d become ill. How helpless he’d felt. How angry at the fates. And he’d felt some small connection with his half brothers.

Still, the distance between them was too long a bridge to cross. He would never fit in with the McKinneys. The way Jim had treated him earlier had driven that fact home with bone-jarring clarity.

When the investigation ended, he would return to his life, and the McKinneys would never be a part of it.

Joey paced the hospital waiting room, anxious for Cole to arrive. She hated hospitals, always had. But she hated being in the dark even more. Anger stirred inside her. If someone wanted to scare her off, they’d gone about it the wrong way. Her Taurus personality kicked in, her resolve to finish the investigation hardening.

The sliding doors squeaked open and Cole rushed in. “Sorry it took me so long. Zane and I decided to run by and get me another car so I’d have transportation. Didn’t think you’d be up for a ride on the Harley.”

"I'd love to ride on it sometime," Joey said. "But it's probably not the safest mode of travel when a killer is shooting at us. Did you find any evidence?"

"No, but hopefully the crime unit will retrieve the bullet casing. Are you ready?"

"Definitely." She clutched her purse over her shoulder, determined not to lose the date book inside.

Ironic that she was putting her life on the line to help a woman who had stolen her father from her mother and ruined her life.

"Are you all right?" Cole tipped her chin up with his thumb. "You look pale, Joey. Do you need to stay overnight?"

"No," she said. "I want to go back to the inn with you."

His breath hissed out, tension vibrating between them. "Then let's go. We'll stop and grab dinner on the way."

Joey tried to relax in the seat as he drove to a steak house on the outskirts of Justice.

At least no one in town would know them here, and they could have a reprieve from the killer and the nosy press. Joey ordered a filet, baked potato and wine. Cole ordered a T-bone, onion rings and beer, and the two of them ate like they hadn't seen food in days.

"What did the doctor say?" Cole asked.

Cole attacked his meal like he did everything else—with strength of purpose. He'd even managed a small moan at the first bite.

She found herself wondering if he would moan like that when they made love. And if he would attack her with the same fervor, savor each bite…

His gaze met hers, and a spark of electricity rippled between them that was so strong Joey shivered. "Joey?"

"Bruises, but no broken bones," she whispered.

"Good." He wrapped his hand around the beer bottle, and she suddenly had an image of him wrapping those long fingers around her. Stroking her face, her breasts, her belly, then dipping lower and sliding inside her. She shifted in the seat, a shot of fire igniting her thighs.

He ran a finger over her hand, stroking softly, his gaze latching onto hers as if he felt the chemistry, too. "You're tired?"

"Today has been…stressful." All she wanted to do was to crawl into his bed. His arms. Taste his kiss and feel him moan her name against her neck.

He nodded. "Are you ready to go?"

"Yes." She swirled her wine in the glass, then took the last sip and rolled it on her tongue. She could almost taste him. Wanted to taste him. All of him. "Definitely."

His eyes turned a smoky-gray. Then he motioned for the waitress and asked for the bill. A heartbeat later, they slipped back in the car. The silence that stretched between them should have been awkward. Instead it was filled with excited anticipation. Today had been hell for both of them. Confronting parents they hadn't seen in years. Parents who had hurt them. And then the shooting and wreck, and the car exploding.

Tonight they deserved to assuage the pain and remember that they were both alive, that circumstances had thrown them together.

That and the raw sexual tension brimming between them. A tension she wanted to absolve while she was in his arms, naked and quaking with his delicious touches.

She tried to remember the reasons that sleeping with Cole was a bad idea as he parked and they walked into the inn. But the ache in her body and soul overrode any reservations, and by the time they reached her room, she unlocked the door and dragged him inside.

Cole silently groaned as Joey pulled him into her room. During dinner, his mind had taken an interesting ride into fantasyland. A land where Joey's endless legs were wrapped around his body, and he was thrusting inside her like a wild man.

He knew enough about police work and near-death experiences to realize that they were both pumped from an adrenaline high. But a deeper need had driven him to forget his resolve.

He hadn't been able to stop thinking about her when she'd left him at the crime scene. And when he'd seen her waiting for him at the hospital, his hands had moved of their own volition. He had to touch her. To feel her next to him tonight. To know that she was alive, and that tomorrow they would both wake to see the dawn.

Feeling like a fool for thinking such nonsense, he paused in the doorway, but Joey caught him by the collar and began to remove his tie. His throat convulsed, and he whispered her name in a ragged tone that sounded far away, as if it had come from a stranger.

"Cole, please. I…need to touch you."

"I know," he said gruffly. A sultry look grazed her eyes, and he succumbed to the yearning and threaded his fingers through her hair. God, it felt more heavenly than he'd imagined. Like fine gold silk across his belly.

What would it feel like across his bare belly? he wondered.

He had to know.

He cupped her face in his hands and sighed with the

knowledge that he'd never met a woman like Joey Hendricks. He probably never would again.

"Joey, tonight—"

"No promises," she whispered. "It's just tonight."

Tonight he could live with. Promises that he couldn't keep he would never make.

But loving her was something he could do. So he let her remove his shirt. The sound of the buttons popping sent a bolt of white-hot lust through him. And when she stood on tiptoe to kiss him, and he lowered his head and claimed her mouth with his own, his sex hardened and pushed against his fly, aching for the sweet haven her body offered.

She parted her lips and took his tongue inside, then suckled him until he thought his body would explode. He walked her backward toward the bed and his fingers moved to her tank top, then he slid his hands down and lifted it over her head. His heart pounding, he trailed kisses down her neck and his hands cupped her breasts. This time she wore a lavender bra that was so lacy her nipples budded through the thin barrier, begging for his taste. He closed his lips around one turgid peak and pulled it into his mouth, licking and sucking the tip.

She moaned and gripped his arms to hold herself upright, then threw her head back in wild abandon. Joey Hendricks was a force to be reckoned with. Unlike any other woman he'd ever been with. Or loved.

Loved?

No, loved physically. Not emotionally. Cole couldn't let that happen…

She stroked his arm, his chest, then moved her hand lower to cup him, and his body told his brain to shut up.

He laved her other breast with his tongue while his

hand inched to her waist, and he ripped her skirt down her thighs. Joey kicked off the garment, revealing a lavender thong that took his breath away. The sprinkling of blond curls at the juncture of her thighs made his mouth water for her sweet taste. He pushed her back onto the bed and stripped her underwear, then stepped back and drank in the sight of her naked body stretched out on the bed. She was an angel in a devil's sultry body, a woman who stole the air from his lungs.

He teased her legs apart with his hands, then lowered his mouth, tracing his tongue along her feminine folds, savoring the heart of her as she writhed beneath him.

"Cole?"

He ignored her tortured plea and continued his ministrations, his body thrumming with raw hunger. Her hips lifted off the mattress, and she clutched the sheets, twisting them in her hands as she cried out his name.

Sweat beaded along his spine as he finished lapping her up, then removed his jeans. His sex bulged, aching to be inside her, to claim her as his own.

But his cell phone rang, a shrill sound that sliced the air and made him pause.

"Cole, don't answer it," Joey whispered.

The shiny metal of his badge twinkled in the sliver of the moonlight, and Cole's instincts and training drove him to reach for the phone. He was a Ranger first, a man second. He always would be. And no woman had ever changed that, or ever would.

Making love to her would have to wait.

He recognized Zane's number, rose and moved to the window and looked out into the dark street. "Sergeant Cole McKinney."

"Cole, Zane. Forensics retrieved the bullet from the car you were driving. Another .38."

"Just like the casing I found in the woods."

"Exactly. And Cole… Donna had a .38 that we confiscated already. She might have bought another."

Cole glanced at Joey lying naked in the bed beneath the sheet, and worry slammed into him. "Anything else?"

"Sloan and Carley have been checking into Donna's bank accounts. For the past ten years, Donna has been purchasing a cashier's check for $1,000 a month."

Cole angled himself away from Joey. He couldn't stare at her sultry body and those still-aroused eyes while he discussed her mother as a suspect. "You think it was blackmail money?"

"It's possible. Maybe someone found out that she killed Lou Anne and she's been paying for their silence."

Unease tickled Cole's neck. How would Joey react to that news?

"Listen, since Joey seems to trust you, maybe you could find out what she knows about the money."

Cole's stomach knotted. "I don't think she knows anything. She's been estranged from her family for years."

Zane grunted. "Maybe that's because she knows they're guilty. Did you ever think that she might be here to sabotage the investigation? That she might be cozying up to you to keep tabs on us and our case against her parents?"

A frisson of unease seized Cole. He had considered that possibility, but his logic had disintegrated when he looked at those mile-long legs and those irresistible eyes. Eyes that mesmerized a man and made his mind turn toward lust and fantasies of long, hot nights doing nothing but riding her.

Damn. He had lost his objectivity.

"Cole?"

Zane wanted him to use Joey. He had come here to prove that he deserved to wear the Ranger badge as much as his half brothers did. Here was his chance.

"Sure, I'll let you know what I find out."

He hung up, and reached for his jeans. No way he could finish their lovemaking, though, not with the sour taste of what he had to do burning his stomach.

Joey sat up, the sheet riding down to reveal those luscious breasts. Breasts that he had teased and loved only a few moments ago. She indicated the bed, inviting him back, her vulnerable but teasing look so enticing he almost relented and crawled on top of her.

Joey trusted him. But he was going to break that trust.

"Cole?"

"It's late," he said in a gruff voice.

"Who was that on the phone?"

"Zane."

"What did he say?"

Cole shrugged. "They dug the bullet from the car. It came from a .38."

She sighed and twisted the covers over her. "Half the state of Texas owns a .38. Heck, even I do."

He nodded. He ached to go to her and climb back in bed. To thrust himself inside her.

But even though everyone in town knew him to be a bastard, he couldn't sleep with her tonight, not knowing that she might be using him. Or that he had to use her, and that he might have to arrest her mother tomorrow.

Chapter 11

Joey's body still quivered with the aftermath of her orgasm. For tonight, she'd wanted to forget the investigation and bury herself in Cole's arms. Already he was the best lover she'd ever experienced. And they hadn't completely finished…

Emotions mingled with the elation of her physical response as she watched him pull on his jeans. His body was magnificent. Bulging defined pecs and broad shoulders. Then that washboard stomach and those muscular thighs. Even his butt was finely sculpted… and his sex. Heavens. She wanted to feel his thick, long length inside her.

Desire heated her body while her chest swelled with another sensation. A tug of affection. Emotions that she had no business feeling for the Texas Ranger. Emotions that scared her to death.

Governor Grange expected her to be the rational, objective one in this case. And how could she do that if her heart turned to mush over one of the McKinney men?

She glanced at her purse and remembered the little black book that had belonged to Lou Anne and itched to check out the contents. Surely her father wouldn't have handed it over to her if it implicated him. But it might contain damning information on Cole's father.

Granted, Cole pretended he didn't care about the man, but deep down she sensed he wanted some kind of gesture from Jim to show that he cared for him. It was only human nature to crave a parent's love.

She certainly had. Heck, she'd realized long ago that her ambition and desire to prove herself in business, her climb to the governor's office, had been an attempt to make her parents proud. Not that they'd ever congratulated her or noticed…

Why had Cole decided to leave her bed? Why wasn't he returning to finish what they'd started?

His blue eyes turned smoky as he grabbed his shirt. Still his eyes skated over her, and hunger burned in his gaze. A tingle of anxiety stole into her euphoria. "Cole? What else did Zane say? Something upset you."

He moved toward her, then sat down on the side of the bed and threaded his fingers into her hair. His touch melted her into a puddle of need again, blatant hunger humming through her bloodstream. "Cole?"

"Sloan and Sheriff Matheson discovered that Donna was buying a cashier's check for $1,000 every month for the past few years."

Joey gasped.

"She hasn't been sending you the money?"

Suddenly feeling cold and exposed, she covered her breasts. "No."

"Do you know what she's doing with the money?"

"I have no idea. I told you Donna and I hadn't spoken in years." Her stomach twisted as she realized the implication. "You think it's blackmail money?"

He shrugged. "I don't know. But we have to find out."

Joey's throat clogged with fear.

He leaned forward and placed a gentle kiss on her forehead. The tender gesture confused her even more.

"Get some rest. We'll look into it tomorrow."

She grabbed his arm to keep him from leaving. "But, Cole?" She rubbed a hand over his thigh, stroked him through his jeans. "I want you to be satisfied."

A grin inched up the corner of his mouth. "Honey, I had a great time." He kissed her again for emphasis, and she tasted herself on his lips. Her cheeks flamed red when he pulled away.

"Cole—"

"Shh." He pressed a finger to her lips. "Let me do the right thing here, Joey."

She didn't quite know what he meant, but she had a feeling he thought sex would interfere with the case. She should thank him for being a gentleman. For stopping her before she gave herself to him completely.

And making love to him just might tempt her to tear down the guardrail protecting her heart.

He walked to the door, turned and seared her with one last hungry look, then closed the door.

But his last comment worried her. Donna had been withdrawing money each month for the past few years. Was she paying off a blackmailer?

It took every ounce of restraint Cole possessed to leave Joey's bedroom. Knowing that she still wanted him drove him insane with desire. Dammit, how had she gotten into his head so quickly?

He growled in frustration. He had done the right thing by walking out. His father had allowed his libido to guide his decisions and look where he'd ended up. If Joey discovered that Zane wanted him to use her, she'd be furious.

Just as he would be if he found out she was using him.

He had to accept the fact that it was possible. That she might not be sharing everything she knew about her family.

Too antsy to sleep, he phoned forensics for a progress report. A detective named Simmons answered. Cole had worked with him on prior cases and trusted him.

"We finally got a lead on the fingerprint on the bullet retrieved in the woods. Belongs to a man named Hector Elvarez."

"Do you know where I can find him?"

"He was working on a ranch in Mineral Wells. The Lucky S."

The Lucky S? Hmm. Mineral Wells, about thirty, forty miles from Justice. And not far from Dallas where Donna bought her cashier's checks each month.

"I'll pay him a visit in the morning. See who hired him to shoot at Sheriff Matheson," Cole said. "My guess is he's the same guy who also shot at us."

An uneasy feeling snaked through him. Donna was looking more and more guilty.

If she was covering up for murder, and had hired this guy to shoot at them, then tough girl aside, Joey would be devastated.

* * *

Joey yanked on a nightshirt. The thought of her mother being a murderer and blackmailing someone to hide her guilt shattered her night of euphoric bliss.

Panic washed over, but she tamped it down, grabbed her purse and removed Lou Anne's little black book.

Maybe Sloan and Cole were wrong. Maybe she'd find something inside to exonerate her parents.

She flipped on the lamp, propped herself against the mound of feather pillows and began to flip through the pages. As expected, she discovered various dates where Lou Anne had rendezvoused with Jim McKinney. The last one on the day she'd died.

Had Leland not cheated on her mother, Joey might have felt sorry for him. But she had adopted her mother's bitterness over his infidelities. Not only had he destroyed their family and Donna, he had taken her and Justin from the only home they'd ever known to be raised by servants.

She flipped back to the beginning, then studied each page more thoroughly. The name, Sly Jones, drew her eye. She tried to recall who he was, then realized he had been her mother's tax attorney. If she remembered correctly, he died a few years back. She searched through several more pages, then gasped.

No. It couldn't be.

Another man's name that she recognized. She turned several more pages and found his name again. Notations to meet at a hotel in Dallas.

Anger mounted on top of shock as she realized that Lou Anne's other lover had been Clayton Grange.

The current governor of Texas.

The man who'd sent her here to handle the media.

She fell back against the covers in stunned silence, her stomach convulsing. Governor Grange had been a young man then, an up-and-comer in politics. A man from a prominent family. A man who helped handle the investigation of her brother's disappearance and Lou Anne's murder. And he had been married at the time, a newlywed. The last thing he would have wanted was a scandal.

Lou Anne had been disgusted with Leland's financial situation. Had she sought out the governor? Seduced him? Maybe threatened to expose their affair if he didn't leave his wife for her? Or maybe she'd wanted money to keep quiet?

Could Governor Grange have killed Lou Anne to save his reputation?

And if he had, would he expect her to cover for him?

Between his body yearning for a night with Joey, his mind replaying various scenarios about the case and his guilt over possibly using the only woman he'd been attracted to in ages, Cole suffered a sleepless night. He took a cold shower the next morning, then dressed in his jeans, white shirt, standard tie and Stetson and pinned on his badge, reminding himself that his job was all that mattered. Being a Ranger was what he lived for. He had no family, no ties, and he didn't need them. They would interfere with his head when he needed to focus. The sooner he cracked and closed this case, the sooner he could leave town and be done with the McKinneys. They'd made it clear they didn't want him here.

And Cole McKinney didn't hang around where he wasn't wanted.

Bracing himself for the sight of the blond beauty who'd haunted his dreams all night, he knocked on her door. She answered, already dressed. A pale blue sundress showcased her sinful legs, and her long hair swung free making him itch to sink his fingers into the silky tresses.

"Good morning, Cole."

Her smile seemed a little too bright and fake. "Is it?"

She shrugged. "I don't know yet. But let's go talk to my mother."

He nodded. He understood her trepidation. He wasn't exactly looking forward to the confrontation, either. Which disturbed him.

He shouldn't care about an interview or how it might affect Joey.

Early morning sunshine beat down on them as they walked to the diner, drilling home the fact that he was actually worried about her. The sound of hushed voices of early morning locals filtered through the strained silence as they entered the diner. Two elderly ladies sipped coffee at a table near the door and a family with four kids fought over the pancake syrup.

The bell tinkled, announcing their arrival and Donna glanced up from the counter. A hesitant smile lit her eyes as if she was happy to see her daughter but wondered why she was with the likes of a bastard like him. Rosa flitted over to Joey and hugged her.

"Joey, are you okay? I heard about the accident."

Her thick accent slowed her down, but Joey seemed unfazed. "Yes, I'm okay."

Rosa's eyebrows furrowed in concern as she examined Joey for injuries. "I saw on news where you in accident." She lapsed into several sentences of heated

Spanish that Cole tried to discern. But she was so upset he couldn't follow. "Are you hurt?"

"No, Rosa, I'm fine." She smiled and squeezed Rosa's hands. "Don't worry."

Rosa clucked, shaking her head from side to side. "It is too dangerous for you here askin' questions. Please, my little bebé, leave things alone."

"Rosa, everything will be fine." Joey waved off her concern and slid into a booth. "Now, we want some breakfast, then I need to speak to my mother."

Rosa's eyes darkened. "*Sí.* I get you breakfast. Omelet or empanadas?"

"Coffee and empanadas would be great," Joey said. "I've missed your cooking."

Rosa smiled although tears glittered in her eyes as she scribbled Cole's order and bustled to the kitchen.

Donna appeared at the register to handle several customers and watched them warily as Joey and Cole ate. When they'd both finished their second cup of coffee, Joey stood. "It's time."

Cole nodded, threw some money on the table, then followed her to the counter.

"Donna, we need to talk," Joey said matter-of-factly.

Donna appeared calm as she finished stacking the bills by the register. "All right. Let's go to my office."

Joey and Cole followed, the air between them fraught with tension. When they reached her office, Donna seated herself in her desk chair, crossed her legs and gestured for them to sit in the two adjacent chairs. "To what do I owe this honor?"

Cole had read that Leland was a hothead under pressure and Donna the calm one. She was proving that correct. At least for now.

"Mother, it's come to our attention that you've been going to Dallas and buying a cashier's check each month for $1,000." Joey fisted her hands in her lap. "What is the money for?"

Donna ran a finger along the edge of her desk, seemingly undisturbed by Joey's bluntness. "I donate it to a children's home, a charity," she said in a low voice. When she looked up at Joey, a well of anguish filled her eyes. "I know it won't bring back your brother, but I wanted to do something in honor of Justin."

Cole chewed the inside of his cheek, studying her while Joey's expression softened. "That's a nice gesture, Donna. Really."

Cole shuffled his boots, kicking the toe against the edge of the chair. Was Donna telling the truth? "What's the name of the charity?"

"It goes through a church in Dallas. St. Francis." Donna scribbled the name and address of the Catholic church on a notepad. "There, check it out yourself."

Cole nodded. He intended to do just that.

Donna excused herself to freshen up, dismissing them.

Outside the door, Rosa cornered Joey and pulled her to the side.

"Joey, I see your mama. She upset. Crying. Said you askin' questions?"

"Yes, Rosa. The sheriff found out about Donna purchasing a cashier's check each month. They thought she might be paying off a blackmailer to keep quiet."

Rosa's coffee-colored skin paled slightly. "Listen to me, little one. I help raise you, and I know you care about your mama. Please don't keep askin' questions.

You are only hurtin' your mama more, and endangering yourself."

Joey clutched Rosa's arm. "Don't worry about me, Rosa. I'll be fine. Maybe I'll even find evidence that will clear Donna once and for all."

Rosa shook her head. "Leave it alone, Joey, *sí?* Please, for Rosa."

Joey hugged her. "I promise I'll be careful."

Cole frowned at the glint of worry in Rosa's eyes. Did she know more than she'd told them? Was she covering for Donna and trying to dissuade Joey because she knew Donna was guilty?

Joey desperately wanted to believe Donna. And she had to talk to the governor. She'd really prefer a personal meeting, but she didn't know how to escape Cole without making him suspicious, so she'd called and left a message. "Where to now?" she asked as they climbed in the sedan.

"I talked to forensics last night. They traced the bullet slug I found in the woods near the inn to a man named Hector Elvarez."

"The bullet fired at Sheriff Matheson?"

"Yes. Elvarez works at a ranch near Mineral Wells. I thought we'd ride out there and talk to him."

"Finally a real lead." Joey's heart raced with adrenaline. "But why would Elvarez want to kill the sheriff?"

"He was probably a hired gun."

Joey nodded and stared at the landscape as they drove toward Mineral Wells. Maybe this man would give them answers. But she still had to question Governor Grange. She'd worked for him for four years now, had thought his marriage proof that happily-ever-after existed. That there was a man or two in the world who could be faithful.

Now that notion and her image of him were crushed. She admired the governor's political views, his fairness in dealing with issues and his staff, his concern for the state. And he'd given her a chance even though her family name preceded her.

But had he hired her in order to keep tabs on how much she knew about the past?

And how would the governor's supporters feel if they knew he had committed adultery when he spouted old-time family values as part of his campaign?

She glanced at Cole's firmly set jaw. They had a half hour drive, and she wanted to know more about him. "What was it like for you growing up?"

A flash of anger shadowed his blue eyes. Anger that didn't quite mask the pain.

"I liked ranch life," he said simply.

He was avoiding the real question. She sighed and rubbed his arm. "Did your father ever try to see you?"

He scraped his hand through his hair. "No. I…never met him or my half brothers until I came to Justice."

"Tell me about your mother."

His expression softened slightly. "She had a great smile. Worked hard. Did the best she could for us."

"Jim didn't provide financial support?"

"My mother told me once that he offered her money, but she didn't intend to be treated like a kept woman." He made a sarcastic sound. "I know people in Justice thought she was a home wrecker, but she loved Jim McKinney." His hands tightened around the steering wheel. "I never understood that. How she could love him when he didn't take care of her or his own son?"

"We don't choose the people we fall in love with, Cole," Joey said softly. "Sometimes it just happens." She lay her hand over his and he stiffened. She wondered if she'd said too much. Sounded as if she might be declaring her love when he didn't want to hear it.

She was smart enough to realize that this was the wrong time for her to get involved with anyone, too. But she couldn't deny how drawn she felt to Cole, how much she admired him for being a self-made man.

"What happened to your mother, Cole?"

"She had a heart attack." He sighed. "She was only forty at the time, but I guess the stress and hard work were too much for her."

She trailed her fingers through the scruffy ends of his dark hair where it brushed his collar. Maybe his mother had died of heartache. "How old were you?"

He clenched his jaw. "Fifteen. I stayed on at the ranch where she worked as a cook. Tried the rodeo circuit but I was getting into trouble, then Clete, the owner of the ranch, set me straight. Later I joined the service and they did the rest."

"That must have been hard, going on without your mother."

He slanted her a sideways glance. "You didn't exactly have a perfect childhood, Joey. Your parents' divorce, then your brother's kidnapping…"

He let the sentence trail off and she gulped back tears. "No, it wasn't easy. I hated Leland for cheating on my mother. Hated him for breaking up our family and then taking me and Justin from Mother."

"Weren't you old enough to choose who you wanted to live with?"

She dropped her hand to her side, and he twined

their fingers together. "Yes," she said through a blur of emotions. "But I took care of Justin. He would have been lost if I hadn't gone with him. He loved Rosa, but he hated Daddy's housekeeper, and he cried for Mother at night." She tried to keep the memories of the fire at bay, but they crashed into her consciousness anyway.

"You were at Donna's the night Justin was kidnapped?"

Joey nodded, seeing her mother's panicked look in her mind. "It was one of the rare occasions when Leland allowed it." She hesitated. "Later, after the kidnapping and murder charges were brought up, I wondered if revenge was the reason he'd allowed us to stay there. So it would look like Donna was incompetent, and he'd have an alibi."

"How did he react to the fire? Did he seem shocked?"

"That's just it," Joey said, still haunted by doubt. "He did act shocked and devastated. It was the only instance where I'd seen my father cry. And later, when Justin was deemed dead, he seemed withdrawn. Of course, just like in the divorce, they both blamed each other." And Joey had never stopped blaming herself.

They reached a wooden cross post sign with the Lucky S painted in red and black, and Cole steered the car down the driveway. Joey glanced across the acreage noting the beef cattle and horses grazing in the pastureland. The scenery was beautiful and peaceful, although the lush green hillside and grazing cows proved it was a working cattle ranch.

Cole maneuvered down the dirt driveway, then parked at a two-story farmhouse that looked inviting. To the right, sat two barns and a stable with pen and corrals. A couple of ranch hands were training cutter horses in the corral. Another in a dusty cowboy hat groomed a beautiful smoky-colored mare.

Cole parked and cut the engine while Joey surveyed the front of the stable where a young man wearing a white Stetson and jeans cantered up on a tall black stallion. He rode with such skill and confidence that he must have grown up on horses. Just like Donna.

He noticed their car, jumped off the horse and called for one of the other hands. “Rodney, we have company. See that Dante is groomed while I find out who they are.”

Sunlight glinted off his black hat as he approached, nearly blinding Joey as she climbed from the car. The young man was probably around seventeen. His confident swagger reminded her of someone, but she couldn’t quite pinpoint whom.

Then he removed his Stetson and her breath caught in her chest. He had Donna’s eyes. Her coloring. Her chin.

She staggered slightly and gripped the wooden pen rail to steady herself as the realization kicked in. This boy might be her missing brother, Justin.

Or was she imagining things because she desperately wanted him to be alive?

Chapter 12

Cole heard Joey's gasp and frowned. She leaned against the rail, her face pale in spite of the sun blazing a fiery path across her skin.

"What's wrong?" he asked.

"Look at him, Cole. He…he has Donna's eyes."

Cole studied the young man for similarities to indicate she was right.

"I can't believe it," Joey said in a choked whisper. "It has to be him. Justin. He's really alive."

Cole placed a hand over hers as he mentally analyzed the situation. "Joey, be careful. If this is Justin, and he was abducted and adopted by strangers, he may not be aware of what happened to him."

She pressed a hand to her mouth, but nodded in understanding. Although she gripped the rail tighter as if she had to restrain herself from leaping forward and pulling the boy into a hug.

"Howdy, folks. What can I do for you?"

"My name is Sergeant Cole McKinney, Texas Rangers." Cole extended his hand, and the boy shook it firmly. "And this is Joey Hendricks, she's a special investigator for the governor."

Apparently impressed, the young man's eyes lit up with interest. How would he feel if it turned out that Joey was his sister?

"Caleb Sangston. Pleased to meet you."

"Caleb, is this your home?" Cole asked.

"Yeah. Well, the spread belongs to Dad."

Joey flinched slightly, and Cole rubbed her back to calm her. "Is your father here?"

Caleb nodded. "Sure. Come on. I'll show you in." He kicked dirt and grass from his boots as he entered the farmhouse, and Cole and Joey followed. She was beginning to pull herself together, but excitement and other emotions glittered in her eyes.

"Dad!" Caleb shouted. "We've got company."

A graying man in jeans, a Western shirt and boots stood at an old-fashioned sink with a mug of coffee in his beefy hand. When he noted Cole's badge, he stiffened.

Caleb gestured toward them. "Dad, this is Sergeant McKinney of the Texas Rangers. And Joey Hendricks. She works for the governor's office."

"Walter Sangston." The man wiped his work roughened hands on a gingham towel, then waved toward the primitive pine table nicked from use and age, and they sat down. "I know who she is." He gave Joey a small smile. "I figured you'd show up here eventually."

Joey curled her fingers around the table edge. "Really?"

"Yeah." He offered them coffee but Cole declined. Joey accepted some ice water, though, and chugged it down.

"Mr. Sangston," Cole said. "We have some questions to ask you."

Sangston nodded warily. Caleb poured himself a glass of iced tea, then leaned against the sink, his interest obviously piqued.

"Caleb," Sangston started. "Maybe you'd better wait outside."

"Actually he should probably stay," Cole suggested.

Sangston's lips thinned, but then a resigned look fell across his craggy features. "All right."

Once again taking the lead, Cole explained about their investigation. "We traced a bullet casing from the woods where Sheriff Matheson was shot to a ranch hand who works for you."

Sangston's gray eyebrows shot up. "One of mine?"

"Yes, a man named Hector Elvarez."

"Hector hasn't worked here in a couple of months," Sangston said quickly.

Cole glanced at Caleb.

"He's right," Caleb said with a quirk of his shoulders. "He left a few weeks ago without even picking up his last check."

Cole frowned. Now to the other part. "Mr. Sangston, when and where was your son Caleb born?"

A tired but defeated look settled in the man's weary eyes. He glanced at Caleb, then back at them. "Why do you want to know?"

Joey suddenly shifted. "Do you know Donna or Leland Hendricks?"

He ducked his head, avoided her gaze.

Joey removed a photo from her purse, one of her parents when they were younger. One where she and Justin had both been captured in the shot. “This is a photo of my parents,” Joey said. “And that’s me when I was thirteen and my little brother when he was two.”

Sangston swiped at his wrinkled forehead where sweat beaded in a pool. “I…guess I knew some day it would come to this.”

Caleb’s eyes narrowed. “What’s wrong, Dad?”

A sheen of tears clouded the old man’s eyes. “I told you that you were adopted, son, but that’s not really true.” He took the picture from Joey and handed it to Caleb, who studied it with a quiet intensity that reminded Joey of his mother, not Leland with his hotheaded ways.

“When you were two, someone left you on our doorstep,” Sangston said, emotions thick in his voice. “Your mama and I…we’d never been able to have children. We thought you were a miracle God sent to us, and we took you in.”

“Mr. Sangston,” Cole interjected, “Joey’s younger brother, Justin Hendricks, was kidnapped and thought to have been murdered at that time. It was all over the news. Didn’t you call the authorities or even consider that this boy you found might have been him?”

Sangston shook his head. “I…don’t read,” he said in a low voice. “Never learned how. Besides, we were forty miles away from where that happened.” His voice rose with conviction. “Then later, when we heard about the kidnapping and possible murder of the Hendricks child, we heard his parents were to blame. Figured the boy was better off with us.”

“Where is your wife now?” Cole asked.

“She passed on a few years back. Cancer.”

"You mean I might be the Hendricks kid?"

Cole nodded. "It's possible."

Caleb suddenly dropped into a chair with a thud. "Then why didn't those people look for me?" Anger made his voice break as he turned a pained look toward Joey.

"We did." Joey reached out a hand to cover his. "But all this time, we thought you were dead."

Cole gritted his teeth. Joey thought he had died. But if Donna had been sending money to the ranch, then she might have known he was alive.

What about Leland?

"So you don't know who left the baby?" Cole asked.

Sangston shook his head. "We found him wrapped in a blanket on the porch with a note that asked us to please take care of him, that he needed a loving family."

Joey's gaze jerked to his. "Did you keep the note and blanket?"

"The blanket, yes. Caleb loved it as a child." He hesitated. "I'm afraid my wife threw away the note."

"She didn't want the baby to be found," Cole said matter-of-factly.

The old man gave Caleb an apologetic, sad look, then gripped the table to pull himself up. He had bad knees, Joey realized, and he was aging, but he loved the boy.

The boy—her brother.

Caleb/Justin looked confused, in shock as he stared at the photo, then back to her. They were turning his world upside down.

Joey ached to say more, to hug him and tell him how sorry she was that he'd been stolen from her family's arms. But she had to make certain he really was her brother.

Although she knew in her heart that he was. She glanced at his hand and noticed a birthmark on his wrist, and her throat convulsed. Justin had had a birthmark in that same place.

How would he feel when he learned that his parents might have been involved in his disappearance? That one or both of them conspired to fake a kidnapping/murder for insurance money?

"Here it is." Sangston loped in, carrying a small blue blanket. It was tattered, worn and resurrected a mountain of memories that sent tears to Joey's eyes.

She clutched the blanket in her hands, studying the frayed corner that Justin used to press against his cheek at night. "Oh, my heavens. This is it." Tears trickled down her cheeks. "You used to carry this around all the time. You couldn't sleep without it. You called it your binkie—"

"Binkie," Caleb said at the same time.

Joey smiled and swiped at her eyes. "I can't believe it. All this time I thought about you, felt guilty, prayed you were alive, and now you're here."

Caleb wrestled with his hands, the strain of Sangston's declaration and her appearance evident on his face. "If you're my sister, why did our parents give me away?"

Joey's heart broke. "It's a long story, Justin—"

"My name is Caleb," he said through gritted teeth.

Joey tried not to react to his anger. For God's sake, she understood it. Knew forging a relationship with him would take time. But at least he was alive.

"Maybe we should come back another day," Joey

said softly. "Give you and your…father time to talk. Give you time to absorb all this, Caleb."

He sipped his tea, the ice clinking in his glass. "No. I want to know everything. I'm not a kid anymore."

No, he wasn't two. But he was still her baby brother. And all her protective instincts surfaced. "I realize that," she said. "But our family…what happened, it's complicated. Not all pleasant."

A calm anger seemed to radiate over him, reminding her of Donna again.

Joey glanced at Sangston for a cue as to how to proceed. The man was hurting, but he seemed resigned. And he obviously adored Caleb. "He deserves to know about his real family. Then he can decide what to do with the information."

Thankful Justin had had a loving family, she explained about her parents' divorce, their bitter fights, Donna's drinking, Leland's affair then marriage to Lou Anne. Justin listened intently, his hands wiping at the water droplets on his glass as she described the horrible fire that night.

"I searched everywhere for you," Joey said, her voice breaking. "I was so upset. And so were Mom and Rosa. Then Dad heard about the fire and rushed over. He was frantic."

His gaze met hers, and he looked impossibly young again, the same little boy she'd rocked in her arms. "They looked for me?"

"Yes, for months. Donna kept a private investigator on retainer for a long time after that. But the police found blood and they thought you had probably died." She hesitated, then spilled the rest of the sordid story. "After that, the police speculated that Leland, our father, might have orchestrated a fake kidnapping and murder in order to collect on an insurance policy, but there wasn't proof. And when no ransom note came, the police believed that plan had gone awry, or that you had really been kidnapped. But there were never any real leads."

When she finished, he looked torn between anger, shock, bewilderment and confusion. Then affection and fury mingled as he faced Sangston. "I wish you'd told me."

"I didn't know everything. And…your mother and I wanted you to be old enough to handle the truth."

Cole had been quiet, intense while she'd relayed her story. He gestured toward the blanket. "I'd like to take that to the crime lab to be analyzed." He pointed to a small dark stain in the corner. "That looks like a bloodstain. It might be too old to pick up anything, but it's worth a try." He paused, then stroked a finger over his badge absentmindedly. "And we'll need a DNA sample to verify you really are Justin Hendricks."

The boy and Sangston traded looks, then Sangston nodded and Caleb agreed.

Joey pinched her fingers together to keep from pulling Justin's hand in hers and comforting him the way she had when he was two. She knew the DNA would prove he was her brother. Donna's child.

But she didn't think Leland was the father. The more she'd studied him, she recognized subtle nuances of another man's face. A man she knew all too well. A man who had been in Justice the time of the alleged kidnapping and murder. A man who'd helped try to pin the case on her father and Jim McKinney. A man who'd known Lou Anne.

A man who must have also had an affair with Donna…

* * *

Cole studied the boy and man, grateful for the rancher's cooperation. He should have reported the baby's sudden appearance on his doorstep years ago and had impeded the investigation, but on some subtle level, Cole sensed Justin—Caleb—had been just as well off growing up on the ranch.

But he had been denied the truth.

And Joey had been denied her brother, and suffered guilt from losing him that night.

He cradled her hand in his, recognizing the strength it took for her not to wrap the boy in her embrace. Joey was an amazing woman. A survivor.

They had to interview Donna again. And Leland. He'd force the truth from them this time. Joey and Justin both deserved answers.

"We should go now." He stood, carefully assessing the situation. He didn't think the old man would run but he wasn't certain. "Mr. Sangston, if the DNA proves Caleb is Justin Hendricks, you'll have to come in and make a formal statement."

"Will he face charges?" Caleb asked, jumping to his defense. "Please say he won't, Sergeant McKinney. I mean if my parents planned a fake kidnapping and murder, they didn't deserve to keep me."

Joey's expression looked tortured. "Nothing was ever proven," she clarified. "I know they've grieved for you, Justin. I mean Caleb. Just like I have."

His young face fell. "I don't want to lose my dad here or for him to get in trouble."

Joey pressed a hand to his shoulder. "Don't worry, Caleb. I work for the governor. You were innocent in all this, and I'll see that the man who loved and raised you isn't charged."

Cole shot her a warning look. She couldn't make that promise. Then again, he didn't know for sure how much power she had over Governor Grange.

"I'd like to see you again," Joey said softly. "When you're ready, Caleb, I'll be here." She removed a business card from her purse and dropped it on the table, then gave Sangston a genuine smile. "I won't intrude on your family, but if Caleb is my brother as I suspect, I'd like some kind of relationship with him. No pressure, though."

Sangston scrubbed a hand over his craggy face. "Thank you, Miss Hendricks. My wife and I…we loved Caleb like he was our own. I'd do anything for him."

Tears dampened Joey's eyes, but she blinked them away, then leaned over and gave the old man a hug. "Thank you for keeping him safe and loving him all these years. I…owe you for that."

Caleb stood and moved to Sangston's side, but gave Joey a tentative smile.

"One more question," Cole said. "Mr. Sangston, did you receive a monthly check for Caleb? A thousand dollars?"

Sangston's chin quivered as he nodded.

"It came from Donna Hendricks?" Joey asked bluntly.

"I did get a check, but it came through St. Francis church. I…honestly had no idea who donated the money. The church said it was from a Good Samaritan."

Cole shifted and tucked his thumbs in his belt loops but refrained from commenting. "We'll call you when we receive the DNA results."

He nodded, and Joey gave Caleb a last longing look, then walked outside into the hot air. By the time they reached the car, and she'd situated herself inside, her shoulders were shaking and tears rolled down her cheeks.

Cole started the car, flipped on the air conditioner, then drove down the long winding driveway from the ranch to the main road. Damn. He tried to harden himself to her emotions. Had to confront her parents. Maybe arrest them.

And he wasn't supposed to care.

But hell. He'd always been a sucker for a woman in trouble. Especially long-legged blondes with eyes that haunted him. And a heart that was just as beautiful.

Ignoring the fact that Zane had warned him not to trust her, he hauled the car to the side of the road beneath a cluster of sprawling trees, then cradled her in his arms and held her.

If Donna had been sending money to the ranch, she had to have known about the boy. He wanted to strangle her for not telling Joey.

"I can't believe it, Cole," Joey cried. "I can't believe he's really alive." She hated the onslaught of emotions, but she couldn't control them. It had taken all her restraint not to break down in front of Justin.

"I know it's a shock." Cole stroked her back, his voice soothing but troubled.

She let the tears fall until she felt spent and exhausted. But slowly as her shock wore off and she began to calm, the full implications of their visit registered. A sick feeling stole into her stomach as she put the pieces together. Finally she pushed back, dried her eyes and looked up at Cole.

"Oh, my heavens, Cole. You think Donna knows that Justin is alive?"

A muscle ticked in his broad jaw. "It's possible."

Anger and betrayal knifed through her as the realization kicked in. "She sent money to that ranch every month. She had to have been sending it to him."

Cole tucked a damp strand of her hair behind her ear. "Shh, don't jump to conclusions. There may be another possibility."

Rage built inside her. How could Donna have allowed her to believe her brother was dead all these years if she'd known the truth? And Leland? If he didn't know, keeping the truth from him was cruel as well. "What other explanation could there be?"

Cole shrugged. "Perhaps a nun at the church where Donna sends the money told her about a charity that supports abandoned kids. Maybe Donna thought she was helping an orphan, not necessarily Justin."

Joey considered the idea. Knew it was a long shot. But she latched onto it.

"I have to know," she said quietly. "I'm going to call Donna and Leland. Have them both meet us at the lab where we're taking the blanket."

It was a dicey move. But their options were running out. The blanket might just be the straw that would break the camel's back and send all Donna and Leland's secrets spilling over.

"You call Donna. I'll phone Leland."

She nodded and punched in her mother's number, while Cole stepped from the car to phone Leland. Donna's voice wavered at Joey's request.

“What is this about, Joey?”

“Just meet me there, Mother. It’s important.” She hung up without giving her mother time to respond, then punched in another number. She had to talk to the governor. Find out how much he knew. If he had slept with Lou Anne. If he and Donna had had an affair. If Justin might be his…

And if he’d known…

If he had, would he have hunted for him? Or would he have wanted Donna to keep the child’s paternity a secret? What if Lou Anne had discovered the truth and had met with him to blackmail him?

Then he, too, had a motive for murder.

Chapter 13

Cole and Joey had a late lunch on the way to the crime lab in Dallas, taking time to discuss their strategy. Cole's thoughts were troubled as Joey sat stonily beside him, staring out the window, her eyes still red rimmed from her crying jag. She chewed on her bottom lip and curled her arms around her waist as if struggling to hold on to her last thread of hope that her parents hadn't deceived her.

On the other hand, he also sympathized with the young boy. How would Caleb/Justin handle learning his father had planned a fake kidnapping/murder for money? What kind of price did a man put on his child's safety?

Leland hadn't been much of a father to Joey, either. He'd been too focused on his financial problems, on his bitterness toward his first wife and keeping secrets to love his daughter.

Seemed neither the McKinneys nor Hendrickses knew much about raising a family.

Another reason he never intended to get tied down with anyone. He liked women, but he'd never been able to commit, just like his old man. He'd probably make a sorry excuse for a father.

His hands tightened around the steering wheel. Why the hell was he thinking about fatherhood? The subject had never entered his brain before.

Caleb—Justin. Joey. That was the problem.

Joey was getting beneath his skin and making him care about her.

Traffic thickened as he approached the Dallas lab. If the blood on the blanket was Justin's, they'd know they had the right kid. And if there was a second type… maybe they'd learn who had abducted the toddler.

Joey's breathing sounded unsteady as he parked at the lab, and they stepped onto the asphalt. The heat felt oppressive, the noisy traffic sounds deafening. He much preferred the ranches, farmland, woods and open-air spaces.

The freedom.

Yet as they entered the building and the elevator, the urge to comfort Joey was so strong he drew her to him. "Joey, are you all right?"

A flash of pain and worry darkened her expression, but resolve and strength emanated from her. "I have to know the truth. It's past time."

He admired her courage as they went inside. He identified himself as Sergeant Cole McKinney, and they were shown to the lead investigator's, Simmons's, office, the same detective Cole had consulted about the ballistics test.

Cole explained about the blanket, and Simmons secured it in an evidence bag. "I'll get someone on it ASAP."

An hour later, the receptionist appeared at the door to inform them that Donna had arrived. Donna rushed into the front office, her hair perfectly coiffed, her dress a white linen that made her look cool and composed in spite of the soaring temperatures and stressful situation.

"What's this about, Joey?"

"Sit down, Mother. I want to wait until Leland arrives before we proceed."

The first sign of panic lined Donna's mouth as she chewed on her lip. "Joey, I don't know what's going on, but think long and hard about what you're going to say and do today."

"I have, Mother," Joey said through clenched teeth. "Now sit down."

Donna spotted the baby blanket in the plastic bag, and the color drained from her face. She slumped into the chair, twining her fingers together. The silence roared with tension as they waited for Leland, but finally he arrived, his face ruddy from rushing in the heat.

Annoyance and anger colored his eyes as he seated himself in the chair adjacent to Donna.

"Mr. and Mrs. Hendricks," Cole began. "We've asked you here because we may have some new evidence concerning the disappearance of your son, Justin."

Donna's gaze shot back to the baby blanket, and Leland's mouth gaped.

Cole picked up the bagged blanket and held it in front of him. "Do either of you recognize this?"

Donna's lower lip quivered. "Yes, that belonged to my baby. He always slept with it."

Detective Simmons accepted it from Cole. "I'll take it for testing now."

Cole nodded. "Did you see that blanket after Justin was kidnapped?"

Donna shook her head and twined her manicured fingers in her lap again. "No, it was missing. I…whoever took Justin must have taken it with him."

"Where the hell did you find it?" Leland asked.

Joey cleared her throat. "Donna has been sending money to a church every month. For $1,000, to be exact. The nun there sends the money on to a ranch."

Leland stood, his tone rising, "What does that have to do with Justin's baby blanket?"

Cole threw up a warning hand. "Sit down, Leland. We'll get to that."

Leland's look of fury was so hot it could have melted butter, but he knotted his hands into fists and reclaimed the seat.

"We just visited that ranch," Joey said. Underneath her calm tone, Cole sensed the barely suppressed rage and hurt. "And guess what we found, Mother?"

Donna gripped the armrest, then glanced away from Joey. Outside a storm cloud passed, covering the sun, and casting gray shadows across the room.

"Mother, it's time to come clean." Joey gripped the edges of the armrest and shoved her face into her mother's, forcing Donna's gaze back to her. "I saw him."

"I don't know what you're talking about," Donna declared.

"Stop lying. Don't you get it, it's over!" Joey's breath hissed with anger. "I saw him. We have his baby blanket. We're going to test the DNA." She shook the chair, rattling Donna. "Now tell me the truth. You sent money to that ranch because the boy who lives there, the one named Caleb, who was adopted by a couple named the Sangstons, is Justin, isn't he?"

Leland flattened his hand against his heart and made a choking sound in his throat. Donna's hand flew to her mouth but Joey refused to feel sorry for her.

"Tell me, Mother. I have a right to the truth." She gestured toward her father. "Even Leland deserves to know if Justin is alive!"

"Yes," Donna screeched, her calm disintegrating. "Yes, Justin is alive. I c…an't believe you found him."

Joey's heart ached. "How could you have done this, Mother?" She glanced once more at her father, wanting to hate him, too, but the stunned look on his face indicated that he had no knowledge of Justin's whereabouts.

Donna reached for her, but Joey backed away, shaking her head violently.

"How could you have lied to me all these years? Made me believe Justin was dead? You let me blame myself for his disappearance." Joey choked on the last sentence, the anguish from her childhood resurfacing.

"Just listen, Joey—" Donna began.

"Listen to what? Excuses?" Joey wanted to shake her, to make her suffer as she had. "What did you do? Plan the fake kidnapping and murder to keep him away from Dad, then whisk Justin away to that ranch?" Her voice grew colder. "Did you pay someone to cover for you?"

"It's not like that," Donna said. "I did not plan that kidnapping." Donna aimed a suspicious look at Leland. "I'm guessing your father did that. He wanted the insurance money and he wanted to hurt me."

Leland slammed his fist against the desk, jarring

papers. "How dare you accuse me of foul play when you've been caught lying?"

Donna jumped up, waving her arms, her calm disintegrating. "I didn't plan the kidnapping. You did, Leland, to hurt me. You had someone steal my son during that fire, didn't you?" She whirled on Joey. "I was devastated, you know that, Joey. I thought Justin was dead for a long time. You have to believe me."

Joey steeled herself against Donna, not trusting anything her parents uttered.

"But I never gave up looking for him. Even after Leland did, I kept searching. I hired a private investigator with my own money." She pressed a hand over her heart. "I just couldn't let myself believe that my baby boy was really dead. I felt in here, that he was still alive. Out there somewhere." Her voice broke. "At night, I used to wake up and hear him crying for me. Saying Mama. I wanted to die inside, too."

"When did you find him?" Cole asked.

Donna clasped her hands together. "About ten years ago. The P.I. got a lead. He called me and I went to this church in Dallas and saw this little boy there. He was with a man and a woman, a family called the Sangstons. They owned a ranch near Mineral Wells." She inhaled and rushed on. "The minute I laid eyes on that boy, I knew he was my son, Justin. I wanted to tear him away from them."

"Why didn't you come forward then?" Cole asked.

"Because Leland still had custody and you knew you'd lose him again," Joey interjected.

Donna twisted to glare at her, then Leland. "That was part of it. But Justin looked happy with those people, and I could tell they loved him, and I realized that if

I spoke out, it would rock his world upside down. For once, I tried not to be selfish."

Joey cut her a scathing look, but Donna continued, "By then, you hated me, Joey, and Leland…he never cared about Justin. He didn't deserve to know he was alive, much less to have custody of him again."

"And why didn't he care?" Joey said, venom lacing her voice. "I always wondered why it was so easy for Dad to have used his own son in a devious plan to extract money."

Donna's eyes went wild. "Joey…"

"Justin wasn't Leland's son, was he, Mother?"

"Be quiet, Joey," Donna sputtered. "You don't know what you're saying."

"Don't I, Mother?" Joey stared at her mother in disgust. "You blamed Leland for his infidelity and were so bitter, that you had an affair of your own."

"Joey, stop it!" Donna ordered.

Leland collapsed back into the seat and scrubbed his hand over his face, sweating.

"What I don't understand is that if you'd confessed that Daddy wasn't Justin's father, you probably could have won custody of Justin."

"That's not true," Donna said, her voice trembling. "With my drinking problem, no judge was going to give me custody. Justin would have been put in foster care. That would have been awful."

"Or maybe his real father would have raised him," Joey shot back. "Or did his real father even know about him? Did you keep that as another one of your tawdry secrets?"

Cole kept his spine straight as he watched Joey grappling with her feelings. She seemed to be holding her breath while she waited for her mother's answer, but Donna clammed up and refused to talk further. Leland stood and moved toward the door, his expression lethal as he whipped his head toward Donna, then Joey.

"I have to get out of here," he said in a harsh voice. "I'll talk to you later, Joey."

She simply stared at him, a wealth of turmoil in the silence that stretched between them.

"Don't leave town, Mr. Hendricks," Cole said. "We may want to question you again when we get the results of these DNA tests."

Leland gave him an icy stare, then walked out the door and slammed it behind him.

Donna stood and smoothed down her linen suit, touched her hair as if to tuck it back in place, along with her lies. "I want you to think long and hard about how you handle this information," she said to Joey. "I've kept up with your brother over the years, and he's happy."

"I know, I saw him," Joey said.

Donna swayed slightly. "You told him?"

"His adopted father and I did, yes."

"My God." Donna pressed a trembling hand to her cheek. "How did he take it? Do you think he'll want to see us?"

The hope that flickered in Donna's eyes surprised Cole. Maybe Donna really did love the boy and wanted what was best for him.

"I don't know, Mother." Joey wheezed a tired breath. "He's going to need time to process everything."

"I wouldn't contact him yet," Cole warned. "After all, the investigation is not over."

Donna's eyes turned into glaciers as she frowned at Cole. "Hasn't our family suffered enough already?"

Cole towered over her. "What about Lou Anne Wallace and her daughter, Sarah? They suffered. Someone has to pay for their deaths, Mrs. Hendricks."

"I didn't kill them." Donna gave Joey a beseeching look. "Please, Joey. For your brother's sake, handle this with discretion."

"I took care of Justin when he was little and you were drunk, Mother," Joey said bitterly. "I'll do everything I can to protect him now. Even if it means protecting him from you and Daddy."

Joey collapsed into the chair, drained as Donna left the room, leaving a cloud of suspicion in her wake.

"Joey?"

Cole's deep voice barely penetrated the fog surrounding her.

He knelt beside her and cradled her hands in his, warming them with his own. "Joey, do you know who Justin's real father is?"

The million-dollar question. She had a good idea. But could she implicate the governor of Texas without talking to him first? Without proof?

Dread swelled in her chest. She hated to lie to Cole. Still, she couldn't be certain yet. "I… I'm not sure."

Cole's blue eyes blazed a path over her face. "Then how did you know that Leland wasn't his father?"

Joey shrugged, vying for calm. "I didn't. I just played a hunch." She searched Cole's face, praying he'd understand. "When I saw Caleb, Justin, I thought he looked like Donna. The way he rode with such confidence was just like her."

He nodded.

"But then I searched his face for signs of Leland, and I…didn't see any of our father in him." She struggled to recall conversations she'd overheard when she was a teenager. Before Justin was born and afterward. "It always bothered me that Dad could have used his own son for money. Then I remembered my parents fighting. Leland calling him 'your' son." She squeezed Cole's hands, clutched them to her, absorbing his strength. Oddly his presence calmed her, gave her a sense of balance amidst the storm of feelings raging inside her. "Now it makes sense."

"If Leland knew Justin wasn't his, why did he fight for custody?" Cole asked.

"To get back at Donna," Joey said, her mind spinning. "And if Lou Anne suspected or found out Justin wasn't my father's, that would have been another reason she balked against raising him."

"You're right." Cole stroked the palm of her hand. "But if she'd threatened to tell, Donna might have wanted to shut her up. Leland probably wouldn't have been happy about it, either."

Another reason he might have killed Lou Anne. To save face.

"So might the real father," Joey said, her heart in her throat.

The door screeched open, and Detective Simmons poked his head in. "Is it safe now?"

Cole mumbled a yes, and Simmons strode in. "I spoke with our lab techs. They examined the bloodstain and are pretty sure it's too old to pick up anything, but they'll give it a try."

Joey sighed in frustration, then an idea struck her. "We don't have to disclose that information. Why don't we leak that we know who the DNA belongs to and see if we can smoke out the killer?"

Her heart raced although other complications made her rethink the plan. Going public meant that Justin/Caleb would find out the truth. Then again, he was old enough to deal with it, she hoped. She only prayed he'd forgive her part in exposing it.

"Joey?" Cole's deep, throaty voice washed over her. "It's a good plan. But are you having doubts?"

Oh, yeah. But she had to do what was right. "No. I know just who to call. Harold Dennison."

Cole nodded. "And I'll call Zane, Sloan, Anna and Sheriff Matheson and tell them to meet us at the courthouse in Justice. I want everyone there when the news hits town."

He punched in Zane's number, and when he finished, Joey borrowed his phone. She'd left hers at the inn. Harold Dennison seemed stunned by her call, but she promised him an exclusive when the story broke, and he agreed to run the story that afternoon.

A mixture of excited anticipation and dread pitted Joey's stomach as she disconnected the call, and she and Cole walked to the car. By nightfall, they might have the answers to the puzzle that had gone unsolved for fifteen years. Maybe Lou Anne and Sarah Wallace's killer would be behind bars.

But which one of their suspects would it be: Jim McKinney? Her father? Her mother?

Or the man she was almost certain was Justin's father, Governor Grange?

Adrenaline raced through Cole as he drove back toward Justice. Zane had agreed to have all the suspects meet at the courthouse. In light of this new revelation and the leaking of information to the press, they were bound to push one of them into a confession. Although Donna and Leland hadn't broken yet…

And what about Jim? Or Stella?

His stomach knotted as a sickening thought occurred to him. If Leland wasn't Justin's father, and Donna had had an affair, whom had she slept with? Leland had been with Lou Anne and Lou Anne had slept with Jim McKinney. Dear God, what if his father had slept with Donna?

Nausea bolted through him. The connection still wouldn't make him related to Joey, but it would mean that Justin might be his half brother.

He scrubbed a hand over his face, deciding not to alarm Joey with his speculations. He would talk to Jim McKinney, though. Find out if he'd slept with Donna.

The scenario played through his head. Years ago, both Donna and Jim had a drinking problem. Jim claimed he didn't know what had happened the night Lou Anne died. What if she discovered that her lover was also sleeping with Leland's ex-wife? That the child Leland wanted her to raise was Jim McKinney's?

He cut his gaze toward Joey, but she'd closed her eyes and rested her head against the back of the seat. Night was falling and shadows streaked her pale face. He didn't have the heart to trouble her with more theories, especially unfounded ones.

The traffic and noise of the city gave way to countryside, and the road was nearly deserted. He checked the rearview mirror and saw bright lights approaching. Déjà vu from the earlier hit-and-run sent a ripple of anxiety along his nerve endings. Ahead, a tractor-trailer raced toward him. He flashed his lights, signaling for the driver to switch to low beams, but he weaved across the centerline as if he'd fallen asleep.

A pickup truck pulled out from a side road, too, a little too slowly, and crawled across the road in front of him. He swerved to avoid it and the truck, and saw the river approaching. Suddenly the car behind him slammed into him, and sent him into a spin.

Joey's eyes jerked open. "God, not again."

"I'm afraid so." He hit the gas hoping to outrun it, but the car crashed into him again with a vicious thud, and he lost control. The sedan spun a hundred and eighty degrees, then skidded and raced toward the embankment. Tires ground and churned on the asphalt. Metal screeched and splintered.

Joey screamed, and water rushed up to meet them as the car nose-dived into the edge of the river and plunged toward the murky bottom.

Chapter 14

Joey braced herself for the impact of the accident, used her hands to block the force of the air bag, then immediately reached for the seat belt. This time, thank God, the belt slid free.

"Joey?"

"I'm all right. You?"

"Yeah." He released a string of expletives, then tore at her air bag again. "We're sinking. Got to get out."

She tried her door but it refused to budge. "My door is stuck."

He was pushing on his. "Hold your breath. Water will rush in when I open the door."

She inhaled a sharp breath, then did as he instructed while he used his shoulder to shove against the weight. The current swept them up, carrying the car deeper and further into the river. Seconds later, icy water flowed into the car, rising quickly to her neck as he opened the door. Cole reached for her hand, and she latched onto his, grateful for the contact as he yanked her out of the sinking car and through the murky water. A chill slithered up her spine as they battled the current. She kicked and fought, determined to survive. Her knee hit a jagged rock and pain sliced along her leg. She clawed for the surface, propelling her arms forward as the water dragged her and Cole apart. Gasping for air, she broke the surface, but the current trapped her and sucked her back under.

"Joey!"

She struggled under the surface, swimming toward Cole, then finally pushed upward enough to lift her head above the water. He swam toward her, but the current tried to drag her the other way. She was losing steam. Her legs ached, her arms throbbed, her lungs begged for air.

Then suddenly Cole grabbed her around the waist and dragged her upward. She kicked, moving on autopilot, furious that someone had almost killed them when they were so close to solving the case.

The call… Dennison. He had already leaked the news and the killer knew they were closing in. He might be here now. Waiting for them. Watching them, hoping they'd drown.

Determination mushroomed inside her chest, and her strength rallied long enough for her to break the surface again, then she gasped in a breath and began to swim alongside Cole. It seemed like miles as they fought the water and made their way toward a tree overhanging the deepest part of the river. A branch had splintered in a recent storm, and Cole grabbed it and used it to haul himself forward. He thrust out his hand, and she grabbed it and kicked while he pulled her to the branch. She clutched it with shaky fingers and maneuvered her body along the thick length until they crawled onto the embankment.

Joey's arms felt ragged as she collapsed onto the grassy edge. Then they glanced up in horror to see a rifle pointed at them.

Heavens, no. They'd survived the crash only to have the killer waiting.

She blinked away the water and murk, shoving at her tangled hair, then lost her breath when she saw the person holding the gun.

Not Donna or Leland. Or Jim McKinney. Not even Governor Grange.

The one person she'd trusted unconditionally—Rosa.

Cole heaved for air, silently thanking God he had managed to get himself and Joey to safety. But the sight of the rifle barrel and the frantic-looking woman holding it froze the blood in his veins. Her eyes looked wild and panicked, and her arm was trembling so badly he feared she'd accidentally press the trigger.

"You wouldn't leave things alone," Rosa wailed. "I begged you, Miss Joey. I begged you to think of your mama."

"Rosa, put the gun down," Cole said, using a tone meant to calm her but one that reeked of authority.

"You don't want to hurt us, Rosa," Joey rasped. "You know you don't." Joey lifted her hand, but Rosa stabbed at her with the blunt end of the gun.

"Don't move, or I'll shoot you both."

Cole gestured for Joey to drop her hand, and she did, but shock tightened her features.

"You helped raise me, Rosa," Joey whispered. "Justin and I both loved you. You were part of our family. Special to us." She hesitated, cleared her throat. "If you're doing this to protect my mother, it's not worth it. I've already talked to her. I know Justin is alive. I saw him with my own eyes."

Rosa made a strangled sound. "You were never supposed to find him. Never supposed to know. You were free to go on with your own life."

"Go on with my life?" Joey's voice vibrated with pain. "How could I do that when I blamed myself for his death?"

Rosa pushed at the loose strands of her black braid. She looked tired and at her wits' end. "Justin was safe and happy with the Sangstons. Now you mess everythin' up."

"I'm glad he was happy," Joey said in a strained voice. "But he's my family. I had a right to know where he was."

"Family… I did everything for family, to protect little Justin." Rosa's voice broke. "Family is all that matters."

Joey knotted a fist over her heart. "But I was your family, too."

"You don't understand. You were older, Joey. Strong. I knew you would be okay no matter what." Rosa's English became garbled with a few words of Spanish. "Justin, my little boy, Mr. Leland…he was going to have him kidnapped. I had to stop it."

"So you took him?" Cole interjected. "Before Leland could put his plan into effect?"

Rosa nodded, tears tracking down her cheeks. "He

didn't love Justin. Knew he wasn't his bebé. He hated Donna for pretending like he was. He was d…esperate for the money."

"So you heard about his plan and you set the fire that night?" Cole asked.

"The fire! Oh, my goodness. You set it!" Joey staggered. "Rosa, we could have been killed."

"No, no…" Rosa wailed. "I called firemen, get us out. No danger, not really." Her crazed expression alarmed Cole. "My cousin, he got the bebé. Took him to the ranch. I know the family. My cousin, Hector, he work their ranch. The Sangstons, they want bebé of their own. They good people. Love our Justin." Rosa's voice grew colder. "Not like Ms. Donna back then, drinking. Or Mr. Leland. Always think of themselves. Pass bebé back and forth like he sack of flour."

"But my mother found out where Justin was," Joey said, obviously trying to make sense of it all. "Did you tell her, or did she find him on her own?"

"I not tell her." Rosa gulped, the gun wavering. "Not at first. But my cousin—"

"Hector Elvarez," Cole supplied.

Rosa nodded. "He tell me Ms. Donna hire man to hunt for Justin. Then Ms. Donna, she change. She not drinking by then. She make right choice. Leave little Justin be. Best thing for everyone."

"Except I didn't know, Rosa," Joey cried.

"What about Lou Anne Wallace?" Cole asked. "She found out about Leland's plan and called Donna, didn't she?"

"She a mess, too. Mean to our Justin." Rosa's voice shook with agitation. "She going to tell everyone Justin not Mr. Leland's. I have to stop her or little Justin be take away. Foster care. Strangers. Not ever see him again."

Cole tried to inject calmness into his voice. "And you killed Sarah Wallace when she came to town because she found out what you'd done?"

Rosa broke into a sob. "Not want to, but my sister, she sick now, needs Rosa to take care of her. Couldn't go to jail or let Justin be found."

"You tried to strangle Anna, too?" Joey asked in horror. Rosa nodded, tears filling her eyes.

"What about Sheriff Mattheson and the fire at the jail? Did you set that?" Cole asked.

Rosa shook her head. "Hector, but he only wanted to protect me."

"Where is he now?" Cole asked. "Back in Mexico?"

Rosa nodded. Her eyes pleaded with Joey to understand. "I check on Justin, Miss Joey. I see him every Sunday, at church. He growin' up. Big strong man, good rider."

"I know," Joey said, her tone more even now. "I saw him, and he is happy. He loves his new family." She started to rise, and Cole reached to stop her, but she gently pulled away from him. "The Sangstons were good to him, much better than Donna and Leland would have been."

"The mama, Mrs. Sangston, before she go, she tell me how much her son mean to her."

"Did she know that Donna had found him?" Joey asked.

"She guessed. I tell her Ms. Donna different. Only want her boy happy."

"That's right, Rosa. And you did what you did for

our family." Joey inched closer, but Rosa thrust the gun up, and Cole's breath lodged in his throat.

"Rosa, you can't hurt me, I know you can't. Justin has met me now. You don't want him to think that you killed his sister."

Rosa's hand sagged, and she sobbed louder. "I so sorry…so sorry, Miss Joey—"

Joey grabbed Rosa, and they wrestled with the gun. It went off, but the shot pinged into a tree. Cole pushed Joey aside, and pried the weapon from Rosa's hands. She collapsed onto the ground in a fit of tears.

Cole clutched the gun and reached inside his pocket for his phone. But water had ruined it. Damn.

He glanced at Joey, wondering if he should tie Rosa to restrain her, but Joey slumped down by Rosa and cradled her in her arms.

Rosa leaned into her, crying. "I'm so sorry, Joey, so sorry."

"I'm going to flag someone down and call for help," Cole said.

Rosa removed a cell phone from her skirt pocket and slipped it into Joey's hands. Joey handed it to Cole, and Cole stepped away to call Zane and Sloan.

A deep sadness pervaded Joey as Zane McKinney snapped handcuffs around Rosa's wrists. Rosa had loved her brother and her more than Donna and Leland had, yet in her panicked attempt to help them, she'd still hurt them.

And she'd taken two lives during the process and almost taken others.

Did Donna know about Rosa's guilt? Had she covered for her all this time?

"We still have to question Donna," Cole said as if he'd read her mind. "See if she conspired to keep the truth from the police."

"And my father has to answer for the fake kidnapping/ murder plan."

Her body throbbed and ached with fatigue, though. "Could we do that tomorrow? I…don't think I can handle anything more tonight."

Cole pulled her up against him. "I think that can be arranged. It'll take a while for Zane and Sloan to process Rosa. I'll tell them to make some calls, and we can set up the interrogation for the morning."

"By then news of Rosa's arrest will have hit the papers," Joey said sadly.

Cole squeezed her hand, then went to speak to his half brothers. She wiped at tears as they situated Rosa into a squad car. Sloan handed Cole his car keys, and he rode with Zane, while Cole drove her back to the inn. She expected Donna to confront them, but thankfully she must not have received word of Rosa's arrest yet. Joey hoped they could forestall it until morning when she'd had time to absorb the shock herself.

Still damp from the river, she shivered as she entered her room. Cole rubbed his hands up and down her arms. "You're soaked and trembling. Why don't you relax in a hot bath, and I'll grab us something to eat."

She ran a hand over his damp clothing. "You're wet, too, Cole. You need to change."

"I'll grab a shower in my room and meet you back here with some food."

Too weary to argue, she nodded and moved into the bathroom. She found a small bottle of bubble bath on the counter, sprinkled some into the tub, then filled it with water. The day's and night's events replayed in her mind like a movie trailer, and she shuddered. How could her family have gotten so messed up? What would Justin—Caleb—do now? Would he want to see her? And what would happen to Donna and Leland?

In the morning, they'd find out. Then she'd talk to Governor Grange.

Or maybe she should get it over with tonight. She retrieved her cell phone and punched in his number, but received his service again. She left a message that it was urgent, that an arrest had been made in the Wallace murders and that she needed to speak to him privately. Then she hung up, contemplating how to handle the situation as she lowered herself into the sea of bubbles and closed her eyes. Slowly she let the heat melt away the soreness and chill in her limbs. But the ache in her heart couldn't be assuaged so easily.

If Governor Grange was Justin's father, did he want to know? Would he want to meet Justin and have a relationship with him? And what would acknowledging an illegitimate son do to his reputation?

How would that revelation affect Justin/Caleb?

Cole. He understood about being an illegitimate child. But he had overcome the stigma and become an honorable man. A formidable Texas Ranger. He was strong, ethical. Smart. Sexy as hell.

And he had saved her life.

She wanted him tonight.

The hotel room door opened, and his deep voice called her name.

"Joey?"

"I'll be out in a minute." She dried off, drained the water from the tub and donned her pale blue cotton robe. When she'd belted it and towel-dried her hair, she stepped into the room. Cole had showered quickly and shaved. His damp hair clung to the ends of his button-down shirt. On the desk, she spotted two cups of steaming soup he must have bought from the bar.

"It's not much," he said, "but I didn't want to go to Donna's and have to explain about Rosa."

"No, I'm not ready to deal with my mother yet, either."

The two of them ate the simple meal in silence. Joey barely tasted the food, but at least the hot soup and bath soothed her nerves. When she looked up at Cole, he was watching her with an intense look in his eyes as if he expected her to fall apart any minute.

"Thank you, Cole."

"Do you feel better?"

His gruff voice skated over raw nerve endings, reminding her of their close brush with death earlier.

"Yes." But she hurt deep inside and didn't think the pain would ease. "I still can't believe that Rosa killed Lou Anne and Sarah Wallace."

"Shh." He stood, set their dishes aside, then threaded his fingers through her hair and hugged her to him. "Don't think about it tonight, sugar."

She lifted her face, and her heart fluttered at the raw need and desire flaming in his eyes.

"I thought we were going to die tonight," she whispered.

He traced his fingers along her arm, and she quivered with longing.

"No one is ever going to hurt you again," he growled. "I promise you, Joey."

"Cole—"

"Shh." The smoldering look he gave her teased at her senses, made her want to believe that she could trust him. That he would be the one man who would never lie to her. Never hurt her.

That he would always be there for her. Take care of her. Love her.

Love?

Heavens, yes. She wanted his loving tonight. The physical touches. The closeness. Even if he didn't say the words or feel them.

The image of Joey fighting through the water, nearly drowning, then facing Rosa with that gun haunted Cole. He had dealt with life-and-death situations all his life, had put himself on the firing line in the military, had witnessed good men die and taken lives, but not once during those times, had such bone-jarring fear for another person seized him.

He had been terrified of losing Joey.

He didn't like the realization, but he couldn't deny it. Just as he couldn't deny himself the pleasure of taking her to bed now and making her come apart in his arms.

She lay a hand along his neck, teasing him with her fingers, and rational thought fled as a fierce hunger erupted inside him. He had to have her now.

She met his gaze, and raw need flashed in her expression. With a low groan, he cupped her face in his hands. The sweet scent of bubble bath and shampoo invaded his senses as he lowered his head and claimed her mouth with his. She tasted like sultry Texas nights, fiery hot and filled with passion. Enflamed, he deepened the kiss, teasing her lips apart with his tongue and delving inside to play a mating dance with hers.

His hands drifted of their own accord, tracing a path down her shoulders. Then he stripped the flimsy cotton robe from her voluptuous body until she stood naked before him. He drank in the sight of her heavy, bare breasts, nipples rosy and distended; her smooth, flat stomach; and the blond curls waiting for his exploration.

She made a small throaty sound, then pushed at his shirt. He tore it off and threw it on the bed, then claimed her mouth again while his hands covered her breasts, stroking, kneading, twirling the peaks with his thumbs.

"Cole…" she whispered his name against his chest as she lowered her head and spread kisses along his jaw, sucking on his neck and below his ear, then moving her hands down to his belt buckle. Seconds later, she removed it, tossed it to the floor, then his zipper rasped in the darkness. His sex surged hard and aching for her, as she shoved his jeans over his thighs.

He kicked them off, but stopped her hand when she began to stroke him. Instead he lowered her to the bed, climbed above her and suckled her breasts, first one, then the other as his fingers sank deep inside her. She writhed against the sheets, threaded her fingers through his hair, ground her hips up to meet his hand, cried out his name and drove him crazy with her needy sounds of lust.

He licked his way down her belly, planted breathy kisses along the insides of her thighs until his mouth replaced his fingers, and he spread her legs and sank his tongue inside her. She twisted frantically, clawed at his arms and pleaded for more.

"Cole, hmm, that feels so good." She moaned. "I love you…"

Her whispered words made him pause momentarily—had she only been caught up in the moment?

She traced her finger along the tip of his shaft. "I want you inside me when I come this time…"

Her heady request made his body churn with desire, and he rose above her, shucked off his boxers, grabbed a condom from his pocket and rolled it on. He was panting, perspiration dotting his chest and forehead, his mind clouded with wanting Joey. Joey with her sassy smile, her glorious mane of blond hair and those mile-long legs.

Mile-long legs he'd imagined wrapped around him the first time he'd seen her. Mile-long legs he'd finally get to feel as he rode her.

His length throbbed, hard and pulsing for her heaven, and she reached up, stroked him once, then guided him inside her. The smile of elation and cry of ecstasy when he filled her shattered something inside him. A wall he'd built to keep emotions and sex compartmentalized.

A wall he didn't want to think about now.

He wanted nothing between them but bare skin and hot touches.

She clawed his hips and he thrust deeper, bracing his arms beside her head as he watched her eyes change colors when she finally allowed her release to claim her.

He drove himself harder, faster, deeper, pulled her legs up to hug him, burying himself as far as he could go, then even deeper. She cried his name again, and he thrust inside her again, his body jerking and shaking with the splendor of the moment as heady sensations rocked through him.

Joey trembled from the aftermath of her orgasm, and yet, she wanted Cole again already. She splayed her hands along his chest, toying with the coarse, dark hair grazing his chest, and pressed a kiss to his neck as he rolled sideways, cradling her in his arms.

She wanted to shout her love for him again, and hoped that her declaration hadn't scared him. She couldn't, didn't expect him to return the sentiment. He had come here to do a job and he'd go back to it, and she to hers. She kissed his neck again, and he dropped a kiss into her hair.

"That was amazing."

"Uh-huh." He moaned and cupped her bottom in his hands, dragging her closer so their bodies touched. "I wanted you the first time I laid eyes on those long legs."

She smiled against him. "And I wanted you the moment I saw you haul your big body off that Harley."

He chuckled and trailed his fingers over her breast, causing a thousand titillating sensations to take flight inside her. "When I saw you take that shot of tequila, lick the salt and suck that lime, I wanted your tongue on me."

Joey rubbed his muscled bare calf with her toe. She liked this teasing side of Cole. "And when you closed your mouth on that beer bottle, I imagined your mouth on me."

He lowered his head and kissed her again, long, hard, taking all she offered, asking for more. "I fantasized about your long legs wrapped around my waist."

She trapped his shaft in her hand and stroked, feeling heady as it hardened and pulsed between her fingers. "And I wanted you inside me."

He nuzzled her neck. "Well, sugar, tonight, let's make all your wishes come true."

If only that were true. Because, heaven help her, right now she wished he'd tell her he loved her.

But he did something almost as good. He flipped her to her stomach, crawled on top of her and massaged the knots in her shoulders. His fingers dipped lower to stroke and soothe all her aching places, and soon he thrust inside her again, pumping and grinding, shouting her name, filling her, until she cried out with another soul shattering climax.

Finally she fell asleep, huddled in his embrace, with euphoria still washing over her and his kisses still heating her body.

The room phone jangled, jarring Cole from the best damn sleep he'd had in ages. He'd been dreaming about sex and a woman who loved him, a woman who'd never abandon him or cheat on him, a woman who made him want forever.

He shifted, his body flaming again as Joey's curvy backside snuggled deeper against his hard length. His hand snaked out to cup her breasts, and she rewarded him with a soft sigh that only heightened his early morning arousal.

Unfortunately the shrill sound of the phone continued. He cursed, and started to ignore it, but it might be important.

Hell. He really did not want to leave this warm, cozy bed with Joey.

The sound blasted the quiet again, and Joey stirred with a frown. "You'd better get it."

"I know." Reluctantly he dragged his warm hand from her breasts and clicked to answer. "Sergeant Cole McKinney."

"It's Zane. Listen, we've got trouble."

He scrubbed his hands over his face. "What's up?"

"Leland Hendricks has taken Dad hostage."

Cole snapped upright. "What?"

"He's holding him in a cabin in the woods, Cole." Zane's voice reverberated with worry. "You'd better find Joey and tell her. Then meet us at the courthouse ASAP."

The phone clicked into silence with a deafening thud. Cole glanced down at the beauty in his bed, and grimaced. She'd had a hell of a time the day before.

And this day didn't look like it would be any better.

Chapter 15

Joey leaned on her elbow and braced her head on her hand with a come-back-to-bed expression.

But Cole stiffened, his Texas Ranger face back on as he yanked on his jeans. Disappointment ballooned in her chest, along with the realization that something was wrong.

"Who was that, Cole?"

"Zane." He grabbed his shirt and shrugged it on. "We have to get dressed. Now."

His clipped tone sent her nerves on edge. "What's going on?"

He finally paused, and looked at her, his blue eyes smoky with the remnants of shared memories of the night before, but also filled with turmoil.

A half-dozen scenarios crashed into her head. Justin had run away or was hurt. Donna was having a fit at the jail wanting Rosa released.

"Cole, you're scaring me."

He hissed a breath, then lowered himself beside her on the bed and cradled her hand in his. "Leland has taken my dad hostage."

Joey gasped. "What?"

"He's holding him at some cabin. Zane wants us to meet him at the courthouse. Then we'll decide what to do."

"But why would my father take Jim as a hostage? What does he want?"

"I don't know yet. But we have to go."

She nodded, numbness creeping over her as the shock settled in. She flew off the bed, adrenaline churning, then ran next door, dug in her suitcase for a clean pair of jeans and shirt and hurriedly dressed. She yanked her hair into a ponytail just as Cole entered. He clipped on his badge and weapon.

Fear clouded her throat. Rosa had been arrested. Her dad was in the clear for murder charges. What in the world was Leland thinking? Did he have a gun on Jim McKinney?

And what would she do if Cole had to shoot her father?

Cole opened the door, and she grabbed her purse. The date book that had belonged to Lou Anne fell out, and Cole frowned. "What's that?"

She snatched it up and stared at it guiltily. She should have told Cole about the book, but she still hadn't spoken to the governor. "Nothing, let's go."

The lie burned her throat as she followed him to the car and climbed in the passenger seat. Her cell phone rang, and she glanced at it, figuring it was an hysterical Donna. But it was the governor instead.

She didn't want to have the conversation in the car, but she had to take the call or Cole would be suspicious. "Joey Hendricks."

"Yes, Joey, it's Governor Grange. I received your message and I'm on my way to Justice. I should be there shortly. Who was arrested for the murders?"

Joey explained about Rosa's part in the murders, as well as Justin's disappearance. "We have another situation now," she told him. "My father has taken Jim McKinney hostage. Sergeant McKinney and I are on the way to meet the other Rangers now and find out what's going on."

"Dear God. It never ends, does it? What the hell is Leland thinking?"

"He must be desperate," Joey said. "Yesterday was rough. He was upset when he left the crime lab. We confronted him with the fact that Justin wasn't his son."

An abrupt silence followed, the tension palpable.

"Governor?"

"I heard you."

Joey waited for a response, but his shaky breathing vibrated over the line. They had reached the courthouse, and Cole climbed out, his brow arched as if asking if she was coming.

"I need to go now," she said. "But we'll talk later."

"Yes," he said in an unusually solemn voice. "I'll see you soon."

Joey hung up, her heart racing as they rushed into the courthouse. Thankfully Harold Dennison hadn't heard a word yet and was nowhere to be seen. But Donna was sitting in the office in a hard wooden chair, her eyes glazed.

"I can't believe you all arrested Rosa." She gave Joey

a condemning look. "Rosa loved your little brother. I don't condone her actions, but she did what she did out of love."

Joey's throat clogged with emotions. Her mother didn't have to sound so righteous. Rosa wouldn't have had to take such drastic action if Donna hadn't been an alcoholic and Leland so vindictive and selfish.

"Mother, do you know why Leland has taken Jim McKinney hostage?" Joey asked.

Cole knotted his fists by his sides as Donna turned away, and set her lips into a thin line.

He had a sneaking suspicion that Leland had been pushed to the limit the day before, humiliated by the public revelation that Justin was not his, and he might have jumped to the same conclusion that Cole had.

That Jim McKinney was the boy's father. That he'd slept with Donna, given her a son and had then slept with his new wife as well.

Every man had his breaking point, and Cole could almost understand Leland's twisted need for revenge. If another man touched Joey, he'd want to kill him.

Zane approached him, looking in control although the rigid set to his jaw indicated he had his own concerns. Sloan raked a hand through his hair and paced the small room like a caged animal. When he spotted Cole and Joey, he halted midstride.

Cole instantly squared his shoulders, ready to defend her if his half brother pounced.

"Let's all take a deep breath," Zane said as if he'd read the volatile situation and knew it needed to be diffused. He introduced Anna Wallace and Sheriff Carley Matheson to Cole, and Joey and the women spoke quietly, each reserved. From the reports, Cole knew that Joey had once shared a house for a short time with the Wallace sisters when they had all lived with Leland and Lou Anne. And she and Carley had grown up in the same town.

He was the biggest outsider of them all. Then again, Joey's father was in the hot seat now, placing her there along with him.

"Leland is holding Dad in a cabin here." Zane pointed to a map on the wall with a pushpin marking the location.

"What are his demands?" Zane asked.

"He's asked to speak to Joey. Says she's the only one he'll talk to."

"Absolutely not," Cole barked.

Joey cleared her throat. "He wants to speak to me. He gets me."

Cole brushed her arm with his hand. He'd almost lost her the day before. He wouldn't allow her to put herself in danger today. "Joey, please—"

"I know what I'm doing, Cole. Maybe I can talk some sense into him."

"We'll drive separate cars," Zane said. "Let's try to handle this without calling in a SWAT team."

Cole and Sloan agreed, and Sheriff Matheson checked her weapon as well. Two of the town's deputies were asked to follow but to wait for Zane's orders. Zane forced Anna to stay at the jail, and threatened to arrest Donna if she tried to interfere. They dispersed, taking different vehicles but agreeing to meet near the woods by the cabin and go in on foot. Fifteen minutes later they converged in a clearing with Zane taking the lead. Everyone was ordered to stay back until they learned Leland's demands.

Cole and his half brothers moved quietly with Joey beside him, the morning sun blistering hot as they hiked through the woods. When they reached a hill overlooking the small log cabin, Zane phoned inside.

"Mr. Hendricks. Lieutenant McKinney here." He gestured for Joey to make herself visible to the porch, and she stepped into the clearing.

"Joey is with us. Now tell us what you want."

He flipped the phone to speakerphone, and Leland's voice resonated over the line. "I'll release Jim McKinney in exchange for my freedom. I want you to drop all charges against me in the fake kidnapping/murder plan."

Cole exchanged furtive looks with Zane and Sloan.

"As Texas Rangers, we're required to enforce the law," Zane said. "We don't make deals with criminals, Mr. Hendricks."

The door creaked open and a crazed-looking Leland pushed Jim McKinney out onto the porch. He forced him to kneel and pressed a gun to the back of his head.

"Dad, let Mr. McKinney go," Joey shouted.

"He slept with Lou Anne. He started all of this years ago!"

Leland sounded distraught, as if he'd walked off a ledge. Joey started to go to him, but Cole held her back. "Wait. He's not rational, Joey."

Cole and Sloan followed Zane's cue and wove through the edges of the woods surrounding the house. Sloan to the right, Cole to the left.

"Convince them to drop the charges, Joey," Leland yelled. "You have power, Joey, you work for the governor."

"Why would Governor Grange agree to drop the charges?" Zane asked.

"Just get him here. He'll do it," Leland barked.

Cole had nearly reached the side of the house, and he hid in the bushes, waiting for Sloan to surface. Through the brush, he spotted his father on his knees. He thought Jim would be scared, but he squared his shoulders, seemingly calm and resigned. Maybe he figured he deserved to die after the way he'd betrayed his wife and Cole's mother. And if he'd slept with Donna, if Justin was Jim's son, he had another son. Maybe he figured it was time he paid the price for that sin as well.

Cole's finger traced over the edge of his badge, then his hand moved to his pocket where he'd stored the one he'd found in the woods. The one he thought belonged to Jim.

Once upon a time his father had worn the badge proudly, too. Until he'd disgraced himself and his family. Still, he hadn't murdered the Wallace women.

Cole had thought he didn't care if the man lived or died. But faced with this dire situation, he realized he didn't want his father's punishment to be death.

He wanted to know the man who'd once worn that shield, to know if he still existed beneath the haggard surface. And although he'd been a poor excuse for a father, he deserved to have his professional name restored.

Sloan emerged from the brush across from him while Cole mentally formulated a diversion, but Joey suddenly shouted, then descended the hill, walking toward the house.

Leland yelled for her to stop, then stood and waved his gun in the air. Cole's blood ran cold. Dear God. Surely Leland wouldn't shoot his own daughter.

* * *

Joey darted down the hill, determined to stop Leland from hurting Jim McKinney.

"Let him go, Dad. Mr. McKinney had nothing to do with Lou Anne or Sarah's murder or the kidnapping."

"That may be true, but he humiliated me by having an affair with Lou Anne. He started the ruin of everything."

Joey was only inches from the porch now. She recognized the resignation in Jim's face. His wife was in a bad mental state, his sons' lives affected by his actions. And he had suffered for his wrongdoings. But he didn't deserve to die.

"I don't want to go to jail," Leland screeched. "Especially now I know your brother is alive. That Donna tricked me all these years."

"You never cared about Justin." Joey's voice caught. "I always wondered how you could plan to have him kidnapped. How you could use your own son to claim that insurance money."

"I was desperate then," Leland wailed. Sweat beaded and rolled down his face as he ranted and waved the gun in a wide arc.

"But you found out he wasn't your son," Joey said. "I understand now, Dad." She held up her hand, inching closer. From the corner of her eye, she saw Sloan on one side, Cole on the other.

Cole. Heavens, she loved him.

She pushed her own pain aside. Her family might never be whole again, but Cole deserved a chance to know the father he'd never had.

"Let Jim go," Joey said in a placating tone. "Please, Dad, it's time for the violence to end."

"I can't go to jail," Leland said in a panic. "I can't

be shut away like some damn animal, Joey. You have to make the cops see that I didn't carry out that plan so they can't arrest me."

He hadn't carried it out because Rosa had beaten him to it. And now she'd suffer for her actions.

"You can arrange for me to be pardoned," Leland pleaded as he raised the gun toward her. "You work for Governor Grange. Arrange it for me, Joey."

Joey swallowed back her fear. "Let Jim go and I'll call him."

Leland aimed the gun at the back of Jim's head and shoved him down the steps. "Call him first."

Sloan inched from the bushes to reveal his location. "Leland, let my father go. Then we'll talk."

Leland's crazed look terrified Joey.

"You don't want to hurt Jim," Sloan said. "Not for an affair that happened sixteen years ago."

"Or does this have to do with Justin's father?" Cole asked.

Leland spun sideways. "You bastard. How can you protect this man here? He never cared about you."

"Just like you didn't care about Justin," Joey said sharply, dragging his gaze back to her.

He waved the gun back and forth between her and Cole, his hand shaking.

"But I'm your daughter, Dad. You won't shoot me, will you?" She took another step closer, and he jerked the gun toward Cole.

"I'll shoot him unless you call the governor right now! He'll give me a pardon."

"Why would he do that?" Cole asked.

"Because he's Justin's father," Leland yelled bitterly.

Shock registered on Cole's and Sloan's faces. Then

Cole glanced at her with a question in his eyes, and she realized that he'd thought Jim might be Justin's father. Neither had trusted the other enough to tell the truth.

"But he's no better than Jim," Leland yelled. "He didn't want to break up his happy marriage or ruin his career. So he let Donna pawn the kid off as mine."

Joey's chest constricted as more emotions pummeled her. How would Justin cope with this knowledge?

"Call him!" Leland bellowed.

Joey reached for her cell phone at the same moment Cole pounced toward Leland. Leland swung the gun sideways, and Joey lurched forward to stop Leland. She reached for the gun, but Jim McKinney slammed his hand into Leland's arm and sent the weapon flying into the dirt.

She hit the ground, while Cole grabbed Leland and hauled his arms behind him. Seconds later, he snapped handcuffs on her father, and Zane and Sloan rushed forward.

Tears rushed to her eyes at the sight of the Rangers arresting her father. Cole darted toward her, but she shook her head to warn him not to. She needed time to deal with the pain and shock. Time to regroup. Time to figure out how she'd break the news to her new-found brother.

And she still had to talk to the governor.

She glanced at Cole again. She loved him. But men couldn't be trusted. They cheated and lied and used you, then walked away.

So far, Cole hadn't cheated on her. And she didn't know if he'd ever lied. But he would walk away. She knew that in her heart.

And she'd have to let him.

Chapter 16

Cole drove Joey back to the courthouse in silence. Zane had taken custody of Leland and Jim rode with Sloan. The investigation was officially over.

And he was worried sick about Joey. She looked withdrawn, pale and obviously didn't want to talk. Having to snap those handcuffs on her father had been hell.

But at least he hadn't had to shoot Leland.

He'd been prepared to, though. If he'd harmed one hair on Joey's head…

His gut clenched as he parked, and he spotted the media circus on the lawn in front of the courthouse. Harold Dennison stood in front of the camera like a peacock strutting his feathers, and an official car that obviously belonged to the governor was parked in front. Oh, boy, the dog do was about to hit the fan.

"Joey, I'm sorry." He caught her hand as he parked.

"You did what you had to do, Cole." Her voice sounded flat, but Cole realized that she kept a tight rein on her emotions and didn't expect attention or sympathy.

All the more reason he wanted to hold her. She never asked for anything, but he instinctively sensed she needed comfort. Needed him.

Which made him feel even worse. He wished she'd yell at him. Hit him. Scream at him for hauling her father into jail. But this quiet acceptance was killing him.

The next few minutes chaos shadowed every moment. Zane and Sloan and the deputies arrived, along with Sheriff Matheson who helped to part the crowd of locals on the lawn and spirit the necessary parties inside.

Joey paused by the media cameras, and handled herself with a professional detachment as she briefly summarized the situation, answered and fended off questions. Of course, she carefully omitted any comment about Justin's paternity.

"What will happen to Rosa Ramirez and Leland Hendricks now?" Dennison asked.

Joey inhaled a deep breath. "Charges will be filed, court dates set. The town of Justice will finally have justice." She turned the mike back over to Dennison who began to comb the crowd for comments, and Cole whisked her inside.

Donna and Anna greeted them with exasperated but relieved looks.

Zane rushed in and Anna hugged him. "I'm glad your father is safe. And now maybe my mother and sister can rest in peace."

"And we can move on with our lives, finally," Zane said.

Governor Grange stood by the window looking out,

seemingly lost in thought as he studied the curious mob outside.

Joey cleared her throat, and Cole touched her arm. “Would you like some privacy?”

She arched a brow toward the governor, but he shook his head. “It’s going to be public record soon enough. Might as well get it over with.”

“You’re Justin’s father?” Joey asked calmly.

He nodded and sank onto a bench. “How long have you known?”

“Not long.” Joey glanced at Cole, then continued. “I saw your name in Lou Anne’s date book, then when I met Justin, I suspected it was true.”

“You had evidence you kept from us?” Zane asked.

“I just found it and didn’t know if it was important,” Joey argued.

Donna clasped her hands together, looking calmer than she had in ages, as if she was finally relieved to have everything in the open.

“You didn’t want your family to know about your affair,” Cole said, letting Joey off the hook. “You had to protect your political career.”

He nodded in confirmation. “My wife knows everything now,” he said. “I told her last night.”

Joey folded her arms across her chest. “How is Martha taking the news that you lied to her for years and that you have a child?”

He shrugged. “Surprisingly well. She said she’d suspected something years ago. And she…thinks I should contact the boy.” His gaze lifted to Joey’s, and Cole saw a tired man. “What do you think, Joey?”

“I don’t know. Maybe. Sometime. But Justin—Caleb—needs time. He’s just learned that he’s a part of our family." A mirthless laugh escaped her. "As twisted as it is. He has a lot to contemplate right now. I'm not even sure he wants to see me, and I didn't betray him."

Governor Grange nodded in acceptance and ran a hand through his thinning gray hair. "Of course I'll resign from office immediately."

"You don't have to do that, Clayton," Donna said. "You've done wonderful things for the state. People will understand."

He shifted and gave her an odd look. "You were always so rational under pressure, Donna. I admired that about you."

She patted his shoulder. "You were meant for office. If I hadn't known that was the best thing for you and the state, I wouldn't have kept your secret so long."

He flattened his hands on his knees. "Well, I suppose we'll see what the people think. How they feel. In the end, it'll be up to them."

"Is that why you sent me here?" Joey asked. "You wanted me to keep tabs on the investigation because of Justin?"

"That was partly it. I wanted answers about his death," the governor said. "But I also knew you'd do the right thing, Joey. You have integrity. I'm glad my son's alive and has you for a sister."

Zane appeared then with Jim in tow. The badge in Cole's pocket stabbed at his conscience. It was time to return it.

Zane waved them into a small office. Jim shoved a hand through his hair, looking harried, but his eyes brightened as he looked up at Sloan and Zane. Then he gave Cole a smile. "You boys are all good Rangers," he said. "I know I've let you down over the years, but

I want you to know that I'm proud of all three of you. And I'm sorry I tore our family apart."

Cole shifted on the balls of his feet, feeling like an outsider again. He didn't belong here. Never would.

Still, he removed the badge from his pocket. "I found this in the woods that day I was searching for evidence."

Zane frowned. "You withheld evidence."

Sloan made a sound of surprise. "You knew it belonged to our father."

Cole nodded. "I wanted to check it out first."

"You mean you wanted to investigate me?" Jim said with quiet acceptance.

Cole met the man's gaze head-on. "I didn't know if you were innocent or guilty."

"I told the truth," Jim said. "I didn't remember what happened that night. But I must have lost my badge when I was drunk, after I left Lou Anne."

"We know you didn't kill her," Sloan said. "That's what matters, Dad."

"No." Jim threw up a hand. "I made a mess of things years ago. I cheated on your mother and disgraced myself with the Rangers." His expression turned grave as he slanted his gaze toward Cole. "But most of all, I let your brother down."

A knot gathered in Cole's throat.

"I kept up with you, though, Cole," he said in a gruff tone. "All these years, I knew what you were doing. Where you were. And before your mother died—"

"She died still loving you," Cole said bitterly. "I never understood that. Not when you didn't return her love. Not when you didn't even bother to attend her funeral or acknowledge that you had a third son."

"You're wrong about my feelings," Jim said with

more force. "I did love your mother, Cole. I...considered leaving Stella for her more than once. But I had my other two sons to think of." He gestured toward Sloan and Zane. "I'm sorry, boys. Sorry for loving another woman. But Stella ...she was weak. The love just dwindled after a while."

"But you stayed with her," Zane said.

"She needed me." Jim faced Cole. "Your mother, Barb, was strong. I knew she'd be all right. Stella wouldn't have survived. Besides..." He rubbed a hand down his leg. "I'd already screwed up by cheating, and losing my badge. If I could do one honorable thing, it would be to honor my wedding vows to my legal wife. And I was afraid if I divorced her, she might commit suicide."

Cole had hated Jim McKinney for so long, that it was hard to let go of the bitterness. But he was a man now, not a boy, and he recognized the truth in his father's words. Some semblance of admiration stirred that even though his father had strayed, he had stuck to his marriage commitment.

He handed the badge to his father and then shook his hand. It wasn't a perfect start, wouldn't compensate for the isolation and lost years, but it was a beginning.

At least they finally had justice.

Zane, then Sloan, shook Cole's hand as well. "Thanks for holding onto Dad's badge," Zane said.

"And for returning it," Sloan said.

Cole nodded, feeling a bond being forged, as if they were finally welcoming him into their brotherhood.

But what about Joey—could she forgive him for his part in arresting her father?

And was there a possibility that she hadn't just muttered that she loved him in the heat of their passion-frenzied lovemaking, but that she'd meant the sentiment? That they might really have something together?

Joey exited the courthouse, her heart in her throat. Cole and his father and brothers were finally reconciling. Cole would have the family he deserved.

While her family still remained in shreds, totally dysfunctional. Maybe someday Justin would come around, and at least she and he could have a relationship.

Weary and still reeling from the fact that Governor Grange had fathered her brother, she walked toward the bar. A drink would help wash away the pain. Help her get her act together. Force her to prepare for saying goodbye to Cole.

The lunch crowd had filled the parking lot, and Joey was just about to go inside when the sound of a Harley ripping toward her jerked her attention away from the door. Her pulse clamored as Cole skidded toward her. His blue eyes skated over her from head to toe, then his gaze settled on her face.

Her heart capitulated as disappointment ballooned inside her chest. He was leaving town already. Going to ride away and she'd never see him again. Never have his lips on her. Feel his touch. Have him inside her.

Hell, it was better. Men were cheaters, liars and then they walked away.

Or in this case, sped away on a Hog.

"Hey, legs. Thought you might like a ride?"

Temptation thrummed through her. But why stall the inevitable? Better to make a clean break than draw out the pain. "Thanks, but I don't want to hold you up."

His brows shot up. "Hold me up?"

"You're leaving town, aren't you?"

He shrugged, and she remembered how it felt to rest her head on those broad shoulders. "Eventually."

Unwanted tears collected in her suddenly dry throat. "I need a drink."

He patted the bag slung over the back of the bike. "We can take Jose with us. Have a threesome."

"Sounds kinky."

He wiggled his brows. "Might be. I have salt and lime, and know some inventive ways to use them."

A small smile tugged at her mouth as titillating sensations splintered through her. Memories of their first meeting crashed back, then their lovemaking. His teasing comment about watching her suck the lime and wanting her mouth on him.

But one ride with him would only make her crave another. And then she might break down and make a fool out of herself by begging him not to leave.

"Cole…"

His expression grew serious, and he reached for her hand and tugged her close, so that she rested against him. "I know you think that all men are liars and cheaters…"

"They are."

He traced a path along her cheek with his thumb. "And that they use you and then walk away—"

"They do." Although she ached for things to be different.

He pulled her hand to his mouth and pressed a kiss to each finger. "I promise not to cheat or lie to you, Joey."

She pushed at his shoulders, needing distance before she broke down and cried and begged him to love her. "Maybe not, but—"

"No buts." A smoldering intensity underscored his

words, and he tightened his grip, refusing to let her run. “And I’m not walking away, sugar.”

A tear trickled down her cheek. She desperately wanted to believe him. “Our families, Cole…our history. Look at them.”

“We’re not *them,*” he said thickly. “Give us a chance, Joey. We can make our own family the way we want it.”

Hope slivered through her. What was he saying? “Family?”

He threaded his fingers through her hair and yanked her down across his lap. “I love you, sugar.”

“Cole—”

He pressed a finger over her lips to shush her. “I love you, and I want to marry you.”

Joey stared into his eyes, his words echoing in her head. Sincerity mingled with heat and passion in his eyes. A passion that she had known with only one man. A love she’d felt when she’d been in his arms and no one else’s.

He had whispered the words in return. And he’d sounded as if he meant them.

“Now, don’t make me beg.” Emotions thickened his voice. “I almost lost you before, Joey. I don’t want to lose you again. Not ever.”

“I don’t want to lose you, either,” she whispered.

“Then climb on, sugar,” he said with a sexy smile twisting his lips, “and let’s go for that ride.”

“Where are we going?” she asked breathlessly.

He grinned and swung her around until she climbed on behind him. “Someplace where we can be alone, and I can feel those mile-long legs wrapped around me.”

She nuzzled his neck with her tongue. “Someplace

where I can sprinkle that salt and lime juice on your body and lick it off?"

"Oh, yeah, sugar. Someplace where we can make all those fantasies I've been having about you come true."

She clasped her hands around his waist and leaned into him. He had already made all her dreams come true just by loving her. But a shot of tequila off his washboard belly and his length inside her was definitely another fantasy to look forward to.

And she was certain that they could think of others…

* * * * *